PRAISE FOR T[...] OF LORELEI [JAMES]

"Sweet, seductive, and romantic, *One Night Rodeo* is an emotional ride filled with joy, angst, laughs, and a wonderful happily-ever-after. Lorelei James knows how to write one hot, sexy cowboy."
—*New York Times* bestselling author Jaci Burton

"The down-and-dirty, rough-and-tumble Blacktop Cowboys kept me up long past my bedtime. Scorchingly hot, wickedly naughty."
—Lacey Alexander, author of *Bad Girl by Night*

"Hang on to your cowboy hats, because this book is scorching hot!"
—Romance Junkies

"Lorelei James knows how to write fun, sexy, and hot stories."
—Joyfully Reviewed

"Lorelei James excels at creating new and evocative fantasies."
—TwoLips Reviews

"Incredibly hot."
—The Romance Studio

"Beware: Before you read this hot erotic from Lorelei James, get a glass of ice. You are going to need it." —Fallen Angel Reviews

"Think it's impossible to combine extremely erotic and sweet? Not if James is writing." —*Romantic Times*

"Plenty of steamy love scenes that will have you reaching for your own hottie!" —Just Erotic Romance Reviews

"Smokin'-hot cowboys [and] lots of Western charm."
—Fiction Vixen Book Reviews

Turn and Burn

A BLACKTOP COWBOYS® NOVEL

LORELEI JAMES

A SIGNET ECLIPSE BOOK

SIGNET ECLIPSE
Published by the Penguin Group
Penguin Group (USA) Inc., 375 Hudson Street,
New York, New York 10014, USA

USA | Canada | UK | Ireland | Australia | New Zealand | India | South Africa | China

Penguin Books Ltd., Registered Offices: 80 Strand, London WC2R 0RL, England
For more information about the Penguin Group visit penguin.com.

First published by Signet Eclipse, an imprint of New American Library,
a division of Penguin Group (USA) Inc.

First Printing, August 2013

BLACKTOP COWBOYS® is a registered trademark of Lorelei James.

SIGNET ECLIPSE and logo are trademarks of Penguin Group (USA) Inc.

LIBRARY OF CONGRESS CATALOGING-IN-PUBLICATION DATA:

James, Lorelei.
Turn and burn: a Blacktop Cowboys Novel/Lorelei James.
p. cm
ISBN 978-0-451-41396-3
I. Title.
PS3610.A4475T87 2013
813'.6—dc23   2013015673

Printed in the United States of America
10 9 8 7 6 5 4 3 2 1

Set in Janson MT STD

*This book is dedicated to all my
Texas friends and especially those wild,
crazy-assed Texas women
who inspire me every day...*

Chapter One

❧

"*S*weet darlin', what did you say you did for a living?"

Sweet darlin'. Did this dude really think she'd buy into his fake cowboy shtick because he'd shown up at a Western bar wearing alligator boots and a Stetson? *Please.* She was a Texas girl, born and bred. And if there was one thing Tanna Barker knew, it was cowboys—*real* cowboys.

She smiled coyly. "I didn't say. But a shot of Patrón would loosen my tongue a whole lot."

Mr. Alligator Boots flagged down the bartender.

Sucker.

Tanna would've almost felt bad for this guy, except he'd approached her. Buying her a shot was the least he could do after he'd laid on the bullshit so thick she felt it seeping into her boots.

After knocking back the tequila, she confessed, "I don't normally share my occupation because it tends to be viewed as…a bit raunchy. But I'll make an exception for you, puddin' pop."

She saw his gears spinning as he pondered her raunchy occupation. Paid escort? Hooker? Exotic dancer? His eyes roamed over her skintight Miss Me jeans, her pink rhinestone b.b.simon belt and her shimmery ruffled blouse cut low enough to garner interest in her abundant cleavage.

Then Mr. Alligator Boots frowned at the bandage on her forehead. "What happened to you?"

"Hazard of my job." She confided, "I'm a professional Roller Derby girl.

I'm the pivot for the Lonestar Ladies. I hit the cement in the ring last night after some bitch hooked me and I ended up with a skate to the head. It bled like a mother, I guess. I didn't notice, 'cause I play to win. Only took ten stitches this time. Last month I ripped the shit outta my calf and ended up with twenty-five stitches."

Silence.

"I can show you the scar. Bet a tough cowboy like you is into scars, ain't ya?" she taunted.

Mr. Alligator Boots backed away and waved at someone across the room. "Would you look at the time? I gotta go. I see my friends are here."

Tanna held in her laughter until he disappeared.

Within five minutes another friendly guy sidled up. Younger than Mr. Alligator Boots. But he still wore the *Hey, baby, I'm all that and a real cowboy* look of a smarmy douche bag. She smiled and waited for him to strike up a conversation.

Hello, free shot number two.

Talk about shooting fish in a barrel. Over the next two hours, and after multiple complimentary shots of tequila, her injury had been the result of a bow hunting accident, from getting clipped by her gear after jumping from an airplane, from a drunken brawl with her fellow missionaries, from hitting the roll bar during the demolition derby finals and her personal favorite—the whip she'd used on her lover recoiled and sliced her in the face. Truly a classic. As the queen of tall tales, she couldn't wait to share these fun little fibs with her buddy Celia Lawson Gilchrist.

Hopefully pregnancy hadn't affected Celia's sense of humor.

Tanna ordered a Corona, lamenting the lack of Lone Star beer this far north. Still, she was grateful for her friends who'd offered her a place to live in Wyoming while she got her head on straight. Her life had been in turmoil these past two years, more than she'd let on. She just wanted a place to hole up, lick her wounds and figure out what the hell to do with herself.

Rather than imposing on Celia and Kyle Gilchrist or Lainie and Hank Lawson, even for one night, Tanna had checked into a dive motel in Rawlins within stumbling distance of Cactus Jack's Bar. This wouldn't be her last night of freedom, but it'd be her last chance to be anonymously wild for a while.

Right. Tell yourself that. You can't go more than two weeks without getting into trouble.

Another guy, this one with too many tats and too few teeth, slunk up next to her. "What's a looker like you doin' drinking alone?"

"Celebrating that I just got out of jail last week."

His bleary eyes lit up. "What a coincidence. I just got outta jail too. What were you in for?"

A real jailbird was hitting on her? Awesome. That'd teach her to lie. "Arson. I allegedly"—she made quotes in the air when she said allegedly— "set fire to my ex's trailer and blew up his truck with a couple of incendiary rounds. The man has no sense of humor and if I ever see that lyin' bastard again…" Tanna squinted at him suspiciously. "Hey. Come to think of it, you look an awful lot like him. An awful lot." She sneered and poked him in the chest. "LeRoy, I swear to God, if you think you can pull some kind of lame disguise with me—"

"I ain't LeRoy, and lady, you're plumb crazy." He backed away. Ran away was more like it.

She couldn't help but snicker before she upended her beer.

"Word of advice, sugar twang? Bein's the town of Rawlins hosts the Wyoming state penitentiary, there's a higher than average population of ex-cons around. And they're not all so easily conned as him."

Tanna glanced up at the man.

Oh, hello, sweet darlin'.

How hadn't she noticed this giant? At least six feet five, he easily cast her five feet three inches in shadow. And holy frijoles was this guy hot. Like, really hot. After being approached by wannabe cowboys all night, there was no doubt this guy was the real deal. So she shamelessly took in his banging body, from his summer-weight cowboy hat to the tips of his dusty boots—and every inch in between.

His age looked to be mid-thirties. In this part of the country his reddish gold complexion had to be from Native American ancestry. Her avid gaze took in his angular features. A high forehead not marred by a single wrinkle. A slash of dark eyebrows arched over eyes the color of warm topaz. His cheekbones were prominent in a wide-set face. A thin blade of nose. The corners of his lips turned up in an indulgent smile. And check out that ridiculously strong-looking, chiseled jawline. His thick neck tapered into shoulders so wide it appeared he wore football pads, until she realized this hunky man couldn't hide bulky equipment under his skintight T-shirt.

"You done looking your fill? Or did you want me to turn around so you can ogle my ass too?"

"Better to know up front that I'm staring at your package, and not considering the size of your wallet, don'tcha think?" Tanna retorted with saccharine sweetness.

He laughed. A deep, sexy rumble that caused a little flip in her belly. "So will you let me buy you a beer if I pull out my wallet?"

"If you're sure you wanna spend money on an ex-con."

"You're not an ex-con by any stretch of your imagination." He waved down the bartender. "But I *am* interested to hear which lie I'll rate." He shot her a grin. "I'm hoping you'll claim to be a secret agent."

Tanna leaned across the bar. "Got a Bond girl fantasy you wanna tell me about, ace?"

"I'm more a fan of Lara Croft or Sydney Bristow. Chicks who kick ass turn my crank."

"Hot women who know how to kill and how to dress to kill *are* the ultimate asset."

"Oh, those women ain't got nothin' on you in the asset department." His gaze dipped to the deep V of her cleavage.

It didn't bother her that he was blatantly checking out her rack. When he finally dragged his gaze to hers again, the unbridled lust in his eyes sent a wave of liquid heat through her.

"You are trouble," she murmured, unable to look away from him. Something about this man pulled her in and revved her up.

"No more trouble than you are, spy girl." He held out a twenty for the bartender without breaking eye contact. "You wanna grab us a booth and we'll talk about what kinda trouble we can get into together?"

She nodded. Just as she stepped back, a man jockeying for her spot at the bar jostled her, sending her off balance. Her tall, dark and handsome stranger kept her from falling by using a firm arm to pull her forward. Her breasts met the hard wall of his chest and all the air left her lungs in a rush. Good God was he solid.

He sucked in a sharp breath at the sudden intimate contact.

The side of her face smashed against his pectorals. She remained like that, inhaling his scent until he tugged on her hair to get her attention. She glanced up into his eyes, feeling a blast of pure sexual heat.

"Might be dangerous to keep looking at me like that," he said softly.

"Because you're afraid I wanna do more than look at you?"

"No." His rough-edged fingertip traced a line down her neck, from the dent in her chin to the start of her cleavage. "But maybe I want more than you're willing to give."

Tanna stared at him. Normally such blatant sexual talk so soon after meeting had her stepping back. But something about this man kept her right where she was—completely entranced by him.

"Say the word, sugar twang, and I'll walk away."

"And if I don't want you to walk away?" she countered boldly.

"Then our night just got a whole lot more interesting."

"Sounds good to me." Opening her mouth over the hard curve of his pectorals, she blew a stream of hot air through the shirt, then lightly bit down. "I'm game for whatever you've got in mind."

"Grab your beer." He led them to the only unoccupied booth, by the front door.

She slid into the bench seat opposite him and raised her bottle for a toast.

"What're we toasting to?"

"Ex-cons and little white lies." She smirked. "And a guy with a big… bullshit meter."

"I'll drink to that." He grinned.

Sweet Lord. There was damn dangerous wattage in those pearly whites of his.

He rested his massive shoulders against the back of the booth. "So, what's your name besides Hot Trouble?"

Tanna shook her head. "How about if we keep it simple and don't exchange names?"

He didn't even blink. "Because you'd probably give me a fake one anyway."

"Yep. I see this ain't your first go-round in this type of rodeo either, cowboy."

"I'm good with no names—I like 'sugar twang' better anyway—but there are a couple of basic questions I've gotta ask first."

"Shoot."

The twinkle vanished from his eyes. "You're not married and out on the town looking for one night with a stranger to cure your marital boredom?"

"No, sir. I don't cheat. So no boyfriend either." She pointed with her beer bottle. "Back atcha."

"No significant other in my life. Or in my bed on a regular basis."

"That clears that up. Next question."

His eyes flicked to the bandage on her forehead. "What happened there?"

"Nothin'. It's a prop to garner sympathy, start conversations and con men into buying me drinks."

That seemed to amuse him rather than annoy him. "What brings you to Rawlins, Wyoming?"

"Just passing through on my way to start a new job." Not exactly a lie. "What about you?"

"I'm on the road a lot too." He let his bottle dangle a couple of inches above the table and swung it like a pendulum. "You're not really on the run from an ex?"

Tanna snickered. "Nope. I'm just killing time in a honky-tonk before I move on."

"So you're not looking for Mr. Right?"

"More like looking for Mr. Right *Now*."

His handsome face remained skeptical.

"Let's cut to the chase. I like sex. There isn't a substitute for the way naked flesh feels sliding together in the heat of passion. There isn't a substitute for a long, wet kiss. There isn't a substitute for a heart-pounding, blood-pulsing orgasm. There isn't a substitute for sex. Period. I'm not sup-posed to admit I get antsy and snappish if I go too long without it. I'm not supposed to admit that satisfying the craving for intimate physical contact is all I want. I don't want messy emotional entanglements. Just. Hot. Sex."

He leaned forward and took her hand, staring deeply into her eyes. "I think I love you."

She laughed.

"In all seriousness, it's refreshing that you're so up front about what you want."

"Or what I don't want." Tanna swallowed a mouthful of beer. "So, you interested in taking me for a tumble?"

"Oh yeah." His smile turned decidedly predatory. "But I'm not gonna shake your hand like this is a business arrangement." He lifted their joined hands and kissed the inside of her forearm, from her wrist to the crook of her elbow. "I'm gonna seduce you."

"Right here, right now?"

"Just giving you a sneak peek at my playbook." His thumb lazily swept an arc from her knuckles to her wrist. "But I won't attempt an all-out blitz. I'd rather make the plays drive by drive. Trust me. I'll still get us to the goal line."

Tanna squirmed in her seat. "I've never been turned on by a football analogy before."

He chuckled. "I'm happy you caught the right sport reference."

"Bite your tongue. I'm a Texan. Football is not a sport; it's a religion."

"My mistake. That said, I'm gonna jump ahead in the offensive play-book and score us a room at the motel across the street. Be right back."

He slid from the booth leaving her staring after him feeling...what? Guilty? Like she should offer to pay for half? Or tell him she'd already booked a room? Or was she feeling like a skanky ho for picking up yet an-other guy in a bar?

Nah. It'd been a while since she'd hooked up. And what was wrong with acting on her baser impulses anyway? Nothing. Men did it all the freakin' time. Her body, her choice. All pleasure, no emotional pain. Just what she needed.

Tanna ordered another round of Coronas and let her head fall back. Her mind filled with thoughts of roving hands and hot mouths. Of cool cotton sheets beneath her. She imagined the taste of his mouth. His skin. She thought about his hair teasing her as he kissed down the center of her body. By the time she'd finished fleshing out all the sexual scenarios she'd like to put into play, the bench seat creaked. She angled her head and opened her eyes to see her hot stranger sliding next to her.

His big hand curled around the side of her face and he swept his thumb over her cheekbone. "I was afraid you'd be gone."

"Why? I meant what I said."

"I believe you. But me heading off to secure a room before I even kissed you is a little rude on my part."

Tanna's heart galloped when he leaned closer, letting their lips almost touch as he gazed into her eyes with such heat and tenderness. She managed to eke out, "Maybe you oughta prove that you're not a bad kisser before this goes any further."

"Be my pleasure."

His breath continued to flow over her lips, but he didn't kiss her. "Is there a problem?"

"No. You're just so dang pretty," he murmured and pressed his mouth to hers.

A soft, quick brush of moist flesh as his lips teased hers. Then another. And another. When Tanna parted her lips, his tongue slipped inside her mouth.

The kiss started out a slow, sweet exploration. Heat built gradually as their lips moved and tongues dueled. She gave herself over to him and this amazing first kiss.

By the time he eased back, Tanna knew her face was flushed. Her heart raced. A warm throb of need had settled between her legs.

"Damn, woman," he finally said.

"I'm feeling a little buzzed after that too." Good Lord. He'd kissed her with such intensity she was out of breath.

"I take it I passed the kissing test?"

She nodded. "With flying colors."

"Good. Because I want another taste of you."

Heat spread between her thighs. "And then what?"

"Then I'll probably throw you over my shoulder and run across the parking lot." His mouth meandered down her throat. He stopped to trace his tongue along her collarbone before he planted kisses straight down to her cleavage.

Somehow he'd maneuvered her into the corner of the booth. His big body blocked her from view of other bar patrons, which allowed him to leave openmouthed kisses on every exposed inch of her breasts.

Tanna's head fell back, letting his greedy kisses on her skin consume her. When she realized her hands were gripping the booth and not his rock-hard flesh, she reached out and placed her palms on his pectorals.

"I like your hands on me," he murmured against the upper swell of her breast.

She curled her fingers into his torso, allowing her nails to scrape down his belly to the waistband of his jeans. Then she put her mouth on the salty skin beneath his ear. "Imagine me doin' that down your back." She nipped on his earlobe. "At least two times."

He groaned and then his mouth was back, overwhelming hers with passion. Not sloppy, wet, I wanna fuck you kisses. But hot, hungry kisses that drove her to another level of need. This wouldn't be a one-off fuck. The first time might be fast. But the second time wouldn't be. Nor would the third time. The fourth go around would be spectacular.

Looked to be a long, sweaty night.

And she couldn't freakin' wait.

She slapped her hands on his cheeks to pull his mouth off hers. When she stared into his face and saw that devilish gleam, she smirked back.

"What?"

"Didn't you say something about throwing me over your shoulder and getting us outta here?"

"Let's go."

Chapter Two

※

Tanna woke up in a panic, sheet clutched to her naked chest. She looked around wildly until she realized she was in her motel room, not his. She sagged into the pillows with relief when she remembered making her escape after he'd fallen into a deep sleep.

Escape. She'd forced herself to leave because she hadn't wanted to. It felt wrong lumping the guy in with her other one-night stands. The sex had been fantastic. A little hard and fast wham bam—which she loved—and then he'd switched gears, drawing out their mutual pleasure. Words beyond *yes, now* and *more* had been unnecessary. They'd let their bodies do all the talking.

So maybe she wished they'd exchanged names. But it was too late now. She glanced at the clock. Nine a.m. Man, she'd slept in this morning. She headed straight for the shower.

After checking out of the motel, Tanna walked two blocks to the truck stop's gravel parking lot where she'd ditched her truck and horse trailer. Didn't appear anyone had messed with it, which was a good thing since all her earthly possessions were contained within the horse bay. She tried not to feel pitiful; a former world champion barrel racer without a horse. A former world champion without a home. A former world champion barrel racer without anything, really. She'd lost so much in the two years since her mother had passed on it still seemed surreal.

Shaking off the melancholy, she climbed in the cab of her Dodge, cranked up the tunes and plugged in the GPS coordinates for the Gilchrist Ranch.

The minute she reached the nicely kept ranch house, Celia Gilchrist opened the front door and stepped onto the front porch to greet her. Celia's husband Kyle exited the house and stood beside her.

Tanna jumped out of her truck and landed hard on her right leg. She bit back a curse and a cry of pain. She feared she'd never be at one hundred percent again. As soon as she straightened up, Celia was there, hugging her.

"You have no idea how happy I am that you're here, Tanna." Celia stepped back and gave her a critical once-over. "Damn, I forget how gorgeous you are. You don't look like you've been through nine months of hell."

Tanna poked Celia's pregnant belly. "Speaking of nine months... how you feelin', mama?"

Kyle stood behind Celia, setting his hands on her shoulders. "She's ornery half the time and crying the other half."

"Not true." Celia elbowed him in the gut. "I'm feeling great now. I was damn happy to see the ass end of morning sickness."

"You look beautiful." Tanna wasn't just blowing smoke. Celia had a glow about her. A happy vibe surrounded her and Kyle. Tanna would be jealous except Celia and Kyle's road to love, marriage and a baby carriage hadn't been a cakewalk. "So, you're at what? Five months now?"

"Yep. My due date is the first part of September." Celia shot Kyle a wry look. "Be interesting to see how it is with a baby during calving."

"I'm sure you'll do great." Tanna looped her arm through Celia's. "You are up to giving me the grand tour of your ranch?"

"Sure. We've made a lot of improvements in the last two and a half years since Kyle inherited it."

"I can't believe you guys have been married that long."

Kyle grabbed Celia's hand and kissed her knuckles. "Been the best two and a half years of my life."

Celia made goo-goo eyes at him and Tanna couldn't resist making gagging noises.

After a quick tour on four-wheelers, they returned to the house and sat in the cozy breakfast nook. Tanna immediately reached for the sugar upon discovering the iced tea wasn't presweetened.

"When do you start working?" Celia asked.

"Monday. I've got orientation on Sunday."

"If you've got tomorrow off, then you can come to the branding."

"You need help?"

Kyle shrugged. "You know how it goes. The branding itself don't take long. It's the rounding up and we could always use more calf wranglers."

"Sounds like fun. I'll be here unless I have to start work a day early." Tanna broached the subject, no matter how loudly her pride screamed to let it go. "How is it that a Texas girl was offered a job at the Split Rock Ranch and Resort in Wyoming?"

Celia fidgeted. Then she looked Tanna in the eye. "I know you struggled after your mom's death. And then to suffer the type of injury you did nine months ago…" Her eyes brimmed with sympathy. "There's no need to pretend things haven't been rough on you. After the accident you took that job at Billy Bob's Texas because you didn't have a choice. So that means you've got experience with retail sales and tending bar, which makes you the perfect temporary solution to the Split Rock's staffing issues."

"Why is everyone so vague about why these positions are temporary?"

"Are you lookin' for something permanent?"

I don't know.

"All three of the big bosses will be out of commission for a while. My sister-in-law Janie—she's married to Abe—deals with sales and PR for the resort and she just had her second baby. Harper Turner runs Wild West Clothiers and is set to deliver her second baby any day." Celia shook her head. "Harper will have had two kids in twenty-two months. Janie had two kids in two-and-a-half years. Tierney Jackson is in charge of the resort's finances and she's pregnant with her first baby. She's fine to do her job, but she can't pitch in or fill in for anyone else like she's done in the past. Her husband Renner put his foot down and since Renner is the majority owner, what he says goes."

"So Janie and Harper will be coming back to work?"

"Be hard for them *not* to come back since they're both owners," Celia pointed out. "They've each decided to take a three-month maternity leave and summer is the busiest time at the resort, which puts everyone in a bind. Finding qualified people is hard enough around here and no one wants to take a job even temporarily if there's no chance the position will become permanent. When they mentioned their staffing problem, I recommended you as a possible hire for the short term. Lainie vouched for you too."

"I appreciate it. I'll get used to the funny way y'all talk and that you don't put sugar in your tea," Tanna drawled.

Celia smiled. "Tierney's sister Harlow will be filling in at the resort this summer too." Then her smile dimmed and she placed her hand on Tanna's injured knee.

Tanna braced herself.

"I've gotta ask. Have you gotten on a horse since the last time we talked?"

Tanna shook her head.

"You need to."

They'd had this discussion several times and neither Tanna's mind nor her response had changed.

Celia kept pressing her point. "It's part of who you are. You're scared. Which is understandable, given what happened."

Tanna could still hear the horse's high-pitched whinny echoing in her head. That noise haunted her. "My physical therapist said—"

"That you were fine to resume riding."

Her eyes narrowed on Celia. "How do you know?"

"You called me after the appointment."

"I did not."

"You did too. But I'm pretty sure you'd been drinking."

Tanna had done a lot of drinking in the last nine months since the accident—although some people didn't refer to it as an accident. They called it negligence.

God. Even saying the word made her want to throw up. She'd never been negligent with a horse entrusted to her care. Never.

"Tanna?"

She glanced up at Kyle. "Sorry. What did you say?"

"I said I know where you're coming from. You'll know when the time is right to face them demons." Celia opened her mouth to retort but Kyle shook his head. "Leave it be, Cele."

"Fine. But can I at least introduce you to Eli?" Celia asked.

Tanna said, "I guess." No point in adding more fuel to Celia's need to "fix" her by admitting she didn't believe Celia's good friend and longtime horse trainer Eli Whirling Cloud could help her—despite his reputation as some kind of magical horse whisperer.

"You still plan on leaving your horse trailer here while you're workin' at the Split Rock?" Kyle asked.

"If that's okay. I took out everything I'd need and packed it in my truck."

"Let's get it parked and get you settled in up at the resort."

When they caravanned down the highway, Tanna couldn't help but gawk at the diverse scenery. The landscape looked like West Texas for a few miles and then sheer rock cliffs seemed to rise out of nowhere. Followed by miles of sagebrush and scrub cedar. Then miles of nothing.

After turning down a wide gravel road, the topography changed once again to a wooded area with rolling hills and scrubby pine trees. They started up a steep rise and at the top were two stone pillars with a wooden sign hanging between them, denoting the Split Rock Ranch and Resort.

Tanna caught her first look at the place. Wood and stone with metal accents. Bigger than she'd thought. Classy but it had a low-key vibe too. At one time she would've stayed in a place like this. Now she was here as an employee.

Even with Celia and Kyle accompanying her inside she was nervous. She had nowhere else to go so she had to make this job work.

She caught a brief glimpse of the great room before Celia cut down the right hallway, with Kyle's hand in the small of her back. Celia leaned into him and murmured something that caused Kyle to kiss her cheek. Even Tanna's cynical side, which scoffed at the idea of true love and soul mates, thawed the teeniest bit seeing her friends so attuned to each other.

Celia stopped in front of the office and knocked.

The door was opened by a pregnant brunette. She adjusted her glasses after she looked at Celia's baby bump and then at hers. "I don't think we can walk through the door at the same time."

"Funny." Celia stepped aside. "Tierney Jackson, meet Tanna Barker. World champion barrel racer, awesome friend and your pinch hitter for the summer. Tierney is the financial guru around here but don't let that fool you. The girl knows how to shoot tequila."

"Forever branded as a bad girl by one isolated incident."

Someone behind them snorted.

Tierney stepped forward and offered her hand. "Tanna, I'm so happy to finally meet you in person. Celia has said the best things about you."

"Likewise. I'm grateful for the opportunity to work at the resort. It's a gorgeous place from what I've seen."

After they exited the office, a good-looking guy, whose carriage screamed cowboy, stepped up beside Tierney. He offered his hand. "Tanna. Renner Jackson. We've met before. It's been a while though. I've enjoyed watching you barrel race on many occasions."

"Thank you. So, you're the big boss?"

"I'm the majority owner but I'd be skinned alive if I copped to bein' the big boss." He grinned. "I was smart enough to hire the best and the brightest."

Tierney hip-checked him. "Don't you forget it, cowboy."

Renner looked at Kyle. "You wanna drive Tanna's truck to the employee lodgings? She'll be in the fourth trailer. Park in back. We'll walk down."

Tanna tossed Kyle her keys.

Renner offered a brief history of the resort and took her back to the main room. He pointed out the various areas with a promise she'd get a more in-depth tour on Sunday.

They cut through the kitchen, which was surprisingly quiet for a Friday. "We've only got two rooms booked for tonight and the couples made alternate supper plans so we're without kitchen staff."

"You don't have your kitchen staff cooking for the employees?"

"No." Renner held open the door for her and Celia and Tierney who were in conversation, walking behind them. "The Split Rock is run like a hotel and not a bunkhouse where the cook is feeding ranch hands twice a day. Most of the employees go home. With a couple of exceptions. The foreman for my stock contracting company lives on-site, as does our jack-of-all-trades, who'll run my commercial stock-breeding business if we ever get the damn thing off the ground. The head of housekeeping and the groundskeeper are married, so they're livin' here too. And now you."

He'd started down a footpath crafted from flat stones. "There are paths like this everywhere. Most of 'em are marked, with the exception of the way to the employees' quarters."

Tanna looked around, immediately calmed by the peaceful scenery. She knew it'd taken a lot of work to make this look natural. They kept walking until they reached a series of high wooden fences. The angle of each section and cut of the pieces of wood gave the illusion of a see-through fence, but all six segments were solid. "Cool fence."

"Thanks. When guests ask we tell them it's a windbreak and a sound barrier, which ain't entirely a lie. But it's mostly to keep the employee quarters hidden from plain sight. We had a few guests complain early on that they hadn't paid big money to stay at a pricey resort only to have to look at decrepit trailers. So we remedied that."

"Should I be worried about these decrepit living conditions?" she joked.

"Nope. We revamped them too. Of course they ain't nearly as nice as the lodge. But they're much better than when I lived there."

That shocked her. "You bunked down with your employees?"

He shrugged. "I wouldn't ask them to do something I wasn't willing to do myself."

That was a refreshing philosophy.

They skirted the farthest end of the enormous fence and crossed a gravel path. Six trailers were nestled in a straight line. Each one had a small deck that separated it from the trailer beside it. A covered portico arched over each front door. A planked walkway ran from the first house to the last and it resembled a floating dock. All the structures had the same wood siding and looked more like cabins than trailers. A small set of steps led to the slightly raised platform.

"This is yours, the fourth from the left. Tobin lives in the first one, Hugh the second one, and Dave and Yvette in the last one."

"Two are empty?"

"Tierney's sister Harlow was supposed to take one, but she's moved into our old place."

"Where do you and Tierney live?"

"In a new house down the road," Tierney said. "We'd planned to wait until this fall to start building, but Mr. Impatient insisted the house be completely finished before little bean gets here in the next three months."

Renner placed his hands on Tierney's belly. "I take care of what's mine. And it was past time. The cabin was too damn small for us, let alone us and a baby." He kissed her.

"You're fogging up my glasses."

"Mmm-hmm."

All these mushy love vibes were making Tanna's feet itch with the need to escape.

Kyle walked down the plank. "You want all the stuff from your truck carried inside, Tanna?"

"No, if we could just set it on the deck I can get it inside later. Thanks."

Renner pointed to Celia and Tierney. "You two stay put. No lifting anything."

They exchanged an eye roll and resumed their pregnancy complaints.

Tanna was anxious to see the inside of the place she'd be living all summer. Sort of pathetic that at her age she'd never really had a place of her own. She'd lived at home on the family ranch when she wasn't on the road chasing the gold buckle. After her father had sold the place, she'd returned to life on the blacktop, staying in the cheapest motels she could find or she had bedded down in her horse trailer.

After the accident, which required surgery on her right knee and ankle, she'd spent two weeks in the hospital. Then she was transferred to a physical therapy center that specialized in treating sports-related injuries. She'd chosen the intensive therapy option and two months after the accident her range of motion had returned to ninety percent, although she still had the occasional issue with her knee. She probably could've regained that extra ten percent if she'd continued with therapy, but medical bills had depleted her bank account.

Pissed off at her father and too proud to ask for his financial help, she used her celebrity, for lack of a better term, to land a job at Billy Bob's Texas—the world's largest honky-tonk. They'd stuck her in the retail clothing store. Her uniform requirement was wearing her Cowboy Rodeo Association Championship belt buckle and the medal she'd won for back-to-back national championships in barrel racing.

As far as jobs went, it wasn't bad. Management provided one free meal and one free drink per shift. With a women's locker room for employees, she even had a place to shower. The frustrating part of being homeless had been moving her horse trailer every couple of days because she couldn't afford to rent a space in an RV park every night.

"Tanna?"

She glanced up at Kyle and realized she'd been so lost in thought she hadn't moved from the entrance to the trailer. "Sorry. Just spacing out." She dodged Renner lugging her two suitcases and she brought the last of her belongings from her truck, dumping them on the deck. Talk about a pitiful pile.

Leave it to Celia to mention what wasn't in the pile. "So, you left all your tack in the horse trailer?"

Tanna shrugged. "It's been in storage. It'll be fine another few months."

"But the branding—"

"I won't be there if I'm required to be on horseback for the roundup, so get that out of your head, Celia Gilchrist," she warned.

A sneaky smile curled Celia's lips. "Fine. I'll put you to work with the other womenfolk, getting food ready, since I doubt you're supposed to be sliding around, twisting and turning in the dirt on your knee and ankle anyway."

"Wrong. I'll be wrassling calves *and* making killer margaritas. We Texas ranch women are multitaskers." She grabbed the suit bag and ducked inside. Like most trailers, the kitchen was in the front. The color scheme was dark brown and muted gray. The countertops and stainless appliances looked new, as did the linoleum. A bistro-type table with two chairs was situated in front of the far window.

She walked into the living room. The walls were wood-paneled and the windows were covered with heavy plaid draperies. The carpet was a chocolate brown Berber. The tan-colored, oversized furniture and a square glass and metal coffee table took up a good portion of the living space. The big wall across from the couch was bare, probably for a flat screen TV—hers would look like a postage stamp on that wall. She started down the hallway and stopped at the first doorway. A small bedroom with a single bed and dresser. The next door opened into a full-sized bathroom. It appeared the remodel fairies had been busy in here too. A black marble-looking countertop with two sinks was on top of a white vanity. The shower also had a tub and the unit was enclosed by a sliding glass door. Her days of showering in truck stops were done for a while. The second bedroom was at the far back of the trailer. The paneled walls had been painted a soft ivory. The room held a queen-sized bed, built-in dressers and two long, narrow closets.

"So? What do you think?" Tierney asked.

Tanna grinned. "I love it. It's perfect."

"The housekeepers put on fresh bedding this morning. Everything is furnished: towels, dishes, cookware and silverware. There isn't maid service for employees. I wasn't sure how late you'd arrive so I had the cooks leave you a couple eggs, a loaf of bread, a salad and some other odds and ends. It'll hold you until you get to the grocery store. The closest one is in Rawlins."

"This is great. Thank you so much."

"We're happy you're here to help out this summer." Tierney looked over her shoulder and then back at Tanna. "My sister Harlow will be job sharing with you. And to be honest, I don't know how that'll work out. If you have any issues with her, please come to me. Renner will tell you to go to him, but I know how to handle my sister."

"Thanks for bein' straight with me, Tierney."

"No problem. Harlow will be here for orientation on Sunday morning. It worked out that there's nothing going on tomorrow and you can go to Kyle and Celia's branding. I'm sure you're anxious to catch up with her."

"And Lainie. I haven't met her son Jason and I haven't seen Brianna for a while either."

Tierney smiled. "Brianna definitely rules the roost."

"Are you and Renner goin' tomorrow?"

"We'll stay here and deal with the guests. I'm watching Harper and Bran's little boy Tate so she can rest and Bran can help out. Renner is sending our hands, Hugh and Tobin. You could ride with them if you don't remember how to get there."

She preferred to drive. "I have GPS. I'll be just fine."

Renner yelled for Tierney and they returned to the living room. He handed Tanna a set of keys. "Extension numbers for the lodge are by the phone, as well as our cell phone numbers. If you need anything, just ask."

"You've done so much already. Thank you."

"See you Sunday morning at nine in the dining room." Renner and Tierney took off.

"We've gotta get goin' too," Celia said.

Tanna hugged her. "Thanks for everything." She turned and hugged Kyle too. "What time do the festivities begin tomorrow?"

Kyle scratched his jaw. "Eight if you wanna help round up the pairs. Ten if you just wanna jump in on the branding portion."

"Need me to bring anything?"

"Just a big appetite, because there'll be a ton of food," Celia said.

"And a big stick to beat off the single cowboys, 'cause, darlin', they're gonna be on you like white on rice," Kyle said with a grin.

Tanna smirked. "Maybe I'll take one or two for a tumble. Just to see how the local boys stack up to wild Texas men." But part of her already knew one man in particular more than measured up.

Don't think about him. What's done is done.

After her friends left, Tanna brought everything inside and set about trying to make the place her own.

Chapter Three

❧

*A*ugust "Fletch" Fletcher stepped out of his blood- and shit-stained coveralls and kicked them across the concrete floor.

He grabbed the soap and scrubbed his hands and forearms until pink-tinged lather swirled down the drain in the oversized stainless steel sink. When his arms were clean, he washed his face and neck. He needed a shower but getting the dust and grime off from the day spent in pastures and barns would do for now. Grabbing a hand towel, he looked around the cavernous space that was his operating room.

The recovery stalls were empty. The chains and pulley systems dangled from the ceiling unused. He hadn't performed any surgeries in here the last month—his mobile unit was equipped to handle most emergencies. He preferred to work on-site anyway. It was better for the animals, for the owners and for him.

Besides, he couldn't keep an assistant for more than a month and had to beg and borrow one from his local colleagues. So it made more sense to send those types of surgeries to his colleagues anyway.

Fletch wandered down the hallway past his office and the lone exam room to the small reception area.

Cora, his longtime office manager, was gathering her things, getting ready to call it a week. The first year he'd hung out his solo veterinarian shingle, he'd advertised for a receptionist. Cora had taken one look at the stacks of files, paperwork overflowing his desk, and jumped right in, so he hadn't bothered interviewing anyone else. That'd been nine years ago.

Now the woman was five years past retirement age, but if he even mentioned the R word to her, that sharp tongue of hers would slice off a layer of his skin. As good as Cora was at her job, Fletch was glad his practice kept him out of the office most days.

"So, are you in a better mood than when you got here late this morning?" she asked.

"I'm the boss. It's my prerogative to be late. Maybe my mood was because I was running behind."

He'd woken to an empty bed in the motel room across town. Normally he'd be relieved his hookup from the previous night had bailed, sparing him awkward morning-after conversation. But he was actually a little pissed off. He'd agreed to her *no name* rule only because he didn't think she'd stick with it. After the intensity of their connection he definitely wanted to know more about her, and he'd lost the chance.

"Maybe your mood had something to do with you waltzing in wearing the same clothes this morning that you'd had on when you left last night?"

He laughed. "Possibly."

"It's not funny, Doc. I worry about you."

"Why?"

"Because it takes more than just one night to find a good woman."

Don't get your back up. "What makes you think I'm looking for that?"

She peered at him over the tops of her glasses. "Because if you didn't want that you'd never go out. You'd be content staying home by yourself. Which you are not. You are out all the time. If you're not working—which you do, all the time."

Fletch wanted to argue with her, mostly out of habit, but he refrained because he knew she was right. His options were getting more limited. There weren't many single women working on the ranches that made up the majority of his business. Being a large animal vet had its own set of problems, mainly being on call and on the road. He didn't have walk-in customers like in a regular veterinary practice where the job entailed neutering, spaying and keeping family pets healthy.

"The one last night must've had...some merit if you stayed all night with her."

"She did."

"So you'll see her again?"

"I hope so."

Cora smiled. "Good. Now, did you sign off on my vacation request?"

Dammit. If he admitted he hadn't even looked at it, Cora would read him the riot act because she'd also know he'd merely moved the papers from his in-box into his bottom desk drawer. So he lied. "Yes, I did."

Her eyes narrowed.

Before she asked specific questions, Fletch said, "You deserve a vacation, Cora. I don't know what I'd do without you."

The hard line of her mouth softened. "Such a charmer. Just like your father."

Fletch grinned at her. Score one for diversionary tactics.

"I'll see you Monday." Cora's helmet of gray hair disappeared beneath the plastic hairstyle protector she wore rain or shine.

"Night, Cora. Have a good weekend." Fletch locked the front door after her and grabbed a bottle of water before he headed to his office. Seated in his padded chair, he let his head fall back and closed his eyes.

Maybe it made him a fool, rewinding the events from last night, but he'd done it several times during the day. Each flashback a montage of her beautiful face. Laughing, lost in passion, teasing, her eyes dark with need. Then his thoughts would skip to the satiny smoothness of her flesh beneath his hands. The sweet taste of her, from her generous breasts to the slice of heaven between her thighs. Remembering the feel of her hands on him, how she hadn't left any part of him untouched.

Outstanding sex aside, they'd clicked on a deeper level.

Wishful thinking. You didn't do a whole lot of talking. She's not from around here anyway. Chalk it up to a good time and leave it at that.

But he couldn't. When Fletch had woken up alone, he'd quickly put on his clothes and checked every car in the parking lot for a vehicle with a Texas license plate and found nothing.

Then again, maybe their night of steamy sex hadn't meant anything to her. She had warned him up front she wasn't looking for more than one night. And honestly, how many times had he done that to women? Banged them and left with a hasty good-bye, and sometimes they didn't even rate that. Too many times to count. So no wonder that bad behavior was coming back to bite him in the ass.

Maybe it was a sign he needed to change his ways.

He dropped his feet to the floor and moved his neck from side to side, hearing a satisfying pop. He still had an ache between his shoulder blades, which was a reminder he was overdue for a visit to the chiropractor. Months overdue.

Putting aches and pains and mistakes out of his mind, he buckled down and updated his files. He took his laptop everywhere with him and was able to document diagnoses on the spot, but he liked to flesh out the cases while they were still fresh in his mind.

Fletch didn't notice three hours had passed until his stomach grumbled. He'd mostly gotten caught up from the last month. With the always busy calving season behind him, he looked forward to a slower pace. At least until he had to start preg testing cows in another few months. Switching over to the answering service to deal with after-hours calls, he set the alarm and left through the back door.

Regardless of how many times he told himself he wouldn't find his mystery woman at Cactus Jack's, he drove there anyway. He sat in a booth with a clear view of the main entrance and ordered a burger and a beer. A few women approached him, and he was polite but cool. He killed two hours before he gave up.

Usually it didn't bother him going home to a dark house, but it did tonight.

～

During a break in the action at the branding the next morning, Tanna leaned against the wooden corral and drained half a bottle of water. She'd been to plenty of brandings in her life, but most of them utilized a rancher's roping skills by getting the calf into the position using the "rope and drag" method. Once the calf was on the ground, then a ranch hand would tie the feet together, immobilizing it for the brand, vaccination, dehorning and castration for the baby bulls. Or she'd been part of a chute operation. Where the calves were crammed into a loading alley and were moved into the chute one at a time, assembly-line fashion, with a propane-fired branding iron and the vaccinating, castration, dehorning all happening in one fell swoop.

But the Gilchrist and Lawson ranches employed the "chicken catching" method of branding. Holding the calves in the big corral and releasing them into a smaller pen ten at a time. It'd take two hands to catch the calf and wrestle it to the ground. One person held the head, the other held the feet during the whole process. If Tanna had to choose a more efficient method—and it pained her Texas cowgirl ranch roots to admit it—the chicken-catching technique was definitely a lot more fun, even if it was a throwback to the good old days.

None of the guys down in the dirt blinked about a woman in the trenches. But Kyle kept an eye on her and had signaled for her to take a break. Tanna appreciated his concern and that he didn't make a big deal about it. She didn't mention to anyone how badly her knee ached after only a few hours.

As soon as Celia saw her resting, she strolled toward her, chatting with a Native American guy who had to be Eli Whirling Cloud.

People who claimed Mexicans and Indians were the same ethnicity had been talking out their ass. Eli looked nothing like the Mexicans she'd been raised around in Texas—certainly nothing like her Mexican uncle from her mom's side of the family. Eli was tall—over six feet, with a rangy, lean build. He dressed like a cowboy, wearing boots, jeans, long-sleeved shirt. His hat was shaped differently and he'd jammed an eagle feather into the hat band. Eli's dark hair spilled into a long braid down his back. He appeared to be in his mid-thirties—a little young to be some kind of Indian wise man.

He aimed a kind smile at her and offered his hand. "Tanna, I'm Eli. Sorry we haven't had a chance to meet officially before now. Thought I'd wander over during a break in the action. It's been a hectic morning, eh?"

"I'll say. Never been to a branding like this before."

"I've done my part. The rest is up to you," Celia said to Tanna before she flounced off.

Eli chuckled. "No pressure."

Tanna relaxed and smiled at him. "She is pushy."

"Celia hasn't always been that way. She's come into her own the last few years, so you won't hear me complaining about the change in her, 'cause it is for the better."

"I've only seen her as the feisty Wyoming cowgirl who doesn't take any crap." Tanna paused. "I'm curious to know what she told you about me."

"That you are a gen-u-wine Texas ranch girl. Tough as dirt. So I was happy to see she hadn't exaggerated your livestock-handling ability. You were a real asset today."

She appreciated his compliment. "Thanks. But I'll point out that you sound surprised."

He shrugged. "I was. I've met a few supposed Texas ranch women a time or two."

"Consider yourself lucky that you've only run across those types. They were the bane of my existence growing up in Texas on our ranch. Those girls whose daddies owned the biggest spreads and ran thousands of heads of cattle, never set foot in the corrals, pastures or barns, let alone helped out during branding. They took private horse riding lessons. So even if they wanted to ride one of their expensive horses on their family land, they had ranch hands to saddle up. They were all about the Texas experience, but not the work."

"So your folks raised you to do ranch work?"

"Not originally." She took another pull off her water bottle. "My mom cooked, sewed and ran the household. She wanted me to be like those girls—proud to tell people of their ignorance in what it takes to run a ranch. But I rebelled. Early as I can remember I spent most of my time outside with the horses and my uncle who taught me everything about livestock and ranching. Which means I'm hopeless at domestic things." She snorted. "So I'm seriously lacking in *any* career fallback skills outside of chasin' cans. I'm grateful for the chance to work at the Split Rock for a bit."

Eli pushed his hat up higher on his forehead. "I heard about your accident. To hear Celia talk, you're needin' my help."

Tanna felt him looking at her but she focused on the grooved edges of her water bottle. "I don't know if anyone can help me."

"Why's that?"

She pointed to the group of horses at least two hundred yards away. "This is the closest I've been to any horses in nine months." She finally met his gaze.

His eyes were gentle, but shrewd. "On a scale of one to ten, how scared are you to get on a horse?"

Tanna imagined herself holding her tack, standing outside the paddock. And just like every time she'd imagined it in the last few months, her stomach roiled. "One hundred."

He nodded. No judgment. "Before the incident, you had daily interactions with horses?"

"Yes, my whole life. I started helping my uncle feed when I was three. I was riding by myself at age five. And I started running barrels when I was eight."

"Besides that one specific barrel horse, have you regularly ridden other horses over the past few years?"

"When I used to go home, I'd help with the livestock, which usually entailed me bein' on horseback. I rode Daisy, a real ranch workhorse." She looked away, across the pasture. "Now, some days— hell, most days—the thought of bein' in a pen or a stall or even a damn field with horses makes me physically ill."

Eli remained contemplative for about a minute. "So I guess my question is ... since you feel that way, do you want my help to overcome it?"

"I'm not hedging when I tell you I don't know."

"You don't need to decide right now. The offer will stand."

"Thank you. I'm not blowing off your generous offer. I'm just in an odd place right now, in so many ways. I'm broke. My family has splintered. If not for the generosity of my friends, I wouldn't even be here."

Eli gave her that soft smile. "Your friends care about you enough to want you here so they can find a way to help you. That's more support than a lot of people have. Besides, I've spent most my life broke. It ain't all that bad. The upside is no one ever hits me up for a loan."

She laughed softly.

"And there's that," he said with quiet intensity that was oddly calming. "Never take for granted your ability to feel something good and laugh."

Tanna had the sense he was speaking from personal experience.

"If and when you're ready to tackle some of the issues, feel free to call me. I don't have business cards with me, but I'll get you my number before you leave today."

She stared into his serene eyes but there wasn't a spark of sexual attraction between them, which meant she couldn't stop the question that tumbled forth. "Why are you offering a total stranger your help?"

"Because you need it and you're too proud to ask for it. Besides, what do you have to lose by trusting me?"

Nothing, because she'd lost everything already.

Kyle shouted for Eli, and he walked away.

Well, now. That conversation wasn't what she'd expected.

As she was contemplating Eli's confident, yet gentle, vibe, two hands landed on either side of hers on the fence. Then a hard male chest connected with her back and the man's hips did a little bump and grind on her backside. Warm lips brushed her ear.

"Hey, hot stuff. Wanna get down and dirty with me?"

Tanna spun around to find herself body to body with Devin McClain. A couple million women across the world would give anything to be this close to the smoking-hot country music sensation, with his soulful blue eyes, infectious grin and that deep sexy voice. Tanna liked Devin, liked drinking with him, but the man didn't do it for her at all. A fact Devin attempted to change at every opportunity. "Devin, you horny devil, when you gonna give up and realize I'm not interested?"

"Never." He rubbed his whiskered cheek across hers on the way to whisper in her ear, "Why you still playing hard to get with me, Miss Tex-ass?"

"Because fucking me would ruin you for all other women since I'm so fantastic in the sack, and I think there's a few ladies in the far reaches of

Maine that haven't sampled the love machine that is superstar Devin Mc-Clain."

Devin threw back his head and laughed. "Have I mentioned how much I love that you bust my balls?"

"Even when they're blue?"

"Even then. But I'll admit that's a rare day. It's good to be me." He gave her a smacking kiss on the mouth. Then his too-handsome face became serious. "How you really doin'?"

"I've got a job and a place to live for the summer."

"Maybe I shoulda thought of hiding out at the Split Rock this summer. No one would think to look there."

Strange comment. "Dev? What's goin' on?"

"Fame bullshit. I feel fucking stupid even saying that. Nothin' major, just a few overzealous fans forcing me to be cautious. Which is why I'm happy to be here, covered in cow shit, hanging out with people who happily bust my balls." His smile didn't reach his eyes. "So after the branding work is done, let's you and me put on some music, do a little two-steppin' and get totally hammered."

"In your dreams, superstar manwhore."

He laughed again. "Let's partner up for the next bunch of calves."

Tanna smirked. "I'm assuming you'll be on the ass end since you're so good at chasin' tail?"

"And I hear you're an expert at giving head, so you got the front end, Miss Tex-ass," he shot back.

Then Bran opened the gate, the calves rushed in and they got to work.

Chapter Four

❦

$\mathcal{F}$letch showed up at Kyle and Celia's in the early afternoon. They'd just branded the last calf and were running the pairs back into the pasture. So he hopped in Eli's truck and rode along behind the guys on horseback and manning ATVs.

Several minutes passed when they didn't speak. Finally Eli said, "Did I do something to piss you off that I ain't aware of, cuz? You're awful quiet."

"Nope. It's stupid but there's something I can't get out of my head."

"Ah." Eli shoved his sunglasses on top of his head. "Not *it*. So who is she?"

"I don't know." He gave Eli the lowdown, and his frustration on why this woman had gotten under his skin. After he finished speaking, he said, "So, got any sage advice?"

"Nope."

That made him laugh. "That's gotta be a first." As the truck bounced through the pasture, Fletch wiggled to get comfortable. These regular-sized passenger cabs were torture for a big guy like him—his knees were smashed against the dash, his shoulders hit the wrong part of the bench seat and his head touched the roof of the cab.

He stared out of the dirty pickup window. He'd purposely shown up after the branding, vaccinating and castrating portion had ended. His friends wouldn't razz him for appearing when the hard work was over. They understood that his profession as their veterinarian and their personal friendships straddled a fine line. So far none of his buddies had taken advantage of his good nature and expected his help without compensation. Hank and Abe, Bran and the Split Rock were decent-sized operations and Fletch depended on the income.

Not that he was getting rich. But he had been restless the past few months and had closed himself off from his friends. Cora blamed it on his lack of downtime for any length of time. His dad suggested he try one of those lateral career moves—going to work for someone else. Despite the demands of his grueling job, Fletch enjoyed his clients. He enjoyed the challenges of diagnosing and treating large animals, as much as he enjoyed the familiarity of performing the same procedures day after day.

But wouldn't it be nice to have someone to share the burden with? At least professionally?

His married friends dropped hints that he should focus on his personal life and actively look for a woman to settle down with.

The Texas hottie from two nights ago popped back into the forefront of his thoughts—which provided all the proof he needed that he was nowhere near ready to settle down.

"You're still awful quiet over there," Eli commented.

"Sorry I'm not great company. Just wondering if I should've gone home after that last call instead of coming here."

"Because of her? Your mystery woman?"

"Seeing all these happy couples makes me worry I'm starting to suffer burnout from one-night stands."

Eli looked at him sharply. "You? Damn, Fletch, that scares me."

"Me too. And being here makes me feel guilty about how far behind I am in helping Renner and Tobin with their potential commercial stock-breeding program." Fletch ran a hand through his hair. "I need to devote at least a month to it—just on the research side."

"You're headed into a slower season with calving done. I heard Bran sayin' he planned to turn the bulls out in the next two weeks."

"Some of my clients already have."

"So that gives you, what, two months before you start preg testing?"

"Yep. Even if I manage to take one full day off a week during the slower season, that's not enough time. And I don't want to be the one holding up the project—then I realize I already am and I probably need to back out. I freakin' hate bein' that guy who lets people down."

"Hmm."

Hmm from Eli never boded well. Fletch returned his sharp look. "What?"

"Nothin'."

"Bullshit. Say it."

"Just thinking how it's gotta suck for you, always bein' so dedicated and responsible. And I'm pretty sure there ain't no one you've let down recently."

Fletch snorted. "You oughta talk. Your dedication to the people and animals in your life makes me look irresponsible."

Eli grinned. "I gotta one-up ya when I can, *Dr. Fletcher.*"

"I've definitely one-upped you in the vehicle department. This truck of yours is like riding in a tin can."

"Stop fidgeting. I swear you're worse than the rez kids."

"Doubtful. I've seen how wild your charges are."

The caravan pulled around and they followed as the second to last vehicle out, passing Kyle so he could make sure all the gates were closed.

Eli parked at the edge of the road down from the house. "About time to eat, I reckon."

"Good. I'm starved. Maybe there'll be leftovers to take home."

"Says the bachelor," Eli said dryly.

"Says the *former* bachelor who now has a woman fixing his meals *and* warming his bed."

"Your jealousy is fully warranted because my Summer is damn good at both."

"Don't rub it in." Fletch hopped out of the truck and took in the trucks and SUVs as they walked toward the tents. "Seems to be less people here than in years past."

He shrugged. "Ain't that the way it goes? People say they're gonna help and then they don't."

Was that a poke at him? Before he could ask for clarification, Eli spoke again. "There are new faces here. Well, Devin ain't new, but he did show up."

"Why in the hell would Devin show up at a branding? He never has time for this stuff anymore." Fletch squinted at the people clustered in groups of two or three. No surprise he saw Devin talking to some woman by the corrals.

"Mebbe he needed to connect with his roots. Spend time with his friends who don't care that he's a country music superstar. He had a great time. Threw down a lot of calves today. He partnered with Celia and Lainie's friend." He pointed to the woman chatting with Devin. "That girl knows her way around ranch work. She impressed me."

High praise coming from Eli.

Ike motioned to Eli and he jogged up the hill to meet him.

Tobin Hale, Renner's jack-of-all-trades whiz kid, entered Fletch's peripheral vision and handed him a beer. "Heya, Doc."

"Thanks for the beer." He cracked the can open. "What's goin' on?"

"Not much. Wishing there were more single chicks here. We had a blast last year, remember?"

"Parts of it. Other parts . . . kinda hazy."

"You ended up with that Carla chick from Montreal." He sighed. "She was hot. You ever hear from her?"

"Nope. I don't recall why she was even at the branding."

"Seriously?" Tobin glugged down his beer. "She was a photojournalist on assignment for some cowgirl magazine. She kept snapping pictures of chaps and asses. Maybe she got your buck-nekkid butt on film. What if you're on some Wild Men of Wyoming hunk-of-the-month calendar?"

"Fuck off."

Tobin laughed. "Easy for you to say when you're getting laid all the time."

"You're not?" Fletch gave him a lewd once-over. "You ain't that bad lookin'. You packing a peanut or something?"

"Fuck off, old-timer. Ain't a lot of opportunities to meet women when I spend ninety-five percent of my time at the Split Rock with Hugh and Renner. And the guests are off-limits."

Sipping his beer, he watched Devin and his mysterious female branding partner cozied up. "Who's she?"

"Hard not to notice, her, huh? She's the Split Rock's newest employee."

"What's her name?"

"Tanna. I brought a cup of coffee to her trailer this morning, you know, to welcome her, since she only showed up yesterday. She was real sweet. She even laughed at a couple things I said. So I thought I might have a shot at her, but it appears she's fallen for movie-star good looks, fame, money and charm."

"Be easy to hate McClain if he wasn't such a great guy."

"He sure wasn't afraid to get dirty today."

"Devin may be all slicked up when he's onstage, but down deep he'll always be a rough Wyoming cowboy." He considered wandering over and introducing himself, but like Tobin, he couldn't compete with Devin's fame, PR training and practiced charm. But for some reason, he couldn't look away from the couple.

Tobin kept talking and Fletch half listened as he finished his beer.

He watched this Tanna chick flirting shamelessly with Devin. She looked great from the back. Long legs. A tight ass. Curvy hips and a small waist that he could span with his hands. She wore a beat-up straw hat pulled down low that put every part of her face in shadow. She wore dusty, muddy jeans with some greenish substance smeared across the back of her shirt. She held a beer in one hand, gesturing wildly with the other. Whatever she'd said made Devin laugh.

An odd buzz started in the base of his spine as she leaned forward to set her empty beer can on the ground and her hat fell off. Her freed hair fell in a waterfall of mahogany-colored silk.

The same silky tresses that'd trailed across his chest two nights ago.

It was her.

Holy. Fucking. Shit.

It was her.

Fletch immediately stalked across the yard.

Devin's eyes widened when Fletch stormed into view. But Fletch barely spared him a glance; he was entirely focused on seeing the face of the woman who'd been haunting his thoughts for the last two days.

He stepped in front of Devin, forcing her to look at him. "I thought I might be hallucinating."

She gasped. "What in tarnation are you doin' here?"

God that Southern drawl alone made him half hard.

"Please tell me you're not some kind of freaky stalker who's been following me."

Stalker? What the hell? "Be pretty hard to do since you left without a single word or any clue where you were goin'."

She poked him in the chest with her finger. "Those were the parameters we *both* agreed to, big guy. So don't blame me."

"I am. Because you didn't give me a chance to change those parameters." His gaze roamed over her face; he couldn't believe she was here. "You left without a word ... why?"

"What was I supposed to do? Leave you a note?"

"Something, anything would've been nice ..." He offered her a slow, steady smile. "Tanna."

Her eyes narrowed at his deliberate use of her name.

"I'll leave you two alone to talk since you obviously know each other," Devin said behind them.

"No, Devin, stay," Tanna said. "He and I don't have anything to discuss."

A sassy little head shake and a dismissive look wouldn't deter him. Fletch growled, "Get lost," to Devin, while keeping his eyes locked on hers.

"Okay, man, I get it. I'm gone." Devin chuckled. "Although, this could probably give me some new songwriting material."

Fletch snarled, "Go."

Devin walked away.

"Unbelievable. Why did you do that?" Tanna demanded.

"I didn't think you'd want to broadcast that we were screwing like minks the night before last, especially since we didn't exchange names."

"I didn't think you'd act like a caveman if we did cross paths again."

When she tried to sidestep him, he latched onto her upper arm. He pulled her behind him, herding her against the corral and boxing her in. "Wrong answer, sugar twang. You know firsthand that I give in to my baser impulses without apology."

She blushed.

They stared at each other.

"Do you remember when I said you looked familiar and you accused me of feeding you a line?" Fletch asked. "Now I know why. I must've seen you in pictures. I've heard about you, Tanna Barker, Celia's sometime traveling partner. Wild child on the circuit, according to Lainie."

She lifted her chin. "And?"

"And you're so damn beautiful you take my breath away."

Her stiff carriage softened slightly. "You are far too charming and knowledgeable about me, Mr. . . . ?"

"Fletcher. August Fletcher. Everyone calls me Fletch."

She drilled him in the sternum with her fingernail. "Aha! Celia's talked about you too. So has Lainie. You're a vet, right? Veterinarian, not a military vet."

"Yep. Now that that's out of the way, can we go someplace and—"

"No."

Fletch moved in closer. "Why did you immediately say no before hearing my suggestion?"

"It either had something to do with us getting naked, or with us talking."

"Oh, I wanna strip you to skin all right. Then spend the rest of the day and all night reacquainting my hands and mouth with your body. But talking is a good place to start."

Her eyes turned defiant. "We have nothin' to talk about."

"We have everything to talk about now that I know you're sticking around, working at the Split Rock. And you oughta know that I tried to bribe the desk clerk to give me your name after I woke up alone. I walked through the motel and the bar parking lots looking for any vehicle with Texas plates. I couldn't stop thinking about you. I even went to Cactus Jack's last night, hoping that you'd show up."

"Really?"

"Yes. Did you think of me at all?"

She seemed reluctant to answer.

He heard the boot steps and then Eli stepped into view.

"Hey, Fletch. What's goin' on? Looks like you're browbeating this lovely woman."

"We're just having a conversation. A private conversation. Everything is fine."

"Is that right?" Eli asked. But he wasn't looking at Fletch; he was focused on Tanna.

Tanna sidestepped Fletch. "I'll catch up with you later." And she bailed.

Fletch got right in Eli's face. "What the hell was that about?"

"You looked like you were gonna throttle her. People were taking note."

"Remember when I told you about the woman I met? That's her."

Eli's eyebrows rose. "No kiddin'? And she's here? How'd that happen?"

Fate. "Guess it's my lucky day. Get this: she's working up at the Split Rock."

"Look, I ain't one to meddle. But will you go easy on her? She's had a rough year and still hasn't found her footing."

Fletch gave him a suspicious look. "How do you know that?"

"I pay attention."

"You gossip, you mean."

Eli shrugged. "Not gossip if it's the truth. But the truth is, she and I had a conversation earlier."

"What's goin' on with her?"

"Ain't my place to say. You'll have to ask her."

"I would have asked her, but *you* chased her off," Fletch reminded him.

"Like you said. She'll be around. Don't hound her today and give her a reason to avoid you." Eli walked off.

Fletch considered that option for roughly four seconds before he went to track her down.

But she'd disappeared once again.

Chapter Five

❧

*T*anna ducked into the barn from the rear entrance. Hopefully no one had seen her and she'd have a few minutes to think.

Holy, holy shit. In all the wide-open spaces of Wyoming what were the odds that her last hookup would be...a Muddy Gap homeboy?

Fletch—God, the name fit him perfectly with that wickedly naughty grin of his.

The barn door opened and she stepped deeper into the shadows.

Lainie stopped just inside the doorway and called out, "Tanna?"

"Over here."

"Aha. So you were hiding."

"I was just looking for a little quiet time. Why? Did you or Celia need something?"

Lainie plopped beside her on the long wooden bench. "No. I saw you talking to Devin, then Fletch horned in and appeared to be chewing your ass. Then Eli interrupted and you took off. So, what's the deal? Because, dude, this is way better than *The Bachelorette*."

At one time Tanna could've talked to Lainie about anything. But in the years since Lainie had married Hank and settled down as a ranch wife with two kids and a part-time job, they now lived in different worlds. As Tanna internally struggled with her answer, Lainie poked her arm.

"No way, missy. You don't get to pull that silent crap with me. I told you about the wild sex stuff that summer I traveled with Hank and Kyle."

"Which was years ago."

"So, because I'm not single I can't possibly understand your love life anymore?" Lainie said with an edge to her voice. "That's crap. We're friends. Friends talk."

Tanna released a slow breath. "Maybe I don't wanna tell you because I'm embarrassed about my most recent one-night stand."

"With who? And how recently?"

"With Fletch. Thursday night."

"Fletch?" Lainie cocked her head and stared at her. "How'd that happen?"

Tanna met Lainie's gaze. "I wanted to cut loose and he was the guy holding the scissors. I didn't tell him my name and refused to let him tell me his."

She laughed. "You guys really didn't exchange any personal information?"

"Nothin' besides we were both single and we don't have any sexually transmitted diseases." Tanna braced herself for Lainie's reaction.

But Lainie just whistled. "You've always been a braver soul than me. So, with the angry way Fletch loomed over you, I take it you snuck out before he woke up?"

"That was our deal. He had no right to act all pissy and territorial."

"Fletch never acts that way."

She offered Lainie a shrug. "Fletch just needs to realize I meant it when I said I wasn't interested in any kind of relationship."

Lainie opened her mouth. Closed it. Opened it again. "Why not?"

"Because I need to figure out where I'll go and what I'll do after this job ends."

"Does that include thinking about returning to barrel racing?"

Tanna fidgeted. "I don't know."

Lainie patted Tanna's thigh and stood. "It's too bad, though. Fletch is a great guy. Crazy busy with his practice. I swear he puts as many miles on his vehicle as you do each year. And he's not the type of guy looking for a permanent thing either."

Rather than continuing to hide in the barn, Tanna followed Lainie outside. Two tables had been set up in the backyard and she felt guilty watching Celia bustling about. "Celia, is there anything I can do?"

"Nope. Our neighbor Ronna had everything organized ahead of time. She and Kyle's mother practically threw me out of my own kitchen." She rolled her eyes. "I'm pregnant, not helpless."

A woman with fiery red hair, sharply dressed in a rhinestone dotted Western shirt and jeans, came up behind Celia and hugged her. "It won't hurt you, my darlin' girl, to take the help when you can get it. Because as soon as my grandbaby is here, you're gonna wish you'd taken the time to put up your feet when you had the chance. Now why don't you sit down and I'll bring you a plate?"

Celia kissed the woman's cheek. "You spoil me, Sherry. I've got a couple things to do and then I promise I'll sit."

Tears welled in Tanna's eyes at seeing that sweet moment between Kyle's mom and Celia. She missed so much about her mother, especially the casual affection they had shared.

All around her, conversations rose and fell. Kids cried. Chairs scraped against the cement. A radio played country tunes. Just a typical gathering on a ranch. She could be on any ranch anywhere in the country. So her sense of the familiar warred with her disconnected feeling. Somehow she found herself wandering to the fence that housed the horses.

The sunny day had become cloudy and the wind had picked up. She rested her elbows on the top of the fence and watched the horses in the distance. At least a dozen milled about, starting to get spooked by the weather. She didn't see any foals, but the new mamas and babies might be in a different pasture.

Boots scraped behind her, but she didn't turn around, expecting it'd be Fletch. But it wasn't. Eli propped a boot on the bottom rung and stared across the landscape.

She fought a ridiculous pang of disappointment. "You don't have to hard sell me on accepting your help, Eli. I said I'd think about it."

"That ain't my style at all. I came to apologize that I interrupted earlier with Fletch."

"You didn't interrupt."

"That's not what he said." Eli's dark brown eyes met hers. "He mentioned you to me."

"He did?" Tanna couldn't keep the surprise out of her voice.

"Yep. Before he knew you were here. Before he recognized you."

That startled her—and pissed her off a little—so she tossed off, "Was he bragging about his most recent hookup?"

Eli shook his head. "Girl, you are defensive. But no. Fletch ain't like that."

"What did he say?"

"That he was an idiot for letting you get away without having a way to contact you."

"Oh."

Eli said, "Fletch is a really good guy."

"You don't have to warn me off your friend. I won't drag him into my drama. That one night was it."

"Fletch is one determined cuss. He'll aim to change your mind."

"He can try. But there's a reason I was named 'Most Stubborn' on the circuit."

Eli grinned. "Ironic that his football nickname was 'Muley' because of his stubborn streak. It's gonna be fun watching you two."

Tanna threw up her hands. "There's nothin' to watch!"

"Keep telling yourself that." He offered another quick grin. "Let's see if there's any food left."

They walked back to the house in silence. Tanna felt Fletch's eyes on her, but he didn't approach her. She filled a plate and listened to Devin entertaining Hank, Abe, Kyle, the two guys she'd met this morning who worked at the Split Rock, Tobin and Hugh, and two other men she'd met earlier, Bran and Ike.

Devin said, "She don't look nothin' like in her videos where she's always glammed up."

"I'd still take her for a tumble," Tobin said.

"You'd have to get past her two bodyguards. And they are mean SOBs."

"Why don't you have bodyguards?" Ike asked Devin with a snicker.

"Fuck off. I don't need one, let alone two. At the bigger venues I get assigned a security detail, but they're more like drivers herding me into the car, getting me where I need to go."

Someone's cell phone rang, forcing a pause in the conversation.

Bran answered. "Hey, darlin'. I was just . . . what? When?" He moved out of line abruptly. "Come on, sugar. Take a deep breath." He listened. "That's it." He frowned. "You're sure Tierney and Renner are okay with takin' care of him for that long? Uh-huh. I'll tell her. No. I will. I promise. Harper," he said sharply, "calm down. Remember to breathe. We've been through this before and you did great. Yep. I'm on my way. Love you, baby." He hung up.

"What's up?" Hank said.

"Harper's water broke. And she's already had contractions. So I gotta get her to the hospital." He looked around. "Where's Celia?"

"I'll grab her," Kyle said and left.

Bran paced. Stopped. Looked at Hank and Abe. "How long's it take to deliver a second baby?"

"Usually way less time than a first baby," Abe said. "Why?"

"I might need one of you to check cattle for me in the morning."

"No problem. Just keep us up to date."

Celia rushed forward. "Harper's in labor?"

"Yeah. She wanted to know if Tierney and Renner can't watch Tate all night, if you'd mind picking him up and bringing him back here."

"I'd love to. But Tierney is great with him and I know she won't mind keeping him. Don't worry. Now. Go." She shoved him a little. "Harper needs you. But I'd suggest you wear protective hand covering in the delivery room this time."

"Thanks." Bran jogged to his truck.

When Celia wandered over to the picnic table, Tanna said, "Why would he need protective hand covering?"

"Because when Harper was in labor with Tate, she squeezed Bran's hand so hard she dislocated his knuckle," Fletch said and sat down beside her. *Right* beside her.

Tanna didn't say anything but her stupid heart skipped a beat.

"I should've asked if I could get you a beer. Corona, right?"

"No. In fact, I'm done."

Fletch's hand gripped her thigh under the table. Then he slid his hand down to her knee and squeezed gently. "Don't go on my account."

It'd look like she was running from him if she left now. And Tanna Barker didn't run from any man. She glanced up to see Celia's gaze winging between them.

"You two know each other?" Celia asked.

"We've met." Fletch didn't elaborate. Neither did Tanna.

Hank, Abe and Ike left, distracting Celia long enough for Tanna to hiss, "Stop it."

Fletch leaned a fraction closer and whispered, "Make me."

"What are you, an eight-year-old boy?"

"More like a sixteen-year-old boy," he murmured in her ear. "I've had a hard-on since I first saw you today."

"Really? That's an original line. *Not.*"

He chuckled. "Sugar twang, that wasn't a line but the gospel truth. And I'll keep throwing you lines all damn night if I thought you'd bite."

"What are you two whispering about over there?" Celia demanded.

Tanna smirked. "Fletch was just confessing that he'd rather deal with a hundred pregnant heifers than just one human woman in labor."

Celia's mouth dropped open. "Omigod, August Fletcher, I oughta reach over and smack you for that."

"Calm down, brat. Tanna was kidding. She likes to get folks riled up. The last time we were together, you gotta rise out of me, what? Four times? In one night?"

Double entendre much?

And dammit. She blushed. Again. She never fucking blushed.

"What are you two talking about?" Celia complained. "I'm lost."

"Inside joke. You up for a little honky-tonking tonight?" Fletch asked Tanna, changing the subject.

That grabbed Devin's attention as he plopped down with a plate piled high with food. "Hey, I wanna come dancin'."

Tobin and Hugh took seats at the table.

"I might have to pass," Tanna said. "I've gotta work in the morning. Wouldn't do to show up hungover on my first day."

"There is that possibility, given how you and I are when we drink to-gether," Devin said.

"Huh-uh. You ain't pinning that on me, hillbilly rock star." She pointed at him with her fork. "You were the one who bought the whole damn bottle of Jaeger. I'da been fine with just one shot."

"So you and the country superstar are drinking buddies?" Fletch asked tightly.

"Not often, thank God," Tanna retorted.

"Not often enough for me," Devin volleyed back with a sexy growl.

"Do you remember the first night we drank together? After Celia and Kyle tied the knot?" Tanna laughed at Devin's perplexed look. "See? You don't remember."

He shrugged. "I'll admit some of that night is a little hazy. So lay it on me, baby. What sort of bad/nasty/wrong things did we do together?"

Fletch stiffened and Tanna felt his eyes boring into her.

"Don't worry. You weren't interested in doin' none of that bawdy sex stuff with me." She mock-whispered to Tobin, "I could've been buck-assed nekkid dancing on the bar top and he wouldn't have reacted."

Tobin made a whimpering groan.

"See?" Devin said. "In my defense I must've been drunk because sober I'da been all over that. All over you, sweet Tex-ass."

She rolled her eyes. "Let's see . . . we were dancing. Then we were up at the bar having another celebratory shot in honor of the happy couple, when these two barely legal chickies horned in. They were all *I can't believe you're Devin McClain! I love you. Can you sign my big, fake tits?*"

Laughter broke out and Hugh choked on his beer.

"The next thing I knew, bimbo one and bimbo two were ordering blow job shots and Devin said he'd rather have the real thing. Then he blew me off so his groupies could blow him on his tour bus."

"I'm sure I had a blast. But as Tanna so tactfully pointed out"—Celia and a couple others snickered—"my excessive alcohol consumption had blocked those memory banks from that night."

"You don't remember bein' with two chicks at one time?" Tobin said, horror on his face.

"Nope."

"Dude. I don't know whether to be jealous you've been in that situation so many times it's normal for you, or . . . pissed off that you can't give us a play-by-play."

"And with that, boy wonder, it's time to hit the road." Hugh stood and asked Celia, "Where's Kyle?"

"In the kitchen talking to his mom."

"We'll catch him on the way out." Hugh nodded to the guys at the table. "Nice seein' you all."

"I'll come with you," Celia said, and they trooped into the house, leaving Tanna, Fletch and Devin at the table.

Fletch swallowed a drink of beer but kept his mesmerizing eyes on her. "So, what do you say? Wanna do a little dancing?"

"You do realize if I say yes, it won't be mattress dancing, right?"

Fletch laughed, reminding Tanna that he had a great laugh. "A man can hope."

She ran her hand over her hair. She needed a shower, but she wouldn't have to fend off the advances she knew were coming from Fletch, if she smelled like a barnyard. "Fine. One drink. One dance."

"Good. Let's go," Devin said.

A funny looked crossed Fletch's face but he nodded. "You're riding with me."

A little high-handed of Fletch to expect that Devin wouldn't want to ride with her. But to be honest, she needed a few minutes alone to clear her head. "I gotta go rub it in el preggo's face that she's missing out on all the fun and say good-bye. I'll follow you."

Chapter Six

They'd barely made it out of the driveway when Devin jumped him. "What the fuck is wrong with you, Fletch? You're a grumpy dick today."

"Then I'm surprised that you fucking bulled your way into hanging out with me and Tanna tonight."

"Jesus. So your asshole attitude is outta jealousy?"

"No." Fletch's hands tightened on the steering wheel. "Maybe. Fuck. Probably."

Devin turned toward him. "Tell me what's going on with you two."

"Nothin'."

"Bullshit."

"This goes no further than us. Thursday night we hooked up in a bar in Rawlins. Had a few drinks, some laughs, followed by awesome sex. Like off-the-charts-awesome sex. When I saw her today—"

"You didn't call her the day after? Man, Fletch, I warned you to knock that shit off."

"Says the manwhore who lives by the *no names* rule," Fletch said dryly.

Devin flipped him off.

"So it was supposed to be one night. I was kicking myself for not getting her name or number because we connected . . . I saw her today and I just wanted to beat the hell out of any guy talking to her, because *I* wanted to talk to her. That's never fucking happened to me before." He exhaled a frustrated puff of air. "Then I find out you know her pretty damn good."

"We've crossed paths a bunch of times. I like her. She's fun. She's wild. She ain't afraid to let her hair down. I've been trying to sweet-talk her into my bed for two and a half years."

Fletch shocked both of them and released a little growl.

Devin laughed. "Somehow that woman has resisted my charms. But I do feel the need to warn you."

"About what?"

"Her. One Tanna Barker, three-time national barrel racing champion, is very much into threesomes. She's also very much the *no names* one-night roll in the hay kinda chick."

"I don't give a damn about how many guys she's slept with before now. But the fact remains she'll be living in Muddy Gap for the summer and I want all her one-night stands to be with me from here on out."

Devin whistled. "You're serious."

"Completely."

"Fletch. Come on. You live in Rawlins, forty miles from the Split Rock. You are a workaholic. You've been in a relationship…never as I recall. With the exception of Miss King Kong tits."

Fletch snorted. "King Kong tits? Her name was Karen. And we dated for four months, so that qualifies as a relationship."

"What was that? Seven years ago?"

"I've been busy building my practice."

"Which leads me back to the workaholic point. Don't try and pressure Tanna into giving you something that you can't offer in return. The surest way to kill any chance with her is to act like a possessive douche bag the first fucking night she's in town."

Fletch hated that Devin was making sense.

"See how tonight goes. If she's into you, wanting you to go home with her, I'll take your truck and leave. But if she doesn't want you, then you will not goddamn badger her, okay?"

"All right. Fuck. I'm not a rapist stalker. I do comprehend the word *no*, asshole."

They parked in the back lot at the Buckeye.

Tanna seemed nervous as they walked up to the front entrance. When Fletch placed his hand in the middle of her back, she seemed to relax.

But once they were inside the bar she shook him off.

"You guys grab a spot up front," Devin said. "I'll get the first round."

After they sat, Tanna was too busy gawking at the unique space for conversation. When he caught her trying to discreetly straighten her clothes and fluff up her hair, he placed his hand on her arm, staying the motion. "You don't need to fuss, Tanna. You are beautiful. Even after rolling around in the corrals all day, wrassling calves."

She leaned closer and warned, "Don't use that fake bullshit flattery on me."

"Not bullshit, sugar twang, that's what I see. Don't lump me in with losers who spew that stuff hoping it'll get them laid."

"Oh, so you're *not* here hoping you can sweet-talk me into goin' another round with you?"

Fletch stared at her mouth. Remembering the hotness factor of seeing her lips wrapped around his cock. And how her eyes would lock on his and then flutter closed damn near in ecstasy.

"That is so not fair," she hissed.

"What?"

"Looking at me with those sexy bedroom eyes, stripping me naked like you're deciding which part of me you want to devour first."

He grinned. "Good to know one of your talents is mind reading."

Tanna looked annoyed for two seconds before she smiled. "Okay, I will just shut the hell up now. Although, I do wanna ask you one thing before Devin gets here. Why did you rent a motel room Thursday night? When you live in Rawlins?"

"Would you have gone home with me if I'd asked you to?"

"No. That's also why I didn't offer up the room I'd rented before I hit the bar."

"No wonder you snuck off so quickly. You had an escape hatch." He didn't want to ask the question but he did anyway. "The thought of facing me, learning my name and me learning yours was so terrifying that you scurried off?"

Devin interrupted her response by setting three bottles on the table. "Here we go. A round of Coronas." He held his bottle up and waited for them to do the same. "Cheers."

Tanna spoke to Devin. "So, when you come in here, do people recognize you? Since you're a hometown boy?"

"Yeah."

"They don't bother you for autographs?"

"Depends. I'm pretty sure the twelve people who live here who wanted my autograph already have it."

She laughed.

"Did you think they'd throw confetti or mob me when I walked in?"

"I didn't know what to expect; that's why I asked." Tanna sipped her beer. "I've been with you when you've been spotted by fans. Remember Apalachicola?"

"Apalacha-what?" Fletch said.

"Apalachicola. It's a town in Florida. Superstar here played a county fair and I was entered in the rodeo, so we met up after his concert. His fans followed him and chased us all over. Finally we lost them and ended up sitting on the beach until sunrise."

Devin reached out and squeezed her hand.

An unspoken communication passed between them and Fletch found himself grinding his teeth.

Then Devin said, "When we go out around here, it's usually Fletch who's mobbed. People wanting an on-the-fly diagnosis for Lassie. For free."

"Does that happen often?" Tanna asked.

Before he could answer, *All the damn time*, Bill Leckland swung by to ask about a heifer not producing enough milk. Soon as Bill left, Charlotte St. Croix asked if he knew anyone selling blue heeler puppies.

"See? What'd I tell you? Around here, Doc is the superstar."

Fletch bit back a comment that he didn't need Devin to build him up. "Tell me what you'll be doin' up at the Split Rock."

"Working in the clothing store and bartending." Tanna swigged her beer. "Temporary gig through the summer."

"Start of county fair season means I'm on the road through the first part of October," Devin said. "Gonna be brutal."

"Don't lie. You look forward to it."

Devin smiled widely. "I love it. There's nothin' like the rush of bein' onstage. Except for sex."

Fletch glanced at Tanna the same time she looked at him. He didn't bother to bank the heat in his eyes.

Silence descended between them. Normally Devin would fill the air with chatter, but he too seemed preoccupied.

After two more interruptions, which required Fletch's attention, Devin sighed. "Tanna, put this man out of his misery and dance with him. At least out there no one will cut in and demand an on-the-fly diagnosis."

Thank you, Dev.

Tanna seemed torn. But someone must've been about to approach him from behind because she grabbed his hand and abruptly tugged him to his feet. "Show me how well you dance vertically, Doc."

On the dance floor Tanna attempted to keep a proper distance, but Fletch didn't allow it. He clasped her right hand in his left and wrapped his right arm across her lower back, pressing them chest to chest.

"Close enough for you?" she asked with a tinge of sarcasm.

"It'll do." He paused. "For now."

"Fletch—"

"Damn, I love the way my name sounds flowing from your tongue." He shuffled backward and spun them away from the bar.

She tipped her head back and looked at him. "One beer. One dance."

"One kiss?" he asked hopefully.

"No. As awesome as the other night was, it can't happen again."

"Why not? Because, sugar twang, it was awesome. I imagine we could get it to spectacular if we practiced a lot more."

Tanna laughed and beat her forehead into his chest with mock frustration.

He nuzzled the top of her head. "What's really goin' on?"

"I've got a few things to work through this summer. I promised myself I wouldn't get distracted." Those dark brown eyes connected with his again. "And you, Dr. Fletcher, would be a huge distraction."

That didn't sound complimentary. But it hadn't sounded insulting either. He could work with that.

"I've barely been here twenty-four hours. I haven't even started my job yet. I need to get my bearings. Seeing you at the ranch…threw me off."

After that admission, Fletch pressed his point. "Because you felt it that night too."

She smirked. "I can feel it now. But I can't offer you anything but friendship."

Fletch waggled his brows. "Friends with bennies?"

"You never give up."

Not when it comes to you. He kissed her forehead. "I'll give it a rest."

A slow song came on next and she didn't pull away. He closed his eyes and enjoyed the moment. When the song finished he stepped back. "Thanks for the dance, friend."

"See? You didn't choke on the word."

Back at the table, Devin appeared to be fighting off the advances of a woman and her daughter.

Devin stood. "There you guys are. For a second I worried you'd run off with my girl."

Before he said anything, Tanna plastered herself against Devin's side. "No way. You are my only love muffin forever and ever amen." She kissed the corner of his mouth and the hand she'd placed on his chest moved down the center of his body toward the waistband of his jeans.

Devin laughed a little too heartily. "Can you at least wait until we get outside, bunny boo?"

Bunny boo? Fletch didn't know whether to groan or gag.

Tanna pouted. "As long as we can go right now."

"Your wish"—Devin kissed her temple—"is my command. Excuse us, ladies."

Fletch followed an entwined Tanna and Devin out of the bar, reminding himself it was a con, shoving down the temptation to knock the smooth-talking superstar on his ass for having his hand on Tanna's ass.

They ducked between the pickups.

Tanna let loose a loud whoop and Devin clapped his hand over her mouth to stifle her laughter.

"That was not fucking funny at all, Tex-ass."

"What the hell happened? We were gone from the table ten minutes."

Devin released Tanna and slumped against the pickup. "The mother and daughter duo pounced on me because they are my biggest fans. They offered..." He shuddered. "I don't wanna think it, let alone share it with you. So come on, Fletch. I know there's good scotch at your place that'll completely scrub this incident from my brain."

Fletch and Tanna exchanged an amused look. In light of their shared camaraderie, he said, "You wanna come over for a nightcap?"

"Nah. First day of work tomorrow. But I'll take a rain check." Once she realized what she'd said, she backtracked. "You know. One of these days this summer."

"I'm holding you to that."

All Devin had to do was open his arms and Tanna was right there, hugging him.

Fletch should've given them privacy, but he couldn't make himself step back.

"Take care, hillbilly rock star. If you can't keep it in your pants at least wear a love glove, okay?"

"Will do. Loop me in on your wild summer exploits."

"Wild. Right. I'll be as mild-mannered as an old school marm."

He snorted. "That'll be the day."

"You know how to get back to the Split Rock?"

"I've got GPS."

"Good."

Fletch couldn't think of anything else to keep Tanna from going.

She said, "Drive safe," and climbed in her truck.

He realized he'd been standing there like an idiot, watching her drive away, when Devin cleared his throat. "We leaving or what?"

"Yeah. Get in the truck."

"Fletch, if you wanna talk about it—"

"I don't. But that scotch is sounding better and better."

❧

An hour later, Tanna sat in her living room, startled when three loud raps sounded on the door. Then the door opened and a female voice said, "Knock, knock."

Tanna peered around the edge of the room divider. "Who is it?"

"Harlow Pratt. We're coworkers. Can I come in?"

Aren't you already? "Sure."

The woman bounded forward like a puppy. "Hey! Tanna, right?"

"Right."

"It's great to meet you." Tanna scrutinized her. Harlow looked nothing like her sister Tierney. Maybe it was the shocking pink hair, cut in funky, chunky layers. Maybe it was the nose piercing. Or the eyebrow piercing. Or the dozen piercings lining each ear. She wore a gray sharkskin-looking dress, ripped black fishnet stockings and vivid orange hiking boots with neon blue laces.

Her first thought? No way could this woman sell Western clothing in a punk hooker *Tron* meets *Mad Max* getup.

Harlow plopped on the couch and pulled a bottle out of her gigantic Hello Kitty purse. A bottle filled with a green liquid, the color somewhere between NyQuil and Midori melon liqueur. "I thought we could have a shot to celebrate and kick off our summer right."

"What the hell is that?"

"Absinthe. Ever had it?"

"No. I'm not sure I wanna tackle it now."

Harlow giggled. "It used to be illegal but they must've changed the formula or something because you can buy it. Do you have glasses?"

Tanna started to refuse, until she realized Harlow had taken the first step for them to get to know each other. The least she could do was have a drink with her. "I doubt I have shot glasses. Is that poured over ice or anything?"

"Drinking it straight means you don't really taste it."

"That doesn't sound good, Harlow."

"Oh, it's not good. But it's the only booze I had left."

Tanna grabbed two small Dixie cups and set them on the coffee table. "I take it you drove here?"

"Straight through from Chicago. Normally I don't travel with liquor, but I moved out of my apartment and I'm too thrifty to toss the bottle out, so I brought it along." She poured two generous slugs and nudged a cup toward Tanna.

Tanna peered at the green goo, then sniffed it.

Harlow lifted her cup. "To a great summer."

"Cheers." Tanna closed her eyes and drained the contents with one swallow. She fought a shiver when the liquid hit her stomach like battery acid. When she opened her eyes, she noticed Harlow wore a grimace too.

"Nasty shit."

"Yep. And I bet it's an ugly color when it comes back up too." Harlow waggled the bottle at Tanna. "Feeling up to one more?"

Tanna grinned. "What the hell?"

"Good woman." Harlow poured refills and said, "You get to make the toast."

"To not barfing in our sheets tonight."

"Or on our shoes."

They toasted and drank. The shot wasn't any better the second time.

"That's enough of that," Harlow said with a shudder.

"I can't even offer you a beer since I haven't been to the store yet."

"Too bad we can't sneak into the lodge for a drink, but I'm sure my big sis would frown on that. Since we're employees and all."

"So, tell me how you ended up working at the Split Rock," Tanna said.

"I've been on a walkabout all over the world the last three years. Working with some humanitarian groups in third world countries and generally fucking off on my dad's dime. He got tired of it and cut me off. Then he said I should learn to be more like Tierney, which is ridiculous because, *hello?* She's a genius. She's got like four advanced college degrees and she makes type A personality people look like slackers." Harlow propped her hiking boots on the coffee table. "My big sis is the greatest person in the world and I'll never come close to being like her, even if I...I don't know... *tried.*

"It's really funny because my dad was so furious when Tierney quit working for him and took over property management for this place. Then she went and did the unthinkable—she married a cowboy. For love." She gasped dramatically. "Tierney cut Dad out of her life completely. Somehow that caused him to wake up and realize he was an asshole—and would be a lonely asshole if he kept it up. They've been trying to get along ever since. Which is great for them, but shitty for me because now, Dad wants her to help me 'make something' of myself. *You're almost twenty-six, Harlow. It's time to become a responsible member of society. When I was your age* ... blah, blah, blah. So here I am. What about you?"

Tanna gave Harlow the condensed version of the past two years, finishing with, "We'll see what happens after Labor Day."

"I'll be sticking around at least until Tierney's baby is born. I cannot wait to be an aunt. I'm gonna spoil that baby rotten."

"If Renner will let you," she said dryly. "He is awful protective of Tierney."

"I know. She's so lucky." Harlow sighed. "Not only is Renner unbelievably hot, he gets my quirky sister. And the way he looks at her ... Maybe someday I'll get a guy to look at me like that, huh?"

"Maybe."

"I've resigned myself to kissing a lot of frogs before I find a prince." She winked. "How fortunate we've got a pond full of 'em so close by."

Who would Harlow try to sink her hooks into first? Fletch's gorgeous face came to mind. Would Tanna have an issue if Harlow set her sights on the hot vet?

Hell, yes.

But you're just friends, remember?

Harlow stood and stowed the bottle of absinthe in her purse. "Great meeting you, Tanna. I promised I'd get rid of the punk hair, so I'm off to see what color my hair will turn out when I bleach out the pink."

"Good luck with that."

"See you at the ungodly hour of nine a.m."

Tanna followed her to the door. "Which trailer are you staying in?"

"None. I'm crashing at Tierney's old cabin. I'll admit I wasn't too proud to beg for it. Probably the only time I can play the I'm-your-baby-sister-card and get away with it." She grinned. "Night."

It'd be interesting to see what kind of worker Harlow would be. Her attitude and Tierney's warning suggested Miss Harlow would try to rule the roost.

Huh-uh. Not happening. There was only one cock of the walk in this place and Tanna had better make sure Harlow understood that it wasn't her.

Chapter Seven

$\mathcal{S}$unday morning Tanna showed up in the dining room on time.

She and Renner were on their second cup of coffee when Harlow strolled in, yawning.

"Sorry. I overslept."

Renner frowned. Tanna figured he'd let her tardiness slide, but he waited until she had her coffee to speak, so he had her full attention.

"There ain't any special privileges for you here, Harlow, so get that outta your head right now. You're here to work. Which means bein' on time according to the *lodge* schedule, not your personal whims. Got it?"

Harlow saluted. "Yes, sir."

He scrutinized her face and her clothing choices. "Let's talk about uniforms."

"What? We have to wear some stupid uniform?" Harlow demanded.

"If you're serving in the lounge, yes. You'll wear black pants and a long-sleeved white shirt. The dress code for Wild West Clothiers is casual. What you've got on"—he pointed to Harlow's clothing: a tie-dyed tank top, cutoff jeans and flip-flops—"is not appropriate."

Tanna was relieved Renner would keep an eye on his sister-in-law for dress code violations so she wouldn't have to.

"The clothing store is open from ten to five, Monday through Saturday, but inventory and restocking need to be done every morning, which means you'll need to be here at eight. The lounge is staffed from four to ten every night. Slowest night is Sunday. So it'll depend on the reservation situation, whether we'll staff it. No guests check in until tomorrow, so you're both clear tonight. Any questions?"

Harlow raised her hand. "Are we paid hourly or are we on salary?"

"Hourly. I'll show you where the time clock is."

"Is there commission on clothing sales?" Harlow asked.

"No."

"Are meals included the days we work?" Harlow asked again.

"No. But you can use the fitness center after ten at night. The pool is off-limits if there are guests here."

Tanna bit back a laugh at the sour look on Harlow's face.

"Let's go over the lodge rules." Twenty minutes later, Renner said, "Any questions?"

They both looked at Harlow. She shook her head.

"I'd like to have you both workin' at Wild West Clothiers tomorrow. It'll give you time to look over the merchandise. Harper is a helluva sales-woman, so you've got big boots to fill for the next couple months. Then I'll have you both workin' in the lounge too. There's a meeting here tomorrow night but it won't go past ten."

"Is that a regular occurrence? A group renting out the lounge for a private meeting?" Tanna asked.

Renner shook his head. "Usually it's something I've set up, like a Split Rock shareholders meeting. I will say that Harper has two or three groups of women that come here to shop from Casper, Cheyenne and Rock Springs. Since we know ahead of time, we set up a private luncheon for them."

"Bet that's good for sales."

"Yep. There's nothin' like handselling." He stood. "Let's take the grand tour."

It took three hours to see everything, including the barns, the riding stables and two of the shorter walking paths. They backtracked by way of the barn and Tanna was relieved they didn't approach the horses. It'd be embarrassing if she freaked out in front of her new boss.

Tobin, the cute ranch hand with twinkling eyes and deep-set dimples, leaned over the fence. The ranch foreman, Hugh, a stoic guy with a scruffy beard and his face hidden beneath his hat, stood alongside Tobin.

"Pretty ladies," he said with a grin. "And Renner."

"Hey, Tobin," Harlow cooed. "You're looking too good to spend the day torturing cattle. What do you say we pack a picnic and go frolic by a stream or something?"

Tobin laughed. "I appreciate the offer, but I'm already spoken for today."

Harlow sauntered forward, parking herself in front of Hugh. "What about you, Grumpy? You ready to drop your pickax and hi-ho away from here for a little R and R?"

"No." He spun on his heel and stalked off.

"You'd be wise not to taunt him, Harlow," Renner warned. "You might need his help with something and he'll leave you high and dry because you're such a tease."

Tanna and Tobin exchanged a look.

"I just won't talk to him at all. If the tour is done, I'm going back to bed." She flounced off down the hill, slipping and sliding in her flip-flops until she disappeared behind a cluster of trees.

Renner sighed. "Tanna, you'll need to tell me if she's not pulling her weight."

"I will. But I do have to ask. She has held a job before?"

"She worked in restaurants and bars and clothing stores through college. No idea how long she lasted at any of those, but she ain't a total greenhorn." He looked at Tobin. "You're all right with hanging out in the lodge today?"

"Yes, sir. I'll change before I head up there."

Renner looked at Tanna. "What are your plans?"

"Grocery shopping."

"If you get bored, you could always hang out with Tobin in the lodge. I'm sure he'd appreciate the company." He grinned. "Later."

When Tanna glanced over at Tobin, his face was bright red.

"I hope you don't think I put him up to that. Because I'd never—"

"I know. Don't sweat it, Tobin."

He relaxed.

"I'm heading to Rawlins for food. Which is the best grocery store?"

"Super-Valu. They have a decent deli." He grinned. "Hey. I'm a bachelor. I eat a lot of sandwiches."

"Me too. My fridge in my horse trailer is pretty small."

"I saw you talkin' to Eli yesterday. Are you gonna work with him while you're here?"

Did everybody know about her situation? "Do you know something about him that I should?"

"Not at all. He's just really good with horses and riders. The best I've seen, actually. And I saw a lot of guys pretending they were horse whisperers and all that crap and none of them come close to what he can do."

"Good to know."

During the forty-minute drive into town, Tanna wondered if she'd be spending a lot of time alone this summer, after her shift ended. That was a depressing thought.

You could spend as much time as you want with the oh-so-sexy animal doc.

That was tempting. They'd been in perfect synch that night. She'd had more than her fair share of great sex, but that encounter ranked in the top five. Maybe even the top three. So why had she said no to him yesterday at the branding when he asked to see her again?

Her conversation with Lainie swam front and center. Everything she'd said had been true. But it'd been bold talk when she was surrounded by people. She'd change her tune right fast when she returned to an empty trailer every night. She had spent years on the road, driving from event to event by herself, so she should be used to miles of blacktop and no one to talk to—except her mom and didn't that just make her a pathetic mama's girl?

Maybe after she returned from her store run she'd make Tobin a sandwich and take it up to the lodge.

❧

Fletch was restless. Not an entirely unfamiliar feeling, but he wasn't sure how to handle it. After spending time with Tanna, he realized he had to convince that little gal they'd be good for each other. Even short-term. And he wasn't sure how to do that.

Maybe his dad had an idea. He called him, giving a heads-up he was on his way over.

His father lived in a retirement community in Rawlins, in a one-bedroom with a view of the golf course. Bruce Fletcher didn't play golf, but he liked looking out the big picture window across the sloping green hills. Fletch paid for that premium view, but his father's happiness was worth it. He'd raised Fletch alone, for the most part, since Fletch's mother, Darla Fast Dog, had a habit of disappearing for months at a time.

Fletch hadn't asked how Bruce, an oil field worker, had knocked up a twenty-two-year-old Indian woman from the reservation—at the time his dad had been forty. Sometimes his father spoke fondly of the year Darla had lived with him, prior to Fletch's birth and shortly after.

His parents hadn't married. Wedding vows would've meant nothing to Darla anyway. Throughout his childhood she'd appear whenever the mood struck her. She'd attempt to be a partner and mother, staying as long as she could stand it, but she always ended up running back to the rez.

The year he'd turned ten, she'd shown up looking like death warmed over. His father had taken her to the hospital and the doctor diagnosed her with late-stage breast cancer—past the stage treatment could help her or save her. Bruce, being a kind man, a man who did right by his family, cared for her until she passed on. He didn't argue with her family about Indian burial specifics, but he insisted he and Fletch be allowed to attend the ceremony.

It was the first contact Fletch had with his Native American relatives. He still remembered their skeptical eyes as he marched to the front pew. They whispered about him, some blatantly questioning whether he was Darla's kid—he looked too white. He remembered wanting to turn around to tell them to shut up. But his dad had held him steady. Fletch understood as long as he had his father, he didn't need anyone else.

Shaking off his melancholy, he scaled the steps to the entrance and waited in the entryway for his dad to buzz him into the building.

And as usual, his father leaned against the doorjamb, waiting for him. He wasn't as spry as he used to be, but he looked good for a seventy-seven-year-old man.

"Heya, Dad." Fletch hugged him.

His dad returned the embrace. "Son, how was your week?"

"Busy. Yesterday was the branding at Kyle and Celia's place."

"How are the Gilchrists?"

Fletch followed his dad into the living room and flopped into the easy chair. "Good. I guess Celia was wanting to rope and drag calves but Kyle put his foot down."

His dad chuckled. "True cowgirl, that one is. Think that baby of theirs will be born with a rope in hand."

"Probably. While we were eating, Bran got a call from Harper. She went into labor."

"What'd she have?"

"Another boy. Named him Jake. Mom and baby are fine. Hank and Abe were there. So were Ike and Devin."

"Sounds like they had a good crew. Was Eli there?"

"Of course."

"Was Summer with him?"

"No."

His father sighed. "Eli's choice? Or Summer's?"

"Summer's, I think. She's still adjusting. And Eli isn't one to push. Even when he should."

For the next hour they talked about their respective weeks, sports, politics, Fletch's upcoming schedule and some weird comment about potential vacation plans that made zero sense. He'd always been able to talk to his dad about anything, so when the conversation hit a lull, he wondered why he hesitated to mention Tanna.

"Something on your mind, son?"

"Yeah, but I feel kind of stupid bringing it up."

"Then it's gotta be about a woman."

Fletch's gaze snapped to his dad's.

His father chuckled. "You're a private guy when it comes to that stuff. I imagine it's behavior you learned from me. So, what's going on?"

He shoved a hand through his hair. "Thursday night I met a woman at a bar. There's something between us. She denies it. But I know she felt it too. I don't understand why she doesn't want to get involved ... ah, romantically, since she'll be working up at the Split Rock all summer." Fletch leaned forward, resting his forearms on his knees. "So why did she mention that we could be friends?"

"Maybe because she'll only be here temporarily. Potential messy breakup and all that. So my advice is to take her up on the friend offer."

"But that's not all I want from her."

"So lie."

"Excuse me? I thought I heard Mr. Never-Tell-A-Lie suggesting I do exactly that."

His father gave him a half shrug. "Convince her you're fine being her friend. She'll at least agree to spend time with you. Take her out for coffee. You can casually wear down her resistance. You'll be back in funny business with her before you know it."

"Huh. You really think that'll work?"

"What were you planning to do?"

Storm her house, kiss her stupid, strip her naked and after an orgasm or ten, beg her to date me.

Maybe the coffee thing would work better. To start with anyway.

"I believe I'll skip my plan for now and go with yours." He grabbed the remote. "So, what game are we watching first?"

⟨⟨

Fletch hadn't taken an emergency call all day, so when Hugh at the Split Rock had called concerned about a new foal, he hadn't hesitated to hop in his truck.

Not just because Tanna lived there and he had a chance to put his "friend" plan into play after he dealt with the animal. Which he was pretty sure was a dire diagnosis if Hugh contacted him on a Sunday afternoon.

It wasn't until he'd gotten ten miles down the road that Fletch realized he hadn't combed his hair, shaved or changed out of his ratty UW tank top. Yeah, he was some slick operator.

He took the dirt road to the left of the entrance that led to the barn. He snagged his medical bag and entered the barn—the cleanest he'd ever been in. Renner was a stickler about that.

Hugh was leaning over one of the last stalls. "Hey, Fletch."

"Hugh. What's up?"

"Pepper's foal won't get up. It's been sitting in the same spot since early this morning. And Pepper knows something is wrong with it because she keeps pacing."

"Did she let you get close?"

"Once. But all the other times she's chased me off."

"How long have they been in the barn?"

"Renner said she was actin' funny yesterday afternoon when we were at the branding, so he brought her in. She didn't have any problems with the birth."

"The foal stood on its own?"

"It appeared to. It started to suck all right so I left 'em alone. That's where it's been since I got here at five this morning. Makes me sick to think I shoulda stayed and didn't."

Fletch clapped him on the back. "Pepper ain't a first-time mother and I imagine you were whupped after branding yesterday, so cut yourself a break. I'm gonna get her to move back and then you'll have to keep her there with a bucket of oats." Fletch opened the gate. Before he got into the stall, Pepper blocked him, her big body protecting her baby.

He rubbed her neck. "Hey. You're a good mama, aren't you, Pepper. Watching out for your baby. Such a good girl. But I'm not gonna hurt it. We're just talking here. I'll bet you're hungry. Been pacing and fretting. I just wanna have a little look-see. We'll take it nice and slow. There's a girl." He kept stroking her, talking to her, gently urging her deeper into the stall. She didn't balk or bolt when Hugh entered, but she stopped moving for a moment. When she deemed it okay, she allowed Fletch to maneuver her.

Hugh inched along the inside of the stall, holding a bucket. As he slowly approached Pepper, the bucket held by his side, Hugh started talking to her and Fletch stepped back. By the time Hugh reached Pepper with the oats, she'd forgotten about Fletch entirely.

He dropped beside the foal. It didn't acknowledge Fletch at all. He waved his hand in front of the face. It didn't flinch. Son of a bitch. It was blind. He ran his hand down the spine to the rump and felt the misalignment. The foal's hip was broken. He patted the legs. They were cold and stiff. Most likely a piece of the broken hip rested on the spinal cord, which would account for why the foal initially stood but couldn't now. He looked at the chestnut-colored filly and sadness washed through him. He patted her neck.

Pepper had finished the oats and was making chuffing noises at Hugh.

Fletch stood. "Sorry, man. It's blind and paralyzed."

"Shit. Seriously?" Hugh paused to stroke Pepper's neck. "We've never had a problem with Pepper's foals before."

"Who was the stud?"

"I'm not sure. Tobin would know. So, what now?"

He reached the gate and pulled the handle to let himself out. "Pepper might stay calm now that she's eaten. I'll get the meds to put the poor little thing down. That'll ease some of its misery. Try and get Pepper outside."

"Not what I wanted to hear, Doc, but thanks for coming out."

"No problem. Where's Tobin?"

Hugh exited the stall. "Up at the lodge. Guess there ain't guests registered but Renner wanted someone there in case they had walk-ins, since he and Tierney had plans."

After he administered the meds and stayed to make sure there weren't other issues, Fletch drove up the hill, saw the empty lot and was tempted to keep going around the bend to the employee housing. He had a legitimate reason for being at the Split Rock. Wouldn't it be only natural if he stopped in to say howdy to his friend, Tanna?

Nah. Maybe that'd come across as stalkerish. Not something a friend would do. So he whipped into the main parking lot and killed the engine. He was thinking about the foal as he scaled the steps and cut through the hallway to the great room.

A loud female "Yes" was followed by a long groan and it echoed to him.

Fletch froze. He'd heard that before. That exact same pitch. But the last time he'd heard it, he'd been naked. With Tanna.

He entered the main room and saw Tobin and Tanna on the couch, her bare feet in his lap and her head thrown back over the arm of the couch. He tried to keep his cool. But somehow he barked, "What is going on?"

Chapter Eight

❧

𝒯anna looked at Fletch coolly. And pressed her foot against Tobin's chest in warning when he tried to stand up. Too bad she couldn't tell Tobin to wipe that guilty look off his face; they hadn't been doing anything wrong.

What gave Fletch the right to just waltz in and holler at them anyway?

She smiled sassily. "Tobin is massaging my ankle because I twisted it walking up the path."

Fletch stomped over. "Let me look at it. I *am* a doctor."

Tanna rolled her eyes. "You're a veterinarian. Big difference."

"Not in this case. A limb is a limb." He motioned to Tobin. "Scram."

But Tobin held his ground. "No offense, Fletch, but Tanna does have the right to refuse medical treatment. You can't make her let you look at it."

"Fine." He plopped his butt on the coffee table and rested his forearms on his knees. "I'll just watch how *you* treat her."

Tobin's lips twitched. "See what I get for bein' a nice guy? A load of criticism and attitude."

"Not from me," Tanna said sweetly. "The world needs more nice guys. Genuinely good guys like you."

"Bull."

His vehemence shocked her. "What makes you say that?"

Tobin frowned and used his thumb to rub the outside of her calf, gently rotating her foot with his other hand. "Nice guys get trampled on. Women claim they want a nice guy, but that's not true. They want a bad boy, regardless if those men treat women like shit."

"Not all women are like that, Tobin. I steer clear of domineering assholes." Tanna shot Fletch a haughty look.

"No offense, Tanna, but I'm betting you don't go for domineering types because you pick guys you can boss around and control."

She felt Fletch studying her and she met his gaze.

Fletch drawled, "I think Tobin's hit it on the head."

"So I should apologize for bein' a strong woman and speaking my mind?" she demanded. "For knowing what I want?"

Fletch shook his head. "No, but you're doin' the same thing as those other women."

"Which is what?"

"Putting the type of guy that doesn't fit your criteria in the friend category," Fletch said.

"A category that I'm very familiar with," Tobin grumbled.

Tanna looked at Tobin. "Were you planning to ask me out on a date?"

Tobin's cheeks reddened. "Maybe." He blew out a breath. "Okay, yeah. I wanted to ask you out. So sue me. I'm a guy. You're hot and you'll be living next door to me all summer. But when I brought you a cup of coffee, you immediately demoted me to that friend zone." He laughed self-consciously. "Which now that I think about it, is a double whammy hit on my masculine pride. You just admitted I'm the type of guy you usually go for—nice, easygoing, I don't mind letting a woman call the shots. But that's not enough for you."

This conversation was going nowhere fast.

"I'll bet you're never shoved into the friend category," Tobin said to Fletch.

"Wrong. But know what's worse? If I've got a woman in my bed, then afterward she changes the parameters and wants to go back to bein' friends—talk about a swift kick to my male pride. Especially when I know the sex rocked her world."

She looked away from Fletch's accusing eyes and wondered how she could keep herself from blushing. Or keep Tobin from noticing.

But Tobin was focused on Fletch. "I gotta admit that sucks worse. I mean if the sex was blah…that happens. But if it was awesome and she still bailed? She's running scared."

"Interesting theory, wouldn't you agree, Tanna?"

Her gaze snapped to Fletch's of its own accord. They engaged in a heated eye fuck that raised the temperature in the room at least ten degrees.

Tobin's sigh broke the moment. "I just remembered something I forgot to do." He set her foot on the cushion as he got up and vanished down the hallway.

Before Tanna moved, Fletch slipped into Tobin's place and picked up her foot. "How about if you let me take a look?"

Those big, rough-skinned hands were cupping her foot, gripping her calf and rotating her ankle. His eyes remained on hers as he maneuvered her foot.

"Does that hurt?"

Tanna mooed.

Fletch threw back his head and laughed. And damn damn damn why did he have to have such a sexy, carefree laugh?

"You are ornery. You know what I do with ornery patients?"

She shook her head.

"I hobble them. Tie them up with straps or ropes or chains. Then I can keep them right where I want them and they can't get away. Or run away."

"How long are you gonna beat on that dead horse?" she asked with annoyance.

He froze; his hands, his body, everything stilled.

"What?"

"I hate that phrase. A dead horse is serious, sad business in my line of work. Especially since I just had to put one down a little bit ago."

That made her feel like shit. "I'm sorry. After what I've been through, I oughta know better than to use that awful phrase too. Consider it forever struck from my vernacular."

"There's that contrite side I remember." His fingers started caressing her shin again. "But I surely do like it when you get all kinds of fired up, sugar twang. Makes that Texas drawl more pronounced. More fiery hot and sweet."

How was she supposed to respond to that?

"Answer the question in English," Fletch prompted. "Does that hurt?"

"Actually, no. It didn't hurt that much to begin with. Tobin overreacted." *Such a lie. You just don't want the good doc to know your recent injury history.*

"Tobin is a smart man. He saw an opportunity to play a little footsie with you. If you'd wrenched your neck he would've volunteered to give you a back rub. Anything to get his hands on you."

"So you're saying all men are dogs?"

He grinned. "Like you didn't already know that. And I don't blame him. I'd do anything to get my hands on you, because I know firsthand how amazing it is to have your hands on me."

"Fletch." He was *not* wearing down her resistance saying such sweet and sexy stuff.

He pushed both his thumbs into her instep and began to massage her foot.

"Omigod."

"Like that, do you?"

Say no. But what tumbled out was a long, "Yes."

Those magic fingers kneaded and poked and rubbed the ball of her foot, across the center pad and over to her pinkie toe. Then back down the outside to her heel. The circuit he made became tighter and more focused on the center of her foot.

God. Now she knew why some dogs' legs shook when their tummy got rubbed in the right spot. But it wasn't just her leg that wanted to shake uncontrollably.

"Ever heard of reflexology?" he asked in that husky bedroom voice.

"Right there. God. That feels good." She lifted her head and squinted at him. "Umm. What did you say?"

"Reflexology. It's a practice where applying pressure to specific spots on your body directly fires certain synapses in the brain. Pressing one place can alleviate pain. Pressing on another spot brings pleasure."

"FYI. I'm not feeling any pain right now."

"Good to know. But to keep everything in balance I oughta work on your other foot too."

Tanna pulled her left foot free from where it'd gotten lodged in the cushions. She so wanted to slide her heel up the length of that muscled thigh and walk her toes up his broad chest. But that would send him mixed signals.

And you moaning and sighing when he's got his hands on you . . . isn't?

"I don't think—"

"Don't think. Just close your eyes and let me do this for you."

She couldn't argue with that.

When he dug those marvelous thumbs into her instep she nearly purred with pleasure. Although she tried to concentrate on the foot massage, other things kept distracting her. The slow, steady sound of his breathing. She peered at him from beneath her lashes. Fascinating, the way the muscles in his forearms and biceps moved. His dark hair fell forward, hiding half his face. His lips, those perfectly full lips, were parted and she remembered how expertly he used his mouth.

"Tanna?"

"Hmm?"

"Will you have coffee with me some night this week?"

Tanna groaned softly when he hit a sweet spot.

"Can I take that as a yes? We could meet at the diner in Muddy Gap. Or in Rawlins. Whatever works for you."

She looked at him. "You're serious about us having coffee?"

Fletch's thumbs stopped moving. "Why wouldn't I be?"

"I don't know. Coffee seems pretty sedate after how we met." *Way to point that out.*

He leveled that wild man grin at her. "Shoot. I knew I shoulda gone with my first instinct and asked you to go skinny-dipping in the creek and then let me have my wicked way with you in the mud. Or over a rock. Or against a tree. Or better yet, all three."

Her belly fluttered. "Ah. Coffee is good."

"Excellent." Keeping his eyes on hers, he angled his head and placed a soft kiss on her instep. Then he playfully bit down.

"Fletch. Stop."

"I don't think I can." He rubbed his lips over the shallow indent below her anklebone. Twice. "You have the softest skin." His palm followed her shinbone up to her kneecap. His smile dimmed when he saw the ugly red scar. "What happened?"

Tanna stared at the side of his head as he inspected the gash. He really didn't know her sad history and bad luck? She'd assumed someone in the Muddy Gap gossipy group of friends had told him.

Why would they? Maybe Lainie, Hank, Celia, Kyle and Devin would talk about her injury and the fallout among themselves, but Tanna wasn't part of their group, so it wouldn't come up in casual conversation. It was just another reminder that she'd lost that hometown connection when her father rid himself of the burdens of his family and the family ranch.

"Tanna?"

Her gaze met his. "If I told you all the gory details now, what would we talk about over coffee?" She scooted back, and spun around to set both feet on the floor. "Thanks for the foot massage. It was awesome."

"I still don't have your number."

She stood and retrieved her flip-flops from beside the coffee table. She pulled her cell out of her back pocket. "Give me your number." He rattled it off and she poked at the keys. Then his phone buzzed in his pocket. "Now you've got it."

"Thanks. I'll call you when I have a firmer grasp on my weekly schedule."

With that, she made her escape.

Halfway back to her trailer she wondered what she was escaping from. Chances were high that coffee would lead to more. She should've said no.

But the problem was . . . she didn't want to say no to Fletch.

❧

Tanna and Harlow worked together at Wild West Clothiers on Monday.

Tuesday she worked alone. Business was slow, giving her time to look over the merchandise—a lot of merchandise. Funky, cool, retro Western clothing, as well as some conservative pieces sprinkled in. Racks of accessories lined one entire wall. She figured out Harper's coding system for when items arrived in the store and it looked to her like nothing was over six months old. Which meant she moved merchandise. That'd been Tanna's biggest complaint working at Billy Bob's. She swore some of the clothing had been on the racks since the place opened.

On Wednesday blond bombshell Harlow popped in fifteen minutes before her bar shift started. She'd donned sedate black clothing as well as a jaunty fedora that she pulled off, in the way so few women can.

"So, Tanna, I have to ask you a favor."

"What?"

"I know I'm scheduled to work in here Friday and you're in the bar, but could we switch?"

"Why?"

"Because I have a date Thursday night. An overnight date, which means I'd have to leave Casper at six a.m. to be here to work by eight."

"So I have to suck up another two hours on shift so you can have a booty call?"

Harlow cocked her head. "Yes."

"This is the first week on the job and you're already asking for schedule changes. You don't see anything wrong with that?"

"I'd switch with you if you asked," she said mulishly.

Tanna tapped her fingers on the counter. "Fine. I'll switch with you. But when I need to swap a shift, I'd better not hear you bitch. At all. You don't get to pull that *Oh, I'm sorry, I'd really love to fill in for you, but I've made plans* bullshit. Understand?"

"I understand. Geez. You're a real hard-ass."

"No, I'm just older, wiser and I've worked with people like you before."

"People like me?" Harlow repeated snippily. "What's that supposed to mean?"

"You skate by with the minimum amount of work, but you expect to be treated with the same respect as those of us who work our asses off and do our damn job." Tanna realized how harsh that'd come out and backed off. "I like you, Harlow. I think we'll work well together as long as you act like you need this job, not that you're entitled to it."

"There goes my chance to fuck off and use the experience in my master's thesis on how I spent my summer vacation," she said breezily.

Tanna rolled her eyes. "Get to work, smart-ass."

Harlow smirked and flounced off.

God. If she didn't throttle that kid it'd be a miracle.

She's not really a kid. Remember what you were like at that age?

Worse than Harlow. Spoiled when she went home, pampered at events by her sponsors, hell on wheels on the road. Not giving a shit about anyone else's issues. Doing whatever she wanted and answering to nobody.

It was hard to stomach that she used to be like that. How long would she have gone on that way if her life hadn't changed so drastically?

Pointless to ponder . . . but she found herself thinking about it off and on all day.

Late Friday afternoon she counted out the till and secured the money and the day's receipts in the safe. After locking up, she exited out the side door.

The air had a bite—surprising for May—and she hustled down the hill to her trailer. So much for her plan to sit out on her deck and enjoy the end of the day. Texas had nothing on Wyoming when it came to how hard the damn wind blew.

Inside her trailer, she grabbed a beer and settled on the couch. Déjà vu hit her. Then it occurred to her it wasn't déjà vu—she'd done this exact same thing the last four nights. Parked her ass on the couch. Popped a top. Flipped through crap on the TV. Then she crawled between the sheets.

Was this how her days would play out over the next three months? She'd work hawking clothes or booze, return to her quarters, knock back a beer, and eat a sandwich while she watched the boob tube and then toddle off to bed?

Fuck that.

She was Tanna Barker. She didn't have to go balls to the wall crazy. No impromptu wet T-shirt contests. No dancing on the bar. No showcasing her pole dancing skills. But she could head to the closest watering hole. Soak up a little local culture. Check out the claim that Wyoming cowboys were a breed apart from Texas cowboys.

You already know that firsthand. Didn't one night with the good doc prove it?

Yes. And he claimed he wanted to prove it over and over again.

So why hadn't Fletch called her about their coffee date this week?

Tanna knew he was busy. She ought to cut him some slack.

Then again, when had she ever waited for a man to make the first move?

Never. And she wasn't about to start that meek and mild routine now.

She drained her beer and changed into a lace cami the color of ripe raspberries and a long-sleeved cream-colored Western shirt decorated with vines of hot pink roses. She slipped on her favorite pair of Miss Me jeans with the white angel wings on the back pockets and big rhinestones on the front. She opted not to wear one of her championship buckles. She shoved her feet in a short pair of orange and pink Old Gringo cowgirl boots decorated with cacti.

Tanna fluffed up her hair—making it big, Texas style. She added more eyeliner, more mascara, more lipstick and spritzed on her favorite perfume. She debated on putting in a pair of colored contacts. Growing up with brown eyes, like everyone else in Texas it seemed, she'd wished for an exotic eye color. When she'd discovered colored lenses, she'd bought a set in every funky hue. Most people couldn't tell when she had in her "fake eyes" and it amused her when they tried to figure out what was different about her.

Ready, she hit the road. She didn't need her GPS to find the closest bar—Buckeye Joe's was the only one in town.

Inside, Tanna saw one familiar face—Kyle's mom, Sherry.

The smiling redhead hugged her. "Tanna! I was hoping you'd come into the Buckeye for a drink. We didn't get to chat much at the branding."

"That's understandable since you were busy running the chow line."

Sherry smiled. "I appreciated everyone coming out and helping Kyle and Celia. The last two years I've seen firsthand how much hard work goes into running a ranch. So, what can I getcha tonight?"

"I don't suppose you've got Lone Star?"

"Nope."

"I'll take a Corona."

Sherry reached into the cooler, then popped the top on the bottle and slid it over. "First one is on me." She lowered her voice. "But keep that under your hat or the locals will think I've gone soft."

Tanna grinned. "Thank you." She took a sip of the icy brew. "You own this place?"

"Part owner. I bought in when I knew Kyle was settling here permanently. Owning a business has been more work than I'd imagined, but I love it."

"Do you see much of Celia and Kyle?"

"As much as I can. They don't go out much anymore and in a few months it'll be even less."

"This baby stuff is so exciting. They'll make great parents."

"And I'll be one of those annoying grandmas who goes on and on about the precious grandchild." Sherry wiped a spot down the bar. "How's it going up at the Split Rock?"

"So far, so good."

"And... here they come. That didn't take long." Sherry's eyes twinkled. "Don't turn around, sweetie, but a few guys are headed this way."

Tanna groaned. "The 'see a single woman in the bar and assume I want company' type of guys?"

"No, they're friends of Kyle and Celia's you met at the branding."

Butterflies took wing in her belly. Was Fletch with them?

Ike, the fast-talking cattle broker, sidled up and offered her a sly smile. "If it isn't my favorite Texas transplant."

The man was so easy on the eyes. Blond-haired. Tall and lanky. Dressed casually, but impeccably. Blue eyes, which wavered somewhere between devilish and intense. Tanna knew there'd be no leading this guy around by a string. "Ike, you slick operator."

His eyebrows rose. "Alls I do is say hello and I'm slick?"

"Dude. You're a salesman. You're *always* selling something."

"But I'm not," came from behind her.

Tanna faced the darker-haired man. Shorter, stockier. More mellow. "Heya, Holt. You flying solo tonight? Or are you Ike's wingman?"

"Both. Come sit with us. Max secured a table. Damn crying shame we didn't get to talk to you much at the branding. But Devin, Fletch and Eli hogged our newest, most beautiful resident."

"Lordy, lordy, darlin'... You sure you're not a salesman?" she asked Holt.

"If you're buying it, then I'm a better salesman than I thought."

She laughed.

"We're your captive audience, hanging on every word that comes out of your mouth," Ike said. "I could listen to you talk all night with that hot accent. But if you just wanna sit there and look pretty, that's good too."

She wasn't immune to flattery from two attractive guys. She winked at Sherry and picked up her Corona. "Check on me in an hour to see if I'm drowning in their sweet bullshit."

Chapter Nine

❧

Fletch had intended to ignore Ike's voice mail that asked if he was around Muddy Gap and had time for a beer. He'd had a long day. Two horse surgeries—one a major repair job on a colt that'd tangled with a mountain lion. All he wanted was to hit the road for home, jump in the shower and wear clothing that didn't reek.

But he had neglected his friends lately. Most of the guys in their group had paired up and married off. Between his unpredictable schedule and the demands on his friends' time, it was a rare night they were all in the same area at the same time, so Fletch agreed to meet them at the Buckeye if he finished his last call before eight o'clock.

Despite his buddies being used to his "fresh from the farm" scent, he scrubbed himself up as best as he could and switched out his sweaty, stained ball cap for a summer-weight cowboy hat.

More people crowded the bar than he'd anticipated—then he remembered it was a Friday night. Man, this week had been such a time suck he didn't even remember what damn day it was. Kyle's mom was busy mixing and pouring at the opposite end of the bar. He saw Ike, Max and Holt at their usual table.

His heart leapt at seeing Tanna sitting with them.

His sarcastic side pointed out that of course Miss Sexy Thang would be here on the night he looked like shit. His practical side reminded him that Tanna liked to have a good time and her bar-hopping choices were limited in Muddy Gap, so he should've expected to run into her. And guaranteed a beautiful woman like her would be surrounded by male admirers.

So why did he have an immediate flash of jealousy and the urge to rip her away from the guys who'd been his friends for years?

Rather than curbing that urge, he gave in to it. After the cocktail waitress brought him a beer, he sauntered over, taking note that Ike hung on her every word. Max's attention was firmly focused on Tanna's cleavage. Even Holt, a confirmed bachelor, seemed mesmerized by her.

Join the club, guys.

Tanna's surprised gaze hooked his as he took the empty chair right next to her, causing a little hiccup in her conversation with Max. Then she was back to telling whatever story required her hand gestures and beautiful smile.

She finally acknowledged him. "Dr. Fletcher."

"I know I told you to call me Fletch, darlin'. No need for formal titles between us, is there, Miz Two-Time World Barrel Racing Champion?"

She cooed, "Would it be bitchy of me to point out I've won *three* world titles?"

"I stand corrected." He lifted an eyebrow. "You gonna make me pay for that oversight?"

Tanna laughed. "Of course. I like seeing a big man squirm."

Goddamn, she had a laugh that pulled him in, a carefree sound that was sexy as sin.

Max gave him a once-over. "I see you're still wearing your barnyard clothes. Finish your last call late?"

Leave it to Max to point out Fletch's less than stellar appearance. "Yeah. If you sat a little closer you could get a whiff of barnyard. Welcome to my world." His eyes met Tanna's. His job was messy and smelly. No reason to pretend it wasn't. Most days he fared a helluva lot worse than this. Question was: would she balk and move away?

"All's well in the world of veterinary medicine?" Ike asked.

"I'm busy as all get-out—not that I'm complaining. But I didn't get home before ten o'clock a single night this week. Those five a.m. starts make for a really long day."

Tanna blinked at him. Hopefully she understood he'd directed that answer at her. Pushing her to have coffee with him and then not contacting her this week . . . not cool.

"How long have you guys been here?" he asked Ike.

"An hour and a half. Ran into this lovely lady right after we arrived. She was sitting all by herself up at the bar."

Fletch kept his focus on her. "Getting wild on a Friday night?"

"No. I'm on clothing store duty tomorrow and I've been warned that Saturdays are busy," Tanna said.

"No wildness for me either," Holt said. "I've got a roofing job to finish tomorrow. Which means I'll be up at the ass crack of dawn before it gets too damn hot."

"I assume you're on animal patrol even on weekends?" Tanna asked Fletch.

"Most Saturdays are busy. Was kind of a fluke last weekend that I didn't get called away after the branding."

"You get called away on Saturdays and Sundays, sometimes night and day," Ike scoffed. "I can't remember the last time you talked about having a full day off. He's a regular workaholic," he added to Tanna.

Fletch felt his face heat. Was it his imagination, or were his friends trying to make him out to be the type of guy who preferred four-legged animals to the two-legged variety? He opened his mouth to protest, but Tanna beat him to the punch.

"You must love your job if you work that hard at it," Tanna said. "Your clients are lucky you're so dedicated."

"Fletch wouldn't know what to do with himself if he wasn't working," Holt said.

"That's not true. I just have to prioritize who I want to spend time with when I do get a break—which didn't happen at all this week, unfortunately."

"So we should consider ourselves lucky that you graced us with your presence," Ike joked.

"I consider myself lucky that you guys haven't written me off as a lost cause when I'm so lousy at keeping in touch." His eyes never wavered from hers.

Tanna's gaze turned thoughtful but she didn't speak.

That's when Fletch noticed her eyes were brown tonight. Not gray like the last two times they'd met. Interesting little quirk, that she changed her eye color.

The music kicked up a notch and Max held out his hand to Tanna. "You promised me a dance."

She tore her gaze from Fletch's and stood abruptly. "So I did. Let's hit it."

Three pairs of eyes followed the couple to the dance floor. Fletch's fist tightened on his beer can when he saw just how close Max pressed his body to Tanna's right off the bat.

"So that's how it is," Ike said.

"What?" Fletch answered distractedly, keeping his focus on the too-close couple on the too-crowded dance floor.

"You. And her."

Fletch offered a halfhearted shrug.

"Don't give me that bullshit innocent act after how you were when you first sat down."

"And how was that?"

Holt leaned forward, snagging his attention. "Like you wanted to crack our skulls together for even lookin' at her. And she gave off the vibe that she'd like nothin' better than for you to bend her over the table."

Fletch choked on his beer. Then he looked at Ike, who nodded agreement with Holt's comment. What the hell? How had these guys picked up on that?

Because you're usually the most laid-back guy in the room and tonight . . . you're not.

Ike sighed. "Why does this always happen? You get there first. I really like her."

So do I.

"What's goin' on between you two?"

"We're just friends," Fletch said with a slight snarl.

Ike's eyes narrowed. "Her choice? Or yours?"

"Let it be," Holt warned Ike.

That shut Ike down immediately.

So they'd drifted into a neutral conversation by the time Max and

Tanna returned. Well, Ike and Max had. Fletch had gotten intercepted by another person requesting animal care advice. He attempted to end the conversation, but the guy didn't get the hint.

After five minutes, Tanna drained her beer and looked pointedly at Fletch. Then at the stoop-shouldered interloper. "Come on, Doc. You're off the clock and you promised to prove that your barbecue skills put Texas boys' skills to shame."

For once Fletch's blank look wasn't feigned. "Shoot. How could I have forgotten?" He pushed back from the table and the old-timer finally shuffled away.

"Devin wasn't kidding when he said that happens to you a lot," she said softly. "And yet, you never act like it's an intrusion."

Half-embarrassed, he shrugged. Then before she could comment on that, Fletch stood. "Sorry to cut this short, but I'm whupped. Good seeing you guys."

"No worries," Holt assured him. "We're about to head out shortly."

Tanna rolled to her feet and offered his friends a smile. "I'll be taking off too. Thanks for the company and the beer. First round is on me next time."

When she glanced up at him, Fletch's heart raced. "I'll walk you out."

If his buddies made sarcastic comments, he didn't hear them. He had eyes only for the petite cowgirl. He placed his hand in the small of her back to navigate through the crowd, trying like hell to ignore the warmth of her skin heating his palm.

Tanna didn't attempt to dislodge his touch or put distance between them as he escorted her outside. "Where'd you park?"

"Close to the exit."

He chuckled. "Planning your escape route before you even entered the building?"

"That's how I roll."

They didn't speak again until reaching her truck. "Tanna. Look. I'm sorry I didn't call you this week about that coffee date."

She faced him and his hand fell away. "I know you've got a busy practice, Fletch. But I will point out that you're the one who insisted we be 'friends' and it was your responsibility to let me know a coffee night wasn't in the cards for us at all."

Chastised, he softly bit off, "Waiting by the phone, were you?"

"Maybe."

"Then I promise it won't happen again. I'll call you even if it's ridiculously late."

"Deal." Tanna stepped closer.

Fletch automatically backed up two steps. "Ah, you probably don't wanna get that close to me, sugar twang."

The crazy woman erased the distance between them and sniffed his shirt. Twice. She wrinkled her nose before breaking into a smirk. "Relax. You don't smell. I'd be more offended if you doused yourself in Axe body spray. Now that shit is really rank." Her fingers traced the row of buttons that stopped between his pectorals. "Nothin' wrong with honest sweat, Fletch. I actually prefer a man who's not afraid to let me see his dirtier side."

Fletch's flip "I'm all about getting down and dirty with you" masked his relief that Tanna wasn't turned off by his less than flowery scent.

She laughed. "You never give up, do you?"

"Nope. And consider that your warning." He grinned. "So, you giving me a second chance on that coffee date? Say . . . on Sunday?"

"How do I know you won't stand me up?"

Fletch placed his hand over hers, which still rested on his chest. "Since my Sunday rates are triple my normal weekly rates, it's gotta be a real emergency for a client to call me."

"Smart. So if it looks like you won't make it can you at least text me?"

Dammit. He so didn't want to admit this.

Her eyes turned suspicious. "What?"

"Does it make me a techno-loser if I admit I don't text?"

Tanna cocked her head. "You're a doctor. I doubt you're a technophobe and don't know how to text, and with all those confusing pharmaceutical names, it's unlikely that you misspell words."

"Not intentionally." Fletch held up his hands. "See these huge mitts? Even the tips of my fingers cover about three letters at a time so I'm a fumbling fool. It takes me three times as long to send a text as it does to dial a number. So if I can't call, I don't bother."

Her eyes were on his fingers and the hungry look on her face suggested she was thinking about how well he used his fingers, not how badly. "Tanna?"

She refocused. "Fine. Where should we meet? Someplace in Rawlins?"

Tricky woman. She didn't consider it a real date if they met up instead of him picking her up.

Wrong. But he'd let her think that if it meant she'd show up.

"Sounds good. There's Dot's Diner across from the Super-Valu. Around eight?"

"That'll work."

"I'm looking forward to it." Fletch pressed his lips to the back of her hand before letting her go. "Drive safe."

❧

Sunday night, Fletch showed up early at the restaurant for their date. He thought he'd prepared himself to act cool and friendlike. But the instant he caught sight of the sexy Texas cowgirl, he knew this "friendship" experiment was doomed to fail from the start.

So yeah, maybe he had a predatory look in his eye and a wolfish twist to his mouth when every delicious inch of Tanna sauntered toward him.

She stopped at the end of the table, propped her hand on her hip and loomed over him—as much as the petite woman could loom—and warned, "I'm fixin' to walk right back out the door if you keep staring at me like that."

He couldn't stop the tiny grin or from asking, "Staring at you … like what?"

"Like I'm on the damn menu."

"I wish."

"Sweet Lord, are you *tryin'* to test me today?"

"Yep. I've already made it clear I'd like a second helping of you. And you are testing *my* willpower, sugar twang, because you always look so tasty."

She whapped him on the shoulder. "I swear, August Fletcher—"

"I love the thick and sweet way my name rolls off your tongue," he half growled. "Say it again."

Tanna purred, "Dr. Pervert," before she dropped into the chair opposite his and smirked at him.

"I guess I deserved that. Still . . . I'm glad you came."

"Since I didn't hear from you beforehand I assume you've not dealt with emergency calls today?"

"Just one. Early on. So I'm all yours." *Stop with the come-ons, Fletch.* "I wasn't sure if you wanted coffee or tea so I ordered both."

"Tea is fine. But pass me the sugar."

He slid the packets closer. "I didn't get a chance Friday night to ask how it's goin', working up at the Split Rock."

Tanna stirred three packs of sugar into her iced tea. "Busy. I had no idea the retail store had that much traffic. I sort of expected I'd be sitting around bored. But that hasn't happened so far."

Fletch wrapped his hands around his cup of coffee. "Did you bartend much?"

"Twice. Harlow kind of took over the bartending gig this week."

"You okay with that?"

"It's only the first week so we'll see how it goes from here. The bar is really sedate." She winked. "I like bars that are hoppin'."

"We oughta head to Buckeye Joe's again one of these nights. Just you and me."

"You and me get into trouble in bars, Fletch."

He grinned at her. "All the more reason for us to go."

"I'll take it into consideration, since my usual choices of drinking buddies are currently knocked up. Or nursing."

She stirred her tea again. Almost like she was nervous.

"What was your week like?" she asked.

"Same old, same old. Horses, cows and bulls. I did help deliver a baby llama. Cute little bugger, but the mama ain't interested in it, so the owners will have to bottle-feed."

"Did you do anything fun?"

He shook his head. "I worked around Laramie Monday and Tuesday. I spent Wednesday and Thursday in Rock Springs. Friday I had nonemergency visits around here I'd postponed. Yesterday I got a couple of calls but the problems had resolved themselves by the time I got there."

"Does that happen a lot?"

"Yeah. But I can't really know if the call was made outta panic or if there's a valid concern for an animal without physically checking it out in most cases. They know they'll be billed for my services regardless if there's something wrong or not. I knew when I started my practice if I didn't take a hard-line stance on billing for my time for all calls, it'd look like my time wasn't worth nothin'."

"Didn't want to be known as the nice guy?" she asked.

Fletch flashed his teeth. "There's a difference between bein' accessible, bein' nice and a bein' a chump. But I must not be too nice because I can't keep a veterinary assistant to save my hide."

A smirk played around the corners of Tanna's mouth. "This might shock you. I went to trade school for a year to become a veterinarian assistant."

Fletch leaned forward. "Seriously? Come to work for me. I can double what they're paying you at the Split Rock. Hell, I'll triple it."

"I didn't graduate."

"I don't care. I can teach you how to do everything the way I like it."

Tanna laughed. "Nice try. But I already learned a lot of the ways you like it in just one night. Which is why you keep doggin' me."

"Partially true. But I'm talking about business here, Tanna, not pleasure."

"What makes you think we could work together?"

"First of all, because you're a born ranch girl. You've been around large animals so you've got some idea what to expect. You don't have as many misperceptions about what I do as some dewy-eyed new vet assistant school graduate."

"I'll bet you've had problems with that. Animal-loving girls who wanna snag a hot veterinarian for a husband."

Fletch thought back to his last assistant, Ashley. She'd dressed nicely, if a bit provocatively, for her interview. She seemed to grasp that his practice wasn't puppies and kitties. He'd hired her on a two-week trial period. She'd shown up the first day in a miniskirt and four-inch heels, with a low-cut shirt that highlighted her D cups. She'd lasted four days. And she seemed really surprised he hadn't offered a marriage proposal.

Before he could toss off a sexy remark, she said, "Besides, I'm only in Wyoming temporarily. You need an assistant who's sticking around for the long haul."

"Why'd you go to school in the first place? Weren't you already on the circuit?"

She wiped the condensation from her glass with a napkin. "I raced on weekends. I hadn't gotten into my groove yet and my dad wanted me to have some sort of skill, so I chose a two-year degree. After I finished a year, I rewarded myself by attending a private barrel racing camp. That's when everything changed."

"How so?"

"The woman who ran the camp hadn't personally won any world championships, but several of her students had. She was this wonderful, grizzled old cowgirl who knew horses and barrel racing. She lived it. The first time she watched me run barrels, she told me why I wasn't increasing my time. One little trick of hers and I shaved seconds off my time."

His eyebrows rose. "Full seconds?"

"Yep. She took a serious interest in my riding style and made me unlearn everything and start from scratch. It worked. I learned so much from her—first off that the horse does matter. Shitty horse, shitty time. When my folks picked me up, she took them aside and gave them the hard sell about letting me compete full-time because I had the talent. Offering to train me exclusively."

"You jumped at the chance?"

"Yes, and I haven't looked back. She tracked down my first competition-grade horse."

When Tanna pursed her lips around the straw and sucked, Fletch's cock stirred. What she could do with that mouth . . .

Focus, man.

"I immediately started winning. I moved up in the standings and people—meaning sponsors—began to notice. By the time I was twenty-two I was ranked top ten in the world and by twenty-nine I'd won back-to-back world championships." A fleeting smile crossed her lips. "I was so thrilled she was in the audience in Vegas when I won. She and I went out and got rip-roarin' drunk. It was a blast and a little bittersweet to think back on now, because the next year she died from a brain aneurysm."

"So it's not like you can go to her, return to basics, and get your riding mojo back." He spun his cup around and decided head-on was the best approach with the fiery cowgirl. "I read about what happened to you last year."

"Where?"

"Online."

Tanna's eyes became guarded. "You could've just asked me."

"I figured I needed to suss out some details before I'd know what to ask."

"So what do you want to know?"

Fletch picked up her hand. "Everything."

"That's a pretty broad subject."

"You're a pretty broad."

She laughed softly. "You don't ever react the way I expect you to."

"I hate to be predictable." He grinned. "Start talking, barrel racer."

"How far back do you want me to go?"

"To when everything fell apart."

"That's easy to pinpoint. When my mother died." Tanna took a long drink of iced tea. But she didn't let go of his hand. "Now I see how spoiled I was. Of course, I took it all for granted then. I never bothered to move out on my own. Why should I? When I went home between events, I had a mini-suite to myself with a big bed, a big screen TV and a bathroom. I had home-cooked meals, someone to do my laundry, a place to train my horse. I had someone to talk to who thought I hung the moon and stars."

He threaded his fingers through hers. Tanna's hands weren't pampered;

hers bore the marks of hard work, like his did. But her fingers looked delicate in his big paws.

"I've always been a mama's girl. My mother, like so many Texas mothers, had dreams of her daughter bein' a beauty queen. She entered me in my first and only pageant when I was eight." The corners of her lips turned up. "I got last place. Mama claimed it was because I hadn't grown into my looks. But I knew even then that big-haired blondes with blue eyes would be crowned the winner. I'm too ethnic-looking for some things and not ethnic-looking enough for others."

"Astute observation."

She shrugged. "My mother was half-Mexican; my father a white Texas good old boy. Anyway, I'd only agreed to the pageant because I'd struck a deal with my mom. I'd compete in the pageant if she let me sign up to learn to barrel race at the fairgrounds." She snickered. "I'm sure she thought I'd win the beauty contest and I'd forget all about barrel racing. But I won and was hooked. On the back of the horse and in the arena, it didn't matter if I was dark skinned or light skinned—it was about skill." Her gaze locked on to his. "I don't need to explain ethnic issues to you."

"No, you don't. My mother was Native. My dad is white. I never spent time on the rez. There weren't any Indian kids at our school. Eli and I suspected we would've been thrown together even if we hadn't been related."

"Wait. You and Eli are ... ?"

"Cousins. His mom and my mom were second or third cousins. Although, I didn't meet Eli until he moved in with his aunt and we started goin' to the same school." That was a situation she'd have to ask Eli about. "Has your family always been in Texas?"

"I'm ... third generation? My grandfather and his brother ran away from their family in their late teens and crossed the Mexican border into Texas. They became U.S. citizens and worked any and every job they could until they earned enough to buy a small ranch. My grandfather was quite the vaquero. He caught the eye of my grandmother Bernadette, a white girl. They married against her father's wishes and she gave birth to my mother,

Bonita. Bernadette died when my mother was eleven. My mom took over running the household."

"At age eleven?"

Tanna nodded. "She didn't have much of a childhood, taking care of my grandfather and my uncle Manuel—who never married. They bought more land and started running cattle. Which is where my dad came in. They hired him as a ranch hand. That's where he and mama met. He ended up taking over everything after my grandfather died. I never met my grandfather. My mama always said he worked himself to death.

"I always assumed my dad liked ranch life. So it shocked me and my brother, Garrett, when he sold off all the horses and cattle within two months of Mama's death. We even had a good friend of his intervene, trying to get him to see how irrational he was acting in grief. But Dad told him to butt out. Then he just looked me and Garrett right in the eye and said he hated everything about living on a ranch. He had for quite some time, but my mother refused to consider selling or moving. Now that she was gone"—those beautiful brown eyes welled with tears—"he had no intention of keeping it."

"So in addition to dealing with your mother's death…you found out your father wasn't the man you thought he was?"

Tanna pulled her hand from his and grabbed a paper napkin to blot her tears. "That's a nice way of putting it. He told me and Garrett that we were spoiled brats and that it was coming to an end. I understand where he was coming from where I was concerned. I was a thirty-four-year-old woman who hadn't left home. But the land succession should've gone to a blood relative descendant. Dad said since my mother had left everything to him, to do as he saw fit, we had no say in any decision he made. It was such an ugly situation."

"Aw, darlin', this is breaking my heart."

"It broke mine too. And my spirit, which is how I ended up on a long losing streak on the circuit. Six months after we'd buried my mother, my father had rid himself of the ranch, married Mama's best friend, Rosalie, and bought beachfront rental property in Florida."

What a selfish asshole. "Did you and your brother get anything?"

"He gave us each one hundred K." Tanna's eyes were burning with rage when she looked at him. "Not that I'm ungrateful or greedy, but that money was an insult. He sold the ranch for ten million dollars. Ten. Million. Dollars. And he couldn't part with less than that amount for his only children?"

Fletch whistled.

"So in some ways, I lost both my parents that year. He never even called me after I got injured. It's like that part of his life ended with my mom."

Silence stretched between them.

When Fletch couldn't stand it any longer, he stopped her restless fingers from ripping the napkin to shreds. He brought her hand to his mouth and placed a kiss in the center of her palm. "I'm so sorry for what you've gone through."

"Thanks. As tired as I am of talking about it, that's not the whole story. During that time I tried to maintain my standings but kept falling further and further down. I didn't qualify for CRA World Finals. My sponsors understood. The breeders who owned the horse understood but they took Jezebel back to their stables. Which I found a relief. I was too embarrassed to tell anyone that I didn't have a place to go, so I hid out in my horse trailer. That was a wake-up call. I realized just how spoiled I'd been."

"I'll bet your mother loved having you home to spoil."

She smiled wistfully. "Maybe. By the time the new year started, I was rarin' to go. But because I didn't have a good showing the previous year, my sponsors cut my funds in half. So I had to curb the number of events and only entered ones with a decent purse and points. After months of limited winning, I decided to enter every event I could. I didn't tell Jezebel's owners and I stopped answering their calls."

"Not smart."

"Yeah, but I wasn't pushing Jezebel too hard. I took extra precautions with her and had her checked out by a vet at least every two weeks. I sent those health reports on to the owners like I always did." She took a breath. "Labor Day weekend I was scheduled to compete in Dallas at an outdoor venue. I'd drawn last, which I usually prefer. It sprinkled a little off and on. Nothin' to be alarmed about. The other competitors said the dirt was fine. My turn rolled around and we shot out at a good clip. Made the first barrel and she didn't feel slippery. On the second barrel . . . she spun out. We both went down. Hard. Jezebel landed on top of me, knocking the wind out of me. So it seemed like minutes that she was crushing me when in all actuality it was only seconds.

"Somehow my boot slipped out of the stirrup or I might've broken my tibia or fibula and cracked my femur instead of just ripping the shit outta the ligaments in my right knee and fracturing my ankle. I thought Jezebel was okay because it didn't take her long to get up after the spill. Her body was a blur as she raced off. Then she made the most god-awful high-pitched cry I've ever heard. I freaked out, and tried to chase after her, but I crumpled into a heap. Somehow I forced myself to get up and walk."

Fletch had read the online articles about what'd happened, but even knowing how it'd played out didn't lessen the impact or the horror of what Tanna was about to say.

"Jezebel had kept goin' after she got up, running out of the arena like she'd always been trained to. No one knows for sure if her initial injury happened in the arena or if she'd stumbled into a hole during her break for freedom and made it worse, but her hind leg snapped above the hock—as you know a compound fracture isn't fixable. The only thing that did stop her was her reins got caught on a metal fissure in the pens behind the arena—which was just another freaky thing. She panicked even more when she couldn't get free. She couldn't rear up. She didn't know what was goin' on and I wasn't around to calm her down."

His heart dropped to the tips of his boots.

Tanna swallowed hard. "Jezebel was a high-strung horse. The worst part was I saw the whole thing happen. I couldn't save her. I couldn't even help her. When the med techs came over, they were all fired up because they thought I'd just dislocated my shoulder when I hit the dirt—they didn't know my right leg was useless because of multiple injuries and I wouldn't let them touch me."

His guts twisted into a knot. She'd suffered through three major injuries at one time. "I dislocated my shoulder in high school during a football game. Hurt like a bitch when they reset it."

"I don't even remember them resetting my shoulder. They knocked me out. I'd become hysterical after they wouldn't let me near Jezebel. When I woke up, no one would tell me what'd happened to my horse. Finally, the next day, Ralph Costas, the rep for the owners, showed up in my hospital room and laid it out for me. I guess one of the bulldoggers who also used one of the owners' horses for competition had called them." Tanna's hands balled into fists. "Ralph told me after the accident, Jezebel was confused and in a lot of pain so the vet tranqued her to reduce her stress level. They had no choice but to put her down. Everyone says it was easier—better— for me not to be there, but dammit, I should've been. After all we'd been through . . . I let Jezebel down.

"I spent the next two weeks in a fog of pain meds after the ACL tear repair surgery on my knee, having my arm in a sling and my ankle in a cast." Tanna dropped her chin. "I'd lost everything, so in some ways, bein' out of it for those two weeks was a blessing. I haven't been able to get on— or even near—a horse since."

Fletch didn't offer her platitudes. But he did know how to offer her comfort and that's what she needed right now. He scooted out of the booth and threw cash on the table. He held out his hand to her. "Come on. We're getting out of here."

She didn't protest. She grabbed his hand, letting him lead her outside.

Rain fell softly, in a foggy mist rather than a steady downpour.

As soon as they were out of the glare of the diner's front windows, he gently folded her into his arms. Tanna squirmed. He merely pulled her closer and murmured, "Hush. Let it go. There's nobody here but us."

"I can't."

"You can."

"Why are you bein' so nice to me after I told you—"

He kissed her forehead. "Because I am a nice guy. And because I really like you."

She buried her face into his chest. She didn't sob, even when he suspected she wanted to. Tanna just held him tightly, her palms flat on the middle of his back. Her fingers flexing and kneading like a cat digging its claws into his flesh.

Finally she raised her head. "Thanks."

"You're welcome. And I'm sorry."

She looked confused. "For what?"

"This." He dropped his mouth over hers, taking the kiss he'd been dying for. Her surprised gasp gave him easy access past her trembling lips and he slipped his tongue inside her mouth.

She tasted so sweet—tea and Tanna. And she gave herself over to the kiss, just like she'd given all of herself over to him the night they'd wound up in bed. Part of him wanted to crank the kiss to the combustible stage, where the steam rising off their bodies wasn't from the rain, but from lust. Yet, for all her bold sex talk, right now Tanna was as skittish as a new colt. He wouldn't give her a reason to flee. So he kept the kiss easy. Slow and thorough. A first-date kiss, because in his mind, that's what this was.

Tanna retreated first. She tipped her head back to look at him.

Tiny drops of mist clung to her long eyelashes. With those enormous brown eyes, dark hair curled around her heart-shaped face and her well-kissed lips, she was so damn beautiful, looking at her stole his breath.

"That went beyond a friendly kiss, Doc."

"Yeah, well . . ." He had no real defense so he didn't offer one. "You're the prime example of why the words *hot* and *mess* go together so well."

She looked shocked for a second. Then she shook her head. "You're possibly the only man on the planet who could say that to me and I'm not tempted to knee you in the 'nads."

That sassy mouth made him smile. "That's why we should hang out more often. In places besides bars."

"Anything but horseback riding."

Fletch framed her face in his hands. Before he could assure her that she didn't have to be flip with him, that he'd be there for her anytime she needed him, she spoke.

"You're not laughing."

His thumbs swept across her cheekbones. "Because I don't think you were trying to be funny."

Tanna moved her head, forcing his hands to fall away. "What is it with you?"

"What do you mean?"

"You like to badger me about stuff and I let you. But it doesn't piss me off like when other people do it to me."

"See? We've already got that goin' for us. The only way we'll know if this"—he hated to say friendship, so instead, he emphasized—"*thing* will work is to spend more time together."

Her eyes searched his. "No pressure to hit the sheets."

A statement of fact? Or a request? "If that's what you want."

"I do."

But Fletch definitely heard the *for now* that hung in the air between them.

"It's late and I know you get up at the crack of nothin'." Tanna started across the parking lot and he fell in step beside her, watching water splashing across the black asphalt.

"Do you have any full days off this week?"

"Tuesday. Harlow is working in the clothing store and Tierney is handling hostess duties with Renner in the lounge. The rooms are booked Monday and Tuesday night with people he knows from the world of rodeo. And I'd rather not be there slinging drinks; know what I mean?"

"I do. I'm glad Renner's conscientious about it."

"He's a great boss—as far as bosses go. I'd probably be worthless in the lounge anyway since I'm supposed to go to Eli's on Tuesday."

"You decided to go to Eli's on your own?"

She shrugged.

"Or is the brat railroading you into it?" he demanded.

"Celia *strongly* suggested it. Several times," Tanna said dryly.

There were so many things he wanted to say but everything sounded trite in his head. "Is that what you were talking to Eli about at the branding? Whether he can help you get back on a horse?"

"He thinks he can help me overcome my"—she waved distractedly—"debilitating fear or whatever the fuck it is. But I think I'm beyond helping."

"Why do you say that?"

"Because I'm reacting like one of those combat veterans suffering from PTSD. I feel this pressure to get back to normal. Everyone says my fear will blow over. It's past time to get over it. But what if...I can't? Ever?" Tanna blew out a frustrated breath. "But the truth is, if I hadn't felt comfortable with Eli, I wouldn't be goin'. I'm not exactly a pushover, in case you hadn't noticed."

So Tanna was one of those women—she showed him her vulnerability but then she'd snap at him if he showed concern. "I noticed. But if my cousin is mean to you, it'd be my pleasure to beat him up for you."

Tanna laughed. "You are the most unpredictable man I've ever met."

Tempting to kiss her good night, but she'd expect that so he didn't.

Chapter Ten

❧

*T*anna didn't immediately jump out of her truck after she pulled up to Eli Whirling Cloud's place. In fact, she sat inside the cab for several long minutes. Even after she saw Eli leaning against the corral by the barn door, drinking from an insulated coffee mug. Watching her.

Judging her?

No. That much she was sure of.

Eli never moved toward her. Never beckoned her over. He merely waited for her to make a decision.

Jesus. Get out of the fucking truck, Tanna.

So she did. Ambling toward him, she wondered if he could see how fast and hard her pulse jumped in her throat. How hard her hands shook. "Good mornin'."

He smiled and it struck her how welcoming that smile was. "Looks to be a beautiful day."

"That it does." *Cut to the chase.* "So, whatcha got planned for me?"

Eli wandered over to where she stood by the fence. "Do you want to get on a horse today, Tanna?"

She shook her head.

"That's good. Because you ain't ready to ride. We're doin' this a different way because it ain't a one-day fix."

She folded her arms over her chest. "Regardless if I ride your horses or don't ride I can't pay you for your time." Damn, did that hurt to admit. "And you'd better tell me right now if Celia and Kyle, or Lainie and Hank are footing the bill for this."

Amusement danced in his eyes. "Don't wanna be beholden to anyone? Believe me, I get that. But you're wrong in thinking the only thing that has value in life is cash. Experience counts a lot more in my book. And you've got that in spades."

"So you'll need my help at some point in exchange for yours now?"

"Yep."

"I'm good with that. Any other people you're working with?" She stopped at adding, "other broken people like me."

"A couple folks in the late afternoon, teaching them to break colts. Got a bulldogger that trains here some mornings if he ain't off rodeoin'. Teaching riding and other stuff. The rest of the time we're exercising the horses boarded here. So I thought we could take the ATVs out so you can get an idea of the terrain. I'm betting it's nothin' like what you're used to in Texas."

Tanna's gaze swept the vista. The hilly land was strewn with rocks. Chunks of shale rose out of nowhere. Scrub cedar and sage abounded. The area did remind her of home—until she caught a glimpse of mountains in the distance. "Some similarities."

"Did you have a good week?"

"Didn't do much besides working and drinking."

"What about Fletch?"

She tried not to get defensive, but her voice had an edge when she asked, "What about him?"

"Didja see him?"

"We had coffee Sunday night."

"And?"

And he kissed the shit out of me. "And it was . . . nice."

He chuckled. "I saw the sparks flyin' between you two at the branding, so *nice* ain't a word that really applies, is it? You plan on spending time with him while you're in the area?"

Why was Eli being so pushy? "He's really busy in his practice during the week."

"True. But he'd make time for you if you asked."

Putting herself out there any more than she already had might give Fletch the wrong idea.

Or the right idea.

Or cement the idea that she wanted him as much as he wanted her and she oughta quit lying to herself about it.

Eli pushed off the fence. "I won't badger you. Let's enjoy this morning before the sun tries to fry our heads, eh?"

Tanna chose an older model ATV and was relieved when Eli didn't drive a million miles an hour. He made an effort to point out things of interest as well as some of the more challenging trails.

They spent a couple of hours traversing the land. Part of Eli's acreage bordered federal land home to wild horses. Eli handed her a pair of binoculars and she watched the animals grazing. Even from a distance they seemed more skittish than horses she'd been around, ready to bolt at the first sign of danger.

"How long have you been doin' this?" she asked. He had mentioned that he received money from the Bureau of Land Management to care for the wild horses—as much as one could care for creatures that had always run free.

"Eight years. I know what equestrians say about these wild ones as compared to horses that are bred for their breed expectations and limitations. But these beauties . . . there's no greater feeling than breaking one but keeping a part of that wild spirit."

"I take it you're not sending me out there to round them up as some sort of initiation into the Wild West?"

"Nope. But let's head back."

Driving the ridge, something tightened inside her. She had such an overwhelming sense of loss. She felt burdened by the weight of her loss and the sense of futility, even though it was nothing new. It had been happening off and on since her mother's death. Never regularly, always at the oddest moments.

Suck it up. This is your life now. Be grateful for what you've got.

By the time they reached the barn, Tanna swore if Eli asked about her blotchy face and red-rimmed eyes, she'd blame any tears on Wyoming dust and wind.

But Eli didn't say a word. He grabbed a bucket and dumped a few oats in. "Come on. Let's mingle." He started for the horse pasture, leaving Tanna no choice but to follow him.

And sure enough, as soon as the horses noticed Eli held the bucket, they trotted over. All twelve of them.

Her heart was in her throat when they were surrounded. She nearly passed out from fear when a big gray mare bumped into her with those muscled shoulders. Then the horse immediately tried to crowd her into the fence.

Tanna balked. She started to duck and move. But the mare pinned her in place.

"Aggie. Behave." Eli's soft command forced the horse to freeze. "Tanna. You need to get your head on, girl, and remember who's in charge."

"Right." Tanna backed into Aggie's left side and kept the bucket of oats low.

But the horse kept pushing and crowding. Tanna dropped the bucket and scrambled away so fast she fell on her knees in the dirt—causing a sharp pain in her knee. Then she was on her feet, running, not caring how foolish she looked. She just needed to find a place where she could breathe without fear.

Tanna didn't stop running until she cleared the gate and had trekked halfway up a small rise. She noticed a crude bench, crafted from old logs and balanced on two flat rocks. She sat on it and pulled her knees to her chest, wrapping her arms around her shins. That's when the tears fell. Not the silent type that she'd cried on the ATV. But huge, gasping sobs.

She'd never ever been afraid of horses. And that's how she reacted the first time she'd gotten close to one in nine months? A panic attack that'd forced her to flee and left her fucking *bawling* like some big goddamn greenhorn baby?

You're pathetic. Give it up. If you can't even touch a horse how will you ever be able to ride one again? Say nothing of competing on a national level?

Those reminders got louder and louder until she wanted to scream to drown them out.

Instead she curled up tighter, cried harder and wondered why she even bothered coming here. To Wyoming. To Eli's. She should just go back to Texas where she belonged and ... do what? She had nothing there either.

After a while, cried out, tired of self-flagellation, she lifted her face to the sky, not knowing how long she'd stayed immersed in her own misery.

A noise echoed to her and she turned, expecting to see Eli. But an Indian woman of indeterminate age—she could've been nineteen or thirty-nine—rested her backside against an old pine tree stump.

At first Tanna thought she might be an apparition, since she held such a stoic demeanor. But then she offered Tanna a tremulous smile.

"I know how you feel," she said softly. "I have more fears than are healthy. Hiding them doesn't help. Sharing them doesn't help. Ignoring them doesn't help. Sobbing about them doesn't help." She paused. "Maybe this will sound horrible, but I was glad to see you break down."

"Because you get off on seeing other people suffer?" Tanna asked sharply.

"No. Because it proves to me that I'm not alone in dealing with a fear that can be overwhelming. But it also shows me that you're brave enough to face it." She paused. "So, are you crying because Eli couldn't help you?"

"Maybe I'm crying because it's obvious I'm beyond anyone's help."

She lifted a slim shoulder. "Today, perhaps. That doesn't mean you shouldn't try again tomorrow. Or the day after that. Or the day after that. It's cumulative."

"What? The fear? Or the solution to it?"

"Both."

Tanna had no logical response for that.

Since the woman stared at Tanna so blatantly, she stared back. The woman's coal black hair hung loose, almost to the waistband of her faded jeans. Her eyes were brown. Not golden, or chocolate, but basic brown. She had a prominent nose. Full lips—too full for her angular face. A regal neck. She was rail thin. From nervous energy? She threw off that vibe. She also wore a dingy T-shirt at least three sizes too big. But with the shirtsleeves hacked off, Tanna could see her arms were corded with muscle. She could also see the woman's skin was marked with odd tattoos.

She should be plain-looking. But something about her unadorned nature was striking. Compelling. Ethereal. Yet, as hard and rigid as the rocks surrounding them.

The woman didn't look away as Tanna scrutinized her.

Then their eyes met. Tanna said, "I'm Tanna Barker."

"I know. I'm Summer Red Stone."

"I'm glad to meet you, Summer, mostly because you're not a figment of my imagination so I can cross *going insane* off my list of mental defects."

Summer smiled. "I've been called a ghost on more than one occasion."

Cryptic. And a little creepy.

"You wonder what I want," Summer said.

A statement, not a question. "Maybe. I heard your name at the branding so I'm guessing you're involved with Eli?"

"Not just involved, we're intertwined."

There was the possessive tone. "Are you here to warn me off your man?"

Summer didn't smile or shake her head or laugh. She merely said, "No. You are a beautiful, damaged woman, Tanna. As much as that appeals to my Eli and his penchant for saving souls, well, I got here first. And he's got his hands completely full saving mine." Then she did smile. "But he *can* help you if you'll let him."

"You sound so sure."

"I am. Be patient with yourself. Overcoming fear is one of the hardest things there is and it doesn't have a set time frame."

Tanna stretched out from her protective little ball and sighed. "It's been nine months—"

"Since the fear started," Summer inserted. "And it's been one *hour* since you faced it. Permit yourself to fail. Forgive yourself for the failure. Each time you try it'll get easier."

"Are you some wise medicine woman or something?" Tanna demanded.

Summer laughed. "Not even close."

Eli strolled into view. Summer didn't turn around to greet him. She waited, her body perfectly still, for him to come to her. Then Eli's arms encircled her. He placed a soft kiss on her neck and a smile of pure serenity spread across her face as she closed her eyes.

"You okay?" Eli asked Tanna.

"No. But I had my first little freak-out session and I'm done with it. For today, anyway."

Summer opened her eyes. "I'll leave you two to talk. Nice meeting you."

"You too."

Summer placed a kiss in the center of Eli's palm and disentangled from his embrace. She didn't turn around. She knew she had Eli's undivided attention as she walked away.

Tanna watched her disappear up the path and noticed Eli's house for the first time. Hidden at the top of the rise and surrounded by trees, it'd been easy to miss. "I didn't see your place. It's well camouflaged."

"The wind blows a little in Wyoming, if you hadn't noticed," he said dryly, "and that spot offers the best protection from the elements."

"What did you build it out of?" It looked modern, and yet rustic.

"From materials I scrounged. Which is why it's a mishmash of logs, wood, rocks and metal. The roof joists are from an old building they tore down in Rawlins and didn't cost nothin'."

"It's really cool. How'd you come up with such a personal design for it?"

He chuckled. "I didn't. I revamped the traditional house I inherited, which had started to crumble but it had good bones. So I moved a trailer out here and worked on it whenever I had the time and cash. I've always lived simply, in small houses."

"This is a wonderful place."

"Thanks. It is. It feels like a home, now that Summer is here." He glanced at the house and then back at her. "You wanna talk about what happened today?"

Tanna shook her head. "I need time to think."

"I figured as much. Luckily, I've got stalls that need cleaning, and that's as good a place as any to sort things out."

"I'm shoveling shit today?"

"Yes, ma'am."

After thirty seconds or so, she shrugged. "Fits, given my mood."

Chapter Eleven

❧

*F*letch's phone rang and the caller ID read Eli's home number. He answered with, "You've got great timing, cuz. I'm on the road."

"Hey, Fletch. It's not Eli; it's Summer."

The hair on the back of his neck stood up. "Summer, is Eli all right?"

"Yeah. I'm calling about Tanna."

His stomach churned. "Did something happen to her?"

"No. It's just...she had a rough go of it this morning."

He'd called Tanna last night and she'd breezily reminded him she was riding the hobbyhorse with Eli today. He'd laughed because the woman had such a way with words. Now, it didn't seem so funny. "What happened?"

"That's the thing. You need to ask her."

"How long ago did she leave?"

"Four hours. I thought it'd be best to wait to call you until near the end of your workday."

"Eli knows you're calling me?"

"Of course."

"Thanks, Summer. Tell Eli thanks too."

Fletch glanced at the clock. Four thirty. Twenty minutes from the Split Rock. The procedure at the Ludlow Ranch wouldn't take more than two hours, but he didn't want to risk Tanna making other plans if he waited to contact her after he finished. He called her, hoping she'd pick up.

"Hello?"

"Tanna. It's Fletch. What're you doin' right now?"

"Burning tater tots in the oven and lamenting the sorry state of my cookin' skills. Why?"

"I'm on my way to pick you up. Be by your truck in twenty minutes."

"And if I say no?"

He actually felt her bristle across the phone lines and bit back a chuckle. "You won't. You secretly can't wait to see me. And you're dying to know the surprise I have for you." He hung up.

Thirty seconds passed before his phone rang. He answered, "This is Dr. Fletcher."

"What's with this *I have a surprise for you* bullshit?" Tanna demanded.

"You'll see. Now you gonna let me pick you up? Or should I keep goin' to my original destination all by myself?"

"Fine. You can pick me up. But if I'm giving up hot tater tots, you'd better feed me after this surprise of yours."

Fletch grinned. This was working out better than he'd planned. "Deal, sugar twang."

"I'll warn you I haven't showered."

"Neither have I."

"Oh, and I've been drinkin'."

"Then I'll be sure not to let you drive."

Tanna laughed. "You're a hard one to rattle."

You've rattled me since the moment we met. "Yep." He hung up again.

His cell rang fifteen seconds later. "This is Dr. Fletcher."

"I hate it when people hang up on me. *Hate. It.*"

"So noted."

Silence.

"Why aren't you talking to me?" she demanded.

"Sugar twang, *you* called *me.* So what do you wanna talk about?"

"Nothin'. I just wanted to hang up on you first this time." *Click.*

He laughed. Hard. Such a crazy, funny, ornery woman.

Fletch made it to the back side of the Split Rock in fifteen minutes. When he saw her leaning against the tailgate of her pickup, the sunlight glinting off her mahogany hair, her arms crossed over those ample breasts—pity that—his pulse sped up.

She hoisted herself into his truck. "Monster rig you got here, Doc. I didn't know you operated on elephants too."

"Gotta be a big rig. I'm a big guy, I work on big animals and I gotta have most my stuff with me."

"So what's the surprise?"

He whipped a U-turn. "Hey, Tanna. Damn, woman, you're lookin' fine. How's your day been?" He peered at her over the tops of his sunglasses. "Go on. Take a stab at bein' all polite and shit to me. I'll wait."

Tanna smirked. "Why, August Fletcher, DVM, how very thoughtful of you to ask about my day—sucky day that it was. I'm glad you think I look *fine*. God knows my day is complete with that stunningly original and heartfelt compliment."

He laughed. "I figured you didn't want me to confess you looked so tasty that I wanted to lick you up one side and down the other. Ending with my face buried between your amazing breasts. Then between your thighs." He flashed another smile. "Bein's we're just *friends* and all."

She abruptly changed the subject. "What's the surprise?"

"You're gonna help me with my last official vet duty today."

"Doin' what?" she asked sharply. "Because if this is some sort of forced equine intervention you and Eli cooked up after my disastrous morning—"

"Whoa, there. First off, I haven't talked to Eli at all today, so I have no idea what you're talking about." Fletch wanted to look at her to gauge her facial expression but he refrained and kept his eyes on the road. "Secondly, I'm aware of your discomfort around horses right now, so do you really think I'd force your hand and put one of my client's animals in danger? No, ma'am."

A few seconds passed before Tanna reached out and squeezed his forearm. "Sorry. I'm a little touchy if you hadn't noticed. Especially after today."

"What happened?"

"Eli eased me in to the horse pasture. Or he tried to. I panicked and fled, then berated myself for bein' afraid of horses. It was...humiliating."

Fletch twisted his wrist to clasp her fingers in his. "You tried. That's all you can ask of yourself." Impulsively, he lifted her hand and kissed her knuckles. "So no horses. This client we're helping runs sheep. They're Australian and do things a little differently than the Wyoming sheep raisers, in what's predominantly cattle country. They're more successful, which makes anyone suspect, right?"

"Right." Tanna relaxed and kept hold of his hand. "So, what's different about these Aussie sheepherders?"

"It's two separate operations. They lamb twice a year, with two separate flocks."

"Smart. Continual income. Not all the ranchers in Texas calve in the spring. A lot of them calve late fall. Or spring and fall."

"These guys are brothers, who married sisters. They ran big sheep ranches Down Under and each had their own way of doin' things. So Harland, the older brother, lambs late fall. And Kirk, the younger one, lambs early spring. Which means it's time to preg test Kirk's ewes."

She smiled so widely his damn breath caught in his throat. "That's what you're goin' to do?"

"What *we're* gonna do. So I don't wanna see you off frolicking with Harland's little lambs when we're on the clock."

"Wait. Will I be sticking my hand . . . ?"

Fletch shook his head. "That's the other way the Ludlows are different. We'll use ultrasound on the ewes. Ewes are more prone to twins, or even triplets, and they can keep a better eye on those mamas needing extra feed, et cetera, if they know ahead of time about the multiples. Not many sheep ranchers utilize the service."

"I didn't think sheep were part of a large animal practice."

"They aren't. But the Ludlows had an emergency right after I opened my practice and I was the only vet who'd take their call. They've stayed loyal to me. It's a nice change from working with mostly cows and horses. Keeps me on my toes."

"What else about them? You've got that sexy little smirk on your lips."

He shot her a grin. "You are picking up on some of my quirks already and I don't know whether to be happy about that or nervous. Anyway, Harland and Kirk help out and provide sheep for the mutton bustin' event at the Mountain Springs Indian Rodeo. At first no one wanted to supply stock and take it to the rez because of all the sovereign nation issues. The Ludlow brothers had no qualms. That earned my respect and gratitude."

Tanna frowned. "Sovereign nation issues? What's that mean?"

"To some it means anything you take to a reservation can be confiscated at any time by the tribe. So you can understand why few rodeo contractors want to take their prize horses and bulls to the rez."

"Does that happen often? The tribe just taking over someone else's property?"

"More often than you think, sadly. It's better now than it used to be. The last couple years Renner has brought his best stock to the little rodeo. Before that...the rough stock wasn't a challenge."

"How's the barrel racing competition?"

Fletch wondered if she'd ask. "Honestly? Dismal. One year there wasn't a single entrant. The cowboys can just show up with their tack and climb on a bronc or a bull provided by the stock contractor. But given most Indians on the reservation live at poverty level, few of them have horses. If they do, they're ranch horses, not specialized barrel racing horses." He slowed and hung a left on a blacktop driveway that stretched into the distance. "Here we are."

"Wow. Successful sheep ranchers."

"Very. And two of the nicest families you'll ever meet." Fletch honked twice when he reached the two houses before he headed uphill to the chutes. In the rearview he saw kids and dogs chasing after his truck. He grinned. Guaranteed Miss Ellie would be put out that he'd brought Tanna as his helper.

"God. Fletch. I don't..."

The panic in Tanna's voice ripped him out of his thoughts. "What's wrong?"

"I have no clue what I'm supposed to do to help you."

"I'll tell you everything you need to know, okay?"

She nodded, less than confidently, and bit her lip.

Fletch wanted nothing more than to lean over and kiss her. But that would fluster her, given they had an audience. "Let's go. Meet me in the back and we'll get supplies."

Soon as he exited the truck, he heard, "Doc Fletch!"

"Heya, Harland Jr. What's up?"

"One of my rabbits had bunnies and that stupid mama fox got all of 'em but one to feed to her kits."

Better the fox was eating the rabbits than the lambs—not that Fletch could say that.

"But me'n Dad are building a fox-proof cage," he boasted.

"Smart thinking." He unlocked the back doors to his mobile medical office. Then Tanna was right there. "In that bag on the floor is everything we'll need. But if you'd hop up and make sure there are enough gloves for both of us and syringes in case we need 'em, I'd appreciate it."

"No problem."

Fletch usually kept this particular ultrasound machine at the office, but he'd loaded it first thing today. He set it on the ground and waited for Tanna to move before he locked up again. "Harland Jr. will lead the way to the chutes."

Tanna fell in step beside him. He explained the process and what she'd be doing. She nodded, asked a couple of questions and that was it.

Harland Sr. and Kirk waved, leaving Fletch to his own devices. These ranchers didn't hover or suggest or distract. They knew Fletch did his job efficiently if he wasn't dealing with their constant interruptions. So he had to laugh when Kirk's wife Betsy whistled shrilly and all the kids scattered.

"How many ewes are you—I mean we—preg testing?"

Fletch gestured to the full pen. "I'm guessing two hundred and fifty."

"So we'll be here all night?"

"Nope. It'll take ninety minutes. Tops. If we don't take a break. Two hours if we do."

Tanna smirked. "I'm fully rested. And I wanna see you in action, August Fletcher, DVM. Show me your stuff."

"Prepare to be wowed." After she'd settled opposite him, he motioned to Renee, Harland's wife, who was manning the chute, to open the gate.

Then he slipped into professional mode and got to work.

He didn't realize how much time had passed, or how deep he'd gone into work zone, until Renee yelled, "Last one, Doc."

Tanna said, "Thank God."

"This mama's carrying triplets." The exit chute gate opened and the ewe trotted out. Fletch shut off the machine and stood, moving his neck side to side and then arching back.

"I couldn't believe how many multiples there are," Tanna said after hopping over the metal corral to his side.

"Too many isn't a good thing. A huge percentage of triplet pregnancies end up with all three lambs lost as well as the ewe."

They walked in silence back to the vehicle and ditched the equipment. Fletch noticed Tanna was limping slightly. "Did you hurt yourself today?"

That surprised her. "Not here. I fell in the pasture running away from the horses and wrenched my bad knee."

"Lemme look at it."

"It's not a big deal."

"Then it oughtn't be a big deal for me to take a look at it." He pointed to the back of his truck. "Park it."

"Fletch—"

"Now."

Tanna grumbled under her breath but she obeyed.

He clamped her ankle between his thighs and curled his hands on her leg above her kneecap. "Is it a dull throb? Or a sharp, shooting pain?"

"It fluctuates between both of those."

Fletch pushed her leg up slowly until the point she winced. "Sorry. Just needed to test your range of motion." He forced himself to focus on the movement of her muscles and not how soft her skin felt beneath his hands. "Have you been having flare-ups from your previous injury?"

"Some. But I don't use the muscles in the same way at my new job. I'm standing or sitting or walking."

"You been keeping up with your physical therapy exercises since you moved here?"

Tanna lifted her chin. "Not really."

Fletch got right in her face. "Wrong answer, sugar twang. From here on out I'm gonna make sure you use this time off from an injury ... oh, to re-cover from that injury, by doin' the exercises you're supposed to."

"Like you've got time to be my personal PT/OT?" she scoffed.

"I'll make time. I've been an athlete all my life, so I have a pretty good idea of what the PT/OT were doin' with you."

"Right. You're an animal doctor."

"Humans were part of the animal kingdom the last time I checked. So indulge this backward country vet. Were these some of the exercises you're supposed to be doin'?" He demonstrated six exercises and felt a little smug when she admitted he'd guessed correctly.

But Tanna wasn't done being snarky. "It's pointless."

He locked his gaze to hers as his fingers gently massaged the inside of her thigh above her knee. "So if you brought your injured horse to me and I gave you instructions on strengthening and conditioning to stave off lameness, would you do it?"

"Of course."

"Then it makes no sense that you wouldn't take care of yourself and follow your doctor's instructions. Your agility ain't something to be trifled with, Tanna. Promise me you'll start doin' your exercises again because I hate to see you hurting."

That was the right thing to say, because she sighed. "When you put it that way . . . okay. Thank you for the rubdown. It feels better already."

"Anytime."

Tanna slid out of the truck. "So, what happens now?"

"The Ludlows will ask us to stay for supper. Up to you if we do."

"What would you do if I wasn't here?"

"I'd stay. Renee and Betsy are great cooks. The kids make me laugh. Harland and Kirk have a unique ag perspective, so I enjoy talking to them."

"Then we'll stay."

Fletch looked at her and smiled. "Good. I'll warn ya that Harland's daughter Ellie might be hostile toward you."

"Got her sights set on you, does she?"

"Yep. She's assisted me many times and she's made no bones about the fact she intends to marry me."

A pause. "Well, you *are* quite the catch, Doc."

Was it his imagination, or had Tanna gotten a little snippy? Was she jealous?

Wishful thinking.

"Let's go wash up." When they reached the pump, he warned her, "It's erratic so watch out."

Tanna pushed up her sleeves and rolled her eyes. "Ain't the first time I've pumped something." She pulled on the handle, pumped it twice to get water flowing. She winked at him. "I'll share my stream with you."

"Thoughtful." Fletch cupped water and scrubbed his forearms. This was one of the cleaner jobs he'd done today. He rinsed and retreated, drying off with a disposable towel.

Soon as she stepped closer to the trickle to rinse, water blasted out.

She gasped and leapt back.

Don't laugh.

"I see that I-told-you-so look on your face. Wipe it off right now."

Her shirt was wet enough the material clung to her breasts. And he didn't pretend he wasn't looking. "Appears you're the one who could use some wiping off." Fletch loomed over her. The small size of the towel meant he could feel the heat from her body as he dabbed the water droplets from her chin. Then her neck. The bottom of his hand rested on the firm swell of her breast as he slowly blotted the water from her chest.

"I think you got it dry."

"So it appears I have." He didn't stop.

"Enjoying yourself?"

Fletch put his mouth next to her ear. "Absolutely. I gotta take my thrills where I can get them with you."

"Not fair. The way you whisper in my ear does it for me every damn time."

His dick took note of that. "Tanna—"

"Hey!" sounded behind them.

He reluctantly stepped back and turned around.

A pigtailed blond cowgirl of about eight stood opposite the pump with her hands on her hips. She stomped forward through the water, splashing mud everywhere as she glared at Tanna. "Who are you?"

"Who are you?" Tanna shot back.

"Ellie Ray Ludlow."

Tanna gave Fletch an amused smile. "I'm Tanna, Ellie, nice to meet you."

"Is she your assistant?" Ellie demanded of Fletch.

"She was today."

"I woulda helped you. I *always* help you. How come you didn't ask me?"

"Because your daddy needed your help in the pens."

"That's 'cause I'm good with animals," Ellie said, aiming a smug smile at Tanna, like she expected her to contradict the statement.

"I imagine a ranch girl like you is good at all sorts of things," Tanna offered.

"You talk funny."

"That's because I'm from Texas."

"Are you going back there? Soon?" she asked hopefully.

Tanna laughed. "'Fraid not. I'm here for a while."

Ellie made a disgusted noise. "Mama said it's time to eat and I'm supposed to invite you to supper."

"Both of us?" Fletch prompted.

"Yes. But *you* are sitting by me." She stormed off.

"That was Ellie of the marriage proposal?"

Fletch grinned. "Yes. But she's already warned me there won't be any of that mushy kissin' stuff when we get married."

"She's adorable."

"Let's hope she's on her best behavior tonight. The last assistant I brought out here ended up with a frog down her shirt."

Tanna shuddered. "Maybe I just oughta go wait in the truck."

"You? Running scared from an eight-year-old? That doesn't sound like the kickin' ass, takin' names, shootin' tequila Tanna I've heard about."

"Maybe because I've had my ass kicked today. And I don't know these people…"

Fletch cupped her chin, forcing her to look at him. "Do you want to leave? We can."

"These are some of your best clients, aren't they?"

"Yeah. But they'll—"

Then Tanna's mouth was on his. Too briefly, but she'd kissed him first nonetheless. "We'll stay. Ignore me. I'm hungry and out of sorts."

"Food will help."

"Probably."

The shadows remained in her eyes. "What's up?"

"How are you gonna introduce me?"

"Tanna Barker, the woman who rocked my world from the first time I met her?"

"You are such a sweet-talker."

Fletch liked the way her face and her entire body softened toward him. "How about we stick with the truth?"

"That I'm a washed-up former barrel racer?"

"Stop." Fletch rested his forehead to hers. "That's not true. And that's not all you ever were even if it was true."

Tanna didn't jerk away. She seemed to absorb a little resolve. "Thanks."

"You're welcome." He stepped back. "And if you ask my future wife really nicely, she'll probably let you play with her little lambs after supper."

"I'm disappointed her name isn't Mary."

"I think the Ludlows have heard that crack as often as I get asked *What's up, Doc?*"

"I hear ya. I tell guys I'm from Texas and they ask if all my exes live in Texas."

A dinner bell clanged.

Ellie stood at the base of the driveway and shouted, "Come on. I saved you a seat."

After eating, and chatting, and sneaking a peek at the baby lambs, Fletch took Tanna home.

She paused for a minute before she bailed out of his truck. "Thanks for today, Fletch. It's been a great surprise and exactly what I needed."

It was exactly what he needed too.

Chapter Twelve

❦

*T*anna had just printed Harper's instructions for pricing the two new boxes of merchandise when the doorbell jangled. She looked up as five women, varying in age from sixty on up, surrounded the sales desk.

"Can I help you?"

"So you're Tanna, huh?"

The woman who spoke was seventy if she was a day. She'd dressed in a one-piece romper, patterned with sunflowers, and black high-topped Converse sneakers.

"I'm Garnet. We're shareholders in the Split Rock."

Tanna masked her surprise. "Really?"

"Yep. We're good friends of Harper. And Tierney. And Celia. We've heard that you'd fit right in with us, beings you're a little wild. But you look kinda tame to me."

"What Garnet meant to say," a stylish redhead interjected, "is Celia mentioned you. We wanted to welcome you to Muddy Gap." She smiled and offered her perfectly manicured hand. "I'm Vivien."

"Nice to meet y'all."

"Oh, isn't her accent just the cutest thing?" a tiny, birdlike woman trilled. "I went steady with a guy from Oklahoma. And I just melted when he talked all soft and slow and sweet."

A stout woman next to her harrumphed. "I swear, Tilda, your tall tales keep getting more outlandish. You got married when you were what? Seventeen? When did you date anyone but Robert?"

Tilda smoothed a hand over her thinning pure white hair. "I dated before Robert, smarty-pants. I met my Southern boy Ray at church camp."

Tanna didn't know which woman to pay attention to, since they all started talking and arguing at once. A shrill whistle rent the air.

They all looked at the fourth woman who hadn't gotten a word in yet. Dressed in a mix of khaki and camouflage, including a slouch hat, she looked ready for a safari. Or war. "You all are cackling and pecking at each other worse than the hens in my henhouse." She smiled at Tanna. "I'm Pearl. You met Garnet, Viv and Tilda. Maybelle, why don't you introduce yourself?"

The stout woman held out her hand. "I'm Maybelle Linburg. Most the young folks call me Miz Maybelle. I'm the society reporter for the *Muddy Gap Gazette*. I'd love to do a feature on you."

"Sure. I mean, yes, ma'am. That would be kind."

"So, what did Celia tell you about us?" Garnet demanded. "Because she's full of hooey if she blamed us for the raid by the fire department. We weren't the only ones shooting tequila that night and we had the flames under control."

Flames?

"And we sure wouldn't have wasted empty bottles by throwing them into the fire," Pearl added.

"We recycle our empty alcohol bottles properly," Tilda sniffed. "We use them for target practice."

"We're all pretty good shots now," Miz Maybelle admitted with pride.

Pearl pointed at Vivien. "Don't ever piss her off when she's carrying. The woman is a deadeye."

Vivien blew on her nails and buffed them on her shirt.

Tanna laughed. "So, ladies, now that we've been properly introduced and I know who not to challenge to a gunfight at the Split Rock Corrals, what can I do for you today?"

"We're having a shareholders meeting after regular bar hours Sunday night." Miz Maybelle rested her forearms on the counter. "We pooled our money and bought shares in the resort. We call ourselves the Mud Lilies. We wear a piece of clothing or an article of jewelry to show solidarity at the meetings, but retain our individuality, so we want a theme."

"A theme. For a meeting?"

"We need six pieces, including one for Bernice, who couldn't come today. So wow us with your expertise, honey," Vivien added. "Harper always comes up with something cool."

No pressure.

Tanna stepped from behind the sales desk and wandered through the clothing racks. Too many unique pieces here. The first accessories rack had a bunch of different scarves, but nothing that could be pulled together as a theme. Except if they all wore hats, she could come up with a hat band for each one.

Nah.

As she headed toward a belt rack between the men's and women's departments, she remembered seeing a funky pair of suspenders. Pawing through the belts and ties, she found the stretchy wide strap, shot through with gold and silver thread. She unhooked it and spun around. Now she just had to sell her idea.

"Is that a bungee cord?" Garnet asked. "Looks like it came from a disco."

"No, it's a pair of suspenders. But it's got a really cool pattern. And it's stretchy." Tanna pulled on each end. "See?"

"How were you thinking of using them?" Miz Maybelle asked skeptically.

"As bracelets. You could cut each one to fit and sew it up the backside. Then on the front, you could attach a little something that personalizes each one. Like Pearl's could be pearl themed. Garnet's could be garnet themed. Miz Maybelle's could be bell themed. Tilda's could be dance themed for—"

"Waltzing Matilda!" Tilda clapped her hands. "Those are great ideas, Tanna. What could we do for Vivien's?"

Vivien tapped her fingers on the counter. "My middle name is Rose. So I could fit that in the name theme."

"Perfect. Now did you ladies want to look around some more, or did you want me to wrap this up?"

Pearl said, "Oh, no, sweetheart. You're not close to done. You have to help us fancy those bracelets up."

"I sure hope you're good with superglue, because they won't let me work with it no more," Garnet grumbled.

Tilda patted her hand. "It shouldn't take more than five hours to get this finished. You're not busy, are you?"

Tanna stared at them, frozen to the spot. She had zero talent with crafts. And she had a shit ton to get done today—she didn't have time to cut and paste with the senior set.

"Sugar? Is everything all right?" Vivien asked.

"Ah. Well. Here's the thing..."

The ladies burst out laughing. "You should see the look on your face. Pure panic."

"Bet you thought you were gonna get roped into arts and crafts time with assisted-living escapees, huh?" Garnet asked.

Tanna laughed. Then she snapped Garnet and Vivien in the butt with the suspenders, since they were closest. "Mean, ornery cusses, every cotton-pickin' one of you."

More laughter.

"So what would you have done if I'd said yes to helping you?" Tanna challenged.

"We would've had us an old-timey, quilting-bee-type thing."

"Except we'd have booze. And we'd be talking about sex," Garnet said.

"Garnet is *all* talk, since she's not getting any sex right now," Miz Maybelle whispered.

"I heard that, Maybelle, and I'd like to point out *you* ain't getting any either," Garnet retorted.

"None of us are," Tilda complained.

Vivien nodded. "Which is why we drink."

"And shoot stuff."

"I'll bet she's getting some," Pearl said, pointing at Tanna.

"To hell with some, I bet she's getting *a lot*," Garnet said, giving her a once-over. "When was the last time you rode the hobbyhorse?"

Tanna offered a cheeky grin. "Now, all y'all will need to buy me a couple drinks before I kiss and tell."

"Are you busy tonight?"

"Nope."

"Good. 'Cause all the other girls around these parts are pregnant. They're worthless as drinking buddies," Pearl complained.

"But great as designated drivers," Tanna said.

"That's Tobin's job," Garnet pointed out. "And whoever else he can rope into it, like Max, Ike, Fletch and Hugh."

Tanna felt her cheeks heat at the mention of Fletch's name.

She turned away as the ladies chattered, her thoughts scrolling to the too-sexy vet she'd been thinking about nonstop.

After the evening she'd spent with Fletch at Ludlows', he'd dropped her off without even attempting to kiss her good night. She'd been oddly disappointed. Watching him in action as August Fletcher, DVM, gave her an entirely different perspective on the man. He had near hero worship status with the entire Ludlow family and he'd downplayed it, acting embarrassed, but it was apparent not only did he love his job, he was damn good at it.

Little Miss Ellie had given her what for immediately after supper. Demanding details on how Tanna knew Fletch. Asking all sorts of questions about Tanna's experience with animals. She'd become marginally more friendly upon learning Tanna had been a world champion barrel racer. But Miss Ellie had kept an eagle eye on them when Tanna and Fletch were interacting. Tanna had been tempted to whisper in the young girl's ear that *she* enjoyed the mushy kissing stuff with Fletch. A lot.

Her mind replayed the following night's events in detail. He'd shown up after nine p.m. with popcorn and candy and they'd watched a movie. An action movie where cars blew up, the walls rattled from the constant on-screen gunfire and bodies littered the ground.

There hadn't been much in the way of conversation. Fletch had stretched his big body out on the couch completely, leaving her the recliner. He hadn't invaded her space and compulsively touched her. He hadn't made one suggestive comment. Tanna had no idea how much she liked their verbal foreplay and his sexual teasing until she hadn't had it.

It'd been like hanging out with her brother. Especially when she heard Fletch snoring.

Normally she'd get pissy about such rude male behavior. But she reminded herself it wasn't an actual date. Just two friends hanging out. The good doc had worked a long day. The man was clearly exhausted.

At midnight Tanna perched on the edge of the couch, not sure if she should wake him or rearrange him so he didn't end up with a crick in his neck. She'd reached over and brushed the section of untamed hair from where it'd fallen across his forehead.

Fletch's eyes immediately opened. Took a couple of seconds for them to focus. He didn't bestow a dazzling smile and she'd felt a pang of disappointment.

"Shit. I fell asleep, huh?"

"Yeah."

"Sorry. What time is it?"

"Midnight."

He groaned. "I've got a forty-five-minute drive home."

"You don't have to go. You could stay here tonight."

His gaze had roved over her face, down her neck to her cleavage and back up to meet her eyes. The heat level in his was set to smolder, not burn, but she knew it wouldn't take much to ignite. "I can't."

She said, "Why not?" even when she'd known the answer.

"Because there's no way in hell I could stay out of your bed," he'd said with a low, warning rasp. He paused and kept watching her. "It'd violate the friendship rules."

She opened her mouth to say "fuck the stupid rules" when his front shirt pocket started to vibrate.

Fletch tore his gaze away, muttering about piss-poor timing. Then he sat up with the buzzing phone in his hand. "This is Dr. Fletcher. Yeah. No, go ahead and connect me with the number." He pushed his hair away from his face. Then he tapped his fingers on his knee as he held the line.

Tanna picked up the popcorn bowls and took them to the kitchen.

"Randy? Hey, it's Fletch. No, that's all right. It's why I have an answering service. What's up with Bluebell? Uh-huh. Uh-huh." He listened. "If you've tried all that and it hasn't helped then I'd better come take a look. It'll be forty-five minutes. Tell Annabeth to put on a pot of coffee." He hung up and sighed.

If this were a relationship, Tanna would run her hands up his back and curl her arms around his neck. Instead she said, "Duty calls, huh?"

"Yep."

"How often does this happen?"

He stood. "Depends on the time of year. Calls have dropped off in the last three weeks. The place I'm goin' tonight...the guy's daughter competes in cutting horse competitions. The daughter is easily panicked. Her daddy calls me. Usually it's nothin' major. But there's always that first time."

"I know a little something about being panicked around horses lately."

Fletch stared at her. "You ever gonna tell me what happened at Eli's?"

"I already did. I don't know what good it'll do to rehash it."

"Guess you'd never know unless you tried." He ran his hands through his hair and snagged his ball cap off the coffee table. At the door he turned and gave her a sheepish smile. "Sorry I fell asleep."

"Blame it on the company."

"I could blame it on a lot of things, sugar twang, but never on that. Good night."

"Tanna?" someone said behind her and she jumped, immediately ending the flashback.

She whirled around and smiled at Vivien. "Sorry. I'm spacey today."

"No worries. Just so you know, we were serious about meeting up with you for a drink or ten at Buckeye Joe's."

"But there are stipulations," Tilda said, peering around Vivien's shoulder.

"Like what?"

"Like nothing," Miz Maybelle said, giving Tilda the stink eye. "If you show up, we'll initiate you."

Tanna looked from face to face, each staring at her earnestly and she realized they weren't joking. "If I show up?"

"Hard to believe that not everyone wants to hang out with us, ain't it?" Pearl said with a sigh. "We do scare people off."

"Well, ladies, I'm from Texas. I'm made of much sterner stuff than that. Maybe y'all will learn some new tricks from me."

"I like her already," Garnet said. "But I gotta be honest, if we're teaching this young pup new tricks, I'll need a few hours' beauty sleep."

~

Tanna was starting to feel like a regular at the Buckeye, given she'd been in four times in two weeks. But since this was the only bar in town, chances were high everyone felt that way. And she'd always considered her hometown small.

After they'd gotten settled and ordered drinks, Tanna said, "If I buy the first round of shots, I've got everyone's promise you'll knock it back no matter what?"

Miz Maybelle leaned forward, her eyes a steely blue behind her thick glasses. "Bring it on, Texas."

Tanna's gaze moved from Miz Maybelle, to Tilda, to Garnet, to Pearl, to Vivien, to Bernice. "All right. Clear the table, I'll be back."

Sherry Gilchrist grinned at Tanna as she walked up to the bar. "They've already got you playing fetch and carry for them?"

"No. This round is on me. So I'll need seven shots of tequila."

"Coming right up." Sherry set seven shot glasses on a tray and filled each one without spilling a drop. "Anything else?"

"A bottle of Tabasco sauce."

"Tanna, darlin', you sure you wanna taunt them with this?"

"Yep." She couldn't admit the Mud Lilies had been taunting *her*. She shook the hot sauce until a layer of reddish-orange formed on the top of each glass. She handed the bottle back to Sherry and dug in her jeans pocket for some cash. "How much do I owe you?"

"Nothin'."

Tanna leaned forward. "Bull. I already got my free drink from you last week."

"Don't get your back up. These shots aren't on the house. But they are paid for and that's all I'm allowed to say." She smiled. "Enjoy."

She carried the tray to the table. The ladies looked at the shots, each other, then at Tanna. Pearl said, "What is this?"

"A Texas prairie fire." After everyone had a shot glass, Tanna raised hers for a toast. "God bless my home state of Texas." She downed the breath-stealing shot quickly. Her eyes watered. Her throat closed up. Her nasal passages protested. She sniffed with gusto and said, "Now that's what I'm talkin' about."

When she glanced around the group, she saw empty shot glasses. None of them reached for an icy cold beer to stop the fire trail to the stomach. And how in the hell had they finished the shots faster than she had? She must've worn a confused look because Vivien offered her a grandmotherly pat on the arm.

"That was really a sweet toast, Tanna dear. Thank you."

Sweet? "But..."

"Not the reaction you expected?" Miz Maybelle asked.

"No! My mouth is still burning. Isn't yours?"

Six heads shook in unison.

"If that's how she reacts...maybe we oughtn't give her the Wyoming version of that drink," Garnet said.

"Wait. You've had this shot before?"

"Yep. Didn't do much for us so we tweaked it a bit."

"How?" Tanna demanded.

Bernice grinned. "You want us to tell you? Or are you game to try one?"

A challenge? Bring it. "Let's see whatcha got."

Pearl clapped her hands with glee, grabbed the tray and headed to the bar.

When Tanna looked over, Sherry gave her a *you're in for it now* head-shake.

They had to be bluffing.

Tanna believed that when Pearl delivered the shots. She even believed it during the "to Wyoming, the equality state" toast. But the instant that sweet, hot and blistering heat singed the lining of her throat, caused her lungs to seize up, and every hair on her body to stand on end, she wanted to cry uncle, swear she'd never doubt them again just to make it stop.

Bernice whacked her on the back with a sharp, "Breathe."

She sputtered. Coughed. Sucked in great gulps of air. Luckily she didn't throw up. God. She'd never live *that* down. After she wiped her streaming eyes, she glanced at the faces peering back at her. Not a single one of them had even broken a sweat.

"Oh. My. Lord. Are y'all fixin' to kill me?"

Laughter.

"What was that evil concoction?"

"It's called a Wyoming wildfire. Everclear, cinnamon schnapps, topped with habanero hot sauce."

Tanna drained half her beer in an attempt to vanquish the fire. Then she choked out, "Where'd you get the habanero sauce?"

Pearl pulled a bottle out of her purse. "Always carry some with me. Most food is so bland."

Unreal.

"Who's up for a pink panty dropper shot?" Garnet asked.

"Not me. I need to—"

"Grow some balls?" Tilda intoned sweetly.

What the hell?

"It'll take at least two more shots for you to live up to that Texas wild woman reputation we've heard about," Bernice warned.

Hey. Was the senior set looking at her with pity? Screw that. "Fine. A panty dropper and a…?"

"Zombie killer," they said in unison.

Jesus. "Do I even want to know what's in it?"

"Nope. But I suggest you limit yourself to one."

Two shots later, Tanna decided she was done drinking for the night. She switched to Coke, but drank out of a lowball glass so the Mud Lilies didn't know she'd quit drinking and wouldn't accuse her of being a Texas marshmallow.

Tanna had passed some kind of test and the ladies embraced her like a long lost granddaughter. She hadn't felt this much warmth and personal connection for longer than she cared to think about. She laughed. Listened to outrageous stories that had to be true.

Then the guys showed up, much to the ladies' delight. It was sweet and amusing how these women had wrapped the young, strapping cowboys around their fingers. Tobin, Hugh, Ike, Max and Holt served as guardians and dance partners.

She felt a pang of disappointment Fletch wasn't with them. And she had too much pride to ask his friends whether he planned to join them later.

At first her misgivings about getting involved with Fletch had been based on her temporary resident status in Wyoming. But now, knowing the doc's brutal work schedule, getting involved with him would likely be a recipe for loneliness.

Tobin caught her eye. "Everything all right?"

"It will be when you dance with me."

He grinned. Lord. Why couldn't she fall for a sweetie pie like him? Tobin was good-looking. Built. Smart. Eager. She could totally train him to be the kind of man she wanted in bed.

But Fletch already is the type of man you need. Experienced. Bossy. Playful. Intense.

"Tanna?" Tobin said softly.

Her focus shifted back to him. "Sorry. I think that zombie killer drink ate part of my brain."

"Probably." Tobin held out his hand, helping her to her feet. "Word of advice. Run if them gals mention pixie dust drinks. Sounds like an innocent girlie concoction, right?"

"Right."

"Wrong." He led her onto the dance floor. "Let's just say I still have no recollection of the deputy sheriff hauling my ass home or why I thought it'd be a good idea to sleep bare-nekkid in a lounge chair on my deck."

Tanna couldn't help but laugh.

"So now that you're in a good mood, can I ask when you're gonna go out with me?"

"I'm dancing with you, aren't I?"

"That doesn't count."

"I'm older than you."

He winked. "Just means you'll be impressed by my youthful stamina."

"True. But it's also true that I've got a lot of baggage."

"Isn't it ironic I used to be a baggage handler at the Split Rock?"

She smiled at him, completely charmed. Too bad she'd met another too-charming guy first.

And Tanna's feet missed a step when she saw him walk in the door.

Chapter Thirteen

❦

*O*ne benefit of hanging with the Mud Lilies? No one approached him for animal care advice because most people in town were scared of them.

In the last half hour Fletch had kicked back and caught up with the women who absolutely cracked his ass up. They'd thanked him for introducing Cora to their group, but Garnet and Vivien purposely distracted him when he'd asked Cora's whereabouts on a Saturday night.

Weird.

The group had split up, leaving him and Miz Maybelle alone. He didn't want to know what the ladies were up to anyway. So he watched Tanna discreetly.

"I'm pretty sure that your hot stare alone isn't enough to burn her clothes off," Miz Maybelle said.

Or maybe his staring hadn't been so discreet. Fletch blushed and ripped his gaze away from Tanna shaking her groove thang as she exited the dance floor. "That obvious, huh?"

"Yes. But don't think for a second that she's oblivious to how close you're paying attention to her. My question is why are you over here, instead of over there?"

"The path across the bar leads both ways. Why isn't *she* over *here*?"

Miz Maybelle shook her finger at him. "What is it with you young people today and your need to play games?"

Oh boy. Lecture mode. Best if he kept his mouth shut.

"Tanna wants to be dancing with you, but instead of asking you to dance, she's cutting a rug with everyone *but* you. Showing you what you're missing."

Little did she know—Fletch was perfectly aware of how well Tanna moved that lean muscular body in tight quarters.

"Are you even listening to me?" Miz Maybelle demanded.

"Yes, ma'am."

"Why haven't you asked her to dance yet?" She paused, giving him ample time to answer. When he didn't, she tossed off, "As I live and breathe, I think the big, tough doctor...is just plain chicken."

His mouth dropped open. "I am not."

She clucked.

The woman actually *clucked* at him.

"Real nice, Miz Maybelle."

She shrugged. "So, you want a side of coleslaw with your chicken?"

Fletch took another sip of beer, refusing to be goaded.

"I don't mind telling you, Dr. Fletcher, that I've been drinking a wee bit, as our Tilda would say."

"No. Really?"

She whapped him on the shoulder. "Such a smart mouth. I know you didn't get that from your charming father."

"You'd be surprised." Hey. Wait. How did Miz Maybelle know his dad?

"But I share my best advice after I've tipped back a few."

"What makes you think I need advice?"

"Because you're moping with an old fart like me instead of playing slap and tickle with Miss Tex-ass, as Devin calls her. That name suits her. She's got those womanly curves and that wild streak men go gaga over. I bet Devin wouldn't put up with her being passed from guy to guy on the dance floor while he sat back here with his di—"

"Don't say it." There was an image he didn't need from this sweet-tongued woman. "Fine. I get it. I'm going."

Miz Maybelle shouted, "You're welcome," as he passed a table of giggling coeds.

Fletch kept his eye on Tanna as he wove through people heading toward the bar. One of the advantages of his height and his size: people tried to avoid him. The group Tanna was chatting with gave him a wide berth.

Tanna allowed a tight smile. "Fletch. I'm surprised to see you here—"

"No, you're not. Been here half an hour, as you're fully aware." He grabbed her hand and said, "Excuse us," with a smile before he towed her to the farthest edge of the dance floor.

"What are you doin'?"

"Taking my turn to dance with you." Fletch brought her against his body and began rocking them to the beat.

"You could've asked."

He put his lips on her ear. "Sugar twang, will you dance with me? Pretty, pretty please? With a chocolate-covered cherry on top?"

Tanna shivered. "No fair. You know what it does to me when you whisper in my ear."

"Really? I forgot that. Maybe I need a refresher course in what makes you putty in my hands." He let his hand drift from the small of her back down to her butt. "And you fit very well in my hands, don't you?"

"You're in rare form tonight."

"Oh, it doesn't have to be that way. I can be this way with you every night."

"You trying to seduce me?"

"I'm trying to charm the pants off of you. Then I'm hoping the rest of your clothing follows suit and hits the floor in my bedroom. Or my truck. Or hell, even the bathroom."

She laughed softly. "Then what?"

Fletch traced the shell of her ear with his tongue. "Then I give you a refresher course on just what I can do with my mouth and hands. I recall you liked the way I use my tongue."

"Mmm-hmm." She turned her head and nipped the side of his jaw. "I really liked the way you used your cock too."

There she was. The sassy-mouthed sexpot he'd first met. Thank God. "Funny thing. My cock was just thinking about how much it liked you." He pressed his groin into hers. "How much it missed you."

"I had a sneaking suspicion it was happy to see me."

He leaned back and looked into her face. "How long you gonna hold me off? And why do you want to? We were good together, Tanna. Damn good."

"I know."

"Then why are you fighting this?"

She held his gaze for ten seconds and then it dropped to his chin. "Because it wouldn't be a one-nighter. We both know if I went home with you tonight it wouldn't be the last time—it'd be the start, since we couldn't stop ourselves because the sex is so spectacular."

"Why would we have to stop?"

"Because you'll want more from me. And I can't give it to you. Then you'll get resentful and pissy about it and take it out on me, even when I warned you ahead of time that's how it'd be."

That was a harsh assessment. But she wasn't too far off base. He'd been on the receiving end of that type of frustration. Whenever he got involved with a woman, he warned her up front that his job came first. He also let her know he was gone a lot and prone to cancel plans regardless of how long they'd been in place. The woman always assured him she understood. But she never did. First the little barbs would start. Followed by hostility. Then tears and accusations. Ending with the big breakup speech about what an inconsiderate asshole he was and no woman in her right mind would ever want to be with him.

"Fletch?"

He glanced into Tanna's eyes. "Sorry. What did you say?"

"What were you thinking about?"

"Proving you wrong."

"And how do you plan on doin' that?"

He brushed his lips over hers. "By taking you outside and fucking you blind in my pickup. Then after I got us both off, at least twice, I'd head home. I wouldn't even call you tomorrow."

She snorted.

"Isn't that what you want?" Fletch ran his palm over her ass, then up her spine. "An intimate connection only during sex? I can give you that."

"So no more bein' friends?"

"We can be friends, because I like you. But we'd be lovers too." He brushed her hair from her shoulders. "Is that what you want?"

She pressed her body against his and kissed the hollow of his throat.

"Say it," he demanded roughly. "Out loud. So I don't misunderstand."

"I want you as more than a friend."

"And?"

"And . . . how about if we test the suspension on your pickup right now?"

He bent closer. "Only if you swear you're not giving me another taste of how awesome it is between us and then you just run away again."

"I ran the morning after because it was supposed to be a one-night thing. Hot sex with a hot man. I didn't expect that within a day of moving to Muddy Gap I'd see you." Her fingertips grazed his smooth cheekbones. "And still want you."

The song ended. Keeping hold of her hand, he skirted the stage and led her out through the side door. He started toward his pickup at a good clip.

Halfway there, Tanna said, "Stop."

When he whirled around to ask what was wrong, she launched herself at him.

"Kiss me. I want you to fuck me but I want you to kiss me first, because you know how to kiss."

His mouth met hers immediately. Hungrily. Her tongue sought his, sliding and stroking. Her head moved to deepen the angle.

Her hands were all over him. He wanted more. Skin on skin would be a good place to start. He forced himself to let go of her mouth. "Come on."

"My truck is right here." And, he noticed, it faced away from the front of the bar. She unlocked the passenger door and said, "You first."

Fletch climbed in, grateful she had a big diesel that gave him plenty of room in the cab.

She straddled his lap and slammed the door shut. She rested her forearms on his shoulders. "Now, where were we?"

"About to get naked."

"Race ya."

Shirts off, he captured her mouth, kissing her with the same zeal that his hands used roaming her soft skin. His fingers found the front clasp of her bra and then her abundant breasts were his for the taking. He released her mouth in tiny increments and followed the sexy curve of her neck down to her cleavage.

"Put your hands on my knees and arch back."

She hissed, "Yes," when his wet tongue lashed her nipple.

He pushed her breasts together and used his mouth to drive her wild. Sucking her nipples as deep into his mouth as he could. Easing back to rub his face over the smooth globes. Using his teeth to nip the tips. Letting his thumbs caress the undersides of the heavy flesh. He buried his face in her cleavage. "I want to slide my cock here."

"Fletch. Please."

"Please what?" He lapped at her right nipple, watching as it pulled into a rigid point.

"Please can we take off the rest of our clothes so you can fuck me?"

"It'll entail some maneuvering."

"I don't think either of us are strangers to sex in pickup trucks." Tanna leaned sideways and twisted until her shoulders were on the seat and her feet were on the passenger-side window. Raising her hips, she unbuttoned and unzipped, tugging her jeans to her knees.

Fletch yanked them off the rest of the way. When he glanced up, she'd started shimmying her underwear down her thighs. Once the scrap of lace reached her knees, he bent down and latched onto them with his teeth, lifting her legs off the window one at a time to remove them.

Laughing, she sat up. "Need help with your jeans?"

"Nope." Unbuckled and unzipped, he yanked his jeans and boxers to his ankles. He managed to keep his wits, even with a hot, naked woman squirming on top of him, and retrieved a condom from his wallet.

Tanna snatched it from his fingers. "Let me." She ripped it open and watched his eyes as she rolled it down his shaft. Then she kissed him crazily and tried to climb on.

His hands on her hips stopped the motion. "I want you facing forward." Fletch slid his hands down, his thumbs met her clit. "So I can touch you like this."

Lust returned to her eyes. "Oh. Good plan." She spun around.

"Hang tight for a second." He scooted until his ass was half off the seat. Her feet were by his hips, her knees spread wide outside his. He held his cock at the base and aligned it with her soft, wet hole. "Reach for the dash." Then he pushed into that tight heat. As soon as he was inside her fully, he brought his legs closer together.

Her head lifted and moaned. "I like this."

"Thought you might." He swept her hair aside, baring her skin. He dragged an openmouthed kiss from the ball of her shoulder to her nape. "Ride me, cowgirl."

Tanna lifted herself off his cock so just the head remained inside her. She pushed back, driving his shaft in fully. "How's that?"

"Awesome." He nipped her ear. "Use me however you need to. You've got the reins."

She made a growling noise. Rocking back. Rolling forward.

Watching the sinuous movement of her body—bliss. Feeling her wet pussy clamping down on his cock—such heaven that his toes clenched in his boots.

He spread his hand over her pubic bone, following her slit down to where they were joined. Coating his middle finger with her juices, he placed it on her clit, rubbing circles on the bundle of nerves as he kissed her back.

The windows had fogged up. The seat squeaked with her every backward thrust. The air was filled with harsh breathing and the perfume of sex. They were in their own little world and it was a damn fine place to be.

"Need it faster," she panted.

"Like this?" he murmured, using short, fast strokes.

"Exactly like that. God, that feels good."

Fletch captured her left breast. Pinching her nipple with the same rhythm he flicked her swollen clit.

Tanna gasped and threw her head back. Her cunt tightened in the sweetest, hottest pulses as her clit throbbed beneath his stroking finger. Her gasp became a long moan as the pleasure overtook her.

Her movements slowed and Fletch took his cue from her. Backing off. Caressing her skin with his hands and mouth. "You're so sexy, Tanna. Goddamn. I could come just from hearing you come."

She rubbed her cheek along his, the lower half of her body still. "How about if I help you with that?" She dislodged his cock and turned around to face him, tucking her knees under his armpits. Bracing her hands behind her on his thighs, she propelled herself forward.

He hissed. "Sugar twang, that's gonna do me in."

"Good. Show me. Lose control for me."

He bent closer, wrapping one hand around her nape to take her mouth, the other hand on her ass, urging her to move faster. Her upper torso was arched so that her nipples only brushed his chest every other roll of her hips. As hot and sexy and necessary as this quickie was, he wanted more of this. Wanted her arching and writhing beneath him. Her strong hands gripping his ass as he fucked her mindless. Her breathy moans hot in his ear as he teased and tortured her, bringing her to the edge again and again.

Those images, along with the deep, steady thrusts, and her fingernails digging into his thighs pushed Fletch to the point he didn't have another coherent thought in his head as he exploded in a white-hot burst of pleasure.

Little nips to his jaw returned him from the hazy state of postorgasmic stupor.

Tanna whispered, "Well, that took the edge off."

He laughed against her throat. "You up for more?"

"Mmm-hmm. No goin' back, remember?" She arched her neck, giving him full access. "Come home with me. Stay with me all night. And tomorrow. We won't have to get out of bed at all."

"Sounds like heaven." He didn't break the mood by warning her that he could—and probably would—get called away at some point.

She sighed and purred as he nuzzled the vulnerable skin below her jaw. "I don't want you to stop doin' that. Sweet baby Jesus, that mouth of yours is deadly. But I'm getting a cramp in my calf."

"So dismount." Fletch kissed the tip of her chin.

"Help me."

He clamped his hands on her ass to stabilize her. Why he held on to her ass and not her back to accomplish that task . . . well, he really loved her ass. Especially her *naked* ass.

She scrambled into the driver's side. Before she asked for her clothes, he handed them to her and kissed her bare arm and palmed her breast.

"Unless you want the next go to happen in my truck again, you'd better stop touching me." She snatched his wrist and rubbed his knuckles against her nipple. "I do like these big hands of yours and can't wait to have them on me again." She smooched his knuckles. "And again."

Christ. He was getting hard. "Soon enough. Do you have...?" He pointed at his crotch.

"Yep." Tanna passed him a napkin from a fast-food joint.

After ditching the condom, he righted his clothing. He glanced over to see her tucking in her shirt. "So, I'll meet you at your place?"

She frowned. "I know you can't leave your vehicle here with all the horse tranquilizers and stuff, but why doesn't it sound like you'll be right behind me?"

"Oh, I plan to get behind you at least once tonight." He grinned. "But first, I'm goin' back in to make sure the Mud Lilies gals have rides home. They really seemed to be ripping it up tonight. That worries me."

"You're telling me," she muttered. "And it's sweet of you to be concerned about them."

"Just doin' what I'd do for any friend."

Tanna smirked. "Well, not any friend, I hope. Not like what you just did to me, *friend*."

"Smart." He kissed her hard. "Ass."

"I like that growly caveman side of you." She sighed. "Don't be long, okay?"

Chapter Fourteen

⋙❦⋘

As Tanna waited for Fletch to show up, her bare feet beat a path in the linoleum and she wondered why she was so nervous. They'd had sex twenty minutes ago. And even then it hadn't been the first time they'd been together.

She'd brushed her teeth. She hadn't taken her clothes off. Should she be wearing her satin robe and a smile?

God. What was wrong with her? She never fretted about this stuff.

An engine revved outside before it shut off. Tanna froze, listening to the sounds. A door slammed. Then heavy footfalls echoed across the deck. A pause at the door before he knocked.

"Come in."

Then Fletch stood on the rug. His hands hung by his sides. He looked gorgeous with that hot, turned-on male glaze in his eyes. The flush to his cheeks. His ragged breaths. The bulge in his jeans.

Tanna nearly lost the ability to breathe when he said, "Come. Here."

Her legs seemed to give out in the face of such passion as she plastered her body to his. Her fingers were in his hair, holding on as he kissed her with abandon. Fletch's hands landed on her ass and he lifted her, urging her legs to wrap around his waist. He did all this without missing a beat, or a kiss or a step as he walked them down the hall to her bedroom.

He didn't toss her on the bed. He pressed her back against the door and broke the kiss.

Tanna's heart beat harder. No sign of the playful Fletch at all in the heated depths of his dark eyes.

"I've been dying to get my hands on you since the moment I woke up alone in that crummy motel room. Fucking you in your truck took the edge off. But I'm nowhere near done with you. And this time, there's no rush."

She rubbed her cheek against his and whispered, "But I love it hard and fast."

"I'm gonna try my damndest to make you love it long and slow too." Fletch kissed her again and lowered her feet to the floor. He popped each button on her shirt until it hung open and he tugged the material free and the blouse floated to the floor.

Her fingers tightened on his biceps as his hot mouth cruised down the center of her throat. While his lips and tongue teased her breasts pushing out of her lacy bra cups, his palms slid to the front of her rib cage. One quick tug and he relieved her of her bra.

Fletch eased back to watch her face as he bared her upper body. She had the unusual urge to cover herself seeing the intimate way he looked at her.

"You're perfect, Tanna." He nuzzled and teased her breasts, using his hands, his mouth, the roughness of his beard bristle and the smoothness of his cheeks. Touching her everywhere except her nipples.

She squirmed and arched, trying to force his mouth to brush the constricted tips.

He buried his face in her cleavage, then he placed hot kisses in a line straight down her belly, dropping to his knees. Those big hands of his were so gentle on her hips. He brushed his warm mouth above the waistband of her jeans and kept making that same, maddeningly slow pass until her entire body quivered.

"Take your jeans off," he murmured against her skin. "Panties too." Then he rested on his haunches, waiting for her to do his bidding.

Tanna unbuttoned, unzipped and shoved the denim and lace panties to her ankles and kicked them aside. Her heart jumped and her body twitched when his rough-skinned hands landed on the inside of her thighs and pushed them farther apart.

Fletch dipped his head and licked her slit. He made a growling noise and did it again. And again.

On the fourth pass she instinctively put her hands on his head and pulled him away.

But he dodged her hands and returned to where he'd been, focusing his swirling tongue round and round on her clit and then zigzagging that wickedly fast tongue to the entrance to her body and plunging it in deep.

God, she loved this. So much. Except for the out-of-control feeling. Which she had right now. Her fingers gripped his hair and she nudged his mouth upward and off her tingling girl parts.

He pulled back and looked up at her. "Is there a problem with me goin' down on you?"

Don't blush. "Why—"

"Because you are wiggling away from me like a damn worm on a hook and you keep shoving at my head." His fingertips squeezed the tops of her thighs. "I remember you did that the first night we were together too. Am I doin' something wrong?"

She turned her head away.

"Look at me."

Her eyes met his. "No. You're not doin' anything wrong. It's me. It's my problem. It just . . . feels so good and I'm always so wiggly. I get off so fast this way and it's embarrassing."

Fletch rolled to his feet. His jeans-clad legs brushed her bare ones. His soft cotton T-shirt rubbed against her nipples and her belly. His mouth grazed her ear. "Then it's my problem too. See, I want to spend a whole lot more time sucking, licking and kissing your pretty pussy. I don't like it when you shove me away. I wanna stay right there, until you come all over my face."

Tanna made a soft whimper.

"So, I've got a solution to help you with that squirminess issue . . . if you'll trust me."

She buried her face in his neck. "I'm sorry that I've already made this awkward."

"It's only awkward if one of us leaves because we can't handle the other's...needs, for lack of a better word. Okay?"

"Okay."

He kissed her, pulling her shoulders from the door and walking her backward until the creases of her knees hit the mattress.

"Crawl up on the bed and stretch out."

Tanna tried to tune out the warning voices in her head as she scooted into the middle of the mattress. She stared at the ceiling and then Fletch was on all fours above her, wearing that wicked, wicked grin. The man moved as fast and quietly as a predator on the hunt. And his very posture screamed that he intended to conquer her.

"Think sexy thoughts, sugar twang. Try and stay still. And close them pretty eyes." As soon as she did, the bed jiggled.

She braced herself for the warm swipe of his tongue or a soft suck. Maybe his callused fingertips would dance across her body. Thinking about all the possible sexy scenarios had the desired effect. Her mind and body were primed.

So where had he gone?

She heard him breathing in slow measured breaths. Then she recognized the scratch of a dresser drawer being closed.

"Do you know how fucking beautiful you look lying there waiting for me?" The location of his voice indicated he'd moved to the other side of the bed. Then she heard plop, plop, plop as pillows hit the floor.

He jostled the mattress. First he tapped the inside of her calf, as a signal to open her legs wider. Then he placed feathery light kisses on the inside of her ankle and her anklebone as his fingers stroked the skin above and below where his mouth worked. "Now we're getting to the part where you need to stay still, okay?"

"Ah. Yeah. Sure. Piece of cake—omigod, what are you doin'?"

Fletch performed the same teasing and caressing on her left ankle and she felt him hanging above her, his knees pushing against her thighs. His breath teased her lips. "Only thing you need to think about is my mouth on yours." He brushed soft kisses across her parted lips. His hand circled her bicep and moved up the length of her right arm. He threaded his fingers through hers and squeezed before releasing her hand. Something soft circled her wrist.

Before she thought to ask what it was, he cranked up the intensity of the kiss. Those wonderfully rough fingers stroked her left arm as his mouth controlled hers.

She wanted him naked, feeling that skin-on-skin connection. She reached up...or she tried to but she could lift her arms only a few inches. She broke the kiss and wiggled more vigorously but nothing happened. "Fletch?"

"Thought I told you to stay still," he murmured and planted kisses down the side of her neck.

"Why can't I move?"

"Because I tied you down." He nonchalantly circled her nipple with his tongue, keeping his eyes on hers.

"What!" Tanna attempted to lift her legs but they were immobilized too. "How...Why would you do that?"

"Because you said you trusted me." He suckled hard on the rigid point and her skin broke out in a mass of goose bumps. "Because I don't want your hands or your knees shoving me out of the way when I'm tasting my fill of you." He chuckled. "But first, test those knots."

Tanna saw that he'd trussed her arms up with a pair of nylon knee-highs. "Sweet Lord. Did you get these out of my dresser?"

"Uh-huh."

"And you tied me to the headboard?"

"Yep. I warned you that hobbling is an effective technique. Wouldn't you agree?"

She watched his dark head moving across her chest.

"I love this spot right here." His cheek followed the inside curve of her right breast. "The skin is so soft and pale." His mouth meandered across her ribs and she gasped. "Ticklish here too, I see."

"Fletch."

"Tanna."

She liked the different ways he said her name. Sometimes drawn out.

Sometimes a short syllable. But she really, really liked when he growled it against her skin.

He inched down her body, a kiss at a time until he had to stretch out between her thighs.

She tried to squirm away, but between the ties and Fletch's iron grip, she had little movement.

And that amused him mightily. "Might as well relax and enjoy this because I'm gonna be here for a while."

At the first wet swipe of his tongue, she moaned. As Fletch pressed sucking kisses down the seam of her sex, she stopped trying to get away. She stopped thinking about being ticklish. Her body seemed to melt farther into the mattress with each soft suck. Her mind fogged at the delicate lapping. He brought her focus back to him with a sudden scrape of his teeth.

Her pulse pounded in her throat. The ties binding her wrists weren't overly tight, but she felt her pulse jumping there too.

When that little tingle started at the base of her spine, she canted her hips and said, "So close."

Then Fletch made that sexy rumble against her sex, and his need to give her this pleasure freed her. She came in a gasping rush of fast contractions. His hungry mouth absorbed every one.

Her hearing went a little wonky, like she'd left a loud concert. She forced air into her lungs because she'd stopped breathing. As soon as her eyes focused, she lifted up and looked down her body.

The depraved man sucked her pussy lips and released them with a loud pop. He waggled his eyebrows. "Better when you can't wiggle, huh?"

"Cocky much?"

"Only when it's justified."

"Are you gonna tie me up every time so I can't touch you while you're blowing my . . . mind?"

"Maybe. That mean you want me to untie you?"

"Yes." She added, "Please."

"Too bad." He grinned and kissed the inside of her thigh. "Because you're gonna go again."

"I can't. It's too much."

"It's never too much. And I warned you I planned to get my fill of you."

"Fletch—" She ended on a short gasp as he blew a raspberry right on her clit. Odd as that was, it kind of felt like a vibrator.

"Shut up, Tanna, and enjoy this. I sure as hell am." He flattened his tongue and lapped at her pussy with long, slow licks. "Do you have any idea how many times I jacked off thinking about the night I spent in bed with you?" More thorough licks as the tip of his tongue rimmed the opening to her pussy. "I should check to see if the motel billed me for the lamp you broke."

"It wasn't my fault . . . oh, God, do that again." Fletch did some tonguing thing over her clit that made her insides and her outsides quiver.

"Completely your fault. I had one hand pulling your hair and one between your thighs, so it wasn't my flailing arms that knocked it over."

"Because you had me bent over the dresser! And you kept doin' that twisty thing with your hips, which made me come so hard I couldn't see. So it's your fault I needed something to hold on to so I didn't float into sexual unconsciousness."

He chuckled. "The sound of that lamp crashing to the floor as you started to come was one of the sexiest things I've ever heard." He stopped nuzzling and teasing to look up at her. "Enough talking."

Her body erupted in gooseflesh at his very intense, very male look.

Fletch dove back in, his mouth busy on her pussy.

When she squirmed at the continual attention, he pressed down on her lower abdomen and pushed a finger inside her. Feeling how wet she'd become again, he added another.

His fingers tunneled in and out of her as his tongue fluttered on her clit. Not constantly, but fleetingly, teasingly. Making her want the unbroken contact.

He blew a stream of air across the sensitized tissues and then licked up one side of her slit and down the other. Stopping between to suckle her pussy lips.

As her mind was chanting *so so so close*, the orgasm rocketed through her. Not as powerful as the first, but longer.

Then his breath in her ear was as hot as his words. "Need it fast." He untied her right wrist, then her left.

Her hands were immediately on his head, her fingers diving into his hair as she tugged his mouth to hers for a deep kiss. Tasting herself on his lips and tongue had never been sexier. Never made her hotter.

Fletch must've untied her legs because she could wrap them around his waist and press her body completely against his as he impaled her. His hips were bucking so hard the headboard slammed into the paneling with every thrust.

This man had so much passion. He showed every bit as he made love to her—in every way he'd shown her it could be the hottest sex of her life, if she'd just trust him.

And so she did.

Moving her legs from around his hips, she put her feet on the bed and raised her pelvis up, giving him a deeper angle.

He broke the kiss on a groan, reaching his hands beneath to grab her butt, holding her there as he pumped harder, faster. He muttered, "Jesus, Tanna, so fucking good," burying his face in her neck as he came with a harsh grunt.

But as he lay there, catching his breath, squishing the air out of her lungs, she had a moment of panic. Remembering her accident and Jezebel's weight on her for those few awful seconds.

Fletch sensed something and moved off her. "You all right?"

I'm just a freak. She smiled and kissed him. "I'm fine. You're just . . . solid."

"Shit. Sorry."

"Don't be."

"Mmm . . ." He nuzzled her neck. "There is a way to fix that."

"How?" She released a little shriek when he rolled them and grinned.

"This time you get to be on top."

❧

Something was buzzing on the nightstand.

Stupid alarm. She forgot to turn it off. She didn't have to work early.

And she definitely didn't want to move since she had a hot, naked man in her bed.

The vibrating stopped.

Thank God.

Then four loud chimes sounded.

Immediately the strong arms holding her vanished. Fletch lifted up and leaned across her. "Sorry. That was mine."

"What time is it?"

"Seven."

Tanna groaned. The last time she'd looked at the clock, after a sweaty bout of sex in the shower that'd made her eyes cross and her throat sore from moaning, it'd read almost three a.m. "I need—"

"Hang on just a second. I'm calling my answering service." He pushed up and sat on the edge of the bed.

She rolled over. His bare back faced her and she allowed a little smirk at seeing the scratches. Such a sexy, muscular back and the most gorgeous color—golden tan with the tiniest red tint. She wanted to run her lips along the scratches for a healing kiss. She wanted to drag her tongue from the base of his neck—starting beneath that silky hair—down his spine to the crack of his ass. She wanted to breathe in his morning scent as her mouth tasted his sleep-warmed skin.

But she behaved when he put on his official veterinarian voice.

"Larry? It's Fletch. I listened to your message. Has there been any change? Uh-huh. Still bleeding or has it closed up? Uh-huh. No. If you think she's savable, then I'm on my way. To be blunt, if there's a chance she'll be dead by the time I get there in two hours? You might wanna discuss it with Sharon. We're on Sunday rates. With travel time." A few more "uh-huhs" and he said, "Let me know. Sure. I doubt I'll get another emergency call in the next fifteen minutes."

He dropped the phone from his ear and sighed.

Tanna scooted behind him, wrapping her legs around him, and laying her cheek between his shoulder blades. "Duty calls for Dr. Fletcher?"

"Not yet. My client needs to discuss treatment options with his wife, since they'd be facing a big vet bill, so I'm in limbo until I hear back." He ran his hands over her bare thighs. "I'd hoped to get to spend more of the day with you. I'd like to say this never happens, but it happens a lot."

No apologies. This was who he was. Tanna knew he was turning this into a make or break moment.

"I could pout because my playtime with you has been shortchanged. Or we could have a quickie to start your day out with a bang. You know. To kill some time while you're waiting." She kissed his spine.

"A quickie, huh?"

"I'll even let you tie me up again."

"Can I spank that fine ass of yours?"

"Umm. No."

"Damn."

She laughed. "Grab a condom."

After he rolled one on—he was already hard, big surprise—he stalked her across the mattress. "This isn't a pity fuck?"

"Fucking you is no chore, trust me." Tanna wreathed her arms around his neck. "But if you want, I can try a pitiful wail and moan real loud."

Fletch said, "You'll do that anyway," and drove into her to the hilt.

After he'd scrambled her brain and put a big smile on both their faces, she watched him, pacing by the side of the bed.

While they'd been in the moment, skin to skin, mouth to mouth, Tanna knew Fletch hadn't been thinking of anything else but pleasing her. Making her forget everything except how well he could make her sing.

But now . . . his focus had shifted.

It was weirdly hot and absolutely endearing.

You can't fall for this man, Tanna. Remember that.

His phone rang. "Hey, Larry. No, that's fine. I'm on my way." He hung up and dialed another number. "Dr. Fletcher, 2295." He paused. "Requesting addendum to standard message." Another pause. "Due to remote site call, wait time for emergency response will be longer than four hours."

Fletch gathered his clothes. Jamming his feet into his socks first, then stepping into his underwear.

"Too bad you can't run your vet practice naked," she murmured. "Such a pity to cover up your bangin' body, Doc."

"Hilarious. That's just what I need. A horse taking a bite outta my cock, thinking it's a carrot."

"It *is* a big, juicy carrot," she cooed. "And I know firsthand how good it tastes."

He laughed. As he dragged on his jeans, he asked, "What are you doin' today?"

Needing a physical connection with him after the intensity of the past few hours, she rolled out of bed and took over buttoning his shirt. "I have to work in the lounge at four. Split Rock shareholders meeting. What about you? If you finish your call early?"

"I doubt that'll happen. If we are gonna save the mare, it'll require surgical repair. I'm wiped out after that. And if I have free time on Sundays, I stop by and hang out with my dad."

"Saving wounded ponies. Doting on your father. And you're a beast in the sack? You're too good to be true, August."

He retorted, "Hardly," and blushed anyway. That reaction appeared to annoy him, so he trapped her face in his hands and kissed her. Her lips buzzed a little when he finally pulled away. "Not too good to be true, sugar twang. I'm just a man doin' his job. And right now? I'm wishing I was a janitor so I could spend all day with you."

"Be safe."

"I will. I'll be in touch. Soon, okay?"

"Okay."

Tanna waited for the door to close before she snuggled under the covers and went back to sleep.

Chapter Fifteen

❧

"*I* need to speak with you, Dr. Fletcher."

Fletch's gaze moved from his computer screen to Cora. "Sure. What's on your mind?"

"I'd prefer to have this discussion in the reception area." She spun on her orthopedic shoe and left his office.

A summons on top of being holed up, browbeaten into dealing with paperwork he'd been putting off forever. This day wasn't off to an auspicious start since it wasn't yet noon. Fletch pushed his chair back and followed her.

But Cora wasn't in her usual spot, sitting primly behind her desk. She stared out the front door, a sheaf of papers in her hand.

"All right, Cora, what's up?"

She turned around. "I've worked for you for nine years."

Crap. Was she giving notice?

"In that time I've asked for a week off here and there. I appreciate the extra paid time off at Christmas. But the truth is, I've wanted to take an extended vacation for quite a while."

"You should've said something—"

"Ah, ah, ah. I'm not done and I will have my full say before you get to jump in, Doc."

"Fine. Go on."

"Even when I take time off, you do not. Not one time in nine years. You have all the calls transferred to your cell phone, so when I'm not in the office it's actually twice as much work for you."

"That's part of the gig since I own my own business." Why was she telling him something he already knew? "Besides, I'm not the vacationing type."

She stabbed her bony finger at him. "How can you know you're not the vacationing type if you've never tried it?"

He'd started to get a bad feeling about this discussion, beyond the fear she might be handing in her resignation. "You do have a point to all this nagging, right?"

Rather than skewering him with a haughty look at his snappish response, she laughed. It sounded a little mean, which scared him, quite frankly. "I wish I was going to be around to see how you handle it, Dr. Smarty-pants."

"Handle what?"

"Your vacation."

Had he somehow missed the signs that she'd started going senile? "Cora. You're confused. I'm not taking a vacation."

Cora crossed her arms over her chest. "Oh, yes, you are. Remember a few weeks back when I brought up my vacation request form and you told me to do whatever I wanted? I did."

"What? I never said that!"

"Hah! You did so and I have the recording on my iPhone if you'd like to hear it."

Shit.

"I filled out the vacation request and told you to read it. Several times. I can tell by the blank expression on your face you didn't bother—even when you assured me on several occasions when I've specifically asked, that you had indeed read the document."

Fletch nervously ran a hand through his hair. "Fine. I'll admit I didn't read it. But I didn't need to, because you've always scheduled your time off over a summer holiday so you can maximize the vacation days. And you take a few nonpaid days. I'm good with that."

Her lips stretched into a smile. "Excellent. Because I'm taking a few more nonpaid days than I usually do."

"How many?"

"Thirty-five."

"What?"

"On Wednesday I'm leaving on a six-week trip to Europe. And while I set up my time off, I cleared your schedule for six weeks. The mail has been stopped. The bills have been paid. The standard medical deliveries have been suspended. The answering service has been switched over. Dr. Arneson, Dr. Anderson and Dr. Eriksen are covering your calls. All your calls. I didn't see a need to put out a memo to your clients that you'll be on vacation because we both know they'd try to contact you at home."

"Cora. What the—"

She raised her hand to stop his protest. "You've covered for your colleagues for the last seven years. They've all three managed to take at least two full weeks off every year in their practices. So by their estimation—not mine—they each owe you a week of reciprocity for every year. We're talking twenty-one weeks. Since it is the slow season, it was no problem for them to step up to the plate and each take two weeks as payback. So you're also on vacation for six weeks."

Fletch knew his jaw hung to the floor. Who did she think she was arbitrarily deciding he needed a vacation? This was *his* business. She was *his* employee. She didn't have the right to make that decision.

"I recognize the anger in your eyes, Dr. Fletcher. Before you start bellowing at me, I'll remind you that I am your office manager. Not just some floozy secretary. I've been with you since the beginning of your career. In the last year I've started to see signs that scare me. You're snappish. You are skating very close to burnout. You have no life outside the care you give other people's animals." Sadness filled her eyes and she lifted her chin. "You're a good man. And a fine vet. But you need to find some balance in your life."

"So you're forcing the issue?" he said testily. "Forcing me to find balance?"

"Yes. And this will tick you off even more when I tell you that I discussed this with your father. He agreed with me the only way to get you to see the importance of making changes in your life was to stage an intervention." Cora hit the intercom button on the phone. "Bruce? You can come out now."

Fletch whirled around to see his dad amble in from the operating room. Another shock rolled through him when he stood next to Cora. "You're in on this too?"

"Yes. Cora has been worried about you for some time. As have I. We've discussed it several times. Since you constantly brush both our concerns aside we joined forces."

"Listen, Dad—"

"No, you listen."

Yikes. Fletch hadn't heard that sharp parental tone in years.

"This is a done deal. You're officially on vacation. Drastic measures were necessary, but the only ones who know we had to force this time off on you are the three of us in this room. As far as your colleagues and clients are concerned, you're taking a scheduled break. As your office manager, I just handled all the details and set it up."

"Did you set up a vacation package for me too?" he demanded.

"God forbid we'd ever presume that much," Cora said with a sniff.

Yeah, she'd already presumed a helluva lot.

"No prepackaged vacation, son. You've got the time to do with it as you wish while Cora and I are in Europe—"

"Wait. *You're* going with her?"

His dad grinned and winked at Cora. "The cat's out of the bag now, muffin."

Muffin? No. Oh, *hell* no. This wasn't happening.

Fletch's gaze winged between them and he couldn't believe his eyes. His seventy-seven-year-old father and his seventy-year-old office manager were looking at each other with...dear God, was that lust?

My eyes. Please. Make it stop.

"I know it's surprising," his dad offered.

Talk about an understatement. "How long has this been goin' on?"

"A few months."

"A few months?" Fletch repeated.

"Give or take. And it's more proof of how preoccupied you are that you didn't even notice."

Just another point he couldn't argue.

"I've had my eye on Cora for a few years, but I figured a smart, classy woman like her would turn down a busted-up former oil rigger such as myself."

"Oh, you and that silver tongue. There's not a busted up thing about you, Bruce Fletcher. You literally run circles around men half your age," she volleyed back.

"I ran after you pretty good, huh?"

"I sure didn't mind getting caught," Cora practically cooed.

Holy. Fuck. He'd have to jam stakes in his ears to keep from hearing shit like that again.

"I also have to thank you for introducing me to the Mud Lilies," Cora said. "They offered me great advice that bolstered my courage to let Bruce know the attraction was mutual."

Damn Garnet. Always trying to play matchmaker. Or was that Pearl? Vivien was a sneaky woman. And Tilda. Not to mention Miz Maybelle... dammit. They were all in on it. They were all about to get an earful about their damn meddling.

"So Cora and I booked the vacation together," his dad said.

"*Together* together? Like sharing the same...?"

"Room? Yes. And we're beyond needing the lecture about practicing safe sex, son."

"Bruce!"

His dad leaned over and whispered something in Cora's ear that made her laugh. And blush. And whisper something back that made his father blush.

Fletch flopped into the closest chair, wondering if he was hallucinating.

Calling his colleagues and claiming to be the butt of a joke would make him look like an idiot who didn't have control over his own practice or his only employee.

A hand landed on his shoulder and he looked up at his father. "Son? You okay?"

"No. You couldn't have...oh, *mentioned* this last night when we spent two hours together watching the game?"

"What would you have done?" his dad demanded. "Argued? Fought this—us? No. This was the only way. Even if you do nothing but catch up on your sleep and the medical journals, it'll be time well spent."

The thought of sitting around in his house, doing nothing for days on end made every muscle in his body seize up.

Then again, the idea of hopping on a plane, living in a hotel, traipsing through some touristy hot spot in the name of relaxation made him break out in hives.

But it was apparently a done deal; he'd have to find a way to deal with it.

"When do you two leave?"

"We're driving to Denver tonight. Cora's convinced me to spend Tuesday at the Natural History Museum. Our plane to Heathrow leaves at four a.m. on Wednesday."

Suck it up. Your dad is excited about this. Weren't you just worried he wasn't getting out of his place enough?

Yes. But hopping on a plane to Europe seemed a drastic way to curb his addiction to cribbage and *Judge Judy*.

"I'd say something witty or profound, but I'm at a loss for words right now and the only thing I can think of is you'd better send me some damn postcards."

⟀

After he left his work office, he immediately went to his home office.

Six weeks.

How the hell was he supposed to fill forty-two days?

He didn't golf. Or fish. Or play tennis. Or hike. Or mountain bike.

His father and Cora had been right in pointing out his lack of outside interests.

He blew out a breath. *Think, man.*

His gaze snagged on the gigantic pile of medical journals and bovine and equine practices updates. He could tackle a couple of those every day.

Good. Keep going.

He could finish the paper he'd started about the Ludlows' Australian sheep-raising philosophy on U.S. soil. They'd gladly give him hard data.

Another good idea. Tedious, but necessary since it'd been a few years since he'd had anything published.

If he could do anything, how would he fill his time?

Easy. He'd spend all of it with Tanna.

Fletch stopped pacing. Why was he just thinking of her now?

Because even after the amazing night they'd had, duty had called. So he wasn't sure if they were technically seeing each other.

And he wanted to see a lot more of her.

Problem was, his house was in Rawlins and she was staying forty-five minutes away.

So move. Go to her. You can read anywhere. As long as you've got your laptop you can work on your research paper.

Brilliant.

Also, here was his chance to make good on his promise to help Renner determine whether a commercial stock-breeding program was financially viable. Jackson Stock Contracting purchased rough stock strictly for their own use, but with the company garnering tons of national awards, other stock contractors had approached Renner about expanding into a commercial breeding program. Genetics was Tobin's area of expertise. Fletch was supposed to delve into specific rules and regulations of a semen collection facility, interstate transport, and equipment needed. Now with all this free time . . . Renner wouldn't say no to him. Especially if the man wasn't paying for his time.

He scrolled through his contact list on his cell phone and hit CALL.

The man answered on the second ring. "This is Renner Jackson."

"Renner? It's Fletch."

"Hey. What's up, Doc?" Renner snickered.

Fletch groaned. "Like I haven't heard that a million times."

"I'm sure. So I'll admit it's weird that you're callin' me. Usually I'm the one in a panic callin' you."

Probably he should've gone out and talked to Renner in person. But at least he wouldn't have to look the man in the eye when he explained the situation. "I need to ask you a favor."

"You've pulled my ass out of the fire more times than I can count. So anything you need? Name it."

"You've still got an empty employee trailer up at the Split Rock?"

"Yep. Why?"

"I'm taking a six-week sabbatical from my practice."

A healthy pause followed. "Shit, Fletch. Is everything okay?"

"Yeah. It's fine. Except for the burnout factor." He sighed. "I haven't taken any personal time off since I graduated from vet school. My office manager has been making noise about wanting to take an extended vacation, so I'm giving it to her."

Silence.

"Renner? You there?"

"Uh-huh. I'm just surprised. Although I think it's great," Renner added hastily. "Why were you asking about the trailer?"

Fletch paced to the big picture window at the rear of the house that boasted a view of the meadow and the rolling hills. "There are a couple of things I've been putting off. I can't concentrate at the office and I'm too easily distracted at home. I need to be somewhat isolated, so my clients can't get in touch with me and let the other vets covering for me actually fill in. But I don't want to get too far from Rawlins. My other option is to live in Eli's horse trailer out at his place, but I doubt he wants me crashing with him and Summer even for a short while." He paced to the kitchen. "Then I thought... the Split Rock is a resort. Maybe I could stay there, but not in the lodge because I can't afford it. Staying in the employee trailers would be like renting a quiet cabin. Wouldn't it?"

"Not a lot of wild parties goin' on at the employee's quarters, that's for sure," Renner said dryly.

"That's what I'm looking for. Somewhere I can come and go as I please. Keep to myself and work at my own pace."

"Some days it sucks bein' your own boss, doesn't it?"

"I'm a slave driver to myself, to hear Cora talk."

Renner chuckled. But he didn't say yes.

"Plus, the benefit for Jackson Stock Contracting would be me bein' on-site if there was an animal emergency."

Another beat of silence passed.

"I'd intended on paying rent," Fletch said. "And I wouldn't expect to eat at the lodge."

"Whoa. I haven't said yea or nay yet, so you don't hafta hard sell me, Fletch."

So what was the holdup? "You need to run it past the shareholders?"

"I don't need their approval on something like this."

"But?"

Fletch could almost see Renner jamming his hand through his hair. "But part of me hopes that if I say no you'll go to a tropical island somewhere and take the time off you need. Find a hot chick in a bikini, get drunk and get laid."

Wasn't like he could confess his thoughts were running along the same lines. But he wouldn't have to go farther than the trailer next door. But he retorted, "Given the chance . . . would *you* jet off to an exotic locale for six weeks?"

"Hell, no. I probably wouldn't know what to do with myself."

"That's where I'm at. This vacation seemed like a good idea at the time and it's sort of embarrassing to admit I don't know what to do with myself either. Which is why I haven't mentioned it to anyone." Hopefully Renner bought that little white lie. "I know I've been lax doin' my part with researching the commercial stock-breeding program, so I figured I could invest time in that venture while I'm there."

"If you ever leave your vet practice, I want you goin' to work for me, because, man, you can really sell it."

Fletch laughed. "So do we have a deal?"

"Absolutely. As long as you give me the real reason for leaving your beautiful house in Rawlins to move into a dumpy trailer in the middle of nowhere. And I ain't talkin' the examples you gave me—valid as they are. What's the biggest reason you want this?"

Fuck. So much for his life as a con man. "Tanna."

"What about her?"

"I'm crazy about her. Tanna and I have been seeing each other off and on since before the branding. With this break, I've got the chance to be with her without phone calls interrupting me all hours of the night, or trying to squeeze time to see her after I've worked a seventeen-hour day. If she's not interested, so be it. But I wouldn't be asking if I didn't believe there's something between us worth exploring…if we had the time. And now we do."

Renner sighed. "I know exactly what you're saying. Before I met Tierney, I had no life besides work. While I love how I make my living, I love my wife more. And I hear her voice in the back of my head, telling me this is one of those romantic gestures women love so much. So I'll agree to it. But if you and Tanna part ways, *you'll* have to leave, not her."

"Understood. And thanks, man, I owe you."

Chapter Sixteen

❦

Fletch looked longingly at his big-screen TV, his state-of-the-art computer system, and his custom-made bed as he packed for his odd adventure. Then he reminded himself there were more important things at stake than creature comforts.

He loaded medical magazines and reference tomes in two duffel bags. His laptop and Wi-Fi connection ended up in his overnight bag along with cords for all his electronic devices. Glancing at the pile of stuff at his front door, he thought to himself, *So much for packing light.* He'd have to come back for the rest later. He wanted to be sitting on the deck of his trailer when Tanna walked by after work. Maybe he'd act all casual-like—kicked back in a lawn chair, wearing board shorts and a puka-shell necklace, strumming a guitar in his bare feet.

Hey, the laid-back image worked for Devin McClain and Tanna had seemed to like him a whole helluva lot.

She likes you a whole helluva lot—she said so, remember?

House locked up tight, supplies laid in—at least enough to get him through supper tonight and breakfast tomorrow, he started toward the Split Rock.

As he reached the outskirts of Rawlins, he debated on stopping by his dad's place to say good-bye. The devil on his left shoulder reminded him that his father had conspired with Cora behind his back. The angel on his right shoulder reminded him his father would be gone for six weeks.

The devil won out. No surprise, he usually did.

Fletch let his mind wander on the drive. When he was on duty, driving from ranch to ranch, he focused on what the issues might be at his next stop. His focus was so absolute he barely noticed the scenery, reminding himself he'd lived in this area nearly all his life. So this time, he watched the topography change, marveling at how fast that change occurred. Although most of his friends were in the ranching business, their land was vastly different from one another's.

No one was in the office besides Renner when Fletch stopped in to pick up the key to the trailer. They spent very little time talking specifics on what Renner considered priorities with the breeding program. Fletch wasn't surprised to learn that Tobin was in charge. Wouldn't that be a change, having a coworker? He hadn't been forced to mesh personalities or differing ideas with anyone since he'd started his own business. Preferring to do things his own way, at his own speed, was the major reason he'd gone into business for himself in the first place.

But he liked Tobin. He respected him. Now if he could just stop thinking of him as a kid. Tobin was only three years younger than Hugh, and Fletch didn't consider him a kid.

He'd managed to avoid Tanna as he'd left the lodge. After unloading his stuff, he stared at the queen-sized bed and his back spasmed in protest. Guess he'd add furniture store to his list of places to stop in Rawlins tomorrow.

Three cans of ravioli and four pieces of wheat toast served as supper. He tried organizing his reference materials, but he was too antsy.

Since Renner had given him the green light for a small grated fire on the deck, he traipsed through the wooded area behind the trailers, looking for deadwood. Took three trips until he had enough to last a couple of nights. He busted the dry limbs into manageable pieces and figured he'd start the fire at dusk.

No surprise Tobin stopped by. As well as Hugh. They didn't question his sudden change of residence and they both seemed happy he'd be around for a while. When pressed on his daily plans, Fletch remained vague, not wanting to commit to anything until he'd had a chance to talk to Tanna.

After the guys left, Dave and Yvette, the property caretaker and his wife, who headed up the housekeeping and laundry for the lodge, wandered over. They'd been married forty years and relocated to Wyoming after Dave retired from the military. With Yvette's years of experience in the housekeeping side of the hotel industry, they'd seized the chance to get to work together at the Split Rock and live in the gorgeous Wyoming countryside. Of course, Fletch hadn't known any of this at the outset of the conversation. Surprised him sometimes at how easily people just told all to a stranger.

His heart beat a little harder when he heard the creak of footsteps on the planked walkway. He kept his focus on the crackling fire.

The footsteps stopped.

He glanced up at her, standing at the edge of his deck.

"Fletch? What in the world are you doin' here?"

Man. He loved that honey-thick drawl of hers. "Nice evening, isn't it?"

"Uh. Yeah. But..." Her eyes narrowed and she crossed her arms over her chest. "You have cattle stuff to do early in the morning and Renner is making you crash here?"

He shook his head.

"Were you out drinking with Tobin and Hugh and you're too shitfaced to drive home?"

He shook his head again.

"Okay. I give up. Why are you parked in a lawn chair in front of a fire with your feet up? At ten at night? Drinking a . . . is that a wine cooler?"

"Tropical berry flavored. It's what I had left over in my fridge at home. And since it'd been a particularly trying day, if I stopped at the liquor store to pick up a bottle of something, I'd be tempted to drink the whole thing. So I'm stuck with this 'bitch beer' as Bran calls it. I have more in the cooler if you're interested in having a drink with me."

Tanna squinted at him. "I need to change clothes."

Fletch's eyes wandered over her. He liked what he saw and he made sure she knew it. "Sugar twang, you always look fantastic. No matter what you are—or ain't—wearing."

"Sweet-talker."

He hooked his foot around the plastic leg of the lawn chair, dragging it closer to the fire. "Have a seat."

She plopped down, propping her feet next to his. "Now gimme a damn drink."

He pulled out a cold bottle, twisted off the cap and passed it over. Clinking his bottle to hers, he said, "To the ass end of this day."

"What did you do today, Dr. Fletcher, that made it so trying?"

Telling her that he got the smackdown from his office manager and father might give her the wrong impression, so he stretched the truth. "I wrapped up a few things before I closed down my office for six weeks."

She choked on her drink. "Seriously? You're taking six weeks off?"

"Yep."

"Why?"

"Because I haven't taken time off for an extended period...ever. My office manager wanted to book a long tour to Europe and I can't run my practice without her, so I'm using the time to write a couple of articles for ag industry journals. Reading material that's piled up in the last year. Resting up."

"Is there a reason you didn't share this tidbit when we were together this weekend?"

The look he gave her reminded her they'd had other things on their minds besides discussing schedules. Tanna blushed and he bit back a grin. "I wasn't sure where I'd end up. This was just one of my options." He bumped her knee with his. "And I didn't want to get your hopes up."

"Thoughtful of you." She cocked her head and took a drink. "So, you'll be here at the Split Rock the whole time?"

"If I stay at my place I'll watch too much TV. Or I'll head out to the bar. Or my clients will pester me. This place is a good hidey-hole. I can get my work done and if I have the hankering to get wild, well, I can always peg Tobin." He locked his gaze to hers. "Or you."

"I have to behave. I need this job."

"I wasn't suggesting we play strip poker in the main room of the lodge. Or go skinny-dipping in the new pool."

"The cement pond is off-limits to employees unless there aren't any guests around."

He shrugged. "I prefer the lake, anyway."

"Me too."

"Yeah? I have access to a lake house. Rustic, but the fishing is good."

"Bet the skinny-dipping is good too," she said with a smirk.

"I haven't tried it since I've only ever gone there with my dad. But if you're interested, let me know and we'll head up there for a day or two."

"That does sound nice."

Silence lingered.

Tanna glanced up and caught him staring at her, because he couldn't stop. "You're beautiful. The glow of the firelight looks good on you."

She squinted at him. "Sweet Lord. Are you drunk?"

Tempting to laugh, but he merely shook his head. "Just observant."

"You are surely tryin' to rattle me."

"Maybe." He drummed his fingers on the arm of his chair. "You aren't gonna get all indignant on me now that I've complimented you, are you?"

Tanna shook her head.

"Can I ask . . . were you upset that I left on Sunday morning?"

"It wouldn't have done me any good to get upset and it just would've made you feel like shit. Lives are at stake in your job. Do I wish the day would've played out differently? Some. But you did give me a memorable good-bye."

"There is that. But then, I didn't call you."

"So? You knew I was working."

"You providing excuses for me . . . that's novel."

She tipped her bottle at him. "I try to be memorable."

The perfect opening. "I want more than just a memory, Tanna." His heart sped up. "I'm sitting here acting all polite like, making conversation with you, while my brain keeps flashing to the image of your naked body. I keep hearing those sexy sounds you make when I'm inside you. I'm remembering how you taste. So, gorgeous, I'm just gonna lay it on the line. I want to be your lover for however long you're in town."

"You wanna be fuck buddies?"

He shook his head. "I can have that anytime I want and I'm sure you can too. I want something different. I'd like to try"—he gasped with complete exaggeration—"dating."

"Really? Why?"

"It'll be fun."

Tanna didn't look convinced. "Can I think about it?"

"Sure. I'll give you fifteen seconds starting right now."

"You are such a caveman."

"You seemed to like that side of me well enough three times on Saturday night and once on Sunday morning."

"Lord almighty, you never give up."

"Not when I've found something worth keeping." Fletch reached out and twisted a hank of her hair around his finger. "You also oughta know I'm not the sneaking around type. If we're sleeping together then we're together in public and private."

Tanna closed her eyes and ducked her head.

Since Fletch had kept hold of her hair, he didn't have to tug hard to get her attention. "What's wrong?"

She looked at him. "It's just been a while since I've heard that. I've gotten used to bein' the wild girl a guy wants in his bed, behind closed doors. You know, the dirty girl, dirty little secret, hidden away in the light of day."

He smiled, knew it looked predatory and didn't care. "Oh, trust me, sugar twang, we're gonna get plenty dirty behind closed doors. But everyone will understand that we're together in every sense of the word when we're out." A look he'd never seen settled on her beautiful face. "What?"

"You are so fuckin' hot when you say stuff like that."

He brought them closer until they were within kissing distance. "What do you say we put out this fire so we can go inside and start another one?"

"With body friction?" she murmured, rubbing the side of her face against the stubble on his jaw. "I bet you can supply the wood."

Fletch stood and grabbed the fire-dampening cover to snuff out the embers. When he glanced over at Tanna . . . all he could think was *want*. He hauled her to her feet and kissed her.

She twined herself around him and tried to scale his body.

Her passion kicked his into a higher gear and his cock pressed against his shorts. He clamped one hand around her hip and one in her hair as he herded her toward the door.

Reluctant as he was to break the kiss, he didn't want to accidentally smack her in the head with the screen door because he was focused on getting her naked. He tore his mouth free. "Inside. Now."

She rested her forehead against his chest. "Good idea. Tobin and Hugh need to pay for a show this hot."

Damn woman cracked him up with her sass.

Once they were inside, he plastered her against the wall, slipping his thigh between hers, tugging her hips forward.

Tanna kissed him harder. Her hands were roving from his shoulders to squeeze his pecs, sliding down his stomach and then dipping below the waistband of his camo shorts.

His dick jerked, trying to jump into her hand.

Placing his hands over the tops of hers, he slipped them beneath his tank top, wanting to feel her touching more than his cock. He made a growling sound when her fingertips connected with each rib and her thumbs strummed his nipples. Then her hands dipped beneath his armpits and she clutched his back.

Tanna slowed the kiss, letting her tongue tease the seam of his lips. "I want you."

"Good to know we're on the same page."

"I couldn't believe my good luck in seeing you at the Split Rock."

"So you were just playing hard to get?"

Those talented lips of hers followed the edge of his jaw to his neck. "Does it seem like I'm playing hard to get now?"

"No. God, no." He groaned when she sucked on the section of skin below his ear.

"I want to nibble on you. Lick you. Suck on you while my fingers learn every ripple in this hard body of yours." Her hands moved around to his chest. "I can explore later, right?"

"Uh. Right."

"Because you have plans for me right now."

"The more I hear that sexy drawl as your hands are on me, the more I'm losing my train of thought completely. All I can think about is bending you over the arm of the couch, because it's closer than the bed, and fucking you until you scream."

Tanna's mouth grazed his ear. "So do it. I'll even help you get started. Lift your arms." She pulled off his tank top and tossed it aside. Her mouth enclosed his left nipple and she sucked hard. "Your move."

Somehow his thick fingers managed to get the buttons on her blouse undone and he peeled the fabric off her shoulders and down her arms.

Fletch groaned softly when he saw her simple white bra. It set off her skin tone, and the low cut allowed him to bury his face in that soft cleavage.

"No fair. I didn't get to play with your chest very long."

"It's easy to get off track when I'm faced with these." He followed the edges of the satin piping with his tongue and breathed in her scent as his fingers unhooked the back clasp. His palms skimmed her luscious tits and swerved to the outside of her hips as he dropped to his knees.

He pulled off her boots. Then he removed the dress pants that were covering up her skin and his favorite warm, soft, wet girl part. Hook unfastened, he lowered the zipper and they fell to the floor. Tanna also wore plain white panties, which were far sexier than he'd ever imagined.

He placed his mouth over the cotton, both inhaling her scent and blowing hot air over her mound, waiting to see if she tried to get away.

Tanna looked down at him, keeping her body still.

"Very good. Not squirming at all today."

"Maybe I'm just worried you're gonna tie me up again. I'm too impatient for you to fuck me to mess around with props this time."

He sucked on the skin surrounding her clit, and let his tongue trace the slit through her panties. And imagine that. She was already wet in one spot. Such a chest-beating moment that she got so wet for him so quickly.

Her head fell back and she groaned. "Why does it seem naughtier when I have my panties on than when your face is pressed into my bare pussy?"

Keeping his eyes on hers, he used his teeth to tug her panties to her ankles.

She laughed and crooked her finger at him.

But as soon as Fletch got up from his knees, she fell to hers. She gave him the exact same treatment he'd given her. Putting her mouth on the bulge in his Jockeys. But since his had an opening in his underwear, that sneaky tongue of hers just slipped right in.

"Dammit!" He jumped back at the wet swipe on his shaft. "No fair."

"Aw, I was just having a little fun."

Fletch shoved his jockeys to the floor. He wrapped his hand around his cock and stroked as Tanna scrambled to her feet.

Instead of moving back, she moved forward, placing her hand over his and standing on tiptoe for an intoxicating kiss.

Curling his free hand around the back of her neck, he pushed her toward the couch.

Tanna broke the kiss to whisper, "Condom."

"Right. Hang tight." Fletch grabbed the condom from the front pocket of his shorts. He quickly had it on and returned to where she waited. Her brown eyes were enormous and glazed with lust. Her mouth ripe from his kisses.

"Knees on the edge of the couch arm and your hands on the cushions."

"You like bein' bossy in the bedroom," she challenged, tossing her hair.

Fletch wanted that soft silk wrapped in his fist as he rode her. "Do it." As soon as she turned around, he pressed his front to her back and grabbed her hair, putting his mouth on her ear. "To show I'm not bossy, I'm gonna let you choose how this plays out, sugar twang." He blew a stream of air into her ear. "A fast hard fuck." He nipped the lobe. "Or drawn out until we're both sweaty."

A shudder rolled through her. "Hard and sweaty."

He held on to her hips as she placed her knees on the edge of the couch. She set her palms on the couch cushions, solidifying her stance.

Before he rammed into that tight cunt, he ran his fingertips down her back, gentle as raindrops. Then he smacked the perfect white globes hard—twice on each side.

Tanna's gasp of surprise turned into a soft groan when he put his mouth on those red spots. Then brushed his lips and smoothed his cheek against the hot skin.

Stepping behind her, he watched her arch as he fed his cock in, inch by inch. He waited, just absorbing the sensation of the wet heat surrounding his shaft and the quiver of anticipation in his legs; the tiny squeezes of her channel that were intimate kisses.

The slow, slow, slow withdrawal.

Then he snapped his hips, driving back in fully.

"Oh God."

Since she'd asked for fast and sweaty, he fucked her with long, hard, deep strokes and then switched to short, hip-gyrating swirls.

Sweat began to bead on his forehead and he noticed those sexy dimples above her ass carried a sheen. He pulled out completely and bent to lap at those damp indents as he slid his long middle finger in and out of her pussy to keep her primed. Then he followed the seam of her sex with his other hand and rubbed her clit, alternating between a side-to-side motion and a quick flick. Rotating the hand plunging in and out of her pussy, he stretched his thumb, slick with her juices, to sweep across the pink rosebud of her anus and pushed it inside the tiny opening.

Tanna detonated. Her initial cry was quiet compared to how hard she came, her cunt spasming, her swollen pearl pulsing beneath his finger and the sphincter tightening around his thumb.

Fletch realigned his dick, bottoming out deep into her core on the first thrust. And the next. And the next. Driving into her tenaciously.

He was close. She was close again. Grabbing a handful of her hair, he said, "Keep your head up. Imagine you're wearing a bridle. I wanna hear you when you come this time."

Four more hard thrusts and Tanna was climaxing again, her cunt a vise around his cock, squeezing and squeezing until he came with a roar.

As soon as he'd regained his lucidity, he realized he'd slumped over Tanna completely. He wasn't exactly a small guy and he knew she sometimes panicked. "You okay?"

"I'm perfect." She turned her head and nuzzled his cheek. "You know what? I think we're gonna be great neighbors."

Chapter Seventeen

❦

*D*ead tired after finishing her shift at the bar, Tanna trudged down the path to the employee living quarters.

Conversation echoed back to her.

She stood at the edge of Fletch's trailer, looking at the people gathered around the ceramic fire pit. Tobin, Hugh, Harlow, Dave and Yvette.

Fletch.

That ticklish sensation started in her belly at seeing the sweet, sexy man who'd been on her mind more than was probably wise, given her temporary status in Wyoming. Fletch had been staying at the Split Rock only a week and they'd already spent most of their free time together.

At a pause in the conversation, she said, "So, did my party invite get lost in the mail?"

Tobin jumped up. "Tanna. Here, lemme get you a beer." He pulled out a bottle of Bud Light and passed it over. "We're short a chair, but you can have mine."

Tanna looked at Fletch. He raised a questioning eyebrow. Here was the moment of truth.

She held her hand out to Fletch. "Keep your seat, Tobin. The doc and I can share."

He took her hand and tugged her forward, settled her on his lap, her back to his chest. Then he pressed his lips to the side of her neck. The kiss spoke of their intimacy in a way that even a full-blown make out session wouldn't have.

She felt all eyes on them.

Tobin laughed and his gaze met Hugh's. "Now it makes sense."

Hugh nodded.

Harlow grinned and raised her bottle in a silent toast.

Dave and Yvette just looked at each other with a knowing smile.

"So, busy night at the lodge bar?" Tobin asked.

"Crazy busy. This group likes to drink. After I finally kicked them out, they headed to the Buckeye. Their pregnant DD didn't want to go, but none of them were sober enough to drive." She looked at Yvette. "I don't envy the mess you'll deal with tomorrow. But I'm betting it'd be safe for you to sleep in because none of them are gonna leave their rooms very early."

Yvette shrugged. "They've been decent so far. Family reunions aren't nearly as wild as college reunions."

Tobin groaned. "Don't remind me. Last year the University of Wyoming's rodeo team held their twenty-year class reunion here. Not only did them guys demand rough stock competitions every day, they partied hard afterward. I swear there was wife swapping goin' on. Me'n Hugh had to take turns acting as security guards because we caught couples goin' at it everywhere. Doin' it in the laundry room. Another couple was making carpet angels right in front of the fireplace in the main room." He nudged Hugh with his knee. "But your discovery was the best. Tell 'em."

"I had a colicky horse in the barn so I did a final check before bed. I heard the damndest noise. In the last stall I saw the former Miss Rodeo Wyoming on her knees...ah, servicing the former All-Around cowboy, while her husband watched and cracked a bullwhip."

Harlow's eyes grew wide. "Omigod. Did you intervene? Did he plan on using the bullwhip on her?"

"For all I know, he might've been warming it up for the guy to use it on *him*. None of my business either way, as long as they weren't messing with my livestock. Different strokes for different folks."

Fletch laughed and Hugh grinned.

Holy crap. Hugh had a beautiful smile. First time Tanna had ever seen it from the gruff-natured foreman.

"I ain't the type to one-up ya," Dave said, "but I saw the champion tie-down ropers showing off their rope skills...not on a calf. But I gotta admit the woman they had trussed up sure sounded like she was enjoying herself. Gives new visuals for the terms *header* and *heeler*."

The guys laughed.

Harlow said, "Bullcrap," with a sneer. "That sounds like something you guys made up, doesn't it, Tanna?"

"Nope. Sounds like a typical Saturday night on the rodeo circuit to me."

More laughter.

"You saw wild things like that?" Harlow said with disbelief.

"Darlin', I participated in those wild things and then some. Heck, I acted as ringleader most of the time."

"So the rumors I've heard about what goes on on the road are true?" Tobin asked.

"Completely true. And usually toned down in the retelling." She swallowed another drink of beer and looked at Hugh. "You've hauled stock to rodeos all over the country. Tell Miss Chicago over there we aren't exaggerating about what goes on behind the chutes."

"No, ma'am, we are not."

Harlow still didn't look convinced. "These women are so hot to get with a cowboy that they just let these guys rope them up? Who likes that sort of thing?"

Tanna raised her hand.

The guys chuckled and Fletch made a growling noise in her ear that traveled straight to her core.

"It ain't only girls who like that sorta kinky thing," Hugh said. "A few years ago, I'd forgotten some paperwork, so I had to go back to the rodeo grounds after everyone had left. Or so I thought. I heard *whack whack whack*. Naturally I got a little closer to the noises and I saw this couple banging by the buckin' chutes. The guy's jeans were around his boots and he's got the woman pinned against the corral, goin' to town on her. Then I heard *whack whack whack* again and realized she was smacking his ass with a ridin' crop. Them barrel racers got a serious thing about getting their money's worth outta their crops."

"Hey, I didn't think anyone was around that night," Tanna protested. "That was a private moment."

Everyone laughed again.

Tobin shook his head. "I knew I shoulda joined rodeo club instead of chess club."

"Chess is much more civilized," Harlow assured him. "And I'm sure *you'd* never misuse your knowledge of ropes and stuff to hold a woman against her will."

"Don't be too sure about that."

Harlow looked at Hugh. "What about you, Grumpy?"

Hugh leaned back and cocked his head, measuring Harlow from head to toe. "I've been complimented on my tie-down skills a time or two. Never had a lady complain or try to get away."

Harlow's mouth fell open.

Hugh, who laughed as rarely as he smiled, emitted the sexiest and most evil-sounding laugh Tanna had ever heard. "Don't knock it 'til you try it, hippie-girl. And if you wanna try it sometime...all's you gotta do is ask me real nicely."

"Don't hold your breath," Harlow retorted.

Tanna wondered how much Hugh had been drinking. He never gave in to Harlow's taunts. Poor girl should've known better than to poke the bear. It's the quiet ones you had to worry about.

"And with that..." Dave and Yvette said good night.

She took another drink of beer and set the bottle on the ground.

Fletch caressed her arm and murmured, "Tired?"

"Yeah. Working and today's physical therapy session was killer." He'd kept his promise to make sure she did her PT at least every other day.

He gently draped her legs off to the side of his chair, curling her body into his. He kissed the top of her head. "Rest your eyes for a bit."

She nestled her face into his warm neck. He smelled so good. She'd never been with a man who coddled her like Fletch did and she liked it way more than she wanted to admit. When she sighed softly, his hold on her tightened.

He and Tobin and Hugh talked livestock stuff that would've lulled her to sleep if she hadn't already been halfway there. She wasn't the type to doze off in a man's arms in public, but the deep cadence of his voice soothed her. Rather than question her sudden, uncharacteristic reaction to this man, she just accepted it.

Sweet kisses roused her, followed by sweeter words. "Wake up, sleeping gorgeous."

"But I'm so comfy. You make an awesome pillow."

"I'll let you sleep on me all night." His warm mouth grazed her ear. "Come to bed with me, sugar twang."

"Okay." The sleep haze lingered and she fought the pull back into slumber.

Fletch stood, keeping her enfolded in his arms, cradled to his chest. "Thanks for the beer and the company, Tobin. I'll see you in the morning."

Tobin chuckled. "I'll be surprised if I see you before noon. God knows I wouldn't get outta bed if I had her in it."

"Point taken. See ya next year."

Tanna smiled against Fletch's chest.

The night air had bite and she shivered.

"Almost there. Hold on." He opened and closed the doors and set her down in the bedroom doorway.

"Sweet Lord. What in God's name is that?"

"You were busy this afternoon when they delivered my new bed."

She blinked and couldn't believe her eyes. "This mattress takes up the whole room."

"California King, baby. A double bed kills my back and my feet hang off the end."

"You'd really suffer if we had to sleep on the bed in my horse trailer."

"I'd never use the word *suffer* when bein' in a bed with you."

"Are you just leaving the bed here when your sabbatical is up?"

Standing behind her, he nuzzled the side of her neck as his fingers worked the buttons on her blouse. "No. My guest room will get an upgrade."

"Lucky guests."

"Won't matter. I never have guests anyway." He tugged the blouse down her arms and tossed it aside. Followed by her bra. "You still tired?"

"He asks with fake concern, as he's stripping my clothes off."

Fletch chuckled. "You caught me. But all that talk of ropes and spankings got me hot and bothered. Plus, we need to christen the bed with smokin'-hot sex before we sleep on it or we'll have bad sex in it."

Tanna snorted. "That is a load of crap."

"No, I heard that from an Indian mystic, so it has to be true." He placed his hands on her hips and his thumbs stroked her bare belly. "So, what do you say?"

"Well," she forced a yawn, "if you can promise me this christening won't take long, so I can get some shut-eye, then I *suppose* I'm game."

"You . . . suppose?" He pushed her on the bed. She landed face-first and as soon as she scrambled around, he depanted her. He shucked his clothes and jumped beside her, but she barely bounced—which said a lot about the quality of the mattress.

Then his mouth reclaimed possession of hers, his fingers dove between her legs. Teasing her clit until it spasmed beneath his stroking thumb. Fletch fucked her with two fingers while sucking on her nipples. He'd turned her inside out in such a short amount of time that her thighs were sticky and her need for him was a physical ache.

He paused in his erotic torment only to roll on a condom. He pinned her arms above her head and impaled her.

Tanna's moan was lost in his hungry mouth. He fucked her relentlessly with a sort of mad finesse. Pushing her to the tipping point and backing off—three times. By the time he whispered, "Come for me, Tanna," her body was damp with sweat, her legs shook and she gasped with each pounding thrust as she unraveled.

Afterward, she lay trapped beneath his big body, listening to his stuttered breaths. Then he brushed kisses on her forehead down to the shiver inducing section of skin in front of her ear. "Sorry, darlin', that took a little longer than I thought. But I *suppose*," he blew in her ear, "that those loud moans meant you didn't mind losing a little sleep."

"Such a bratty, cocky man."

"You hate that I'm always right."

"Always? In your dreams."

Fletch ditched the condom and crawled back in bed. "Speaking of dreams...now you can use me as a pillow and get some shut-eye."

Tanna snuggled into him, content on too many levels to count. "Okay. But don't let me sleep late. I have to go to Eli's in the morning."

"Don't worry; I make an excellent alarm clock."

Chapter Eighteen

After a restless night filled with dreams of her mother, mixed with nightmares about Jezebel, she'd awoken in a cold sweat, her body shaking so hard she feared it'd wake Fletch. She'd managed to calm down on the drive to Eli's, cranking the tunes and singing along at the top of her lungs— her personal type of scream therapy.

At Eli's she watched as he trained with a bulldogger. Summer worked the chute, releasing the steer. Eli served as the guy's hazer, racing out on horseback on the right side of the bulldogger, keeping the bulldogger's horse in line with the steer until the moment the steer wrestler hung off the right stirrup with one toe and launched himself off. Skidding in the dirt, the bulldogger grabbed the steer by the head and flipped it on its side.

Dust flew and the bulldogger got up and squinted at the chute.

Summer yelled out, "Five point six two, but you broke the barrier."

"Dammit."

Eli held the reins for the bulldogger's horse and waited for him to trot to the end of the arena. He pushed the steer through the back gate before he mounted up. The guys were lost in conversation and hadn't noticed her, so Tanna didn't interrupt.

They exited the arena, returned to the chutes and did the practice run four more times until Summer was out of steers. Something about the bulldogger seemed familiar. His fluidity on his horse, the determination in his repeated attempts. She'd eat her hat if the guy wasn't a pro. She couldn't see his face, but like most bulldoggers, he was a substantial guy.

Not as big as Fletch, but few guys were as supersized as the veterinarian.

Finally Eli sauntered over, talking animatedly to his bulldogging buddy. But Summer yelled at the mysterious guy and Eli cut toward her.

"Hey, Tanna, how long've you been here?" Eli asked.

"A while. I thought I'd get an early start on whatever torture you had planned for me today."

Eli laughed. "I haven't planned nothin'. To be honest, I musta got my days mixed up. I wasn't expecting you this morning."

"Really?" That explained the bulldogger.

"But as long as you're here, got someone I want you to meet." He whistled loudly and the guy started toward them.

The bulldogger kept his eyes on the dirt as he wandered over. He raised his head. Beneath the brim of his hat was one of the most beautiful men Tanna had ever seen.

Holy. Fuck. Somehow she kept her tongue in her mouth when the guy thrust out his hand.

"Tanna Barker, right? I'm Sutton Grant."

His gigantic hand dwarfed hers. "Hi, Sutton. Good to meet you." Sutton Grant... why did that name sound familiar?

"You probably don't remember me," Sutton said, "but we have met before."

Her eyes took in every detail of his stunning face. His eyes were an exotic shade of bluish-green usually seen in the water on a tropical beach. Dark eyebrows. Bone structure that might seem feminine if not for the wide expanse of his chiseled jaw and the ruggedness of his facial features as a whole. Then he smiled. Yep. He even had two dimples. "Not to contradict you off the bat, but, darlin', I surely would've remembered meeting you."

Sutton laughed. "Probably not. I was a little shy. A little intimidated by your championship buckles and the guys flocked around you."

"When was this?"

"The season after your second win. We ended up at a couple of the same meet-and-greet after events."

She didn't remember all the guys she'd slept with—most of them—but there were a couple of nights where the veil of alcohol masked her hookup's face.

"Jeez, Tanna, you looking at him like that is making *me* uncomfortable," Eli complained.

"Sorry. I've had some wild times, and a few...ah, *meet and greets* that aren't crystal clear."

Sutton grinned. "No worries. I would've been too shy to approach you anyway, even if I hadn't been in a relationship at the time."

Summer shouted for Eli and he took off, leaving her and the compellingly sexy Sutton staring at each other.

"So, are you from around here?" Tanna asked. Talk about lame.

"No. I'm from Colorado. Eli's been a family friend for years and he's helping me."

"Helping you do what?"

"Choose a new horse. I've narrowed my choices to two."

Finally his name clicked. "I've been off the circuit, but you won the CRA steer wrestling championship last year, didn't you?"

"Yeah."

"Where are you in the standings this year?"

"Third. There's a wide gap between fourth place and the rest, so I'm feeling confident of my chances of making it to the CRA championships." He studied her. "Are you healed up enough from your injury to compete again?"

She shrugged. "According to my physical therapist? Yes."

"But?" he prompted.

Don't tell him. You'll look weak. Washed up. Pathetic.

Tanna offered him a dazzling smile. "But nothin'—"

Sutton put his hand on her arm, as if to assure her she didn't have to lie to him. "Have you even been on a horse since the accident?"

Indignant, she snapped, "Did Eli tell you—"

"No. You know he ain't the type to break a confidence or you wouldn't be here, would you?"

She shook her head.

"I asked because I read about your wreck online. I knew you'd disappeared off the circuit for rehab. Sucks, huh?"

"Ya think?" She bristled. "And how would you know that, youngster?"

"I know because I've been there. The year you won your third championship."

"Sorry. I just get a little defensive when people tell me they know what I'm goin' through. What happened to you?"

Sutton cocked his head. "How about if we have a seat and swap stories?"

Something about his eyes urged her to trust him. "Okay."

He flipped over two plastic feed buckets.

Tanna sat, sinking her heels into the dirt and resting her forearms on her thighs. "You go first."

He squinted at her. "Why?"

"Beauty before age," she purred, "'cause, sugar, you are one hot-lookin' speci-*man* and I'm your elder by at least eight years."

"I'm betting that cooing tone and them pretty brown eyes get you just about everything you want, don't they?" he teased.

She shrugged. And smirked.

"Short version? Or long?"

"Longer is always better."

He chuckled. "My story's gonna sound tame. I grew up in a ranching family. Got bit by the rodeo bug early on. In high school I was state all-around champion. I competed with the University of Wyoming rodeo team for four years. Senior year I was collegiate steer wrestling champion."

Tanna whistled. "Impressive."

"I had a few rodeo sponsors and the blessing of my family so I decided to try my luck on the pro circuit. I did okay the first year, but I missed home and my girl, so I kept out of trouble, for the most part."

"Sutton, that ain't no fun. Pining in your horse trailer instead of ripping it up?"

"Yep. That was me." He shot her a sideways glance. "Which is why you and me didn't cross paths more often."

She laughed.

"I didn't make it to the CRA first year. I decided I'd give it another year and had a great second season, landing in the top fifteen. Then early on in my third season I had a bad night. Launched off too soon. Hit the dirt and the steer at the wrong angle. Blew out my knee, my elbow and my shoulder. I spent months recovering from surgery to repair a torn patella tendon in my right knee and a torn bicep tendon in my left arm. I moved home. I was worthless. I couldn't help out on the ranch. I couldn't get a job while doin' rehab. My girlfriend saw me as a slug and dumped my ass."

"Sad story. And no offense, but I don't see the parallels in our lives."

"Be patient. It gets worse. Calving season at our ranch means everyone pitches in, including crippled-up sons. We'd moved eight cow/calf pairs into the barn and I was tasked with watching them. Easy, right? I wasn't out checking cattle in the cold and snow. I'm not sure if it was a change in the weather or what, but the calves freaked out, which freaked out the mamas. I was supposed to stop them to keep them from injuring themselves. But the second I got close to one, I fell down in the muck." He fiddled with his gloves. "I froze. I'm not talking a momentary lapse. I stayed in the stall, frozen in fear for four hours before anyone noticed.

"I'd gone into shock. Keep in mind—I'd started helping my dad separate cow/calf pairs when I was five years old. Twenty years of experience and I'm suddenly catatonic around livestock. Not only couldn't I compete in bulldoggin', I couldn't help out at the ranch. And I didn't know how I'd ever get over my fear."

"Obviously you did. How'd you do it?"

"A neighbor of ours, Fife, a grizzled old rancher, called for help with his water heater. When I showed up, he admitted he'd lied to get me over there. My dad had confided in him, because he didn't know how to help me. Fife took it one step at a time. After a month of daily baby steps, I'd conquered my fear enough to be around livestock. By two months I was milling around in the pasture with a hundred calf/cow pairs. Three months I was back to taking down steers. By month four I was throwing myself off my horse like I'd never taken a break. No one outside of my family knew I ever had that fear. I healed up, jumped back on the tour and won the world championship the next year."

"That's a great story. Inspiring. But my situation is different. I don't have the luxury of daily immersion. I have a job. So if I'm only goin' to Eli's one day a week, if I end up on your type of time frame to get this issue handled, I'm looking at a solid sixteen months before I'm even ready to saddle up. I'll be almost thirty-eight."

"You don't need me to point out that you can barrel race well into your fifties and sixties. Some of the best women in the world didn't win until they hit their late thirties and early forties."

"But you can't deny the majority of the winners are young," Tanna pointed out. "I won two of my championships during my twenties."

"I'm just saying that even if it does take you sixteen months? You won't be washed up. I can tell that you feel washed up right now."

Wouldn't you? How can I ever get past this?

"How would you feel if you never climbed on the back of a horse again?"

"Sad."

Sutton nodded as if she'd said the right thing. "That's good. How would you feel if you never ran barrels again?"

That one she didn't answer immediately. "Lost."

"More lost than you feel right now?"

"I don't know." She fought a burst of frustration. "*Why* don't I know?"

"Whoa. There's no right or wrong answer, Tanna. I'm just trying to share some of the same stuff to think about that helped me."

This guy she'd met only a half hour ago was going out of his way to help her. Eli had been the same way. "Is everyone in the West so dang helpful?"

"Southern hospitality ain't got nothin' on us," he offered in an exaggerated drawl.

She managed a wan smile.

"So see, I do know what you're goin' through. If you ever want to talk more..."

Tanna must've looked skeptical.

Sutton grinned at her. "I'm not hitting on you. Give me your phone. I'll plug my number in. That way, if you want to talk, you can call me, but I'll never bother you."

She handed him her phone.

"Sutton, I need your help," Eli called.

"I've been summoned." Sutton patted her shoulder as he stood. "I'm sure we'll run into each other again."

As she watched him amble away, she had the fleeting thought that he looked just as good from the back as he did the front. Sure, Sutton was a very attractive man, but that wasn't his pull for her. He'd been in the darkness and found his way back to the light.

Maybe there was hope for her.

That thought gave her the courage to step foot in the pasture. And when the horses came running, expecting treats, she didn't hide or retreat.

One step at a time.

～

Tanna returned to her trailer more rung out than if she'd run a marathon. Her shift at the bar didn't start for hours and she didn't know what to do with herself so she crawled back in bed.

That's when the nightmare came again. A continual loop of blood, death and horses. She'd lived the events, making the nightmare realistic— right until the part where her horse plowed through her mother, turning her into smoke. She opened her mouth but no sound came out. She tried to call out for her mother. For Jezebel. She gave it one last scream.

And that's when she woke up.

"Tanna?"

She froze at seeing Fletch standing in the doorway.

"You all right?"

"Yeah." She raked her hand through her hair, hoping he didn't notice how much it shook. "Just a bad dream. Guess that'll teach me not to nap in the afternoon."

He frowned. Seemed to want to question her further but didn't.

"What are you doin' here?"

"I was in the neighborhood."

"Ha-ha. You know that's the first time that line has ever rang true." She patted the mattress. "Care to take me for a tumble?"

"As much as I'd love to crawl between your sheets and thighs, I need to make a grocery store run. Anything you need?"

Yeah. Can you pick me up a gallon of courage? And a bottle of fear retardant?

"If you're coming over after I'm done working, we probably need more popcorn."

"Done. And I'll pick out a movie." He leaned over and kissed her forehead. "And if you need to talk about your bad dream—"

"I don't." She gave him a smacking kiss on the mouth. "Better get condoms too; we're goin' through them like crazy."

Chapter Nineteen

⧸⧹

At the end of the week Fletch finally ventured to the big metal building across from the barn. The structure had been jammed in at an angle—the front door was on the side opposite the barn, which meant access to the closest door was through the corral, and he cut through the rough stock horses. Hard to look at these beauties and imagine them trying like hell to buck you off.

"Knock knock," Fletch shouted into the cavernous room.

A chair squeaked and Tobin yelled, "Back here."

Despite the vast emptiness of the space, Fletch's footsteps were muffled.

Tobin leaned against the doorjamb. "Is Hugh having an issue with an animal he forgot to tell me about?"

"No. Since my morning was free I thought I'd take a look at what you've got regarding the commercial stock-breeding program."

"Come in and grab a cup of coffee. I've stored the info on a flash drive." He pointed to a long conference table. "You can set up over there. I have an extension cord if you need to power up."

"My laptop has a full battery so I'll be good for a while."

"Knock yourself out," Tobin said, tossing him the flash drive.

Less than five minutes later, Fletch looked up from his laptop and said, "That's it?"

"Seems like there should be more, huh?"

"Has any other work been done on this *at all*?"

Tobin crossed his arms over his chest. "Not really."

"Because you're short-staffed?"

"More like shortsighted," Tobin muttered. "To be honest, I think Renner has bitten off more than he can chew."

After he finished typing in a few notes, Fletch met Tobin's gaze. "You wanna explain that?"

Tobin shoved his laptop to the center of their shared work area. He took a long sip from the scarred insulated mug before he spoke. "Is there such a thing as doctor-patient confidentiality for vets?"

"Absolutely. Whatever cattle tell me when I'm doctorin' on them stays strictly between them and me."

"I'm serious, Fletch. If I can't share my honest thoughts with you, without worrying that you'll take them to Renner, I'll just keep my mouth shut and take my coulda, shoulda, woulda lumps from you."

First time Tobin had taken that tone and Fletch definitely wanted to hear what was on his mind. "The only way I'd talk to Renner about what we've discussed is if the information you share adversely affects the health of the animals. If there's something he's not doin' that he oughta be doin', or something that he is doin' that he shouldn't be doin'."

"Fair enough."

"So what did you mean that Renner might be in over his head?"

"I've been working here almost four years. Renner is the most ambitious guy I've ever met. First he built the Split Rock. Then he moved his rodeo stock contracting operation up here. Those two businesses, plus we're running a hundred head of cattle, are more than enough to keep Renner and me and Hugh busy. Hugh's even replaced most of the guys who were involved with Jackson Stock Contracting in Kansas with locals. Works out well for these guys because they love rodeo, but they can't afford to be gone from home for weeks on end."

"Renner does have the reputation of bein' more than fair with his wages."

"That said, with the stock contracting business bein' localized and with our current workforce, the maximum amount of distance Hugh is willing to haul stock is twelve hours from here. Keeps costs down across the board, keeps Renner's rough stock in demand."

Fletch nodded. "Which is why he hasn't lost much stock."

"Maybe he's worried about that. The man can pick rough stock like no one I've ever seen. I've gone to auctions with him and he'll buy a scrawny-looking bull and the next year, that sucker is huge. And usually mean."

He laughed.

"Over the years Renner has occasionally sold semen from his best bulls and horses to raise funds. So the idea has gotten stuck in his head that instead of buying bulls and bucking horses, he oughta be breeding them. Then he could act on the demand from other contractors and other breeders. There's huge money in it, if it's done right."

"And that's the part you're worried about?"

Tobin sighed. "We've only talked about starting a commercial stock-breeding program loosely—I mean *very* loosely. We mentioned it to you. That's it. The next thing I know, Renner had . . . some guilt or panic attack or something, because he's leveling the ground to build this place, claiming it's for our *future endeavor.*"

The place in question being a ten-thousand-square-foot metal pole barn. It was unused except for this large corner, which Tobin and Hugh had turned into office space. "My understanding was the reason he did it was because the contractors were already breaking ground on his and Tierney's house."

Tobin gave him a thoughtful look. "I know that's what he says, but I think he had some kind of provider anxiety due to Tierney's pregnancy. Hell, maybe this is his way of nesting. But I believe Renner wanted yet another financial fallback in case any of his other businesses went to hell. He didn't want to be beholden to his wife making all the money."

Damn insightful.

"And I get this building is only a few months old, but I just don't know what the hell he expects to do with it."

"Is he putting pressure on you to figure it out for him?"

"No. Maybe I'm putting pressure on myself because my background and education is in animal husbandry and genetics. But with Hugh bein' mostly gone now that summer rodeo season is in full swing, I'm so damn busy dealing with the livestock and stuff goin' on at the Split Rock, I don't have time to think about it. Let alone come up with a viable business plan that won't waste a whole lot of Renner's time and his money."

Fletch studied Tobin. He did seem stressed, which wasn't the norm for him.

"Now you're here, out of the blue, ready to get to work on what's basically been an abstract idea— and it would've been nice to have a heads-up on *that* from my boss—I feel like I got caught with my pants down and I'm about to get spanked."

He let the pause between them linger for a minute before he said, "I'm assuming this confidentiality thing goes both ways?"

Tobin nodded.

"Renner didn't tell you about me showing up here because it wasn't something either of us had planned." Fletch rubbed the back of his neck, feeling oddly self-conscious about telling the truth, even when Tobin needed to hear it so he wasn't questioning his position and future with Renner. "Here's what happened."

After he finished, Tobin pierced him with a look. "You've *never* taken a vacation."

That's what Tobin chose to focus on? "Besides a few days here and there? Nope."

"Jesus, Fletch, you sound just like my dad." He winced and clarified, "Not because you're old, but that's the same mind-set he has. It's also probably why he's had two heart attacks."

"My old man mentioned that same scenario to me. The issue is I don't know what the hell to do with myself when I'm not working."

"Did you know when you went to vet school your career would be this demanding?"

Fletch shook his head. "Like most thirteen-year-old girls, I'd romanticized bein' a vet just a tad."

Tobin snickered.

"Besides, I went to college to play football."

"So you didn't have the burning need to become a veterinarian because you were constantly bringing home birds with broken wings and had a desire to help four-legged members of the animal kingdom?"

"Fuck off."

Tobin laughed and Fletch was glad to see some of the shadows had cleared from his eyes.

"Like I said, I got a full-ride scholarship to play college football. My grades weren't great; I was a little better than an average student—which probably ain't a surprise to a brainiac like you."

"Fuck off, right back atcha, Doc."

"Prior to college, I hadn't thought much about what career path I'd end up on, even when I knew I'd never play pro ball. I registered late for classes and got stuck in an ag exploration course. I figured it'd be an easy A; I'd hung out with ranching kids my whole life. I ended up liking it and did well enough in subsequent classes that by the end of freshman year I decided animal sciences would be my career focus. Got my undergrad degree in pre-veterinary sciences at Colorado State and went right into their DVM program."

"How long did that take?"

"Total? Six years. After graduation I worked for a large animal vet in Fort Collins for a year who was set to retire. He had clients in Wyoming. I moved back to Rawlins, took over some of those clients and went into business for myself."

"I gotta ask, 'cause I'm still paying off my graduate school loans, but did you get a full ride for vet school too?"

Fletch grinned. "Yep. One of the few times it paid to be Indian. My advisor steered me toward every possible scholarship and I received every one I applied for and some I was just awarded. So not only did I come out of vet school debt free, I came out money ahead because I'd chosen to work in an underrepresented section of animal health care—large animals. And I'd chosen to work in a rural area—I always knew I'd be back in Wyoming. And I was a minority."

"Man. That was smart."

"I also realize that I was fortunate for the financial support. I try and give back, especially to the Indian community, even when I really don't know a whole lot about bein' Indian." He smirked. "Of course, my cousin Eli is more than happy to school me on that every chance he gets."

"Speaking of Eli…" Tobin took a swig from his mug and grimaced. "He called yesterday."

"About?"

"About swapping out our old trail horse Lyle for one of his younger training horses."

Fletch frowned. "Did he give you a reason why?"

"Said he was working with someone who's really skittish around horses and wanted a horse that wouldn't buck or get spooked by anything."

Was that horse for Tanna? Question was, had Tanna requested it, or was it Eli's decision? Whenever Fletch asked her specifics about the time she spent at Eli's, she became evasive. Then she seduced him.

"So, it probably ain't my business, but is Eli wanting that horse for your girlfriend?"

"I imagine so."

"You don't know?"

"Tanna ain't talking. And Eli is the most trustworthy, secret-keeping motherfucker I know, so he ain't talking either. It sucks."

Tobin grinned. "A woman not bein' honest or spilling her guts? I'm shocked."

"Fuck off."

"Tanna is always so upbeat and sarcastic around me. Don't take this wrong, but the raunchy comments that woman makes would make a porn star blush."

Oh boy, you don't know the half of what that dirty mouth can do. "Folks might say the same thing about you, Tobin. You act so laid-back. You're so freakin' happy-go-lucky all the time." Fletch paused. "But that ain't the case, is it? You've got a darker side that no one sees."

Tobin looked startled for a second. "So, Doc, you're an expert on all animal behavior? Or you just guessing about me?"

Fletch smiled.

"And with that," Tobin said, "maybe we oughta talk about the business—or nonbusiness as the case may be—at hand. I've done next to nothin' on this. Far as I know Renner's done even less than me besides having Tierney set up the corporation and constructing the building."

"I'll tell you what—bein's I'm on sabbatical, I've got way less to do around here than you. I'll jump on the research. See what options we've got. I'll see if I can't come up with a concrete plan, or at least a reason to abandon this idea altogether. Then if Renner asks you about it, say I've taken over. That way you're off the hook and I've got a valid excuse for bein' at the Split Rock for the next few weeks."

"Really? You'd do that?"

Fletch shrugged. "It'll be a change for me, if nothin' else."

"Thanks, man." Tobin stood. "I gotta get. Buzz me if you need anything."

"Will do." Fletch reached for his laptop.

Tobin's footsteps stopped. His voice drifted across the cavernous room. "Can I ask you something?"

"I guess."

"Is Tanna part of the reason you're spending all your time off up here?"

No, she's the only reason. "Yep. Something about that woman . . . just got to me from the get-go. Never happened before."

"Does she know that?"

"No. So like you, I'm gonna try like hell to look like I'm busy."

Chapter Twenty

❧

$\mathcal{H}$arper barreled into Wild West Clothiers shortly after noon, blond hair sticking up every which way. She set the baby carrier on the floor, looked around the store and burst into tears.

Slightly freaked out, Tanna gently took Harper by the hand and sat her in the chair closest to her baby.

"Harper? If you hate where I positioned the socks and slippers display, I can always put it back where it was."

That caused her to cry harder.

While Harper cried, a panicked Tanna studied her face. Her skin was blotchy. Her eyes swollen. Her lips puffy. The beautiful, serene, always put-together woman was a mess.

"I'm sorry. It's not the display."

"I kinda figured that. Can you tell me what's goin' on?"

A long pause ensued and Harper leaned over to check on her baby. "Poor Jake. Upset mama turns his whole world around."

The kid hadn't uttered a peep. "He seems to be adjusting."

"The car ride always mellows him out." Her red-rimmed eyes met Tanna's. "I'm losing my mind because I received notification that my sister Liberty was injured in the line of duty."

Tanna's stomach dropped. She reached for both of Harper's hands. "Oh my God, Harper, that's horrible."

"Evidently it's bad enough they brought her back to the U.S. as soon as she was stable. That's all they'll tell me."

"Where was she stationed?"

"Afghanistan. She only had two months left on this tour and she talked about getting out of the service for good." Harper bit her lip to keep from crying—no wonder the skin was so raw. "This isn't the way she's supposed to do that! Then I think, God, at least she's not coming home in a casket."

"Do you know what happened? Or the extent of her injuries?"

She shook her head. "So I have to fly to Walter Reed to deal with this."

"When are you going?"

"Today." She smoothed her hand over her head, trying to tame her hair. "I have to take Jake with me since I'm nursing. It scares me to death to take my baby into a hospital environment where the patients have been exposed to all sorts of weird viruses from all over the world. But that said, I don't know what I'll do if they won't let me bring him into the room with me to see Liberty. As much as I want Bran there . . . as much as I *need* him there . . . he has a ranch to run and a child to take care of. He's a great daddy, but Tate is a handful." She sniffled. "I have no idea how long I'll be gone."

"Don't you have other family that could meet you there and help out?"

She shook her head. "My younger sister Bailey is also in the army and she's stationed in Japan. All my friends are pregnant or have infants so they can't come with me. So I have to do this on my own."

Tanna felt so helpless in the face of Harper's distress.

Then Harper inhaled a deep breath. "I'd planned to be here tomorrow since my largest shipment for the year is arriving. It takes me a solid week to catalogue merchandise and I've always had Tierney or Janie to deal with customers. This can't wait until I get back. The merchandise can't sit in boxes long because there's only a two-week window to decide on returns. I really hate to ask, but is there any way you can catalogue all the merchandise? That'll entail you working in the back every day until it's done. With as busy as we've been, Harlow will have to run the front end by herself."

"Of course I'll do it."

Relief swam in her eyes and she teared up again. "Thank you."

"Hey. I shouldn't have to remind you that it is my job. Do you have sheets or lists from last year that'll show me exactly how you want everything categorized?"

Harper nodded and stood. "My filing system makes no sense to anyone but me, so I'll grab the files. Might take me a bit." Her gaze winged from the baby carrier to Tanna. "Will you keep an eye on Jake?"

"Sure."

Harper disappeared into the back.

Tanna crouched down and looked at the baby boy. Such a cutie. His small head appeared to be covered in white-blond chicken feathers. His lips were curved into a frown and milk seeped from the corner of his mouth. Jake sported a Western onesie in plain brown with fancy white stitching down the center. He wore camouflage pants. On his tiny feet were socks with a monkey face on the toes. Who said babies couldn't be fashionable?

A wave of want rolled over her. She'd always expected she'd have a couple of babies and a husband by age thirty-six.

It could be worse. You could be on your way to some strange hospital to deal with an injured sibling.

Tanna sighed. She really hoped she heard from her brother soon.

She stared at the sleeping baby and willed him to wake up. Maybe she should just scoop him up and hold him anyway. The kid looked lonely.

Ha. You just wanna hold him and absorb that sweet innocence.

The cowbell on the door jangled and she looked up, expecting a customer, but Bran and Fletch walked in.

Fletch smiled at her. As did Bran Turner, but his smile didn't make her heart turn cartwheels like the doc's did.

You fall in love too fast, Tanna. This is a lusty friendship, that's all.

"Hey, guys. What's up?"

"Tracking down my wayward wife." Bran crouched beside Tanna and immediately reached out to touch his son's cheek. "Why is it you'll sleep in public but not at home?"

Not surprising that Jake didn't answer.

Fletch leaned over the baby carrier. "Damn, Bran. He is a cute little bugger. Kid totally takes after his mama."

"Don't I know it."

Tanna glanced around but didn't see Tate the terror. "Where's son number one?"

"In the office with Tierney. Crazy woman is teaching him his numbers and I'll be damned if the kid hasn't learned them. He can count to ten."

She and Fletch exchanged an amused look at Bran's pride.

Jake squirmed and opened his eyes.

The sight made her melt. Baby Jake was a blue-eyed heartbreaker to boot.

"Heya, buddy," Bran said softly. He moved the carrying handle and picked Jake up, bringing him to his shoulder as he stood. Patting the infant on the back, he said, "He'll start fussin' in a second. That oughta get his mama out here right quick."

Sure enough, Jake squalled and Harper practically came running. "What...? Bran? What're you doing here?" Her gaze scanned the room. "And where is Tate?"

"I left him at home alone in the garage with the power tools, a pack of matches, a stack of porn and a bottle of vodka." Before Harper retorted, he said, "I do know how to look after our son, sweetheart. He's upstairs with Tierney."

"Oh." She frowned. "I told you I had to do one thing before I left."

"I came to prod you along. We gotta get on the road so we don't miss our flight."

Harper walked over and took the fussy baby from him. "You mean my flight."

Bran shook his head. "I'm comin' with you. So's Tate. He oughta be real wound up by the time we get to Denver. Don't envy those folks on the plane with us."

"But..." Harper looked completely bewildered.

He curled his hands around her face. "You're not doin' this alone. And you'd have known that, had you not raced outta the house before I got off the phone."

"But the cattle—"

"Will be fine. I've lined up help for Les, which oughta give him an incentive to get his work done and not screw around. Since we both know how much the cranky old coot loves to have helpers underfoot."

Harper laughed and sniffled.

"Nothin' is more important to me than you and our family. Nothin'." He pressed his lips to her forehead. "Liberty is my family too. Bein' a family means we always stick together, got it?"

Tanna probably should've turned away to give them privacy, but the love and connection between these two caused warring feelings inside her: joy for their obvious happiness, sadness that she might never experience that for herself.

At that moment Fletch reached for her hand and squeezed.

She looked up. Whoa. When had they moved so close to each other?

But Fletch was focused on Harper and Bran too.

Bran placed a kiss on Jake's head. "Now gimme back my boy. I'll get Tate and you finish your business with Tanna. Five minutes. That's it."

Harper muttered something and Bran laughed. Then she faced Tanna. "Okay. All the lists from the past three years are in the file on the desk. I'll have my cell phone with me so if you need something, text me."

Tanna hip-checked Fletch. "See? Everyone in the world texts except you."

"Now that I'm living up here for a bit I can just knock on your door if I wanna talk to you."

"Shoot. I forgot to do one thing." Harper raced into the back room.

Bran hefted the baby carrier. "Thanks for easing Harper's mind, Tanna."

"No problem. But it still strikes me as odd. Part of my job is to rotate merchandise. Why is this such a big deal?"

"Because it's Harper's favorite activity of the year and now she won't get to do it." He shrugged. "I don't get why she loves ripping the plastic packaging off shit and steaming out the wrinkles, but I don't question what makes her happy. The fact she trusts you to do it says a lot." He looked at Fletch. "You comin'?"

"Yeah. I'll be right there."

After Bran left, Fletch lowered his lips to hers, giving her a kiss both hot and sweet.

"What was that for?" she said, a little breathlessly.

A secret smile crossed his face. "Just because."

"Well, thanks."

"Anytime. So, you wanna hang out after you're done here? There'll be daylight left so we can shoot skeet. There's a range outside of Muddy Gap."

"You're taking me on a gun date?"

"Yep. Do you have a shotgun?"

Tanna rolled her eyes at the ridiculous question. "Did you somehow forget I'm from Texas?"

"My mistake." He kissed her again. "See you later, sugar twang."

Skeet shooting would take her mind off the change in daily schedule that meant for at least the next week, she couldn't go to Eli's place.

But she wasn't sure if she felt relief or disappointment.

Chapter Twenty-one

⌒✦⌒

𝒻letch pulled up to the fence at Eli's, parking next to a van with Wyoming government plates. He heard happy, high-pitched shrieks a few seconds before he saw several girls chasing after one another, riling up the dogs yipping at their heels. The girls were part of a state sponsored social program—a pet project of his socially conscious cousin—that tried to curb juvenile delinquency in at-risk Native American kids by pairing them with Indian adults who'd successfully beaten the odds. Fletch watched as the young social worker, a spitfire named Andie who ran the program, followed the girls into the barn.

Eli ambled over, wearing his usual grin. "Mornin', sunshine."

"You are entirely too chipper before noon, Eli."

"And I ain't gonna apologize for that either. Has bein' on sabbatical made you one of them lazy types that sleeps until noon?"

"Fuck off."

Eli laughed and Fletch followed him to the fence connected to the chute, mimicking his stance, leaning over the top, gazing across the paddock.

"Not that I'm not happy to see you, but what brings you by?"

No reason to hedge. "Tanna."

"I figured." Eli sipped his coffee. "But swinging by to say howdy to her because you were in the neighborhood ain't all of it, since I'm pretty sure you woke up beside her a few hours ago."

"I did. I could get used to having that cowgirl in my bed. Anyway, I wanted to see how she's doin'. Or more accurately, what she's doin'."

"Well, she hasn't been doin' anything since up until this morning I haven't seen her for two weeks. That aside, you questioning my methods, cuz?"

He shrugged. "Maybe a little."

Eli took it in stride. "Been wondering if I oughta be questioning them methods more myself."

"I know she hasn't been here, but before that . . . had Tanna made *any* progress?"

"Some. Not nearly enough. She don't scale the fence and run away from the horses like she did that first day when she helped me feed."

Fletch frowned. "But she is at least around horses, in close proximity to them?"

"No. I'm as embarrassed as I am frustrated when I admit that Tanna's idea of getting help . . . and my idea of helping her are vastly different."

"Explain that," Fletch demanded.

"She has no problem cleaning a stall. Or the whole barn, as long as there aren't horses in said barn. I'm afraid to go into my own tack room because she's got it so perfectly organized. She'll even grab a bucket and help me feed. But as far as her spending time with any horse? Dropping a lead rope and catching one? Or even just standing by while I'm grooming one? Nope. Hasn't happened yet."

Fletch's stomach knotted. "Shit. It's been weeks since she first came to you, Eli."

"I'm aware of that. I haven't pushed her—we both know that pushing ain't my way. Times like this, I wish it was. But I expected she'd get tired of the snail's pace and take the initiative. A woman like Tanna, made of fire, stubborn as all get-out, shouldn't be content to be shoveling shit. She oughta at least be riding by now. Heck, even having her pet a damn trail pony would be a step forward. Again, it hasn't happened."

"Got a theory as to why that is?"

Eli sighed—a rare sign of his frustration because Eli always excelled where others had failed. "If I was the type to lay blame, I'd point out that

Tanna isn't here every day trying to overcome this paralyzing fear... maybe because she ain't sure if she *wants* to overcome it. Is she goin' through the motions just to keep the folks off her back who think she oughta be over this issue by now?"

"She does have a job," Fletch pointed out. "She's limited on time during daylight hours, and she's worked the last ten days straight."

Eli faced him. "You making excuses for her?"

"No." Fletch blew out a frustrated breath. "I don't know. I don't want to. She tries to hide her fears, but some nights she has nightmares. She won't talk about them to me and I know they've got to do with the accident. I'd hoped maybe she was talking to you."

Eli shook his head.

"Any time I ask what she's doin' out here with you, she changes the subject. I knew something was up, or that her progress had stalled or whatever when I realized she won't even come down to the building where I'm working with Tobin because she'd have to pass through the horse corral."

"I never would've pegged her as the Queen of Avoidance, but that's what it's come to. And I feel like I've helped put the crown on her head." Silence stretched. "You got any suggestions?" Eli asked. "'Cause I ain't too proud to admit I'm doin' her more harm than good right now. Seems I'm better with horses than people."

"Yeah, I'm right there with you most days." Fletch tapped his fingers on the top of the fence post. "What were your plans for today?"

"Nothin'. I sorta wing it when the girls are here. Andie is insistent on them blowing off steam and excitement before I put them to work learning life lessons."

Fletch snorted at the term *life lessons*. The girls were getting firsthand knowledge on cleaning a chicken coop, mucking out a barn, and the daily requirements of having livestock. "So you could've scheduled something for the girls today as a surprise?"

"Whatcha got in mind?"

"A hands-on demonstration about proper horse grooming with a veterinarian, assisted by the lovely cowgirl and expert horsewoman, Tanna

Barker. Followed by a show-and-tell session of what it means to be a barrel racer. Complete with visual aids." Fletch grinned. "Gonna show the Queen of Avoidance that the King of Tenacity is in the house today."

Eli grinned back. "That'll work. But I'm gonna leave it up to you to tell her. I ain't about to get my head chopped off."

The girls were still chattering away with Andie and Tanna as they left the barn. The instant they saw him, they shrieked, "Doc Fletch!" and raced toward him.

Tanna meandered over, waiting until there was a break in their fawning to say, "I see you've got some admirers."

"Me and these girls go way back to last summer, right, ladies?"

"Uh-huh! It was so cool! We were there when Dr. Fletcher rescued a baby kitten that'd gotten lost from its mama."

"Yes, the good doc has a penchant for caring for lost things."

Was that how Tanna saw herself? Saw him? Fuck that.

She smiled at the chubby freckled girl. "So then what happened?"

"After he checked her out to make sure she wasn't hurt, he let her go. The baby kitty ran back home where she belonged."

"Interesting how that happens," Tanna murmured. "She's lucky she had a home to run back to."

He wasn't ready to touch that one. "These two here," he pointed to the two smallest girls, "have sworn to me they'll study hard so they can go to vet school and help save all the animals in the world."

"I've been practicing wrapping my dog's legs in bandages," the freckled girl announced. "And I've gotten really good."

"You wish," the dark-eyed one he called "feisty" argued. "Lady just lays down now when she sees you get the tape out because she's scared. That don't count."

Tanna and Fletch exchanged a grin.

Then the other girls vied for Fletch's attention until Andie let loose a shrill whistle.

"Pipe down or you'll miss the surprise Eli lined up for you." She gestured to Eli. "Go ahead."

"Dr. Fletcher is gonna demonstrate the proper way to brush down a horse. So I know you'll use your best manners and listen to him. Then he'll answer all your questions."

"Who's gonna be his assistant? 'Cause all vets have assistants."

Shouts of "Pick me! Pick me!" rent the air.

Fletch signaled for quiet. "Not all vets have an assistant. Most days I don't. But you're in luck today because Tanna will be my assistant. She's an expert horse groomer. And the extra surprise is she's gonna talk to you about bein' a three-time world champion barrel racer and show you some tools of the trade."

Tanna froze beside him.

Amidst the buzz of excitement, Eli said, "While we're giving Doc and Tanna time to get ready, head on up to the house. Summer baked a whole batch of monster cookies for you little monsters."

The girls said a hasty good-bye and loped off, Eli and Andie behind them.

Fletch stepped in front of her. "You wanna discuss how we're gonna present this here? Or as we're walking to the pasture to round up a horse?"

"Fletch. I . . . *can't.*"

"I'm not asking you to climb on a horse and run barrels, Tanna. I'm asking you to help me show them what good horsemanship is all about. How much time and energy goes into an animal that's entrusted to the owner's care."

"Need I remind you of what happened to the last horse that was 'entrusted to my care'?" she snapped.

"It wasn't your fault." He cupped her face in his hands. "Please, sweetheart, you need to believe that because it's true."

"Fletch—"

"It wasn't your fault," he repeated stubbornly. "You were seriously injured. You need to let go of the guilt that you weren't there for Jezebel in her last moments. God, Tanna, I know you. You would've crawled across glass to be with her if you could have. So, please. Stop punishing yourself."

Tanna shook off his touch and was at a loss for words for several long moments. "I can't. Especially not today . . . in front of . . ."

"Which is why I want you to talk about how you got to be a world champion. Show them the different types of bits and bridles and training harnesses. You've landed on the top of the heap of your sport three times. These girls, who have so little, who most likely don't have many women like you in their lives to look up to—they need inspiration."

Fletch read the questions in her eyes as easily as if she were speaking out loud.

What if I'm a disappointment because I won't get on a horse and show them how it's done?

What if they ask why I'm not doing it anymore?

"They are gonna ask questions. But if you can answer a bunch of curious preteens, who have no filter, imagine how much easier it'll be to answer questions from industry reporters when you get back into the sport."

"That's not the part I'm worried about."

Bingo. "I'll be right there beside you as we're brushing the horse down. *We*, sweetheart. Not just you."

His reassurance didn't help: Tanna's panic was palpable.

Then he was right in her face. "Breathe. Come on, sugar twang. You're a strong-minded woman. Put your mind to this. You're strong willed too. You *can* do this," he said softly. "I know you can. You just need to believe it."

That got her back up. "Is that why you're here? To give me a pep talk before you force me to do something I'm not ready for?"

"That's the thing—you *are* ready for it. Besides, is it so bad, me bein' on Team Tanna? I am here for you, I have been for weeks even when you wanna shut that damn barn door and keep me out at every turn."

"You're full of bad clichés today," Tanna retorted, "and it's not helping."

"Nothin' is helping. So yeah, I'm forcing the issue." He stroked her cheek. "Because if you're not ready to even *touch* a horse after all the hours you've spent out here at a goddamned horse ranch, I'm gonna kick Eli's ass." He smirked. "Then possibly yours."

"Try it."

"With pleasure. And here's another thing I'm gonna force on you." Fletch held her jaw and dropped his mouth over hers for a kiss that reminded her he was in charge.

Tanna didn't try to pull away. She wrapped herself around him, holding on, making those needy moans that made his dick hard.

His little head tried to wrest control from his big head, but Fletch wouldn't succumb to the seductive power of his body's needs. Tanna used sex to distract him whenever he tried to discuss her issues and he'd be damned if he'd do the same thing. So he broke the kiss.

Brain one, cock zero.

He rested his forehead to hers. "Please. Trust me. If this is too much for you, we'll stop. But you gotta at least try."

Her body tensed again. A very long minute of silence passed before she whispered, "Okay."

Thank God. Fletch stepped back and held out his hand. "Come on. Let's go catch us a horse."

Tanna took his hand. "A *slow* horse. And I'd better get a big cookie after this demonstration of yours, Doc."

"Sugar twang, I'll personally feed you all the cookies you can eat."

Chapter Twenty-two

*T*anna was agitated.

The woman could not sit still after they'd returned from Eli's. She prowled silently around the living area of his trailer, her brow furrowed. She'd give him one- or two-word answers if he asked her a question, but beyond that she remained quietly edgy.

Finally she said, "I'm goin' to the pool."

He slipped off his reading glasses and set them aside. He'd reread the same page for the last ten minutes anyway. "Thought the pool was off-limits to employees."

"Only when there's guests. The lodge is empty, which is why I'm not working tonight. I'll see you later."

The screen door banged shut behind her.

Normally he wouldn't care that she hadn't invited him to come along. But it did bother him, given the day had taken a toll on both of them.

During the grooming session with Eli's docile trail horse, Fletch had stayed close to Tanna, offering silent reassurance by touching her as she touched the horse. The girls didn't see her jerky movements or shaking hands, or recognize the higher-pitched tone of her voice. Eventually she calmed and Fletch had been proud of her.

While Tanna showed the tools of her barrel racing trade, breaking down the parts of the saddle, describing the different bits or snaffles, and the headstall—parts that made up the bridle—he remained in the shadows outside the barn, his body tense as if he'd absorbed Tanna's fear.

So yeah, he'd like to blow off some steam too.

And he'd really like to see Tanna in a bikini.

The thought of rubbing oil all over her curvy body had him off the couch, searching for his board shorts.

Fletch gave her thirty minutes of alone time before he draped a towel around his neck and wandered to the pool.

It wasn't a large pool, maybe twelve by twenty feet. The deepest end was only five and a half feet. A high fence enclosed the area, the wooden slats angled to allow air circulation within the space. The metal gate creaked when he entered and the smooth concrete was warm beneath his feet.

Tanna floated on an inflatable neon green lounge chair in the middle of the pool. Her breasts spilled out of her red string bikini top. The matching boy short bottoms showcased the curve of her hips and her flat abdomen.

He could lick her up one side and down the other. Sucking on her sun-warmed skin and tasting her sweat mixed with the chlorinated water.

"What are you doin' here?"

"Came to join you for a little water play."

"No offense, puddin' pop, but I'm not in the mood for any of your games."

Jesus. That haughty twang of hers got him hard as a fucking rock. As did the nearly derisive sneer on her lush mouth. Fletch knew Tanna loved it when he went all "caveman on her ass" and he wouldn't want to disappoint her when she'd baited him first.

"Now I'm hurt. Guess I'll have to play with myself."

"You go right ahead and do that."

"Cool. But, sugar twang, you might wanna close your eyes."

She dismissively flapped her hand at him. "I've seen this particular show before."

Fletch grinned. "Don't say I didn't warn ya." He grabbed her bottle of suntan oil and squeezed a puddle in his palm. Keeping his eyes on hers, he slowly rubbed that oil down his left arm. Taking his time to work it into his biceps, triceps and forearms. Then he switched sides, giving the right arm equal attention.

Was Tanna even aware that she'd licked her lips?

He drizzled oil on his chest, his slick hands leisurely massaging it into his pectorals, the tips of his fingers digging into every ridged muscle. When he reached his nipples, Fletch let his head fall back as his thumbs traced around the puckered discs.

The sound of the float squeaking drifted to him. Was she getting a little squirmy from the show she claimed she didn't want to watch?

Fletch squirted oil directly onto his sternum and ran his hands over his shoulders as one thick stream of liquid slid down, down, down his torso. Before the rivulet reached his belly button, he smeared it across his abs.

Dripping oil on his fingertips, he rubbed his fingers together before he placed them on his lower abdomen and began to inch them beneath the waistband of his board shorts, his eyes locked on to hers. Tanna couldn't miss his cock tenting his trunks.

"Stop," she said hoarsely. "Sweet Lord. Are you really fixin' to jack off right here?"

Fletch feigned a confused look. "You thought I was…?" He laughed. "God, no. I was just adjusting my trunks." He rolled down the elastic band and tugged on the lining. "Why? Is that something you'd like to see?"

"I already told you no," she snipped. "Now that you're all greased up like you're in a body builder's competition, you gonna lay in the sun and see if you can't get that skin a little redder?"

Such a smart mouth. He manufactured a shocked gasp. "You mean that was oil to make my skin darker? Not sunscreen?"

"Nope."

"Well, shit. I'd better wash this oily gunk off right away." He walked to the edge of the pool.

Her eyes widened. "Fletch. No."

He tucked his arms around his knees as he jumped in. A big guy like him could do maximum water damage with a well-placed cannonball.

When he surfaced, he saw that he'd completely drenched Tanna. He'd even knocked her off the float.

Sweet.

"What are you? A twelve-year-old boy?" she demanded, wiping the water from her eyes.

"Yep. I see a girl I like at the pool and I splash her to get her attention. Especially if she's fixin' to ignore me."

"Not nice, makin' fun of my accent." Tanna flipped her hair over her shoulder. When she noticed him stalking her, she warned, "I wasn't kidding, Fletch. I'm in a mood and you really don't wanna be around me right now."

He put himself between her and the steps. "I'm in a mood myself. So how about we just skip the niceties and take out our frustrations on each other?" He'd herded her until her back was against the wall. Then he braced his hands on the ledge beside her shoulders and leaned in. "I wanna fuck you every way I can think up. Hard. Fast. Dirty. Rough. Nasty. I wanna use my mouth, my teeth, my hands and my cock in ways that'll make you blush, make you scream and make you cream. I wanna strip this down between us to pure, animal fucking. It'll take the edge off and then some."

Tanna shuddered. Then she turned her head and bit down on the ball of his shoulder with enough force that he hissed. She licked the line of his collarbone, up to the arch of his neck and whispered, "Big talk. Prove it."

Instant shot of adrenaline. His breathing changed. His focus sharpened.

Her nails dug in to the side of his neck as she yanked his mouth to hers for a ferocious kiss.

Fletch let her have control now—because after this? Control was all his.

When she finally relinquished his mouth, he spun her around so she was in front of him. One hand twisted in her hair and he flattened his other hand against her belly. His lips started at the tender sweep of her shoulder and drifted up, stopping behind her ear. "Do you wear your hair up at work?"

"Ah. No."

"Good." He opened his mouth below her hairline and sucked. Hard. And he kept sucking, marking her with a love bruise even when her knees buckled. He felt the vibration of Tanna's moan beneath his lips and he couldn't help but sink his teeth in a little more.

Tanna moaned louder.

He added two more marks that when he finished looked like a fat letter F. She might not be able to see it, but it was there. And he knew it was there.

Then his lips traveled to her other shoulder and he raised her arm up to nip and kiss the tender skin on the underside.

Another shiver worked down her body and he watched her nipples tighten.

Fletch let go of her hair. "Leave your arm up." He bent it at an angle, keeping her bicep by her ear and putting her palm on the back of her head. "Stay like that." He curled his hands around her rib cage and followed the contour of her body, slowly, pausing on her hips. "Spread your legs."

She complied without protest.

He traced the edge of her suit bottoms. Even beneath the water he felt her abdomen quiver in response. He slipped his left hand beneath the elastic band, following her slit to her opening. He pushed one finger in her pussy, growling, "You're so fucking wet. And I know it ain't from the pool water."

"It's all you," she breathed against his neck.

His dick twitched against her ass and she ground back into it. Fletch nudged her head to the side and fastened his mouth to the skin right below her jawbone as he plunged one finger in and out, then two.

Tanna undulated, bumping her pelvis into his hand.

"Hold still," he warned. Once she'd settled, he slipped his right hand into her swimsuit bottoms too. He stretched the fleshy part above her pussy lips with his index and third finger, while his middle finger began to manipulate her clit.

"Oh God."

His oil-slick fingers rubbed her inner pussy wall opposite her pubic bone. Knowing it drove her crazy, he alternated tapping on her clit with drawing small figure eights.

Fletch drifted into that place where her pleasure was his only concern. He tasted her skin and breathed in her scent, his fingers propelling her toward orgasm. The heat of the sun, the temperate water, her soft body pressed against his, the aromas of coconut oil and chlorine—this had to be paradise.

Just as he put his mouth on her ear to command her to come, she detonated. Her free hand hit the water, gasping moans drifting from her mouth. Tanna's body trembled and he rode it out with her; her pussy sucking at his fingers, her clit pulsing.

She slumped against him after the final contraction. Her arm fell into the water with a splash.

Fletch straightened her swimsuit bottoms. Before Tanna came out of her haze, he spun her around to face him and hoisted her up, wrapping her thighs above his hips. Then he dipped his head, running his razor-stubbled cheeks across the upper swells of her breasts. "Arch back."

"Fletch—"

"Do it."

Tanna leaned back completely in the water and let herself float, arms out in a T shape while her legs were anchored around his waist. Her eyes were dark, sated, yet held a glimmer of lust. The sunlight reflected off her hair, highlighting the red in her mahogany tresses.

Fletch lowered his head and licked a line up her torso from her belly button to the hollow of her throat. His mouth slid to her right breast and he slipped his tongue under the swimsuit top. Her skin was cool and wet and soft . . . except for the hard nipple poking up.

When his hot mouth enclosed that tip, Tanna started to throw her head back, but caught herself at the last second.

He smiled and proceeded to torture her—biting, licking, exposing the wet tips to the air to watch them constrict, knowing she couldn't move. He loved watching the way she parted her lush lips and how her chest lifted out of the water with every hitch in her breathing.

Tanna started to grind her pussy into his abdomen and he realized she was close to coming again.

"Get yourself off while I suck on your tits."

"Yes." He felt her hand delve between their bodies, her knuckles bumping his abs as she rapidly stroked her clit.

Although he couldn't see what she was doing, it was fucking hot as hell knowing exactly what she was doing.

Especially when she started to moan, completely oblivious to everything except expressing her pleasure.

As soon as her hand fell away, Fletch pulled her up out of the water and kissed her. In a full-on onslaught. Teeth and tongues dueling while their chests slipped and slid against each other.

His hands skated from her shoulder blades to her butt and followed the cleft of her ass, stopping where her butt curved into her thigh. He slipped his thumb beneath the fabric of her swimsuit bottoms and stroked her anus.

Her body tensed but she seemed more startled than put off.

He pulled back so their lips were barely touching. "This ass? Mine today."

A shiver ran through her.

"I want to bend you over that chaise lounge, slick up my cock with suntan oil and slam my dick deep into this pretty little asshole." Fletch brushed butterfly kisses across her cheek, stopping at her ear. "I'll ride you hard, Tanna. That's the mood *I'm* in."

She angled her head and scraped her teeth across the stubble on his jaw. "So do it."

Jesus. The way she used her teeth sent a jolt of electricity straight to his balls.

"Just not here. I don't want people to come running to see what's goin' on when they hear me howling."

Fletch growled, clamped his hand on her butt, holding her in place as he exited the pool, his mouth zeroing in on all the hot spots on her neck.

Once they were on the pool deck, Tanna wiggled to be let down.

He slapped her ass. "Stay put. I'm gonna grab the oil and we're gone."

"You don't have to carry me."

"Oh, but I do. I don't give a flying fuck what anyone thinks or sees. So unless you want me to fuck you right here, right now, you'll keep this sexy body of yours wrapped around me tight until I set you down."

"Yes, sir," she said softly.

Fletch handed her the bottle of oil. "Hold this." Flip-flops on his feet, he headed to the gate.

"But the towels—"

He cut her off with a kiss. They stayed outside the gate, dripping water, bodies plastered together, mouths locked in passion. When Tanna rocked her pelvis into his, he released her mouth. "Hold that thought, but I gotta see where I'm walking."

She nodded and buried her face in his neck, her breaths fanning across his damp skin.

Fletch seemed to make the trip to his trailer in five steps.

As soon as they were inside, Tanna unhooked her legs, and stood in front of him. The suntan oil hit the floor. She paid no attention, digging her fingertips into his pectorals as she tongued his nipple.

He sucked in a surprised breath. She wasn't shy about what she wanted when it came to sex, but she hadn't acted this . . . hungry for it—for him— before.

Tanna lavished attention on his nipples and he let her, keeping his hands by his sides, relishing every lick and nip. Her wet hair trailed over his midsection and tiny, cold drops of water kept landing on the tops of his feet, making him flinch.

Enough. He needed her hot mouth and cool hands elsewhere.

Fletch cupped her jaw in his left hand and used his right hand to tug down his swim trunks. He feathered his thumb across her full bottom lip. "Such a pretty mouth. I want it on my cock."

With her eyes locked on his, Tanna sucked on his thumb, swirling her tongue around it. She allowed a cocky smirk before she dropped to her knees.

The instant her lips circled the cockhead, his entire body tightened in anticipation. No matter how many times she'd blown him, he'd never get used to that dizzying feeling of the first wet touch of her mouth.

He stroked her hair as she brought him deeper with every bob of her head. Instead of using her hand to jack his shaft while her mouth performed oral magic, her fingers clutched his thighs. When his shaft was fully seated in her mouth, the tip bumping against the back of her throat, her nose against his lower belly, he held her there.

She didn't balk or try to pull away.

"That's it baby, breathe through your nose. Now swallow. I wanna feel those throat muscles kissing my cock."

Tanna's eyes remained closed as she swallowed.

"Ah fuck. Next time I'll come down your throat like this." He let his hands fall away and she retreated, his dick slipping out of her mouth.

She nuzzled his hip, and planted kisses across his lower abdomen.

Hauling her to her feet, he claimed her mouth while untying her swimsuit top. After flinging it aside, his hands slid down to remove her bottoms. A driving need built inside him with each openmouthed kiss. He wanted to possess this woman, fuck her, mark her, own her, leave an imprint on her so skin deep, so bone deep, that she'd only ever think of him. That she'd only ever want him.

Standing on tiptoe, Tanna broke the seal of their mouths and brushed her lips across his jaw, starting on the left and moving to the right. She whispered, "I'm yours however you want me."

"Couch. Now."

She unwreathed her arms from his neck and sauntered away, aware his eyes were glued to every enticing swing of her hips.

Like he needed additional enticement. The woman was sex on legs.

Bottle of oil in hand, Fletch joined her. "Hands on the cushions, legs spread wide, ass in the air."

As soon as she'd assumed the position, he sat on the floor between her legs. With his neck resting on the edge of the cushion, her cunt was above him.

Fletch poured oil on his fingers. "Put your pussy on my face."

Tanna lowered herself without hesitation.

He feasted on her. Lapping her juices, tickling her clit with the tip of his tongue, burying his mouth in her soft, wet tissues until he was drunk on her taste. High on the scent of her arousal. His mouth wandered to the pink pucker and he flicked his tongue over that tight rosebud until Tanna's moans escalated.

Then he stopped, replacing his tongue with an oil-slicked finger. He teased her pussy with rapid swirls and firm-lipped nibbles as he slowly inserted one finger in her ass.

Tanna was so focused on her impending orgasm that she didn't notice—or didn't care—when he added a second finger. He reached up and squirted more oil on her tailbone. It rolled down her butt crack into her asshole, coating his fingers as he plunged them in and out, preparing her to take his cock.

"Please. Please make me come."

He latched onto her clit and sucked until that sweet moment when her body responded. And he swallowed a very male grunt of satisfaction that he'd brought her there. Again.

Every throbbing pulse caused her to gasp, "Oh God. Oh-God-oh-God-oh-God."

After the last tremor, Fletch gave her pussy a soft kiss, eased his fingers from her back channel and stood on shaking legs.

Want. Need. Now.

It took every ounce of willpower not to ram his cock into her right that second. He grabbed a handful of tissues from the coffee table and wiped his fingers. Then he realized he hadn't brought protection. Tanna was still in a stupor and she wouldn't notice if he slipped away for just a sec.

But when he turned toward the bedroom, she said, "Where you goin'?"

"To get a condom."

She raised her head and looked over her shoulder at him. "No condom."

Shocked, he said, "You sure?"

"You're clean. I'm clean. And it's not like you'll get me pregnant." She shot him such a hot look the temperature in the room seemed to go up twenty degrees. "Bare. Your cock in my ass. Don't tell me you haven't fantasized about it."

"I have. I just wasn't aware that you had." Their gazes stayed linked in a heated eye-fuck as he poured more oil in his hand and slicked up his cock.

He stood behind her, his body tensed, primed, eager, but even in his raw surge of need, he took a moment to string kisses down her spine. Her beautiful skin erupted in gooseflesh when he placed a kiss on the dimples above her ass.

Fletch didn't ask if she was ready; he was too far gone. Although his hands were slippery, he managed to keep hold of her butt cheeks as he pulled them apart. He nudged the tiny entrance with his cock twice, pushing the head in on the third pass. Once those strong muscles constricted around the head, he couldn't hold back. He slammed into her to the root.

Tanna cried out.

That caught his attention. Before he could ask if she was all right, she said, "Don't stop. God. I forgot how much I love that bite of pain."

A possessive noise rumbled from his chest and he withdrew and impaled her again. And again. "Goddamn, I like this without a condom."

After a dozen strokes, he picked up the pace. His hips pumping, her soft butt cheeks a cushion for his increasingly hard thrusts. Then he pulled his cock out completely, the head pausing briefly at the tiny hole before ramming home.

Tanna pushed back into him, each thrust eliciting a "Yes."

A crazy pressure began to build in his head as he watched his dick driving into her ass. Her anal passage was so hot and tight and a different sensation from plowing into her wet and welcoming cunt.

Sweat beaded on his chest. The back of his neck burned. The scent of coconut permeated the air. For a brief instant he imagined they were in the jungle as he fucked her like an animal. Like a mad man. One hand fisted in her hair. One hand clamped to her hip, holding her body steady for his unyielding powerful thrusts.

Tanna moved her hands to the back couch cushions to brace herself against his pistoning hips.

His brain chanted *faster*.

That warning buzz started in his tailbone.

He closed his eyes. His body had demanded this rapid pace, driving him to this point as quickly as possible, and now left him teetering on the precipice. This was a special kind of torture; he wanted it to end, he didn't want it to ever end. "So close. So fucking close."

Knowing what he needed, Tanna contracted and released her inner muscles, increasing the pressure on his dick. His shaft stayed nearly motionless in her snug channel as he came in hot blast after hot blast. He'd never experienced anything like his bare cock jerking against her inner walls with every wet pulse. The abyss opened up and he might've yelled "fuck yeah" a time or two as he fell into sweet bliss. The blood roaring in his ears muffled sounds and gave him a monumental head rush. He'd gripped her so desperately that his hands had cramped. As well as his ass cheeks. And his jaw.

Breathing hard, spent, his mind a little scrambled, Fletch slumped forward, his hands beside hers on the cushion. His chest covered her back, but he didn't let her small frame bear the brunt of his weight. He remained poised above her until he could breathe normally.

That's when Tanna turned her head and whispered, "Boom."

"No kidding. That...you...blew my fucking mind, Tanna." He found his sanity kissing her, drawing out soft-lipped smooches and the glide of wet lips on wet lips.

"Next time I'll know what you really have in mind when you threaten to go all caveman on my ass."

He didn't laugh. He just growled and lightly bit the top of her ear. She wasn't a virgin to anal sex, but no doubt she'd be sore tomorrow after how hard he'd taken her.

Fletch pushed her hair aside and started sucking another hickey on her nape just because he could.

Tanna arched into him and moaned. "Fletch. Stop. I can't take much more."

"Too bad because I'm not done with you yet." He teased her, blowing in her ear, nibbling on her lobe as he cupped her mound. "Baby, you're still wet. And swollen." He pushed two fingers inside her and rubbed her clit with his thumb. "Need some relief?"

"I..."

"I'll take that as a yes." Tanna was so primed it didn't take long until she hit the point of no return. "Come like this for me. With my dick in your ass and my fingers in your cunt."

"Oh, goddamn you, Fletch, I'm..." And she started to come. Violently. Tanna actually released a scream as every intimate part of her contracted around his fingers, his cock, his thumb. She bucked into his hand. And away from his hand. As soon as the intense orgasm ended, she sank her teeth into his bicep.

He hissed at the sharp sting of pain.

"I'm done in," she panted, "worn out."

"Me too. You undo me every time I get to touch you." He removed his fingers first, then his cock and pushed himself upright.

When Tanna straightened up, Fletch wrapped his arms around her belly and kissed the back of her head, just needing to hold her.

She sagged against him.

"Shower?" he murmured in her ear.

"Not right now. I just want to bask in the two hundred orgasms you forced on me."

"Okay." Fletch swept her into his arms and carried her to his bed.

Tanna spread out on the cool sheets and moaned. "My body is so overheated right now. So overstimulated."

He stretched out alongside her. He was so wired he considered putting on his running shoes and hitting the pavement. But he didn't want to leave her. They'd had intense sex before, but this was on a different level.

Unused to silence from her, or physical distance in bed, he placed his hand on the small of her back, half worried she'd shake him off after the overstimulated comment.

She didn't. She sighed.

God. He was so crazy for this woman.

After a bit, she said, "Thank you."

Was she being sarcastic? "For...?"

"For not treating me like I'm fragile. Especially after the stuff that happened at Eli's today."

Not sure if she wanted a response, Fletch remained quiet and his thumb lightly caressed her spine.

"It was hotter than hell. You fucking me, taking me the way you wanted. Not making tender, sweet love to me."

His motion stilled. "You don't like that?"

"Don't get me wrong, I love the way it can be tender and sweet. Or fun and fast. But sometimes...I need it like...that."

Relieved, he said, "I do too, baby, so you're welcome."

"And please don't ruin this by asking me if you were too rough," she warned without looking at him.

"Actually, I was thinking that next time I'm gonna spank your ass until it's hot and pink before I fuck it."

Tanna groaned—a good groan.

For the longest time Fletch petted her and stroked her and she let him. After she drifted off, he dressed and went for a long run. Before he returned he remembered to pick up the towels from the pool.

As far as mood improvement therapy, he'd scored a touchdown.

Chapter Twenty-three

After finishing her physical therapy exercises, Tanna picked up her cell phone and saw she'd missed a call from her brother Garrett, not ten minutes ago. She called him back, hoping he picked up.

He answered on the second ring. "If it isn't my wayward big sister."

"I'm not wayward. I'm untoward, remember?"

Garrett laughed. Tanna had to close her eyes at the hollow feeling that sound evoked. She missed him. During her years on the road they'd spent a lot of time on the phone. She hated that since he'd started a career as a "security specialist" eighteen months ago, she couldn't just call him whenever the mood struck her.

"How're things goin' in Wyoming?"

"Hawking clothes and slinging drinks at the resort is fun so it doesn't seem like work most days. Where are you?"

"I'm in Colorado, actually."

"Hey, you're close to me. So are you done training?"

"I hope so. So much of it is bullshit busywork. I hate playing step'n'fetch. But I gotta pay my dues before I move up to management, which hopefully won't take more than six months, since turnover is so high."

She paused, wanting to ask him a million questions. "What happens now?"

"Checking out my apartment options in Denver."

"Really? But I thought you'd put in a request for California."

"I did. But I've decided to stay with this office rather than transferring to the one in L.A. Colorado…the geography is different enough that I won't pine for Texas here. Goddamn, I miss sweet tea. I even miss the humidity."

Tanna laughed. "I *don't* miss the humidity. And I'm happy there seem to be very few bugs around here. Anyway, I'm proud of you."

"For what?"

"For admitting that you're pining for Texas but adapting to that change better than I have."

"Tanna. First of all, I wasn't in an accident that permanently altered the course of my career. Second of all, I didn't *have* a career beyond hauling hay. Anything is a step up from unemployment."

She snorted. A career hauling hay. Garrett hadn't been some second-generation slacker ranch hand. He'd enrolled in college immediately after high school, signing up for business management classes, computer programming classes. Even theology classes. He'd racked up enough college credits to graduate, but not in any specific major. So if asked, he'd claim a degree in B.S.—which amused him far too much.

"I heard that snort."

"You were meant to. But I'll point out that bein' an unemployed barrel racer doesn't earn me unemployment checks."

"Anything new on the *getting back on the horse* front, sis?" When she didn't respond, he sighed. "Forget I asked."

"So when this Wyoming gig dries up, can I move in with you in Denver?"

"I'd like that. Might make me sound like a pussy, but I miss living with family."

No, bro, that means you're still the sweet, kind boy you've always been. "Speaking of family…Have you heard from Dad?"

"No. Then again I haven't heard from anybody since training started. Have you?"

"Not a word."

"Jesus. What a fucktard. How long has it been since you talked to him?"

"A year and a half. You?"

"About the same. I did get a weird Facebook message from Rosalie's daughter Lucinda, about the same time you had your accident."

"What did she want?"

"She asked if our dad and her mom had joined some kind of weird cult where the new members have to cut off all ties with their family."

"Did you respond?"

"No. I wanted to say . . . that her mom and my dad contracted asshole-itis and I'm staying far away 'cause I fear it's highly contagious."

Tanna couldn't even laugh at that.

Silence lingered between them for a moment.

Garrett sighed. "You know, there are days that I'm still in shock about how it all played out after Mom died."

"But other days?" she prompted.

"Most days I'm not surprised Dad surgically excised us from his life."

"This might be a stupid question, but did you know?"

"That Dad hated everything about the ranch?" A long pause followed. "I had my suspicions."

Not what she'd expected and she said so.

"Don't take offense, but you weren't there most of the time. With the drought takin' a toll on the cattle numbers, you know we had to sell off a bunch of livestock . . . so he'd been in a state of transition five years prior to Mom's death."

"Why didn't you say anything to me? Warn me?"

"It wouldn't have changed anything. And you'd've gotten pissed off at me and confronted Dad about it. Dad would've told Mom to control *her daughter*, she'd've gotten upset and it would've become an ugly deal. There was no reason for it."

How many times had her father called her *her mother's daughter*? And why hadn't she noticed that it'd been an insult to her and her mom? Or at least their close relationship?

"I know selling the ranch upset you, but did you really see yourself giving up your career and settling down to become a full-time rancher after Dad retired?"

She paced to the window. "Dad made that choice for me. Why are you taking his side?"

"I'm not. I'm just pointing out a few things you haven't considered."

"Such as?"

"Such as all you ever wanted was a home base. A place to come back to. The ranch was there for your convenience. You weren't raising livestock on a daily basis. You were competing halfway across the country."

"Did you resent me for that, Garrett?"

"Sometimes. But I also saw the writing on the wall right after you started competing professionally. Why do you think I kept taking all those classes? I knew I needed a fallback position besides ranching. It's why I volunteered with search and rescue, the coroner's office, the police reserves and the fire department."

"I thought you were just trying to one-up me with all that shit."

He laughed. "Well, I never could've competed with the trophies, buckles and saddles you won."

"Do you ever wonder what would've happened if Dad had died and Mom had lived?"

"Mom would've talked to you before she made a decision about the ranch."

"Me? But like you said...I was hardly ever there. You were. Why not talk to you?"

"You're the oldest. If you'd said sell, the place would've been sporting a For Sale sign. If you'd said keep it, she would've asked me how to make that happen."

"After hearing about all this stuff I never knew...makes me question whether we ever were the happy family I remember."

"We were. Even though I worked with Dad every day, I wasn't as close to him as I was to Mom. I think he let us be *her* kids because it made her happy, and when she was gone..."

"He didn't have to pretend anymore." She closed her eyes and experienced that overwhelming feeling of loss and pain again.

Garrett was as quiet as she was.

Then he said, "You've never given any of this serious thought before now?"

"No. At first it was easier not to think about it because it made me miss Mom. Then I had other issues to deal with and, well…out of sight, out of mind." She took a deep breath and confessed, "I have nightmares about her. They get all mixed up with that night with Jezebel. I wake up shaking. Crying sometimes."

"Jesus, Tan. How often does it happen?"

Too often. It'd happened again last night. She couldn't believe the scream that'd woken her up hadn't woken Fletch. Then she'd skulked out of his bed and locked herself in her trailer. "Often enough."

"Have you talked to anyone?"

"I'm talking to you."

"Not what I mean."

"You mean like a therapist? No."

"What about Celia? Or Lainie?" he demanded. "You listened to their tales of woe for years."

"They nag me about getting back on a horse. I figure if I tell them about the nightmare, their advice will *still* be to get back on a horse and I'm not ready. I don't know if I'll ever be."

Another bout of silence stretched—but it was unlike their previous pauses. "What?"

"You know I love you, right?"

"Right. And can I just say *fuck you* ahead of time for whatever you're about to say, because no conversation starting out with those words ever ends well."

"Fair enough. I'll give it to you straight. Quit bein' such a fucking baby about this horse shit. Get your goddamned saddle, get your tack, pick a horse, mount up and ride that fear right out of your head. I realize you suffered a traumatic event, but guess what? You're not the only barrel racer in the history of the world to deal with this. Most barrel racers who don't race anymore *can't*…due to injuries. I'd bet if you asked any one of them, they'd love to have your problem—mental, not physical.

"You're healed up. There's no reason for you to walk around, wringing your hands, lamenting your lot in life and the sad turn to your career. Buck up. Get on a horse and move on. Or don't. Do what Dad did. Excise every bit of barrel racing from your life and find something else to do with your life."

Tanna had to sit down at hearing Garrett's harsh words.

He remained quiet on the line for a long time too.

Or maybe he'd hung up.

"Tanna, I hate to end the call on this note but I've gotta go. I love you. Take care of yourself and I'll talk to you soon."

⁓

She paced and cursed and even cried a little for the next hour. She wouldn't concede any points to her brother, except for one: she did need to talk to someone.

Tanna scrolled through her phone list. Her finger hovered above the CALL button before she pressed it down.

He answered on the third ring. "Hello?"

"Hey. It's Tanna. Do you have time to talk?"

"Of course."

"Where are you right now?"

"Oddly enough, I'm down by the pens."

"At the Split Rock?"

"Yep."

"So we can talk in person?"

"Yep."

"Cool. I'll be there in five."

⁓

It was probably the only time Tanna was happy not to see Fletch hanging around the stock pens.

Tobin grinned at her. "Hey, lady. I think this is the first time you've ventured down here."

"Why would I want to fill my lungs with barnyard scent when I don't have to?"

"Point taken. If you're looking for—"

"Actually I'm looking for Sutton."

Tobin frowned. "Okay." He whistled and waved to a guy in the pens with the baby steers she assumed was Sutton.

"What are Eli and Sutton doin' here today?" she asked.

"We're swapping out a couple horses."

"Do you do that a lot?"

"Not as much as we used to."

Sutton loped over. "Hey, Tex-Mex."

"I don't want to interrupt if you're too busy."

"I'm not." He exited the pens and walked along the fence, brushing dust from his jeans. "Where we goin'?"

She pointed to a bench that sat between the newest metal structure and the barn.

"That'll work." He looked at Tobin. "If Eli asks where I am, would you point me out?"

"Sure."

As soon as they sat, Sutton said, "I was surprised you called me. Not that I wouldn't like to spend all afternoon talking to you, but I might have to leave quickly since I'm here helping Eli."

"Understood."

"What's goin' on?"

Her plan to ease into it vanished when she blurted, "I just got off the phone with my brother. And he said some stuff that hurt, but it's also made me think. Made me wonder if maybe he's right."

"Right about what?"

"About me bein' a big baby and whining all the fucking time about my horse phobia."

Sutton's jaw dropped. "Are you serious? Your brother *said* that to you?"

"Yeah. I know he did it out of love and concern for me, but it still stings. But I have to ask myself if he's right. A mental breakdown isn't as serious as a physical breakdown. He didn't ask if I was milking this phobia for attention, but that's probably only because the conversation was cut short."

"You're close to your brother?"

"Very. He's not the guy who says hurtful things just because he knows what'll slice into me the deepest. He said he's tired of hearing about my indecision. That if I don't think I can ride, I should just purge my life of everything barrel racing related."

"Well, that's just plain damn ridiculous."

"Is it?" She faced him, even though she was fighting another bout of stupid tears. "Do you know there's a barrel racer on the circuit who's broken nearly all the bones in her body? Last time, she broke, like, her neck or something and she climbed back on her horse within two months. Two. Fucking. Months. What does that say about me?"

"Tanna—"

"It's almost been a year and I can barely stand to step boot into a horse pasture. I think about climbing on a horse and all I envision is being trapped beneath it. I'm suffocating under the weight as it's dying on top of me. And the last time I picked up my tack? My hands shook so fucking hard I couldn't even hold it. But that's the issue my brother pointed out—that I'm physically able to do it. I could saddle a horse and ride one if I wanted to. My accident didn't disable me. Didn't physically ruin me.

"I can name a dozen other women, all fantastic barrel racers, who've had injuries way worse than mine, and it was hardly a hiccup in their career. They were back on, training harder than ever, not cowering by the fence. So, back to the question. What is wrong with me?"

"Hey."

Tanna kept her gaze focused on the ground.

"Hey," he said more firmly and she looked up. "Those women are not you, so stop comparing yourself to them. They may be riding in the worst pain of their lives and regret every second they're on a horse. Maybe they lie in bed for a week afterward, physically and emotionally drained. Cowgirls are tough, Tanna. That's what sets them apart. They won't admit weaknesses but you can be guaranteed they have them."

Don't cry.

"I can't—I won't—judge you for your phobia. Neither should he. And yes, I know your fear is real. I've watched you at Eli's. Is it hard—almost impossible to believe, given how you've lived your life around horses? Yes.

I get why he'd say that. But your brother hasn't seen you facing your fear and trying to overcome it. But you are. One step at a time."

Tanna didn't say anything because she didn't know what to say.

Sutton rubbed her arm. "What else?"

Just say it. "I have nightmares. Bad ones. Not every night, but at least once a week. And they're always intermixed with my mother's death. Which is fucked up on several levels. I imagine they'll fade in time. Or if I ever actually get my scared ass on a horse."

"Keep goin'. You need to get this out," he said gently.

So Tanna talked. And talked. Sutton listened without judgment, without interruptions besides to make a comment when she took a pause. When she finished, she did feel better. Even when she felt a little guilty for dropping the burden on a guy she barely knew.

Why couldn't she say any of this to Fletch? By confiding in Sutton, was she giving Sutton the wrong idea?

Don't be an idiot. This is about a shared trauma—a trauma Fletch doesn't understand.

She was saved from the awkwardness of having to apologize when Eli shouted to Sutton that it was time for them to go.

❧

Fletch slumped against the wall by the open window where he'd been eavesdropping.

Eavesdropping. On his own girlfriend like some snoopy neighbor lady that didn't have anything better to do than listen in on private conversations.

As far as hearing a private conversation, this one had been a whopper.

Tanna spilling her guts—and her fears—to Sutton.

Not to him.

That rankled. No, it just plain damn hurt.

Was he a fool to think they'd made any progress a week ago at Eli's? Not only in getting her to touch a horse, but in getting her to trust him?

Probably. What had they done after her small breakthrough?

Screwed like animals in a big way. Fletch so high on victory to prove he knew what Tanna needed that he'd mastered her with rough, raunchy, hot, down and dirty sex.

He scrubbed his hand over his face. So he should've . . . what? Demanded they talk it out instead of fuck it out? Hell no. That wasn't him. With Tanna he could be the overtly sexual being that he hid from most women and she accepted that side of him. She'd wanted that side of him. Needed it, actually.

So if she couldn't talk to you, can you really blame her for talking to Sutton?

Goddamned right he could.

Jesus. What was wrong with him? Could this hollow feeling come from jealousy?

No, not jealousy, not the normal kind, where he wanted to beat Sutton's face in because Fletch suspected the snarky bastard was trying to sweet-talk Tanna into his bed. No, this jealousy was worse because he'd just realized there was an emotional bond between Tanna and Sutton—and that intimacy was more painful to bear. The bulldogger had a part of Tanna that Fletch couldn't reach.

That kicked in a feeling of betrayal.

Why couldn't she let him be the man she needed? In bed and out of bed? Why did she want Sutton's help? Especially when Sutton Grant was a smug asshole?

Fletch would really like to boot the boy's butt back to Colorado.

Nice. Way to get to the real problem with that petty, juvenile chest-beating attitude. Fletch knew that was pointless, but just because he was aware of it didn't mean he could stop it.

When he glanced across the path to see Harlow staring at him from the barn, he quickly ducked back inside.

This shit was going round and round in his brain with no way to stop it. He needed to clear his head. As soon as he finished this afternoon, he'd go home for a few days to try to gain some perspective.

With Sutton as her confidant, Tanna probably wouldn't notice he was gone.

Chapter Twenty-four

※

The following afternoon Kyle was sitting outside on his front deck when Fletch pulled up to his house.

Patches, Kyle and Celia's blue heeler, greeted him with a happy yip. He crouched and ruffled the dog's silky ears. "Heya. You're a good boy. Bit of an attention whore."

"Celia spoils him rotten. But he's a great cattle dog, so I can't complain."

Fletch looked at Kyle. "Where is the brat?"

"Napping. She's still tryin' to do everything, lugging a baby in her belly. Then she's so tired she falls asleep right after supper."

"I never pegged Celia as the type who'd nap during the day."

"Oh, she ain't." Kyle smirked. "But I got my ways of coaxing her into bed. And yes. Them are doctor's orders."

Fletch laughed. He pointed to Kyle's beer. "Got an extra one of those?"

"Sure." Kyle disappeared inside and returned with two bottles. "You wanna sit on the porch?"

"I'd rather walk down by the barn."

Neither spoke until they rested over the fence separating the yard from the horse pasture.

"Not that I'm not happy to see you, Fletch, but I'll admit you got me a little worried, calling out of the blue in the afternoon, asking if I was busy."

"Yeah, this bein' on vacation shit is weird for me too."

"What's goin' on?"

No reason to beat around the bush. Fletch sipped his beer. "Tanna."

"What about her?"

"Well, we're … you know …" Fletch felt Kyle looking at him but couldn't meet his gaze.

"Not to be a dick, but no, I don't know the particulars. What's goin' on between you two? If Tanna's been talkin' to Celia, Celia hasn't been talkin' to me about it."

"Tanna and I are … fuck buddies is a crude way to put it, but that's pretty much all we are." Or so he'd come to believe in the past day.

"You don't sound too happy about that."

"I'm not." Fletch knocked back another swallow of beer. "I've got it bad for her, Kyle. Bad like I've never had it for a woman before and I don't know what the hell to do."

"Have you told her?"

"Nope. She don't wanna hear it. She's all about Muddy Gap bein' a temporary pit stop in her life. She's been clear about that from the start."

"Again, not to be a dick, but that's how you prefer to run your affairs."

Fletch snorted. "Affairs. So you're telling me what goes around comes around and I deserve this?"

Kyle shook his head. "Just making an observation. I'm also wondering why you came to me. Because my wife and Tanna are good friends?"

"No. Tanna's goin' through some stuff and I don't know how to help her deal with it. I offer to talk, but she changes the subject. Then I found out she *can* talk to that smarmy douche bag Sutton Grant, because evidently he understands."

"You jealous?"

"Hell, yes, I'm jealous. But mostly I'm frustrated." He sighed. "I know she's hurting on a much deeper level than she'll let me see. So again, it makes it seem like what we have is only on the surface, but I know better. I just don't know how to get through to her that she can trust me."

"You never got seriously injured during the years you played football, did you?"

"I missed a few games here and there. But something that affected a whole season? No. That's part of the reason I didn't audition for a pro team.

Playing with the big boys pretty much guaranteed that streak would come to an end. Why?"

"It wasn't your life anyway. You loved the sport, but you knew it wouldn't be your career," Kyle pointed out. "Football never defined you."

"No."

Kyle drank his beer and remained quiet for a few moments. "So you don't know what it's like to have the one thing that defines you taken away—not by choice."

"You've been there. Dealing with recovery time after an almost career-ending injury. What was it like? The year you took off from bull riding?"

"One of the worst years of my life."

Fletch's stomach sank to his toes.

"I had to live with my mom and her loser boyfriend. I couldn't work. I had to live off my mom's charity. My friends were busy with their lives and Cheyenne seemed a world away from Rawlins. During rehab, I wasn't sure if I'd ever get on the back of a bull again. I had a bitter taste of mortality and I didn't like it. I had nothin'. I felt like nothin'. Sitting on my mom's couch, day after day, wondering what the hell I was gonna do with myself if I ever did find my balls and get on a bull again."

"Christ, Kyle. I had no fucking idea."

He shrugged. "No one did. I had a lot of pride. Even now when my life is better than I ever hoped, I carry shame about that dark period in my life. And no, I haven't talked to Celia about it. Would she understand? It doesn't even matter because I don't ever wanna be 'less than' in her eyes. It was hard enough bein' 'less than' in my own."

This wasn't what Fletch wanted to hear.

But isn't it what you expected?

"In Tanna's case, not only did she have to deal with an injury and the loss of her horse, right before that she lost her way of life. Tanna has always defined herself as a Texas ranch girl. Now she's not that. Now she's not a barrel racer either."

Fletch chugged his beer.

"I don't know Sutton, but I remember the buzz the year he got injured.

Everyone considered him done for. Some of them bulldoggers can bounce back from surgery and in three to six months they're back in the game. With all the problems Sutton had with that wreck ... like I said, I probably would've walked away. He didn't. He came back stronger than ever. So he has a different perspective."

"Couldn't Tanna have come and talked to you?"

"Tanna is Celia's friend first, and Celia has already told her to suck it up, get back on the damn horse and do what she was born to do—race around barrels." Kyle sighed. "Love my wife, but if I was Tanna, I wouldn't wanna talk to either of us."

"So I'm screwed. Tanna won't take my support, because I don't understand what she's goin' through. But she's fine playing grab ass with me as a diversion until she moves on."

"I think you've hit it right on the head—sorry to say."

"And if I break it off with her because I want more from her emotionally, she'll take it as a sign I don't care enough about her to stick around and try to crack that tough shell."

"Yep."

"Fuck."

Kyle clapped him on the back. "I know *hang in there* ain't the advice you were hopin' for, but it's all I've got."

"Thanks, Kyle. I appreciate it."

They wandered back to the house, exchanging random small talk. After Fletch promised to keep in touch, he climbed in his truck, needing time alone to process everything.

But he had a stop to make first.

✆

As Fletch walked into the barn at Eli's place, he decided there was no reason for niceties. He'd known Sutton for a few years, if only in passing.

So where was Mr. World Champion Bulldogger?

He saw Sutton in the far stall brushing his horse. Of course it was a damn nice piece of horseflesh.

Sutton turned and smiled. "Hey, Doc." Then he wandered over and rested his forearms on the top of the stall. "If you're looking for Eli, he had to run an errand."

"I'm not looking for him. I'm looking for you actually."

Every bit of friendliness evaporated from Sutton's eyes.

"And I can see by the way you're giving me the stink-eye you know exactly why I'm here."

"Yeah, I do. But I wanna hear you say it anyway."

Fletch leaned closer. "Keep your fucking hands off Tanna."

"You know you wouldn't have the balls to say that if Tanna was within earshot because she'd kick 'em into your throat for treating her like a piece of property."

"Maybe I would say it. Because make no mistake, boy, she *is* with me."

"You sure?" he taunted.

"Shut up, right now, or—"

"Or what? You gonna beat the fuck outta me?" Sutton snapped his finger in front of Fletch's face. "Get in line."

Lightning fast, Fletch crushed Sutton's hand in his big fist. "Don't. Ever. Fucking. Snap. At. Me."

"Jesus. All right. Let go of my hand."

Fletch released him. The fear in this son of a bitch's face was worth the momentary lapse in control.

"You are one scary motherfucker." Sutton squeezed his hand open and closed. "Why don't you ever show people that 'me hulk' side of you?"

"I'm the cool-headed professional, remember?"

"But if you could beat the fuck outta someone, you would, wouldn't you?"

"Yep." Fletch flashed his teeth in a non-smile. "And you would be first on the goddamned list."

"I'd tussle with you. It's a little-known fact that cowboys like to fight," he said with a straight face. "You might have size on me, but I've got youth on my side."

The gall of this kid.

"But I'll speak my piece to you. And to her. Because I won't become another guy in her life who enables her."

What the fuck was Sutton talking about? "Enables her to what?"

"Hide behind her fear. Eli does it. You're doin' it. The three-time world champion barrel racer is slinging drinks and selling clothes in a little-known burg in Wyoming. She needs to be in an arena, running barrels. That's what she's meant to do."

"You think I don't know that?"

"No, sir, I don't."

"That's because you don't know me," Fletch snapped. "I realize Eli won't push her. But I *am* the man who will give her back that part of herself that's been missing. I've already laid the groundwork. So I sure as hell don't appreciate you riding in here and fucking it up."

"It's already fucked up. And that's what pisses you off. That I give her something you don't. That you can't no matter how much groundwork you lay."

"Which is what? And you'd better take care with your answer."

"Understanding. I've been *exactly* where she is, so she trusts that I know what I'm talking about. I can help her in ways you can't. You may have her in your bed, but you weren't the first person she called after her brother gave her the smackdown that left her raw. I was. What do you think that means?"

That I was an idiot for running away like a scalded cat after overhearing your conversation. I should've confronted her, made her talk to me, even if I'd had to drag her away kicking and screaming. Even if I'd had to hog-tie her to a damn chair to get her to open up to me.

"It means that we both want the same thing—Tanna to conquer her fear. But I can't help but suspect that *your* reasons for wanting Tanna to saddle up again aren't as altruistic as you're pretending."

"You're reaching."

"Am I? If Tanna gets back into competition, then she'd be on the road, drifting from rodeo to rodeo, which is... *wow*, exactly the same lifestyle you'll be living and on the same circuit you'll be competing on. Coincidence, bulldogger?"

Sutton's fake jocularity vanished. "So you think by keeping her in Muddy Gap that you'll somehow have her? Do you really want to be her second choice?"

Fletch drew back as if Sutton had taken a swing at him.

"Hit a little too close to home, did I, Doc?" Sutton sighed and scrubbed his hands over his face. "Look. I don't have a horse in this race—pardon the pun. Tanna may talk to me, but she listens to you."

He had no response for that.

"So my advice is quit looking at me like I'm the problem," Sutton said.

He turned and walked away, leaving Fletch just as frustrated and adrift as when he'd gotten up this morning.

Chapter Twenty-five

⚜

*L*ate evening the next day, Tanna watched Harlow saunter into the lounge at closing time. She oozed sex appeal just walking across the room, even when there wasn't a man in sight for her to impress. Hadn't taken Tanna long to realize Harlow wasn't putting on a sex kitten act. With her white-blond hair, abundance of curves, big blue eyes, full mouth and breathless way of speaking, Harlow Pratt was an old-fashioned pinup girl in the flesh. And Tanna liked her more than she'd admit—especially not to Harlow.

"Hey, harlot, what brings you by?"

"That is *not* a nice nickname."

"Meant in good fun, I promise."

Harlow looked around the empty bar. "Bunch of early birds roosting at the Split Rock this week."

"Not that I'm complaining. Because next week it could be completely different."

"Since you're off early, you have big plans tonight?"

Tanna wiped down the counter and rinsed the rag before she replied. "Nope. Do you?"

"I was hoping for another bonfire but no one seems to be around to-night. Which is weird because Tobin is always around. Speaking of Tobin . . . I saw you down by the corrals the day before yesterday talking to Sutton and Tobin."

"Really? I didn't see you."

"I got sidetracked looking for Renner." She set her elbows on the bar. "What's going on with you and Sutton?"

"Why would you ask me that?"

"Why would you answer a question with a question?"

Smart-ass. "Nothin' is goin' on. Sutton and I are friends. Why?"

"'Cause it looked a whole lot different than 'just friends' from where I was standing."

"And where was that?"

"Just inside the barn. The one with the big door? It was open. A bunch of us were standing there."

"I'm confused on why you're bringing this up, Harlow."

"Because I think you're making a big mistake throwing Fletch over for Sutton."

Tanna's jaw nearly hit the bar. "Sweet Lord, girl, have you lost your ever-lovin' mind? What in the hell are you talking about?"

"While I was in the barn, I watched Fletch across the way in the other building, watching you. It about broke my heart. He saw you in that intense conversation with Sutton. He looked so . . . sad."

That caused a sudden pang. Sadness was such a rarity with happy-go-lucky Fletch. And to think she'd had any part in causing it, even accidentally? That hurt ten times worse. "I think you misread him. Fletch knows I'm friends with Sutton."

"I think *you've* misread Fletch if you don't think he's bothered by your friendship"—she made air quotes—"with Sutton. Because what I saw? And what everyone else around the corrals saw? Sure didn't look like friendship."

She stared at Harlow, too dumbfounded to speak.

"I know you think I don't know what I'm talking about because I'm considered a cocktease. But part of the reason I'm so good at knowing how far to take the tease is because I know men. I'm all-pro at reading male body language and you might as well have kicked Fletch in the balls. Your actions hurt him that bad, Tanna."

"Then why in the fuck didn't he say something to me?" she demanded.

"Because he's too old to play games. I'll bet you haven't heard from him."

She hadn't. Not for two days. She'd wondered why but she didn't want to seem like one of those pushy, needy, clingy girlfriends that insisted on spending every day with her lover.

Then it hit her and her stomach bottomed out. He'd probably heard the entire conversation between her and Sutton. The fact she'd bared her soul—her fears to Sutton, rather than to him, would slice him a lot deeper than what might've looked like harmless flirting.

"Fletch is the type that'll just quietly stop coming around and vanish from your life." Harlow's eyes searched hers. "Maybe you're used to playing musical cowboys on the road and you don't know any other way to act. It's your prerogative to flirt with any guy who crosses your path. Just as it's Fletch's choice to walk away. I don't blame him. He deserves better than how you've treated him."

Tanna's eyes narrowed. "Is this where you tell me that *you* can treat him a lot better?"

Harlow emitted a sultry laugh. "See that spark of jealousy? That means you're *not* okay with me getting up close and personal with the sexy vet. Why on earth would you think he'd be any different? Especially seeing you holding hands and whispering with Sutton the sexy bulldogger?"

"So if you're not after Fletch . . . is this little heart-to-heart because you want a shot at Sutton?"

She laughed again. "Just between us? I could have Sutton if I wanted him. There's no challenge in that. The challenge is to land the guy who wants you so bad and yet, he acts completely oblivious to you. Maybe even a little rude. That's when things get interesting." Harlow slid off the bar-stool. "With no chance of a bonfire I'm off for a long soak in the tub and a bottle of wine."

Tanna thought of nothing else on the walk back to her trailer. All the lights were off at Fletch's place and his truck was gone. She checked her cell phone.

Fletch hadn't responded to her voice mails.

Just to test Harlow's theory, she sent Fletch an *I missed you today* text.

Thirty-five minutes passed. He didn't call.

He always called, because he refused to text.

Enough. Time to find out what's going on.

Tanna drove into Rawlins. Her GPS seemed to take her on a merry chase, but she never would've found the place without it. She wasn't sure what she'd expected from Fletch's house, but she was pretty dumbfounded when it came into view.

The A-frame was nestled between two hills at the end of a primitive gravel road. The siding was wood. She noticed the back end extended beyond the glass-fronted window and spread out like two wings, giving it a birdlike appearance. A circular driveway curved around a small bunch of bushes.

The light in the front window was on. Fletch's pickup sat in the drive rather than the garage. She forced herself to scale the wide steps leading to the front door. Tanna poked the doorbell and the sound pealed through the house. Seemed a lifetime passed before the door opened.

Fletch looked surprised to see her. "Tanna. What are you doin' here?"

"Looking for you. You haven't been at the Split Rock and you haven't responded to my texts or phone calls, so I got worried and thought I'd check on you." He didn't look like he'd been sick. He wore his lounging clothes—baggy black athletic shorts and a sleeveless T-shirt that molded to his upper body. But he didn't seem particularly happy to see her either.

"So, now that I know you're all right, I'll go." She whirled around.

The door squeaked and two enormous hands curled over her biceps, preventing her escape. Then his arms, those big strong arms, slid around her and his mouth teased her ear. "Stay."

"You don't have to say that if you don't want me here."

"I want you here. I just wasn't expecting you. It threw me off." He nuzzled her ear. "Come in. Please."

"Okay."

Fletch picked her up as if she weighed nothing and carried her inside.

As soon as he set her down, she snaked her arms around his waist and set her head on his chest. Listening to the strong and steady thumping of his heart. Breathing him in—the scent of clean cotton and his spicy musk. The scent she'd missed.

Fletch silently stroked her hair.

"I'm sorry."

"For?"

"For bein' the way I am."

"Sugar twang, I like the way you are. So what's all this really about?"

Tanna tipped her head back. Tempting to dodge the issue and seduce him. He wouldn't say no. But she forced herself to address this head-on. "You know there's nothin' goin' on between me and Sutton Grant, don't you?"

"I'd wondered."

"Why?"

"A couple of things pointed that direction."

"Like what?"

His gaze hardened and his hands tightened on her head. "Why did you leave my bed the other morning?"

He *had* noticed. So she tossed off a breezy, "I woke up early and couldn't get back to sleep. I didn't think you needed to suffer for my restlessness, so I left."

Fletch's hands fell away. She knew he wasn't buying her fib. "Thoughtful of you."

She smiled. "I try."

"So you didn't suspect your bloodcurdling scream before you scrambled out of my bed might've woken me up?"

"What?"

"Don't do that, Tanna."

"Do what?"

"Lie to me. Since you drove over here, and you're so concerned for me, at least give me the goddamned courtesy of being honest with me." He spun on his heel. Paced down the hallway and came back. "I know you're not fucking around with Sutton Grant. But there's part of me that wishes you were."

Her mouth dropped open. "Why would you even say that to me?"

"Because then maybe I'd understand why you're turning to him instead of me. I get your physical affection, but when it comes to any emotional issues, you cut me off. You ran screaming from my bed, Tanna. And the person who gets the explanation for that is ... Sutton? Not me?" Fletch inhaled a slow breath. "Did you really think I wouldn't want to know? I'm just the fun sex guy, right?"

"No! You're so much more than that."

"Prove it. Tell me about the nightmare, because you glossed over it when Sutton asked you about it."

So Fletch had overheard their conversation. Tanna wrapped her arms around herself and backed away. "It's about my mother and Jezebel. I'm in the middle of my run and we skid around the second barrel, just like that night. But instead of crashing like we did, Jezebel gets up and I'm tangled in the stirrups, bein' dragged beneath her. She's bleeding. Broken bones are sticking through her skin. Somehow I know she only has one eye and we're headed toward the gate at breakneck speed. I can't stop her. She's killing herself to finish the run. She's killing me to finish it too. I'm yelling at her to stop. When I look ahead, I see my mother standing in the middle of the open gate. I'm shouting at her to move but she stays right there. Smiling that proud smile ... and when Jezebel hits her at full steam, I hear my mom's scream, Jezebel's scream and lastly mine. Then I wake up. I can't reassure myself it was only a bad dream. The reality is my mom is dead, my horse is dead and I'm wandering around lost."

Fletch enfolded her in his arms, holding her tightly so she couldn't squirm away. He didn't push her to talk or offer platitudes.

Part of her would've preferred that reaction from him. This silent comfort was unnerving mostly because he understood that's exactly what she needed.

He pulled back and wiped the tears from her eyes. "Maybe I haven't said it enough, but I'm sorry for all you've gone through."

"Can you see why some days I just wanna pull the covers over my head and hope I dreamt the last two years?"

"Then we never would've met."

She twined her arms around his neck. "But that might've been for the best. I'm a train wreck, Fletch. Why did you even answer the door tonight?"

"Because I don't think you're a train wreck. You're a hot mess some days, but you've not derailed completely." Fletch traced the outline of her face with the blunt edge of his thumb.

Tanna felt that pull of sexual need from the tips of her fingers to the ends of her toes—just that one, simple gesture filled her with want. But she'd used sex as a distraction with him far too many times and it was time she pointed out he did the same thing. "You need to really think about that statement when I'm not pressed tight against your hard cock. When you're not feeling all soft and sweet and sorry for me." She placed her finger over his lips when he started to argue. "You know I'm right. I'd understand if you've changed your mind about getting mixed up, even temporarily, with someone like me."

"I ain't gonna change my mind about anything, sugar twang. But I won't be compartmentalized anymore either. I don't have a problem with you bein' friends with Sutton. But I do have a problem with you telling him stuff you oughta be telling *me*. You'd better be as comfortable talking to me as you are fucking me. We clear on that?"

Well, then. No misunderstanding those terms. "Uh. Yeah. I...can we be done talking about this right now?"

Those fierce golden-brown eyes narrowed. "Why?"

"Because I really want you to show me this fancy house of yours, Doc."

Fletch smiled. "That, I can do. Come on." He held her hand as he led her into the interior. Light streamed through the windows, falling across hardwood floors the color of warm honey. The entire space was open. Oversized leather furniture was arranged in front of a rock fireplace. The kitchen wasn't enormous but it utilized the space well. It boasted an island with a cooktop surrounded on the front side by a breakfast bar.

"Great kitchen," she commented. "Do you use it a lot?"

He shrugged. "I'm usually not here enough to do much cooking. My dad comes over and putters around."

Tanna admired the artwork adorning the walls. Native American themed, it ran the gamut from scenes painted on leather animal skins, to different types of old weapons, to drawings seemingly painted by children.

She came to a dead stop upon seeing the six-foot-tall metal sculpture. Without searching for the artist's signature, she knew this work was the creation of the same guy who'd done the art at the Split Rock.

The piece was a mishmash of metal parts: chains, plates, pieces of pipe, horseshoes, silverware, doorknobs, mysterious chunks of junk she couldn't name. But somehow, it all blended together to create a tipi. Even the parts that were supposed to resemble billows of fabric or animal skin stretched around the base were forged from sheets of metal. It was one of the most remarkable sculptures she'd ever seen.

She ran her finger over the tipi poles sticking out the top, crafted out of thick, rusty sections of rebar. "This piece absolutely blows my mind."

"Braxton really knocked it out of the park with this one." Fletch chuckled. "I commissioned it when Braxton was an unknown artist and needed cash. He keeps trying to buy it back from me to display at an art gallery, but I keep refusing. It's really the first cool thing I bought for myself that spoke of my race."

"I don't blame you for keeping it private." Tanna glanced at the opposite wall. It held an elaborate family crest, done up like a family tree with branches going every which way. Encased behind glass because it appeared to be hand painted. She cocked an eyebrow at him. "And this?"

"My dad's family is Scottish. He knew I'd taken an interest in my Indian heritage so he wanted to be sure I had that part of me too."

"Sweet."

"You want me to continue the tour?"

"Lead on, MacDuff."

Fletch groaned.

"At least I didn't whoop out an Indian war cry."

He groaned again. "You really have no filter, do you?"

Tanna froze. "Does that bother you?"

He smiled and leaned down to brush his mouth across her wrinkled brow. "Nope. It's one of my favorite things about you."

The wide hallway opened into a great room. "It's too dark to see the back, but there's a meadow, and trees with a small stream."

"You've got water?"

"Yeah. Why?"

"Celia indicated water was a hard commodity to come by here in the high plains desert."

"It is. Probably why I paid a pretty penny for this piece of land. Although, the guy did drop the price when I pointed out it wasn't like I could run livestock beyond a horse or two."

Now that he mentioned it...she hadn't seen any dogs or cats. "Don't you have animals?"

He shook his head. "My practice leaves me no time. If there's one thing I've learned, animals needed tending. Wouldn't be fair to leave a dog alone for sixteen hours and I can't take one with me."

"True." She spun a slow circle in the room. "So. No TV in here, huh?"

"With this view? Nope. That's why it's in the den by the fireplace."

"Oh. I didn't notice." No doubt this was a single man's pad. Big, comfy furniture. Sturdy coffee table overrun by stacks of magazines. "So, is that some of the reading material you needed to catch up on?"

"That's not even half."

Fletch tugged her to a closed door on the right side and it opened into his bedroom.

The gigantic bed was the showpiece in the room. Larger than a king size and at least a foot taller than the biggest four-poster she'd seen. The comforter was tan, the pillows were navy and a star quilt was draped at the foot of the bed.

She touched the tip of one vibrant red star. "That's really pretty."

"One thing my mother didn't manage to hock," he said dryly.

As much as Tanna wanted a more thorough look at his bedroom, she switched to a neutral topic. "How many bedrooms does this house have?"

"Three. We used an A-frame for the forward portion of the house and there's a bedroom up in the loft area. I bump my head on the ceiling, so we needed to expand. Holt built the master suite on one side. On the opposite side is another room I use as a home office and then there's a workout room." He opened a door. "The bathroom's in here."

Tanna stepped into the glass- and black-tiled bathroom and envy burst through her. This reminded her of the bathroom at the ranch. Three showerheads had been placed at different heights and the opaque glass door could slide back for an open shower, or closed for a more intimate one. The vanity had two hammered copper sinks and the countertop height would graze the bottom of her rib cage. But it obviously was the right height for Fletch. The toilet was in an enclosed area with a pocket door. The entire top half of the wall opposite the mirror and vanity was windows. "Doesn't it get cold in here in the winter with all these windows?"

"Not really. The glass is thermo-pane so it keeps the hot air in."

They crossed the expanse of the bedroom back to the hallway and kept walking to another door.

The office was half the size of the great room. One whole wall was floor to ceiling bookshelves, filled with books. "Holy cow. Have you read all those?"

"Most. I have an extensive library of research books. Although I deal primarily with large animals, stuff comes up that I've never dealt with before so I need a frame of reference. And I like to have it at my fingertips."

This office had everything. Plush carpet. Shades that could block out the sun completely. A flat-screen TV was suspended on the wall. A big computer monitor sat on the center of the desk. A fax machine, a scanner, two printers were stacked alongside the keyboard. She glanced at him. "Do you work from home very much?"

"Mostly on the weekends. Some clients have video cameras and can upload live video links to their animals, which is handy because sometimes I can diagnose over the Internet in real time. That ability has saved me several trips." He sighed. "I should work from here more often since this is actually a lot nicer than my office space in Rawlins."

She frowned. So why wouldn't he want all this information at his fingertips when he was doing research? Why would he leave it all behind on sabbatical and shack up in a crappy trailer?

Because you're there.

That awareness froze her in place. Fletch knew she wouldn't make the drive to Rawlins during his vacation time, so he came to her, because he'd made no bones about wanting her.

Seeing all he was giving up? Just for a chance to be with her, even temporarily? Talk about humbling.

She smiled at him brightly to hide her self-consciousness.

His eyes narrowed with suspicion. "What?"

"How long have you lived in this gorgeous place?"

"Four years. Holt worked on the design for six months after I bought the land. We were both happy with how it turned out."

"You should be." Tanna reached up to sift her fingers through his hair. So thick and long. She loved the way it trailed along over her skin as he kissed down her torso. She dug her nails into the back of his neck and yanked his mouth to hers for a hot, wet kiss.

They eased back simultaneously from the kiss that'd left them both breathless.

Then Fletch's hands were cupping her face, angling her head to peer into her eyes. "Have you eaten?"

"No."

"Will you let me feed you?"

Did he mean literally?

His eyes were dark with an odd male possession, as if he'd prefer she turn herself over to his care, but he wouldn't demand it.

"Yes."

"I want you to stay with me tonight."

"I'd like that," she admitted softly.

"Good." Fletch placed the warmest, sweetest kiss on her lips. "Come to the kitchen." Clasping her hand, he led her through an arched doorway. Then he plucked her up and set her on the counter. "Don't move. I'll bring the food to you."

Tanna watched as he sliced peppered salami and a hard white cheese swirled with yellow. He cut heavily grained bread into rectangles and halved cherry tomatoes. He added green olives and tiny sweet pickles. He squirted mustard, mayonnaise and pesto on a plate, spreading the colors out in an artist's palette. He cracked open a dark bottle and held it to her lips.

"It's hard cider. It'll go well with the light bites."

She sipped and the bubbles burst on her tongue. It tasted like fizzy citrus beer. "Mmm."

Fletch knocked back a mouthful. Then he inserted himself between her legs and tugged her forward until their pelvises were aligned. When Tanna moved her palms to his hips, he shook his head and brought her hands up. "I touch you." He kissed her knuckles. "I feed you." He kissed her other hand. "You just sit there and let me see to you."

The indignation she expected never came.

He began to feed her. A piece of bread dipped in pesto. An olive and a piece of cheese. A sip of cider. While he fed her, he touched her. First, a brush of his fingers down her neck. Next he dragged the backs of his knuckles across her collarbone. Smoothing her hair away from her face. Following her jawline while she chewed. Trailing his fingertips up and down her arms. Sweeping his thumb across the crease in her elbow.

Her heart raced. The excitement from his unwavering attention made her pulse pound and she felt it everywhere. On her lips. In her throat. Between her thighs.

The gentle nuzzles, the stolen kisses, the way his breath fanned across her damp skin or teased her ear—every inch of her skin was highly sensitized, eager for his touch.

And Fletch kept nurturing her body and soul. A bite of sweet pickle. A chunk of meat dipped in mayo. A tangy piece of tomato. Interspersing kisses and licks and soft smooches.

Tanna was absolutely drunk on him.

When the plate was empty, he nuzzled the crook of her neck. "Still hungry? I can cut up more."

"I'm good. Thanks."

"Time for dessert."

"Fletch, I'm—"

"Just a couple of bites." He ran his tongue over the shell of her ear. "Sweet bites."

"You can fill me up with sugar bites like this anytime."

"Sugar bites?" he repeated against her neck.

245 TURN AND BURN

The warmth of his breath tickled more than just her damp skin. "That's what we Texans call these sweet little nipping kisses. Sugar bites."

"I guess that fits, 'cause, sugar, I could just eat you up. Bite"—he fastened his teeth to her earlobe and tugged—"by bite."

Yes, please. "Hang on a second. I'm thirsty."

"Let me." He lifted the bottle and offered her another drink. Excess cider spilled out the corners of her mouth and dribbled down her neck. She raised her hand to swipe it away, but he stayed the movement and murmured, "I'll get that."

The sensation of his warm tongue delicately lapping at her skin sent gooseflesh rippling from head to toe.

"Be right back with something sweeter than you."

Tanna closed her eyes and listened to him rummaging in the fridge. What would he feed her? Chocolate syrup? Whipped cream? Ice cream?

She heard him approaching and then Fletch's hips pressed against the inside of her thighs. A hand fisted her hair, tilting her head back and he thoroughly plundered her mouth in a hot, wet kiss that electrified every nerve ending in her body. She whimpered. Arched against him. But he didn't bring her closer. He eased back, his lips a whisper away.

"Look at me."

She slowly lifted her lids. The beautiful man remained inches away, gazing into her eyes.

"Open your mouth."

Her lips automatically parted. His fingers slid between her teeth and he dropped something on her tongue. She pressed the object against her hard palate. The taste of blueberry spread across her tongue. She swallowed and smiled.

"You like?"

"Mmm-hmm."

Fletch held another berry to her lips.

But she caught his fingertips between her teeth, swirling her tongue around the tips before sucking the fruit free.

The heat that flashed in Fletch's eyes sent a surge of warmth through her.

"Another."

Tanna parted her lips, expecting a repeat, but he rimmed the inside of her lip with a fat raspberry, moving it so slowly she felt every seedy contour on the smooth inner flesh of her mouth. He repeated the process on her upper lip, his eyes avidly following the arc of the wet, berry-stained flesh. When he finished, she poked her tongue out and he placed the soft berry on the tip. She brought it into her mouth and sucked, feeling the fruit break apart.

The next raspberry he fed her was coated in sugar. He pressed it against her lips, releasing the juice and turning the sugar granules sticky. He licked and sucked her mouth with such eroticism, she nearly forgot to breathe.

"Tanna," he whispered sexily against the corner of her mouth. "Give yourself to me tonight. Let me take care of all your needs. You don't have to think, just feel." He started kissing straight down her throat as his fingers twisted in her hair.

"Why? I should be—"

His mouth consumed hers until she forgot what she'd been about to say. "Indulge me."

Indulge? In that raspy tone it sounded more like a command.

But she didn't care. She wanted this commanding, yet sensual and nurturing side of Fletch. She liked how he took care of her. No man before had ever bothered so she truly didn't know how to act when he treated her like someone special. Almost with reverence.

Tanna looked into his eyes and said, "Consider yourself indulged."

Chapter Twenty-six

❧

*A*fter a week and a half of sun, the day dawned overcast. Not cold. Or muggy. Clouds covered the wide-open sky—unusual for summer in Wyoming.

Tanna slipped on boots, jeans and a tank top beneath her long-sleeved shirt. She wasn't sure what Fletch had planned for them today, so she grabbed a light jacket from her trailer before she walked back to his.

Fletch was on the deck, talking on the phone. He grinned at her and returned to his conversation.

"I understand. No. That's always worked in the past so I haven't needed to explore other options." He laughed. "Not a miracle worker by a long stretch. Just fire me an e-mail with whatever treatment you decide on. Sure. Tell her you couldn't get in touch with me. No. She'll insist on talking to me and I'm supposed to be off the grid. Mention her daddy. That always gets her back up. No problem. Thanks for the heads-up. See ya." He hung up.

"Problems?"

"One of my clients is being a pain to my colleague who's handling my practice during my sabbatical."

"I thought they weren't supposed to be calling you."

"Emergency only." Fletch pocketed his phone. "But she figures she's a special exception. I assured my colleague she's not. Anyway, it's done with so let's get started on our day."

"Where we goin'?"

"Around," was his vague reply. He took her hand, leading her to the parking area.

"Are you gonna feed me?" In the last week the man had demonstrated a thing for making sure she ate. With his forced PT and concern for her diet, it was like she had a personal trainer and a nutritionist.

"There are muffins and drinks in the truck. That oughta hold you for a little while."

"Are we goin' on a picnic?"

"Nope." Then Fletch tugged her against his body and laid a fiery kiss on her.

When she managed to break the lip-lock, she murmured, "And we're not spending the whole day in bed doin' that...why?"

He chuckled. "Oh, we'll have plenty of time for that after."

"After what?"

Fletch just grinned and boosted her into the passenger side.

They didn't talk much on the drive. She studied the scenery whizzing past. Fletch turned onto a dirt road. After a few miles, he hung a right onto another road that disappeared between a grove of trees. The quaintest ranch came into view. The house had been painted white, the shutters red. A white metal fence stretched from the edge of the red barn and down the pasture. The cattle in the field were Charolais, a breed as rarely seen as longhorns around these parts.

Fletch parked and cut the engine.

Tanna looked to the front of the house, expecting someone to greet them, but the red door remained closed. Odder yet was when Fletch helped her down and towed her to a picnic table beneath a weeping willow. "I'll admit you've got me stumped. Where are we?"

He sat next to her on the whitewashed bench. "This place belongs to my dad's good friends Wally and June Gansett. They're in Jackson Hole. But I have permission to be here." He slowly turned his body, giving himself a panoramic view. "I love this place. It's so peaceful."

"It certainly doesn't look like anything I've seen in Wyoming." Tanna's gaze met his. "So why are we here?"

Fletch straddled the bench, mimicking her position, and took her hands. "I wanted to bring you to neutral ground so we could talk."

An uneasy feeling arose. "What's on your mind?"

"You." He squeezed her hands. "Always."

"That's a little vague."

When Fletch's gaze locked to hers, her uneasiness grew. "Have you saddled a horse since we did the grooming demonstration at Eli's?"

She didn't like where this conversation was headed. "I've conditioned saddles. Does that count?"

Fletch didn't chastise; he just waited for her honest response to his question.

"No, I haven't saddled a horse. But I've groomed them and fed them and that should count for something."

"It does…for anyone else but you. You are a horsewoman to the core, Tanna. I've brought you out here to face that loss of yourself."

Tanna's heart raced and that panicked feeling made every muscle in her body grow tense. If it were anyone else but Fletch she would've stomped off. But the firm way he held her hands and the gentle determination in his eyes kept her in place. "How?" slipped out of her lips.

Fletch kissed her knuckles. "We're goin' horseback riding today."

Her stomach lurched and she tried to jerk her hands from his.

But he held tightly. "Just you and me."

"No," she whispered.

"Yes. On one horse."

"Riding double? I haven't done that since…" She'd first learned to ride. With her Uncle Manuel. She'd been young, but she still remembered his patience. His complete confidence in her abilities. Tears pricked her eyes. She couldn't be certain if her response was from remembrance or fear.

"Hey." Fletch got right in her face. "Don't hide from me, Tanna. I want to help you and in order to do that I need to know everything you're feeling."

Spots wavered in front of her eyes. Somehow she made her mouth work. "Well, I'm scared."

"Okay. Excited?"

She shook her head.

"Angry?"

"Yes."

"At me? Or yourself?"

"Both. I'm mad at myself because it shouldn't be this fucking hard. I'm mad at you because...I don't know why. I just am."

Fletch reached up and wiped her face. "Please, don't cry."

She hadn't realized the tears she'd tried to hold back had escaped.

"Let me be what you need. If only for today."

"And if I lose my shit? What then, Fletch?"

His eyes searched hers. "Are you worried I'll run after seeing you that way?"

She nodded.

"I won't. I promise." He brushed his mouth over hers. "Nothin' will make me run from you, Tanna. Nothin'. You can punch me, slap me, scream at me. You're a little bitty thing. I'm a big guy. I can take whatever you dish out."

"You sure?" Tanna eased back and held her hands out so he could see how badly she was shaking. "I'm this way just at the thought of getting on a horse."

Fletch threaded his fingers through hers. "See? If you have me to hold on to the shaking isn't as bad."

More tears fell. The man was so damn sweet and wonderful and perfect. He deserved a woman who wasn't broken inside.

"C'mere." He lifted her onto his lap. His strong arms wrapped around her and he set his chin on top of her head.

She hid her face in the crook of his neck. Trying to slow down the mad pounding of her heart. Trying to breathe normally. The scent of his skin, being surrounded by him, supported by him, eased the fear somewhat. But not entirely.

He shifted her body so he could look into her eyes. "You can do this."

In that moment Tanna understood why she trusted Fletch implicitly. His praise and kindness, all wrapped up in warm assurance gave her self-confidence a much-needed kick in the ass.

"Okay." She disentangled from him and stood. Or tried to stand but her legs gave out.

"I've got you." Once again he swooped her into his arms.

His long-legged strides ate up the distance to the barn door. After pressing a lingering kiss to her forehead, he set her on her feet.

She curled her hands around the metal fence.

"The horse we're riding today is a twenty-year-old gelding. A Belgian Draft horse. He's big enough to carry both of us. He's gentle and the most even-tempered horse I've ever dealt with."

"What if I can't do it?"

"You can. You will. That's why we're here. No one else is around. It might take you a hundred tries to get on today, but I promise you *will* be on Gus before we leave."

"Fletch—"

"I brought a bandana to use as a blindfold. Your choice if I put it on you or not. Obscuring vision works for some skittish animals." Fletch ducked his head to look into her eyes. "You still with me here?"

She nodded.

"Huh-uh, sugar twang. Say the words back to me so I know you're cognizant of what's goin' on. Are you with me?"

"Yes, I'm with you."

"Good. Do you need a drink or to use the bathroom or anything before I get Gus?"

"No. I'll just ... hang on to the fence and"—*freak the fuck out*—"wait."

Fletch took a blue bandana square out of his back pocket, shook it out and rolled it from end to end before draping it around her neck. "Don't worry. It's clean." He kissed her. "Wear it or don't. Your choice. Be right back."

She let go of the fence and paced. Half tempted to "accidentally" twist her bad knee. Fletch wouldn't make her get on if she had a flare-up of her previous injury.

He'd know you did it on purpose. Do you really want to see disappointment in his eyes?

No.

Tanna scoured the area wondering where she'd need to stand to get a leg up on the horse. Since they were riding bareback, there wouldn't be a stirrup.

Each minute she waited wound her tighter. So when she heard the soft *plop plop* of horse hooves in the dirt, she nearly shot out of her skin.

Fletch led Gus out. The horse was huge with a beautiful shiny light brown coat and a pale, almost blond mane. He didn't act too spirited as he clomped closer. Fletch alternately talked to Gus and watched her. He stopped just inside the gate and tied the lead rope around a fence post. "How you doin'?"

She shrugged. Sharing all her whacked-out physical reactions wouldn't help either of them.

"You wanna come in here and get acquainted with Gus while I round up some oats?"

Tanna shook her head. "Over the fence is fine."

Fletch's face betrayed nothing. He turned and jogged back toward the barn.

Gus didn't pay much attention to her. He didn't dance around impatiently either.

She moved closer. "So, Gus, you're in for a real treat. If I'm even able to climb on you. How am I supposed to hold on with no saddle horn? Will the doc want me riding in front of him? Or behind him?"

Gus just blinked slowly.

"So I'm telling you that the last horse I rode ended up dead. Was it my fault? I don't know. Alls I know is I can't shake the guilt. And the regret."

Fletch approached Gus on the left side. Immediately Gus's head disappeared inside the tin pail. But Fletch's quizzical eyes were on her.

No way would she tell Fletch she'd confessed her transgressions to a horse.

Gus emptied the contents of the bucket in no time. He raised his head and Fletch was right there with the bridle, employing that gentle soothing tone he sometimes used with her. "Are you using the bandana?"

"No."

"I won't insult you and suggest I lead you around the corral before we ride." He raised an eyebrow. "Unless that's what you want?"

She shook her head.

"Good. I'll get on first. You'll ride behind me. Sound okay?"

The blood was rushing through her head so fast she scarcely heard him. His mouth moved but the words were unclear.

Fletch brought Gus close to the fence, climbed to the third rung and threw a leg over.

Just like that he was mounted up.

Easy, right?

And just like that, Tanna had to bend at the waist so she didn't pass out or throw up or both. When the whooshing sensation lessened, she reached out and used the fencing bars to pull herself upright. Took her a few seconds to meet Fletch's gaze.

The muscle in his jaw flexed. His lips were compressed into a thin line. She couldn't read his eyes, shadowed beneath the brim of his hat. He hadn't moved when she'd been discreetly dry-heaving and trying not to black out from fear.

He said, "Better?" after God knows how long she hung back from the fence.

Tanna swallowed twice before she could speak. "I guess."

"Come on, sugar twang. I'm right here. It's just you and me and this old horse."

"If I get on and can't stay on, you'll stop?"

"Yep."

"You promise?"

"I promise."

"No galloping."

"I'll just walk him if that's what you want."

"I do."

Fletch scooted closer to the fence and held out his hand. Tanna latched on so fiercely a lesser man would've been jerked to the ground. "I've gotcha. That's it. One more rung. Now put your hand on my shoulder. That's fine; grip it tight if you need to."

Tanna felt suspended in time as she transferred her weight against Fletch and she swung her right leg over Gus's rump. Fletch leaned forward, keeping a death grip on her hand as she slid her front down his back until her ass met horseflesh. She pressed the side of her face into Fletch's broad back, keeping her eyes closed.

Was it possible that her heart could actually beat out of her chest?

"Wrap your arms around my waist, Tanna."

"Don't go yet," she said with panic.

"I'm not. We're still right by the fence."

She focused on the scent of Fletch's shirt. The moderate breeze. The hard muscles her fingers were digging into. The firm touch of his left hand curled around her left thigh.

Breathe. Come on, Tanna. You can do this.

Sitting behind Fletch, she had no knee control of the horse; it all belonged to the forward rider. Her legs dangled like noodles and she missed the security of stirrups.

Gus shifted sideways and she gasped.

Fletch's hand squeezed her leg. "Easy. It's all right."

No, it's not.

"You tell me when."

Never.

Fletch stayed true to his word. He didn't pester her to buck up so they could get moving. He waited on her signal.

Okay. She was on the damn thing. Through gritted teeth, she said, "Go."

Then they were meandering along. At this speed she could feel every shift of the horse's back legs, which made the ride seem unstable.

"Tanna? You doin' all right?"

Don't think about sliding into that turn.

Don't think about clipping the barrel.

Don't think about Jezebel falling down on top of you.

Don't think about watching her race away.

Don't think of her shriek of pain.

Don't think of her dying alone.

Gus moved into a canter and Tanna's heart zoomed into her throat.

"Fletch? Why're we goin' faster?"

"You kicked your heels in."

She didn't remember doing that.

This pace smoothed out the ride. The instincts were still there.

So she held on. Remembering riding double with her uncle. And then with her brother. Her dad preferred ATVs to horses. In the time she'd had to reflect upon hearing about her father's hatred of the ranch, she could admit the signs had been there. After her uncle died, Garrett had handled all the livestock, while her dad spent more time on the computer. Not at the house with her mother, but in the tiny foreman's cabin her bachelor uncle had occupied her entire life.

Tanna hadn't been overly close to her dad. He didn't attend many of the events she'd entered. His excuse that driving for two hours to watch her compete for twenty seconds still stung. And since her mother didn't drive beyond going into town or her friends' houses, she'd had little in familial support for the whole of her career. But she had that support when she returned home after an event. She trained. Spent time with her mom, or her friends or whatever guy she'd been involved with. She'd only paid attention to those around her when they could do something for her or entertain her.

She'd gotten so lost in self-recriminations she'd almost forgotten she was on horseback until Fletch spoke to her.

"There's a long, flat section up ahead. I'm gonna give Gus his legs, so hold on."

Tanna wanted to tell him, *no, wait, you promised no galloping*, but Gus kicked up the pace. She opened her eyes only to close them again.

She so wanted that big *aha!* moment when everything became clear. When the wind in her hair and the years of conditioning her muscles kicked the memory of what she used to be and she felt a burst of joy. Of rightness.

But neither of those feelings came.

They slowed. Stopped. She could feel Fletch's core muscles working and the muscles in his arms tightening. Such a powerful man. Yet such a gentle giant.

He turned toward her and she lifted her head. "You okay?"

"Yeah."

"Do you want to get down and walk around?"

"How will we get back on?"

"Me Injun. Know how to mount bareback."

Tanna smiled for the first time since they'd left this morning. "Okay, chief."

"Hang on to my arm. I'll help you off first."

Just look at Fletch. Nowhere else.

"Tanna, sweetheart, give me all your weight. You're not gonna hurt me."

She swung her right leg over and slid down until both her feet were on the ground. And she was upright. Not wobbly. Not light-headed. This was good.

Fletch dismounted and immediately circled his arms around her, dipping his head for a kiss.

"Wait. Don't you need to tie Gus off?"

"Nope. He's broke to ground tie. Now gimme that mouth for the victory kiss I'm dying for."

"Victory kiss?" she repeated.

"Mmm-hmm. 'Cause this ride surely is a victory for you. Don't see it as anything less." Their lips met in a sweet, loving, comforting kiss. A kiss he was in no hurry to end. Teasing her tongue with little nips and sucks, gliding his wet lips over hers, coaxing her to relax into him fully. He eased off and completely wrapped her in his embrace, mashing her face against his chest.

"You did great. How do you feel?"

"Lucky."

"How's that?"

"Because you're a pushy bastard. You made me do it because you knew I wouldn't on my own. Maybe ever. If not for you ... anyway. Thank you." Tanna dropped her head back and peered at his handsome face. Something deeper than lust pinched her heart.

And in that moment, she knew she loved him.

"Tanna? Sweetheart, you're looking at me really funny."

She couldn't tell him. He'd attribute her reaction to the situation of his helping her face her fears. So she redirected. "How is it I forgot how unbelievably hot you look in a cowboy hat?"

He grinned. "No clue. Probably I haven't been wearing it much since I've been on sabbatical."

"Pity, that."

Gus tried to poke his head between them.

Fletch studied her very carefully for signs of panic as Gus sniffed her arm, the side of her head and her ear. When she stepped behind Fletch, Gus followed and kept pestering her. But Fletch pushed him back. "Quit sniffing my woman, old man."

Gus gave an indignant snort and meandered a few feet away.

"Are you ready to head back?"

"How far are we from the ranch?"

"Probably a mile."

"Seems like it should be a lot farther."

He cupped the side of her face. "I want you to ride in front of me on the way back."

Her pulse leapt. "Why?"

"This is a pretty piece of dirt and I bet your eyes were closed during the whole ride here."

"Fletch—"

"I'll hold the reins. You don't have to do anything but lean against me and soak in the view." His thumb feathered across her cheek. "You're ready."

Tanna couldn't help the grudging, "Okay."

"I can tell by the stubborn set to your mouth you might just keep your eyes closed to spite me."

She smiled. "Maybe. Just because I rode on the back of a horse for a mile doesn't mean I'm ready to find my seat again."

"We'll go as slow as you want. I'll have my seat on the horse first." He kissed her again, his lips so warm and sure.

Watching him mount without stirrups was a testament to his strength and agility. After his Indian comment she imagined him mounting up bare chested. In a loincloth.

"Tanna?"

Crap. Fletch had his hand out to help her up.

When Gus turned his head to see what was going on, Tanna shied away.

"Don't let him spook you. Show him who's boss."

She felt so damn ridiculous. Retreating from a twenty-year-old gelding. Keeping one eye on the horse, she reached for Fletch's hand and he hauled her straight up as easily as if she'd been on a pulley. Then his left arm snaked around her waist, pulling her back so her butt was snug against his groin and her spine was pressed against his chest. She was at a loss without the reins. "What am I supposed to do with my hands?"

"Hold on to the outside of my legs."

Tanna placed her palms on the midpoint between his knees and his hips.

His deep voice settled in her ear. "You ready?"

"I guess."

Fletch kicked his heels in and loosened the reins and Gus started to move.

Her body seemed to be as stiff as cement.

"Are your eyes open?" he murmured in her ear.

"Yes."

"Close them and lean into me."

It was a relief to slump back.

"Now drop your head to the left. Keep holding on."

When his open mouth landed on the exposed section of her neck she knew why he'd told her to hold on—that one hot kiss was as potent as an electrical charge.

"I've missed you in my bed." Fletch nuzzled the tender area below her ear. "I woke up hard."

"Have to take care of it yourself?"

"Mmm-hmm. In the shower." Whisper-soft kisses drifted up and down the side of her neck. "I used my left hand and pretended it was you jacking me off."

"Did it take long or did I drag it out?"

"Oh, you were a greedy little thing. You wanted to get me there as fast as possible. You worked me hard in your slippery fist."

Tanna was right there. Watching as Fletch jerked himself off. She could hear the *slap, slap, slap* of skin. She felt that breathless moment of anticipation when he stopped breathing and threw his head back. When long ribbons of come jetted from his cock, splatting onto the floor and swirling down the drain.

"I recognize that sexy noise."

"I'm not surprised. I make it a lot around you."

Fletch rocked his pelvis forward and Gus picked up the pace.

Tanna's eyes flew open. Gus's muscles rippled against her inner thighs. She bounced out of synch with the horse's gait. She felt herself starting to slide to the right just like her accident and jerked herself to the left.

Fletch's arm squeezed her lower torso. "Tanna. I've got you. You won't fall. I promise."

"But what if—"

"You won't. Get them thoughts right outta your head." He kissed her temple. "Now where were we? Wrap your arm around the back of my neck. You can even dig your nails in because you know how fucking much I like that."

She maneuvered her right arm back and held on; the pose felt decidedly wanton. Not at all like her usual seat atop a horse.

"Know what I'm thinking about? How badly I want my hands on you. My mouth on you," he murmured. "I'd start on your tits as I'm kissing you. I'd rub my palms over your nipples, until they were diamond hard."

Her nipples immediately constricted.

"As much as I wanna put my mouth on those rigid tips, I'd save that for later. Too much naked skin tempting me to kiss and tease. I love when your breath catches as I touch you here."

His fingers on her belly lightly brushed the skin between her hipbones. A little gasp escaped.

"There's the sound." He adjusted his upper body and bent his head to place a kiss on the tender area on the inside of her arm. "I'd run my fingers along the muscles from your wrist to your biceps. Stopping to trace the bend in your elbow. The ball of your shoulder. Your collarbone. Your neck. Your strong, stubborn jaw. All beautiful feminine places."

"I have other feminine places," she said a little breathlessly.

"Believe me, I know. I like watching your face as I'm kissing a path down your belly to gorge myself on that slice of heaven between your thighs."

Fletch kept telling her all the wickedly raunchy things he planned to do to her. Explicit things. But he didn't touch her beyond caressing her thigh with his thumb.

Rather than being wound tight, Tanna relaxed against him completely. The deep, modulated cadence of his voice was a perfect complement to the easy cadence of the horse.

She felt a stab of disappointment when the barn appeared. She hadn't wanted this horseback ride to end.

Wait. What did that mean?

Imagining strapping on the feedbag, Gus picked up the pace.

Tanna held her breath, expecting that panicked feeling would overwhelm her.

But nothing came.

"You all right?" Fletch asked.

"Yes. I am. I really am. Thank you for this."

"My pleasure. This riding double thing is awesome."

She laughed softly.

"I'm gonna swing down and open the gate."

Leaving her alone on Gus.

Fletch dismounted and walked them through the gate.

He helped her dismount.

Tanna stood in the dirt, watching Fletch deal with the horse.

She'd survived.

In fact, she felt exhilarated.

Alive.

Wanting to celebrate this feeling—this victory—with more than just a kiss.

She paced outside the gate and as soon as Fletch exited, she pounced on him. She kissed him as she tried to scale his body.

Fletch returned her kiss with equal enthusiasm, until she reached for his belt buckle. He released her with a groan, stopping the motion.

She wasn't ready to let him go. She latched onto his neck and whispered in his ear. "I need you, Fletch. Fuck me against a tree or on the picnic table or even in the dirt. But I need—"

"Slow down." He stepped back and took hold of her hands. "Sugar twang, there's no rush. Let's just chill for a minute."

"But...I thought we would..." She knew she looked bewildered and didn't care.

"No." He kissed her knuckles. "When we get back to the Split Rock, we can hit your bed, or my bed and do all the things we talked about. But not here."

"So why would you say all those..." Lightbulb moment. Duh. "You were distracting me."

"Yep."

Tanna fought back tears. For Fletch's thoughtfulness and that she'd become such a basket case that she needed soothing in the way he knew would be effective on her. "I'm sorry."

"Don't be." He brushed his mouth across her forehead. "This is about you. Sex is about us. In this moment we're gonna talk. Really talk about where you think you can go from here. No holds barred, beautiful."

She really loved this man. "Okay."

Fletch led her to the picnic table. They sat side by side, her small hand engulfed in his bigger one, her head resting against his bicep. She took a deep breath. "I was so fucking scared when you told me I was getting on a horse today that I considered faking a recurrence of my knee injury so you'd change your mind."

He laughed. "Clever. But wasn't happening. Go on."

Baring her body was a lot easier than baring her soul. But she did it.

Fletch didn't run. He didn't pass judgment. He just listened. Then he kissed away her tears.

He'd helped her take the first step. The rest was up to her. And for the first time in months, she had a feeling of hope.

The first thing Tanna did when they got back to the Split Rock was call Eli and ask if he had a gentle mount she could ride first thing tomorrow.

The next thing she did was convince Fletch she needed lots of help on reclaiming her riding skills as she led him to bed.

Chapter Twenty-seven

❧

*W*ith the warm breeze drifting through the open windows in the cab of his truck and his sense of anticipation, Fletch could almost imagine this was the beginning of his vacation instead of the end of it.

Where in the hell had six weeks gone? Six weeks ago he'd wondered how he'd fill his time. Now he made a mental list of all the things he hadn't done.

It'd been a week and a half since the horse incident, which Tanna referred to as "the day the horseshit hit the fan" and things had never been better between them. Even when he'd known it was the beginning of the end.

He'd convinced her to spend the last two days of his sabbatical with him at the lake.

"We're not sleeping in a tipi, are we?" she asked, interrupting his thoughts.

Fletch sighed. "You really went there, Tanna?"

She laughed. "Kidding. I just wanted to hear that exasperated sigh. It's sexy as hell."

"I oughta turn you over my knee and paddle your ass. Those yelps *you* make are sexy as hell."

"I'm on board—but only if you pull my hair too," she cooed. "I love it when you go all he-man large and in charge on me."

"Remember you said that." Fletch brought her hand to his mouth and kissed it. "This cabin is rustic. But it does have running water. And a decent dock."

"A boat?"

"An old fishing canoe."

"So no waterskiing? Damn."

"You water-ski?"

Tanna shook her head. "I've always wanted to try, but it'd just be my luck if I wiped out and tore the crap out of my knee again."

"Motorized watercraft aren't allowed anyway." He waggled his eyebrows. "You'll just have to lay on the dock in a bikini."

"While I'm holding a fishing pole. Because I'm a damn good fisherwoman."

"Glad someone is," he muttered. "I brought steaks just in case."

"Buffalo steaks?" she snickered.

"Y'all are fixin' for me to open a can of whoop ass for them Indian comments, ain't ya?" he shot back, imitating her twang.

She laughed. "I deserved that."

With no beach or motorized boats, the small lake didn't attract many people, so the area had remained unchanged since Fletch's childhood. They turned off the main road onto a bumpy, overgrown path one step below a fire trail. The pine trees were sparse. Not much green grew on the forest floor. The road took a sharp curve and they reached the back side of the cabin.

"Here we are."

Tanna bent forward and squinted through the front window. "Where's the outhouse?"

"No outhouse. It has a septic system."

"Whoo-ee Jim-Bob! Then this here is right uptown."

If Fletch had his way, he would've carried in everything. But Little Miss I Can Do It insisted on helping. He kept an eye on her to see if she favored her knee after her recent return to riding.

She set the sleeping bags on the floor and looked up at him, smiling. "This oughta be cozy."

"Let's test it." Fletch pulled Tanna against his chest and landed on the mattress on his back. He took her mouth in a ravenous kiss, keeping her arms trapped between them so he could tease and coax—devour her however he pleased and she couldn't do a damn thing about it. By the time he slowed the kiss, his dick was hard.

He pressed his lips to her forehead. "We'll fit, but one of us will have to be on top. All night."

Tanna angled her head to bury her face in his neck. "Sounds like something fun to try."

He loosened his hold on her, but she remained curled into him. He trailed his fingers up and down her back, more than content to just lie with her like this.

"Fletch?"

"Hmm?"

"Thanks."

"For?"

"Bringing me here. For wanting to spend time with me."

There's no place I'd rather be. No one I'd rather be with.

"My pleasure. I hate that my vacation's about over." He twisted the ends of her ponytail around his finger. "I wish this was longer than two days."

Tanna kissed the pulse point in his neck. The corner of his jaw. The tip of his chin. "Me too. So we'd better make the most of the time we have." She pushed up and stood beside the bed, offering him a hand to help him up. "Let's go explore."

"You go ahead. I'm right behind you."

Her white cover-up blouse fluttered to the floor. She kicked off her flip-flops and grabbed a beach towel.

Fletch stopped at the cooler and snagged two beers.

Barefoot, Tanna wandered to the end of the dock, looking delectable in cutoff jean shorts and a bright yellow bikini top. She sat and dangled her legs over the side. Resting back on her elbows, she aimed her face toward the sun and closed her eyes.

He nearly stumbled over his own feet; the woman was such a vision. He just stared at her while drool formed in his mouth and icy water dripped off the bottom of the cans.

She cracked an eye open. "Why you standing there, breathing hard, blocking my sun?"

Because I love you.

His little Texas cowgirl would run if he confessed that, so he plopped down beside her and said, "Just admiring the view, sugar twang."

"Of the lake?"

"Nope. I've seen that dozens of times."

Her lips curled into a smirk. "You were looking down my top, huh?"

"Yep. Don't suppose I could convince you to sunbathe topless since no one's around today?"

"But what if I burn my nipples?"

"I'll kiss them and make them better."

She laughed. "We'll see."

"Want a beer?"

"Always."

He sat beside her, close enough to touch but not too close to crowd her, and cracked open both beers, sliding one to her.

"So, how often did you come here growing up?" she asked.

"Once a year. Twice if we were lucky."

"Does your dad still come here?"

"Not as far as I know. The older we get, the more we want creature comforts. Dad is in great shape for his age, but he's got a bad back and prefers to sleep in his adjustable bed." He sucked down a mouthful of his beer. "Makes me wonder how he's faring on the overseas trip."

"Haven't you heard from him?"

"Briefly to tell me the schedule was crazy busy and he'd fill me in after he returned home."

Tanna cocked her head. "You miss him."

"Yeah. Probably sounds stupid."

"I think it sounds wonderful." She sipped her beer. "I don't miss my dad and I try not to think about him at all."

"You don't have any happy memories?"

"A few. But now, even those are tainted. Makes me wonder what I hadn't seen as a kid. If he was just goin' through the motions because he didn't have a choice."

"You are a glass-half-empty type."

"In this case it's beyond empty. The glass is cracked and put aside to see if it'll shatter on its own. Anyway, I had my mom and she more than made up for it. Why don't you ever talk about your mom?"

He immediately stiffened up. "Probably because I feel the same way about her that you do about your dad. Except I've felt that way since I was a boy. I didn't know her well enough to be sad at her passing. And I never understood why it'd upset my dad so much."

"He must've loved something about her." She shot him a look. "Even if it was only that she gave him you."

Fletch smiled at her and ran his knuckles down her jawline. "Thanks. My dad never married. I never thought he dated either, so the thing between him and Cora seriously blew my mind."

"I, for one, am happy the old-timers are getting some. I never wanna be that woman who'd rather do ten household things than do my man. I hope to still be bangin' the hell outta the headboard when I'm in my seventies."

"Me too. Though I hope to Christ I'm not single living in some old folks home."

"So you want the wife-and-kids life?"

He kept it light, but honest—besides confessing he wanted that wife and kid life with her. "I do. I've been a little envious, watching my friends settle down. But with the demands of my job, I fear Miss Ellie isn't far off in asking me to wait until she grows up. Maybe things will have stabilized by then."

Tanna rested her head on his shoulder. "Your fears aren't justified, Doc. There are probably dozens of women who'd snap you up as a husband. But I have to ask if this break from your practice has changed anything."

Meeting her had changed everything. "It's reminded me why I don't take time off. You can't miss what you don't have; know what I mean? When

I get back into the groove on Monday, my mind will be on sitting in the sunshine drinking beer with a hot cowgirl."

"Aw. So you'll be thinkin' of little ol' me?"

Always. "I'll also be remembering all the mornings, afternoons and nights we spent in bed."

"Sex is one of our stronger points as a couple."

"Relationships have been built on far less." He drank half his beer, grimacing because it'd already gotten warm. "What about you? Ever been in love?"

"Dozens of times. Mostly in my late teens and early twenties. Every guy I dated became *the one*. Funny how I thought that about all of them and none of them thought that about *me*. At some point—and I can't even tell you exactly when—I stopped looking for a guy to make me complete."

"I'll bet that's when you really started winning on the circuit."

"I'm not surprised you figured that out." She sighed. "What about you? Ever been in love?"

Since the moment I saw you. "Thought I was once. Since then it's been easier to—"

"Compartmentalize," they finished simultaneously and laughed.

"As I was saying, it's been easier to separate the need for sex from the need for a relationship."

"We really are so much alike," Tanna said softly.

"Well, there are a few obvious differences."

"Such as?"

"Such as your accent."

"Please. You Northerners are the ones who talk funny."

"Okay. What about how you phrase stuff. Like . . . I'm fixin' to . . . what does that even mean?"

Tanna laughed. He loved that she laughed so much around him.

"Then there's your blind adoration of any and all Texas sports teams, regardless of how bad they suck."

"The Dallas Cowboys are America's team. No, the Dallas Cowboys are *God*'s team. God said so. It's in the Bible and everything. You can check for yourself."

Fletch snorted. "You Texans are so—"

"Uh-uh, cowboy, I'm fixin' to go all wild-ass Southern woman on you if you slander the greatest state in the Union."

"When did we start talking about Wyoming again?" he said slyly.

She shoved him. "Smart-ass Yankee."

He brushed a hank of hair from her cheek. "In all seriousness, do you miss Texas?"

"Even if I never live there again and I'm a ninety-year-old lady, I'll always miss Texas. I'll always consider Texas home."

Fletch wasn't surprised by her answer, just disappointed.

"How did we get on this subject anyway?"

"Just making conversation."

Tanna swung her leg over his. "Maybe we should be doin' something else with our mouths instead of talking. Make love while the sun shines and all that jazz... or should I say all that *jizz*."

He burst out laughing. "Goddamn, I love your total lack of a filter."

"You bring out my raunchy side. So whatdya say?"

"What if get slivers in my ass?"

"I'll kiss it and make it better." She placed a kiss on his neck. "Please say yes. I just have this... need to feel you wrapped around me."

Sometimes this woman undid him completely. Fletch stood and helped her to her feet. Somehow between the long, slow kisses and the tender caresses, they managed to get their clothes off and he remembered the condom he'd stashed in his pocket, just in case.

He herded her to the end of the dock where he spread out the towel. He sat on it, with his legs hanging over the edge of the dock, and patted his lap.

Tanna bit her lip. "You promise in a moment of abandon we won't plunge into the water?"

"I promise. But that means you'll be doin' all the work."

She perched on her knees over his crotch and slowly lowered onto him. Her breasts were cool against his sun-warmed chest. Her mouth avid against his.

Fletch leaned back on his elbows, entirely focused on the sexy way she moved. Rolling her hips. Tightening her cunt around the tip of his cock before sliding the shaft inside her wet channel.

The sun beat down but a light breeze blew off the lake. It was a surreal experience, making love outside in the middle of the day. But it was damn close to perfect too.

When her movements picked up speed, he sat up and gripped her ass, helping her ride him.

Tanna broke the kiss and started to arch back, but he caught her before she tipped them too far forward.

He planted kisses on the curve of her throat and pumped his pelvis up. "Go over. Go over and take me with you."

She cried out and her pussy clamped around his cock. The contractions of her body launched his orgasm and he rode the wave with her to the very end.

He stretched out on the towel and she followed him down, sprawling on his chest and keeping their bodies connected. His fingertips drifted up and down her spine. Fletch decided he could die a happy man in this moment. At the same time he feared he didn't have many more of these left with her.

⟡

The rest of their time at the lake passed in a blur of fun and laughter, despite that they had no luck fishing. They swam, played cards, stargazed and indulged in spontaneous bouts of sex that were sweet, raunchy, intense and poignant.

In one of his favorite moments yet, they were curled up in bed listening to the sounds of the night drifting through the screened windows.

"What are your plans for next week?"

"Selling clothes, pulling taps. Right after I lock the doors Tuesday, I'm headed to Eli's to work with the girls on horseback. Meaning they're on horseback and I lead them around the barrels. Sometimes I wish I could just cut them loose and let them try it on their own, but until I'm sure Sparky won't balk, we have to go slow and steady."

"I meant, how's it goin' for you?"

"Oh. I'm riding. I can even go around the barrels. Slow but I have picked up some speed."

"Don't you trust yourself to go faster? Or is it the horse?"

"A combination. Then I wonder why I'm even bothering to call this *training* and that doesn't help my mind-set to get back in the game."

"So, getting back into training hasn't made the nightmares worse?"

"No. I still have that bad dream. But I don't wake up screaming..." She poked him in the chest. "As you well know, bein's I've been in your bed most nights."

"Don't remind me." He kissed the top of her head. "I'm gonna miss that."

"Me too. Are you looking forward to seeing your dad tomorrow?"

"Yeah. Be interesting to see if he actually took pictures with the camera he had to buy."

"Will it be weird between you and Cora? You said you had no idea they were together before they went on this trip."

"Oh, she'll be as bossy as ever. I doubt my dad will show up for a nooner, then again...I'm hardly ever around at noon so it could happen."

She laughed.

Just ask her. "Would you wanna meet my dad sometime?"

"Absolutely, if he's as good-lookin' and charming as you."

He released the breath he'd been holding. "He'd claim I was a chip off the old block."

Tanna didn't say anything else and he realized she'd fallen asleep.

But sleep didn't come for him so easily. Fletch didn't know how he'd survive when this woman walked out of his life.

ᴄᴇ

He showed up at his dad's on Sunday afternoon after dropping Tanna off early in the morning at Eli's. He had returned to the Split Rock to load everything from the trailer and hauled it back to his place, then opted to come back for the bed another day. Hauling it out now made his leaving seem so final.

His dad waited in the doorframe, smiling at him.

"If it isn't the world traveler." Fletch pulled him into a big hug and held on for longer than usual. "I missed you, old man."

"Missed you too, boy." He patted him on the back. "Would you like a glass of the whiskey I brought back from Ireland?"

"Of course. And don't be stingy with it."

Drinks in hand, they settled in the living room, Fletch on the couch, his dad in the easy chair.

"Tell me all about it."

"Well, we started out in London." He talked for the next hour, and had Fletch laughing and groaning at some of his senior group experiences.

"Did you take pictures?"

"Not a damn one. Couldn't figure out how to use the camera and I had too much pride to ask for help. Besides, what would I do with pictures anyway? Wallpaper the bathroom?"

He chuckled. "Good point."

"Now you wanna tell me how you spent six weeks of vacation time?"

"I stayed at the Split Rock and did some research for Renner Jackson on a project he has in mind. Caught up on my reading. Wrote and submitted a paper to a veterinary journal."

"You worked the entire time?"

Fletch shook his head. "I had plenty of downtime."

His dad's eyes narrowed. "What else? And please tell me you didn't take a single animal call while you were on vacation."

"Dad—"

"Dammit, boy, what is wrong with you? You were given a gift and a chance and you—"

"Fell in love, all right? I fell in love with the most perfect, beautiful, funny, sexy woman on earth and there's not a goddamned thing I can do to stop her from leaving me." He drained his drink and walked to the kitchen for a refill.

Fletch hadn't meant to say any of that. He'd been away from Tanna less than four hours and he was already moping.

A heavy hand clapped him on the back. "How about if we start this conversation over?"

He nodded.

His dad refilled his own glass. "This woman. She's the one you told me about before I left?"

"Yeah. The last two months have been the best of my life." Fletch talked. And talked some more. He hadn't realized how much he'd needed someone to listen to him. He'd always had Eli as his sounding board. But since Eli was also counseling Tanna, he didn't feel comfortable being so brutally honest about her with him. His other guy friends, well, this wasn't the sort of shit he shared with anyone besides his dad.

"She sounds wonderful. Do I get to meet her?"

"I asked her last night and she said yes, but only if you're as good-lookin' and charming as me."

His dad laughed. "I like her already. Got a day or night in mind?"

"That's the thing. I go back to the unpredictable schedule this week. I could set something up, but guaranteed if I do, I'll be called to some emergency in Rock Springs."

"Have you considered that maybe your job might be one thing that's holding her back from making a commitment to you?"

"Of course. But it's not like I'm independently wealthy and can quit."

"No. But you do have options. Maybe it's time you seriously looked into them." He held up his hand to quell Fletch's protest. "Having the life you want is about sacrifices."

"What's that supposed to mean?"

"I know you think I'm a rambling old man—"

"Dad, I do not think that. Not at all."

"Then listen up. Back in my day..." He grinned. "Kidding. I will say from the time I was a kid I wanted to be an oil rigger. My folks insisted I get an education first so I took business classes for two years and earned an associate's degree. Then directly after graduation I started working in the oil fields in the Southwest as a roughneck, not a pansy-assed suit and tie management guy."

Fletch raised an eyebrow. "So how'd you end up doin' exactly that?"

"Because of you. After your birth, it was obvious Darla wouldn't take to being a mother. I had a child who needed at least one stable parent. Instead of working three weeks on at a remote location and one week off at home, I chose the eight to five, Monday through Friday job." His dad looked at him. "You think I wanted to be management? You think it was easy showing up at the job sites questioning my friends about labor cost and accident ratios after we'd been coworkers for years? No. But I had no choice except to take a different position in the company with less money to start out, but more stability. Would I trade those years for a fatter bank account right now? Not on your life. That change was good for me. Good for my life because I got to spend it raising you. So don't automatically discount a change. Maybe it's time."

In the last couple of weeks, working normal hours with Tobin and having some freedom, Fletch had been thinking along those same lines. So he wasn't as averse to change as he'd once been. And since his dad had brought this up, it was the perfect time to turn this back on him. "So are you mentioning this because there'll be changes in your life?"

His dad frowned. "What?"

"You. And Cora. Are you two dating? Is there a chance you'll be moving in together?"

"No. I like Cora. We had a great time on the trip, but we're both too old, too set in our ways, and too used to living alone to ever combine households. Our independence is important to both of us." He shook his finger. "You, on the other hand, are young. There's a woman in your life now. That should play into any decision you make."

What his dad didn't understand is Fletch didn't have a say in Tanna's decision. After she'd finally had a breakthrough with the possibility of returning to the career she loved, he couldn't put additional pressure on her to stay in Wyoming with him.

"Now that my fatherly duties are done, what're we watching? Europe is lousy for any kind of real sports."

"Gotta be a baseball game on. Or since you're a big-spending international traveler these days, maybe we could see if there's a boxing match on pay-per-view."

Chapter Twenty-eight

❦

"*I* see Eli's still babying you along."

Tanna turned toward Sutton and rolled her eyes. "He wants me to 're-connect' with my love of horses. In the past four hours I've ridden two mares and a gelding." She smirked. "I was gone a while the last ride. Did he send you out here to check on me?"

"Busted. Tell me the truth; were you secretly out cutting a clover leaf pattern around the rocks?"

"No. I just lost track of time."

Sutton grinned. "That's good to hear. So are you running barrels?"

"Finally."

"How's it feel?"

"Slow. But good. I've been gone a couple of days, so I had a moment of panic when I got back in the saddle and wished I hadn't sent Fletch away, because the man can convince me to do anything." They'd been apart for only five hours and she already missed him.

"Eli mentioned something about you and Fletch bein' off on a romantic getaway."

"Yep." Tanna led the horse through the gate.

Sutton fell in step beside her. "So I don't get the down-and-dirty details of your sexcapades?"

"Nope." Tanna hadn't seen Sutton since the day she'd spilled her guts.

As much as she liked him, after her conversation with Fletch, she had to reestablish some boundaries.

"That sucks."

"I thought you were off rodeoin' during Cowboy Christmas?"

He shrugged. "A couple here and there. Nothin' big. What about you? Need some help setting up barrels?"

"I'm done for today. I know Sunday is Eli's day off and I'm determined to ride every day, so I wanted to get riding in early so he didn't spend the whole day worrying about me. Plus, I've got plans for this afternoon."

"With Fletch?"

"With friends." Tanna set about unsaddling the horse, her mind elsewhere.

"You've made a lot of progress since the last time I saw you, Tex-Mex."

"Yes, I have. Still got a ways to go, though."

"You'll get there." Sutton clapped her on the back. "Holler if you need anything. I'll probably be here this week."

She smiled at him. "Will do. Thanks."

⤳

Although she'd been in Wyoming two months, this was the first day Tanna's schedule had meshed with Lainie and Celia's. After Lainie had married Hank almost six years ago, Celia had stepped into Tanna's life to fill that friendship void. But that'd changed once she'd married Kyle and quit the circuit. Their lives had taken divergent paths; still…she'd missed their close friendships the past few years.

Lainie and Hank had a wonderful house. Their home embraced you as soon as you walked in the door. Tanna preferred houses that were homes, not an ostentatious showplace where you couldn't sit on the living room furniture, the dining room got used twice a year on holidays, and the family areas were separated rather than small enough for everyone to be together.

Her childhood girlfriends in Texas who'd married and started families— it was their goal to live in one of those McMansions in a suburb. A large brick and concrete box, with a manicured lawn, two top-of-the-line SUVs in the triple-car garage. The kiddos attended private preschool, suffered through scheduled piano lessons, dance class, club soccer practice and church on Wednesday nights and Sunday mornings. Kids didn't get dirty; they weren't allowed to explore. They lived by the color-coded weekly calendar on the refrigerator.

So it did her heart good to see Brianna, Lainie and Hank's almost four-year-old daughter, spinning and dancing across the open field adjacent to the house, an energetic dog following her.

Celia sat on the porch, her feet on a footstool. She waved. "Hey, stranger."

"Hey, yourself, mama." Tanna stopped beside the porch support and watched Brianna. Her copper-colored curls bounced as she jumped, twirled and sang. "Is Brianna always like that?"

"She's a happy kid. But how couldn't she be? Her mama adores her, she's got her daddy wrapped around her little finger, aunts and uncles who spoil her rotten, a baby brother who worships her and her very own dog."

Tanna grinned at Celia. "The dog was your doin'?"

"Yep. When Patches's mom had more puppies, I gave Brianna the runt of the litter for her birthday. She named him Flutterbee because that's what she called butterflies. Flutter keeps an eye on her because the girl does like to explore."

"She's beautiful. Lucky to be raised around family." Tanna glanced at Celia's rounded belly. "And hopefully lots of cousins."

Celia groaned. "Gotta get through this pregnancy first before we talk about more."

"How you feeling?"

"Tired. Which is stupid because Kyle won't let me do anything while I'm gestating baby G. I've even learned to crochet, if you can believe it. I've turned into this home-cooking, housecleaning, crocheting, waiting-for-my-man-to-come-in-from-the-fields kind of ranch wife."

"And you love every minute of it," Tanna said.

Celia smiled and rubbed her hand over her belly. "It's absolute bliss. I do miss workin' cattle. And I miss riding my horses, but Kyle makes sure I don't lose my riding skills entirely."

"More than I needed to know."

"Oh, pooh. You and I used to talk about sex nonstop. Okay, you talked, I listened and took notes." She waggled her eyebrows. "Which Kyle is very thankful for, by the way."

The screen door opened and Lainie stepped onto the covered porch, her dark-haired baby boy perched on her hip. "Pay no attention to Celia. She's in that 'me so horny' stage of pregnancy."

"That's a real stage?"

"Yep."

"I learn something new every day."

The boy squirmed to get down.

Celia said, "I got it," and started to get up.

"Stay put," Lainie warned. She passed the squirmy kid to Tanna. "Hold Jason for a sec while I get the gate up."

Tanna hadn't spent much time around kids. Tiny babies fascinated her, but scared the crap out of her. Kiddos this age, well, they were fun because they'd started to do tricks. She balanced the boy on her hip. Talk about solid. He was a Hank replica, from his near-black hair to his thoughtful expression.

"All right, the baby jail is in place so he can't escape." Lainie plucked the boy from Tanna's arms and sat him down.

"It won't be much longer and the baby jail won't hold him," Celia remarked.

"Bite your tongue," Lainie shot back. "He walked early, which was bad enough. And he wants to do everything Brianna does."

Jason ran to the baby gate stretched across the porch supports, blocking access to the steps. He grabbed the top of the gate and jerked on it, testing whether he could break it down.

"Oh, shit," Lainie said and ran back into the house.

Tanna looked at Celia. "Was it something I said?"

"No. Something she smelled, most likely. She's pregnant."

"Again?" Tanna said. "Jason is what? A year old?"

"Fourteen months. I doubt you're really surprised because Hank and Lainie want a houseful of ranch hands—I mean kids."

Tanna walked to the opposite end of the porch, resting her hips against the railing. She gazed across the rolling landscape. No cattle within view, but they grazed in different fields in the summertime. The Lawsons and the Gilchrists had roots here that would carry through another generation.

There'd been a time when Tanna figured her life would play out the same way. She'd meet a ranching cowboy during her on-the-road travels, fall in love, take him back to the family ranch and set up housekeeping.

Now she realized her dream had been vague. She hadn't made a plan for how she'd earn a living beyond barrel racing. Her mystery husband... she'd never imagined him having his own life and connections; she'd just expected him to be with her and make her happy.

For all of her supposed love of the family ranch, she'd never considered what her part would be in it. How that piece of dirt would support three families. She'd created a dream life that had as much basis in reality as Brianna twirling through the field, chasing butterflies and playing princess.

"Tanna? Are you all right?"

She spun around. "I'm fine. Just thinking about how quiet it is here."

Then Jason shrieked at the top of his lungs.

"So much for that." Celia patted the chair beside her. "Come sit. Lainie made iced tea and she even remembered to bring sugar for you."

She wandered over, watching Jason dig through a box of toys after abandoning all hope of escape.

"How're things goin' at the Split Rock?"

"Good. The place does a steady business. Except Sundays are quiet. The clothing store is closed and we rarely have to staff the bar."

"What do you do on Sundays?"

Laze in bed with Fletch as long as possible. "Depends. Why?"

"Just curious how often you're goin' to Eli's."

"If I go, it's during the week. He keeps Sundays as a day off for him and Summer."

"What's she like?"

Damaged. Like me. Tanna spooned sugar in the bottom of her glass and poured in tea. "Why're you asking me? Aren't you and Eli tight?"

"We were. Then Kyle and I got married. Since Summer's come into

Eli's life, the way he's always wanted her to, he's been around everyone a lot less."

Tanna shrugged. "I guess it happens when you find the one."

"Is that why we haven't seen you? Because you're with Fletch and he's *the one*?"

The screen door opened and Lainie strolled out, hand on her stomach. "I guess I won't be eating yogurt again for a while. Bleh."

Brianna skipped up the sidewalk and climbed over the baby gate. "Mama, can I—"

"Bri, sweetie, don't do that. I don't want Jason trying it."

Brianna's face was damp with sweat, making her freckles more pronounced. Her pink unicorn shirt bore the imprint of two muddy handprints. She had bug bites on her skinny legs and she wore only one sock. Her deep blue eyes lit up when she spied her little brother smashing plastic trucks together beneath the porch swing. She immediately joined him and dumped the remaining toys out of the box.

Tanna could so identify with the tomboyish spitfire. And the way she bossed her little brother around. She hadn't heard from Garrett since that last phone call and that worried her.

"So what did I miss?" Lainie asked.

"Tanna was about to tell all about her and Fletch," Celia said slyly.

"No, I wasn't. We're . . . hanging out while I'm here. That's it."

"But he's still staying up at the Split Rock?"

"No. He's back in Rawlins as of today, actually."

"What happens now?"

"He'll be busy with his practice."

Celia rolled her eyes. "No. I mean what happens between you guys now?"

"I guess we'll see."

"That's it? That's *all* the juicy insider stuff we get?"

"What else do you want to know?" She dropped her voice. "Yes, he absolutely rocks my world in bed. Happy now?"

Lainie and Celia looked at each other and laughed.

"What?"

"Oh, you've got it bad for Fletch if you don't wanna give us explicit details."

Tanna bared her teeth. "Or maybe I've just grown up and no longer need to brag about everything and every*one* I've done."

"Or maybe Fletch is *the one* and you don't want to admit it to us, let alone yourself."

"I stopped believing in, and looking for, *the one* a long time ago." *Such a liar, Tanna.*

Celia pushed to her feet. "That tea ran right through me."

After she waddled into the house, Lainie leaned over. "You don't have to tell us everything. You don't have to be upbeat, wild child Tanna around me all the time either, okay? I've had darkness in my life, if you'll recall."

"Which is why I'm so thrilled to see you living the dream with your hunky hubby, your beautiful two-point-one kids in this bucolic place. I've missed you. And it's been... I won't say good for me to learn to deal with this stuff on my own, but it's been necessary." She blew out a breath. "So can you please steer the conversation away from horses and Fletch? Celia's like a dog with a bone when it comes to this stuff."

"Only because she cares about you as much as I do." Again Lainie looked at her and seemed to look through her. "You're in love with him, aren't you?"

Tanna nodded, but didn't say anything further.

"I can see by the look on your face you haven't told him."

"There's too much up in the air for both of us right now."

"I understand." Lainie squeezed her hand. "But all this that you see? The hunky hubby, the beautiful two-point-one kids and a home in this bucolic place... you deserve that too. So does Fletch."

"I know. But what if I'm not the one who can give it to him?"

The door squeaked and Celia lumbered into view. "Hey, what are you two whispering about over there?"

Lainie gave her a haughty look. "A pregnant woman shouldn't be asking questions, lest she ruin a possible surprise."

She groaned. "Not another surprise shower. I still haven't lived down the last one." She jabbed her finger at Tanna. "I never did get even with you for the basket of vibrators."

Tanna laughed.

"My mom is the shower queen," Lainie said.

"She did throw a great bash in California for Brianna. I was glad I got to come. No issues from your mom about you naming your son after your late father?"

"None. She was actually pleased. It helps that Jason looks nothing like me or my dad." She shot a fond look at her son. "With the exception of those curls."

Tanna looked at Celia. "What baby names are the front-runners in the Gilchrist household?"

"Since we don't know the sex, we've picked a couple." She scowled. "Kyle nixed Marshall; I thought it would be nice closure to name the baby after his grandfather."

"I think you're having a girl," Lainie said. "So Marshall definitely won't work."

"So how about...Jasmine?" Tanna suggested.

"Stripper name," Celia said.

"Mallory?"

"Too stuffy."

"Gillian?"

"Ugh. Gillian Gilchrist? No. Poor kid. First letter of her first name and first letter of her last name both start with G but it isn't pronounced the same? And it always looks like Gilligan to me."

"I'm thinking Skipper would be awesome for a boy or a girl," Tanna said.

Celia laughed. "We watch entirely too much classic TV. But I can promise you, we won't be saddling the poor kid with a weird name like *some* people I know." She and Lainie exchanged a look.

"What?"

"Our neighbors? Josh and Ronna? They named their little girl Style."

"Style? As in...doggie style?"

"Only you would think of that, Tanna."

"What? You didn't?"

"No. I thought of freestyle, no style, bad style and hairstyle."

"I can guarantee the kids on the playground will have thought of it."

"True."

"Besides, I have the perfect name for a girl," Tanna said smugly.

"Spill it."

"Kyla."

"Oh, my husband will love that one. What else you got?"

"Cecil for a boy."

For the next few hours as they discussed baby names and gossiped about former rodeo friends, Tanna was happy to let the decisions of the real world fade away.

Chapter Twenty-nine

❧

First thing Fletch did Monday morning before he headed out of town was stop by Jet Eriksen's office to pick up copies of client paperwork he'd handled during Fletch's sabbatical.

The parking lot of Jet's veterinary office was empty at seven a.m., but Fletch knew he'd be in the office working. He entered through the side door, yelling "knock, knock" before venturing down the hallway.

Jet grinned at him from behind a massive desk. "Fletch! Good to see you, man. There's coffee in the break room. Help yourself."

"Don't mind if I do." After he filled a mug, he wandered back to Jet's office and sat on the stool by the window. "Thanks for filling in for me. Although since Cora set it up, I'm not sure which weeks you took."

"The first two. Arguably the hardest two because none of your clients wanted to hear you were unavailable. One guy, Les somebody, argued with me for fifteen minutes about your dedication to animals and how you never took time off." Jet sipped his coffee. "Which I happily pointed out was exactly the reason you deserved time off."

Fletch laughed. "So, besides grumpy Les, you have any issues?"

"Only the fact you work so hard all the time, with nothing less than total dedication, that you make the rest of us look like slackers."

"Yeah. I've heard that a time or twenty."

A pause ensued. Then Jet said, "Fletch. How old are you?"

"I'll be thirty-seven in a few months. Why?"

"You've been in business for yourself how long?"

"Almost a decade." He sipped his coffee. "Again, why?"

Jet leaned forward. "I'll cut to the chase. There's plenty of business for all of us in this area, since our 'area' covers well over three hundred miles. I just wondered if you'd ever considered taking on a partner."

That was completely unexpected. Jet Eriksen was a decade older and had been running a successful solo practice since before Fletch had started out. They were friendly colleagues who consulted each other when needed. "All right. Where the hell did that come from?"

"Due to a screwup with the answering service, Arnie, Tasha and I got called to the same emergency. Once we had it handled, the three of us ended up having coffee and realized we're all suffering from being overextended in our practices, despite that we're all at different stages in our lives and careers. Arnie's looking to retire in about ten years and Tasha is still fresh enough out of vet school she's retained that dewy-eyed optimism. I think that's something neither of us has seen for a few years."

"True."

"So, strictly between us, we're kicking around the idea of going into practice together. If you were interested, we could rotate the weekends so we wouldn't all have to be on call, but we could rotate in one weekend a month. Granted, that'd change during calving or other busy times, but I gotta admit, losing some of those late nights has a huge appeal for me."

"Me too," Fletch admitted. "I'm listening."

Jet grinned. "Thought you might be interested. The biggest up-front expense would be combining all our practices into one location. That way all the billing issues, supply stores, equipment and surgical areas would be shared equally. There'd be a minimum buy in, split four ways. We could share staff, which would be good for you and Tasha since you're both working solo. Arnie and I each have two vet assistants, which frankly, aren't necessary but would be for four docs."

"Arnie and Tasha are in fully?"

"Arnie is. He wants to share his load since he's closest to retirement. Tasha is pregnant with her first kid and she's worried about the long hours for the short term. She'd like to talk to you before making a decision. She's a good surgeon, one of the best I've seen, so if she could stay focused on that until she delivers, one of us could deal with the physical demands of this job. She's happy about the pregnancy, but worried about the limitations it will impose in her practice, so I have no qualms that we wouldn't always be doing the heavy lifting for her; know what I mean?"

"I do. That's probably the reason I didn't go into practice with old Doc Sharpe after I interned with him. I figured he'd slave me, dangle that partner status and when it came time to retire, he'd close down instead of selling." Fletch flashed his teeth. "Which is exactly what happened, by the way."

"I felt sorry for that kid who'd worked for him a few years and ended up with nothing." Jet tapped his pencil on his desk blotter. "So I can tell Arnie you're interested?"

Fletch had sworn he wouldn't say no if an opportunity presented itself. Was this the right one? Maybe. He wouldn't jump in without more details and assurances. "Sure. I'll talk to him and Tasha."

Not what Jet wanted to hear, but he masked his disappointment quickly. "How was your time off?"

"Great. I've never taken time off. Too scared to, I guess. Figured I'd lose my clients to you or something."

Jet chuckled.

"So it was a shock to me to realize I liked having a life away from my practice. It showed me I didn't *have* a life outside my practice and I needed to change that."

"We want to give you the opportunity. And I know I sprang this on you first thing after a long vacation, but it's something we've been discussing for almost a month."

His eyebrows rose. "Really?"

"Don't know that all of us have ever been in a room together when we weren't tossing out diagnoses. We clicked that night and everything we've come up with since makes good business sense. We've set up a tentative meeting a week from Saturday night at the Cattleman's Club. I'll warn you it'll be more involved than a discussion over dinner. I suspect it'll go on for a few hours. We're serious about getting this under way. And if we come to an agreement it will impact you—either way."

"Because your operation would have a lock on large animal care for three hundred miles."

"Animal care wouldn't suffer under a merger of four practices. In fact, it'd improve being more streamlined. Plus, the fees would be standard. And no offense, Fletch, but you aren't charging enough for your ranch calls. Trust me, with the near worship I've seen from your clients, they won't balk at a price increase. Regardless if you join with us or not."

Fletch stood. "I appreciate the information and the invite. I'll give it serious consideration before we meet."

"This stays between us," Jet warned. "Until we're ready to go ahead, we're not mentioning it to our spouses."

"That'll be easy for me, since I don't have a spouse," he joked.

"You come into practice with us, you'll have time to go looking for a wife." He laughed. "And with that... all visits, case histories, are on a thumb drive in a priority envelope on my receptionist's desk."

"Thanks." Fletch fought a groan. Cora hated dealing with technology. She was an old-school office manager, which meant paperwork, paperwork and more paperwork.

If you joined their practice, your records would be more manageable.

Records, heck. His life would be more manageable. He hated that he couldn't discuss this opportunity with anyone. Normally he'd pick his dad's brain. But since he'd gotten involved with Cora, he might have a different slant on it.

Back at his office that night, he turned on his computer and scrolled through his schedule. The way it looked, he'd definitely be playing catch-up all damn week.

Chapter Thirty

❦

*T*he following weekend, they were naked in Fletch's gigantic bed, entwined together, half watching TV, half dozing, when Fletch's cell phone buzzed on the nightstand.

He reached over, picked it up and muttered under his breath.

"Is it an emergency call?"

"No. It's Tilda."

"Tilda of the Mud Lilies? What does she want?"

"Probably a ride home from the bar." Fletch answered with, "Tilda, darlin', are you out tearing it up again?"

Tanna snickered. The Mud Lilies cracked her up.

Fletch disentangled his legs from hers and sat up. "Slow down and start over, okay?"

Uh-oh. Fletch was using his vet voice. Not good.

"Last time he ate?" he asked gently. He listened and said, "I can't diagnose over the phone so it'd be best if I came over. Hey, Miz T, I promise it's no trouble. See you in a few." He hung up and stood.

"What's goin' on?"

"Tilda's dog is sick." Fletch slipped on his athletic shorts. He pulled his T-shirt over his head. "So I'm going to check him out."

At eleven o'clock at night. "Do you do that a lot?"

Fletch shrugged. "Not really. But Tilda doesn't have family around here to call, so I don't mind."

Such a sweet, sweet man.

"Plus, she's a little bit of a thing. Although she'd whap me upside the head if she heard me say that." He smiled softly. "Tilda dotes on Ripper. When he's healthy, it's not an issue. But when he's sick . . . she struggles with his size."

"What kind of dog is he?"

"A Newfoundland."

"Holy crap."

He perched on the edge of the bed to put on his socks and shoes. "I don't know what time I'll be back."

Tanna debated all of four seconds before she tossed back the covers and dragged on her bra and underwear. She slipped her sundress over her head and moved to stand in front of him.

Fletch quirked a brow at her. "That doesn't mean you've gotta go home."

"I'm not. I'm coming with you." She stepped between his thighs and ran her fingers through his hair. Damn. She'd really messed it up earlier when he'd gone down on her.

"Tanna—"

"I'll stay out of your way. Or I'll help you if you want. I know this is par for the course in your practice—you headed out at all times of the night. It just makes me sad thinking about you bein' alone."

His eyes turned that beautiful liquid brown and he pulled her mouth down to his for a thorough kiss. "Thank you. I'd love it if you came with me."

Neither said much on the drive to Tilda's.

Even in the dark Tanna could see the gingerbread cuteness of Tilda's house that fit her personality.

Fletch squeezed her hand as they pulled up to the house. He grabbed a large black satchel and they exited the truck.

He knocked once and walked in.

Tilda sat on the floor next to an enormous black dog. She glanced up at Fletch and offered a wan smile. "Thanks for coming, Doc."

"You're welcome. How's he doin'?"

"No different."

He knelt on the blanket and slipped on a pair of surgical gloves. "Let's do a few basic checks."

Tanna took a chair in the living room and watched Fletch work. Taking in his gentle hands, his soothing demeanor with both animal and owner. He asked question after question while performing his exam, taking out his stethoscope, penlight, without stopping to dig through his bag.

The dog's breathing was thready, his eyes were closed. Ripper allowed Fletch to arrange his limbs and palpate his abdomen. After taking the dog's temperature, Fletch patted the furry rump.

"So, is there anything you can do?"

Fletch shook his head. "I'm sorry. The old boy is just plain worn out. How old is he?"

"Twelve years."

He whistled. "Dogs this big don't usually live that long. It's testament to your love and care that Ripper's had such a good, long life."

Tilda's chin dropped to her chest. "I got him the year after Robert died. He was such a cute little puppy and I was so lonely."

Tears prickled in Tanna's eyes.

"How long does he have?" Tilda asked softly.

"A couple of hours. Maybe a day."

"He whimpered a lot this morning. But as the day wore on, he stopped."

"I think... even making noise became too much effort for him." He ran his hand down the dog's side. "Tilda, darlin', he's in a lot of pain."

"I know." She dabbed her eyes with a lace handkerchief. "I hate that." She glanced up at Fletch. "Can you... make it easier for him?"

"Yes." Fletch kept stroking Ripper's fur. "Is that what you want?"

Tilda nodded. "I can be with him until...?"

"Of course. You *sure* this is what you want?" he repeated.

She nodded again. "Yes, it'd be for the best for him."

"I'll be right back." Fletch went out to his truck.

Tanna remained in the easy chair, her heart aching as Tilda petted Ripper's head in her lap. The dog's tail no longer thumped. Still, Tilda kept murmuring and petting.

Fletch returned holding a syringe. He spoke softly to Tilda and her beloved dog.

Tanna couldn't see where he inserted the needle. Ripper didn't even flinch. Then Fletch patted the dog and returned outside. She wanted to run after him, but she stayed in place and turned away, giving Tilda privacy.

She knew the drug was quick acting, but she wasn't sure how much time had passed as she'd sat in silence. When she closed her eyes, it wasn't the horrifying images of Jezebel running away that flashed through her mind, but the good times with the horse who'd been close to her best friend. They'd been partners and teammates for years. For the first time in months she welcomed the flood of memories. The hours they'd spent training and traveling together. Their victories in the arena. Their hard-fought struggles when stubborn rider met stubborn horse. She'd never forget the huffy way Jezebel acted if Tanna somehow changed the status quo in her perfect little horsey world. Or how Jezebel would prance so prettily and then buck so damn hard when she wanted to remind Tanna of her place in the equine world. She thought back to the horrible time after her mother died, and the hours she'd spent with her face buried in Jezebel's neck, the horse's soft hide absorbing her tears and her grief.

Grief. God. Had she even grieved for the horse she'd loved and lost? No.

Maybe her inability to be near a horse after the accident hadn't been only about fear, but the sorrow that *any* horse she got on wouldn't be Jezebel.

A noise permeated the flashbacks and Tanna opened her eyes to see Tilda's shoulders shaking and that Ripper's too-still form wasn't moving.

Fletch came back inside and paused in the doorway, his face heavy with sorrow. His eyes met Tanna's and he motioned her closer. Then he dropped to his knees beside Tilda and put his arm around her. "I'm sorry."

"Thank you. For everything you did."

"You're welcome. Do you need more time with him?"

She shook her head.

"You took great care of him, sweetheart. Will you let me take care of him now for you?"

Tilda released a small sob. "I didn't even think about that..."

"I know," Fletch said softly. "That's why I did. Is there some special place to lay him to rest?"

Tanna was crouched beside them and watched Tilda firm her trembling chin, which only caused Tanna's tears to fall faster.

"The flower garden. On the north corner by the birdbath." Tilda's small hand ruffled the fur behind Ripper's ears as she'd probably done a thousand times. "This big guy could sit there for hours watching birds. He loved to chase butterflies. He'd never hurt them and they liked to tease my gentle giant."

"Sounds like the perfect place for him." Fletch looked at Tanna. "Would you fix Tilda a cup of tea?"

"Sure."

Tilda placed a kiss on the top of Ripper's head and hugged him one last time. She rose to her feet as regally as a queen.

Tanna put her arm around her, throwing a quick look over her shoulder as Fletch lifted the big dog and carried him outside. As she fixed tea, she cried silently for Tilda, for herself, for the animals that came into their lives and changed them for the better. She even cried for Fletch. It went above and beyond his job to bury a client's pet. But he was outside at midnight, doing just that. Such an incredible man.

"There are lemon bars in the fridge," Tilda said after Tanna served her tea. "Would you like one?"

"No. But I know the doc has a sweet tooth."

Tanna sat next to her. "I'd ask you for the recipe, but I'd just botch it."

"I'm not much of a cook either. Vivien made the bars. I had to stop myself from eating the whole pan."

Several more minutes passed.

"Do you want me to call Vivien or another of your Mud Lilies pals to come stay with you?"

"That's okay. It's late. I don't want to bother them."

She leaned closer and took Tilda's hand. "Tilda, darlin', if one of them was dealing with this and called you, would you consider it a bother?"

"Heavens, no. I'd be there right away."

"Then you gotta let them make that decision, don't you think?"

Tilda nodded and more tears fell.

"So who should I call for you?"

"Vivien," Tilda choked out. She pulled her cell phone from her purse on the table and handed it over to Tanna to make the call.

Within thirty minutes Vivien and Pearl showed up. Tanna wandered to the front window while they fussed over their friend. She wanted to fuss over Fletch. Where was he? Should she go out there and offer to help him?

A light bobbed in the darkness and then it disappeared.

She heard heavy footfalls on the steps.

Fletch came through the door and headed straight for the bathroom.

Vivien, Pearl and Tilda returned to the living room.

Pearl said, "Where's the doc?"

"Washing up."

He'd barely left the bathroom before he was surrounded.

Vivien pressed her palms to his cheeks. "You are such a dear, dear man. Thank you for everything you did tonight."

Fletch blushed.

Pearl elbowed Vivien aside. She whispered something in his ear. Then Pearl too, gave his cheek a motherly pat.

Tilda merely threw herself into his arms and sobbed.

His eyes met Tanna's when neither Vivien nor Pearl stepped in to console Tilda.

Tanna moved beside them and patted Tilda's shoulder.

She stepped back and wiped her eyes. "Sorry. I'm just so grateful."

"I know. Try and get some rest tonight."

Pearl held out a bottle of whipped cream–flavored vodka. "We'll all sleep well."

He curled his arm around Tanna's waist. "Good night."

Fletch was so distracted he didn't open Tanna's door.

Once they were speeding down the gravel, she reached for his hand. "You all right?"

"Yeah."

293

"Have you been doin' this long enough that animal deaths don't bother you?"

He looked at her strangely. "It bothers me. I hope I never get cynical enough that it doesn't bug me. But to be honest, this was a reminder of why I didn't go into a regular veterinary practice, despite the more reasonable work hours. People losing pets is about the most heartbreaking thing."

Tanna brought his hand to her mouth to kiss his knuckles. "Have I mentioned what a wonderful guy you are?"

"Jesus. Not you too. Can we please drop it?"

"Fletch. You really have no idea how much it meant to Tilda that not only did you show up, but you eased her dog's suffering and you buried him for her."

"She's in her seventies. How was she supposed to haul a one-hundred-fifty-pound dead dog out of her house?"

"Would any of your colleagues have done the same thing?"

"How should I know? It's done. Now can we please drop it?"

And a humble man too.

"You know, I've been thinking about what you said that day at Eli's when you forced me to groom that horse with you."

He stayed quiet—but a tensed quiet.

"You said that I needed to let go of the guilt where Jezebel was concerned. I guess I've always known I didn't do anything to cause her death, despite the thinly veiled accusations from the owners. But looking back, I realize they were hurting from the loss, and they were just lashing out at me because they couldn't be with Jezebel either. So seeing Tilda tonight, watching her stay with Ripper to the very end? It's like I was finally able to let go too. No more guilt about not bein' by Jezebel's side. From here on out I'm gonna concentrate on all the good years we had together."

Fletch swept his thumb across the inside of her wrist. "I'm so glad to hear that, sweetheart."

Then he slipped back into silent mode. He'd had a long day before this midnight call. "You tired?" Tanna asked.

"I'm a little wired if you wanna know the truth."

"So if you go home alone in this state, what do you usually do to take the edge off?"

"Some nights I drink. Some nights run on the treadmill. Some nights I lift weights. Depends." Fletch shot her a look. "Why?"

"Just taking an informal poll."

He laughed softly.

Her brief attempt at humor vanished quickly and the cab became somber again. Tanna didn't push him to talk. But the death of the animal left a lingering sadness around him, almost like guilt, despite the fact that nothing he could've done would've made a difference.

As soon as they crossed the threshold at his house, Tanna jumped up and wrapped her legs around his waist, plastering her mouth to his.

He couldn't help but grin, given the ferocity of her kiss. "Lucky you're a little whip of a thing or you would've knocked me over. Not that I'm complaining, but what was that for?"

"Because you're amazing. Because you're you." *Because I couldn't be more crazy about you if I tried.*

Fletch rested his forehead to hers. "If you're trying to sweet-talk your way into my bed, sugar twang, it's working."

Tanna slid down his body and grabbed his hand, leading him to his bedroom. Once they stood beside the bed, she slipped her fingers beneath his T-shirt, letting her palms rest on his hard, ripped abdomen. "Take off your clothes and lie facedown."

"Why?"

"'Cause I'm fixin' to give you a massage." Her fingers inched up and she squeezed his pectorals before placing a kiss on his chest, over his heart. "Any other questions?"

He shook his head and stripped, releasing a soft sigh when his overheated body met the cool sheets.

She sat on his butt and dug into his shoulder muscles, earning a heavy sigh of satisfaction. "You always wound this tight? Or are you sore from your stint as a midnight grave digger?"

"A little of both. Goddamn. Yes. Right. Fucking. There."

"I take it I hit a good spot?" she murmured in his ear.

"Yes. Where did you learn to do this?"

"Lainie. I had a massive girl crush on her whenever she gave me a massage. I insisted on a play-by-play, so I could learn all her tricks."

"It worked." He released a deep groan when her thumbs pressed and rubbed his triceps. "If you decide against chasing cans for a living again, you could make a killing doing this."

Fletch never said too much about the snail's pace of her recovery since she'd started running barrels again. When they were together it wasn't about their careers. It was about being a man and a woman who enjoyed each other. Yet, their connection had gone beyond being strictly about sex.

Tanna wasn't sure if she'd ever been so completely herself around a guy. She didn't have to pretend to be too wild or too tame. No curbing her raunchy sense of humor. No feigning interest in a subject that held zero appeal. She looked forward to sharing the stupid little stuff from her day. She looked forward to hearing about his day.

She refocused on his massage. Paying special attention to his hands and forearms. Such strength in these sinewy muscles. Yet, such tenderness. The TV droned in the background—because he always left it on. He'd told her the noise made it seem like he wasn't alone in his house. A mind-set she understood. During her years on the blacktop, she'd constantly had the radio on.

When she finished the massage, she brushed the hair from the side of his face. "Better?"

"Uh-huh. But I need to hit the bathroom."

"Oh." She slid off his body, letting her hand linger on the curve of his butt.

Then Fletch rolled over and his cock—his hard cock—was right there. She reached for it only to have him snatch her hand midair. "Hey. I just wanted to massage it too."

He snorted. "Hold that thought. Stretch out and make yourself comfortable."

Tanna lifted an eyebrow. "Is that a command?"

"A request." He disappeared into the bathroom.

She'd just settled into that happy, almost smug place where she knew she was about to get laid, when the bed bounced and Fletch started to hike up her dress. "I can take it off."

"Maybe I wanted to help." His fingers inched up the outside of her thigh and he rubbed his full, soft lips on the scar on her knee. "You have a problem with that?"

"Yes." She sat up to pull the dress over her head and tossed it on the carpet, leaving her in a skimpy bra and boy short panties. "You can help with the rest."

"Take off the bra."

Tanna let the tips of her fingers follow the plunging lace-edged cups. She watched Fletch's avid gaze as she unhooked the front clasp, whipped the bra aside and stroked her breasts.

"I love it when you touch yourself for me."

"I know. Do you want me to get myself off for you?"

"Another time. Right now, I want you to lie back," he said gruffly.

As soon as her shoulders hit the mattress, his work-roughened hands skated up her belly. His hands covered the fleshy mounds of her breasts. He stroked and caressed, occasionally allowing his thumbs to rasp over her nipples. But he didn't use his mouth.

His hands followed the curves of her body, as he tugged her panties down her legs. His touches on her naked limbs and torso were featherlight. Then she swore she felt his nails scraping her flesh hard enough to leave marks. She tried not to squirm or rub her legs together because she suspected he'd go slower yet.

She must've made a disgruntled sound because he chuckled and kissed the hollow dent above her navel. "Where do you want my mouth? Between your legs or on your tits?"

"Tits, definitely."

"Good answer." He feasted on her nipples with the perfect amount of hard rhythmic sucking, gentle licks and softly pressed kisses. And it was hot as hell the way he kept his big hand on her stomach and pushed her back to the mattress whenever she arched up.

Fletch didn't say another word. He just drove her out of her fucking mind with lust.

Then he withdrew.

Tanna opened her eyes to see him throwing the star quilt aside. Before she could ask what he was doing, he plucked her off the mattress. She shrieked, which made him laugh as he brought them to the floor.

Then six feet five inches of man covered her body and his hungry mouth owned hers. Destroyed her with kisses so blistering-hot she swore she was melting. Fletch pinned her hands above her head and nestled his pelvis between her thighs. No need to use his hand to guide his cock in. He just rolled his hips and the tip prodded her entrance.

Tanna surged up, anxious for that first hard thrust, gripping his waist with her legs and digging her heels into his ass.

He broke the kiss.

"What?" she murmured. "Did you forget a condom?"

"No. I slipped one on in the bathroom." He kissed the corners of her smile, then went back to watching her with those topaz-colored eyes.

"Why'd you stop?"

"Because I want to see your face when I do this."

He pushed inside her so slowly she swore she could feel every pulse of the vein running on the underside of his cock.

She wiggled her wrists to get him to let go and he wouldn't. The man wasn't acting at all like she expected. "We have done this before, Fletch."

"I was rough earlier tonight."

He'd been so...desperate for her after not seeing her for a couple of days, he'd pinned her against the wall and fucked her as soon as she'd walked in the door. She'd loved seeing that side of him. "That's what we both wanted."

"Well, I don't want that now."

"What do you want?"

"You." His lips brushed hers with fleeting kisses. "This."

Tanna tried to chase his mouth for firmer contact, but he wouldn't allow it. He smiled against her cheek. "Woman, you define impatient."

"I don't like to wait. What's the point? We both want to get off."

"I can stop." He pulled out completely.

"Don't you dare stop," she warned him.

He gifted her with that sharklike grin and slammed home to the root.

Tanna arched up, or rather she tried to, but Fletch's big body kept hers in place. He barely moved his pelvis. He nuzzled her neck, nipping at the straining cords as she tried to force him to fuck her harder, faster, deeper—all to no avail.

"You always smell like wildflowers and rain," he murmured. "I want to lose myself in you. Just like this. Slow and sweet."

Maybe she needed a gentle touch tonight as much as he did. And she'd needed affirmation that she could give it to him.

"Will you kiss me slow and sweet while you're lovin' on me that way?" she whispered. She felt him smile against her throat.

"Be my pleasure."

Chapter Thirty-one

❦

"*S*o on your day off, instead of hanging by the pool or shootin' pool in some dark bar, you're out here . . . doin' what exactly?"

Tanna rested her forearm across the pitchfork handle and looked at Sutton. "I wonder why I'm happy to see you when I remember that every time I do see you, you bust my balls."

Sutton laughed. "Missed your smart mouth, Tex-Mex. But really, what are you doin'?"

"Helping out. Eli and Summer went to some big auction out of town. The girls were scheduled to come today and rather than disappointing them, I offered my services. After they left, I went for a ride. Now I'm cleaning up. What about you?"

"I'm here overnight. There are a few rodeos within a day's drive so Eli said I could crash here between events."

"Will you be training while you're here?"

"Doubtful. How about you?"

Tanna shuffled her feet. "I'm riding, and training—if I can even call it that. It's slow goin'."

His eyebrows drew together. "You're slow goin'? Or the training is slow goin'?"

"Both. I mean, I'm no longer trotting around the barrels, which is progress, but I'm nowhere near normal speed."

"You've had no issues galloping and pushing the horse hard when you're out joyriding?"

She laughed. "Nope."

"So what horses have you been working with?"

"Mostly Celia's horse, Mickey. He's a little high-strung, nowhere near Jezebel's level. But at least he knows what to do on the dirt, which is more than I can say for the other horses I've tried. No offense to Eli. But slow and steady is probably all I can handle right now anyway."

"Bullshit. You run barrels yet today?"

"No."

"Why not?" he demanded.

Pathetic to admit, but she needed a cheerleader. Or at least a score-keeper. Or someone around to help her in case she did get injured. "I'm not in the mood."

"Which is exactly why you should do it. Let's kick dirt in the face of those speed demons—or lack of demons—doggin' you, and chase some cans."

Tanna rolled her eyes. "You're a real comedian."

Sutton playfully tapped her arm. "I ain't joking. Getcha tack, Tex-Mex. We're gonna have us a little rodeo."

"Sutton—"

"I'm here, you're here, we ain't got nothin' better to do, right? So catch your horse, get your tack and I'll set up the barrels."

On one hand Tanna wanted to defy his bossy behavior; it annoyed the piss out of her. On the other hand, she needed this push. Hadn't she wanted some-one around to help her today? Besides, Sutton knew barrel racing and wouldn't feed her full of shit about her performance and technique if she sucked.

Oh, yeah, she was gonna suck it up bad. She just knew it.

But there was a spring in her step as she headed to the fence. She tossed two handfuls of oats in a bucket and slipped into the horse pasture.

Mickey's ears perked up when Tanna called his name. She draped the lead rope over her shoulder and shook the oats.

That did the trick. Mickey trotted over, expecting a treat. Tanna looped on the lead rope and Mickey gave a disgusted snort. "You oughta know by now that everything has a price." She led him out of the pasture and tied him to the corral while she grabbed her brush, saddle pad, saddle and training bridle.

When preparing him to ride, Mickey tried to bump her, she reacted instinctively, just like she used to—without fear. She shoved him back. "Dammit, Mickey. Behave."

He snorted and blew out a noseful of snot.

"Thank you so much for that. Jerk." Tanna brushed the dirt from his back and then smoothed her hand over the hide to make sure she hadn't missed anything. She settled the saddle pad, positioned the saddle and fastened the cinch. She slipped the headstall over his head and inserted the snaffle bit into his mouth. Then she tied the reins around the saddle horn while she rechecked the cinch.

Sutton yelled over the fence. "How long's it take to warm him up?"

"About ten minutes since I already rode him today." She mounted up and Mickey went straight for the hay on the other side of the fence. "No way." Tanna reined him back. "Work first. Then food." Mickey continued to fight her; she continued to show him who was boss.

As soon as they were out in the pasture, the other horses showed up to run alongside Mickey. Mostly to taunt him that they could scatter at will and he was tethered. Even though Mickey wasn't permanently boarded here, he'd taken the role of pack leader when he was.

Tanna urged him to a good clip. Bouncing along the rocky terrain, that niggling fear returned. One slip of his hooves at this speed and they could be on the ground, grinding to a halt in a mix of broken bones at the bottom of the ridge.

"Whoa." Mickey stopped with little reining effort.

Then they loped.

Trotted.

Galloped.

Looking over her shoulder, she saw that Sutton had opened the gate to the corral and sat on the inside ledge where the electronic timers were placed at an event. The barrels were set up. Knowing Sutton, even the dirt had been raked.

You can do this.

Run 'em fast, run 'em hard.

Tanna blew out a breath and sat deep in her saddle.

She used Celia's starting command. "Run 'em, Mickey."

They were off like a shot and for once, she didn't pull back.

Mickey knew exactly what to do. At this speed his body quivered with excitement as she directed him to the left barrel first. The corral seemed too close and she had that split-second image of crashing headfirst into it. But when she pulled on the outside rein to direct Mickey's body to come out of the turn, he kept his head up and cut around the barrel. While she kept a decent seat, her body wasn't in tune with Mickey's.

Focus.

Her heart thumped as they approached the second barrel. At this speed it took every bit of courage to keep her eyes open. She gritted her teeth so hard pain shot through her skull.

Not gonna fall.

Not gonna fail.

Then they were in that breathless moment in the pocket where it seemed the horse was nearly on plane with the ground. Tanna kept her shoulders aligned with Mickey's, not leaning too far in or too far out, switching the pressure on the rein from the inside to the outside.

Heading toward the last barrel. Mickey went into his turn too fast, making it too wide and in that instant Tanna knew why Celia'd had no luck shaving time off her scores. Slicing was almost impossible to retrain in a barrel horse.

Even as that thought raced through her mind, she kicked him into a gallop. Mickey tore down the dirt to the arena exit. "Whoa." The horse could stop on a dime, she'd give him that much—and after he settled a bit, they loped to the outer side of the corral where Sutton sat.

She squinted at him. "Well?"

"Twenty-eight point three."

This time last year she would've been devastated with that time—even in practice runs. But now...she'd take it.

Sutton held up his hand. "Slap me some skin, sista. That's what I'm talking about. You did it! You cranked on the speed."

Tanna high-fived him. "Turn and burn, baby."

"Turn and burn," he repeated with a grin. "You ready to go again?"

"Yep. But first, what did you see, as far as mistakes?"

"Until you do a few more runs, I can't separate horse and rider."

"Gotcha." Tanna turned Mickey to the right and they trotted to where the alleyway would begin if they were in an arena. She wanted to test his anticipation level.

Mickey danced sideways, backed up, and tossed his head.

Apparently he'd missed it too.

Tanna signaled him to go.

Her brain shifted the same time as her body and she was focused on getting back in the game.

After the fifth run, Tanna climbed off and gave Mickey a well-deserved break. When she wandered over to where Sutton stood, he had an odd look on his face. "What? Was I really that horrible? Because I did shave four—"

"No, that's not it. You looked great. Better than great actually and that's why I wanna talk to you about something."

She swigged from her bottle of water. "Shoot."

"There's a breeder in Colorado who'd like to talk to you."

"About?"

"About you considering using one of their horses for CRA competition."

Tanna stepped back. More like she stumbled back. "I'm not sure I'm gonna compete again."

Sutton stepped forward. "Don't lie to me, but most of all, don't lie to yourself. I saw you today. If you truly were walking away, then you wouldn't have started running practice barrels. You'd be content that you'd just gotten back on a horse again. Am I right?"

She blinked at him.

"Alls I'm asking is that you consider meeting with these folks. They're good people. Hard workers. They're horse brokers as well as breeders. And I've gotta say, they've been breeding exceptional stock. In a few years, they'll be at the top of the heap. How would you like to be one of the riders who put them there?"

"How hard did you have to lobby on my behalf, Sutton?"

He scowled. "Goddammit, I knew you'd say something like that. I didn't lobby at all. I mentioned you were up here for the summer."

"And?"

"And they asked how you'd fared after your injury. If you'd started training. What your plans were. They mentioned your accident. In fact, they called it a freak accident and said no one should be blaming you for Jezebel's death."

Why didn't she believe him?

"Since I'm such a great guy," he grinned again, "I said your plans were up in the air. That's when they really put the boots to me. So I promised them I'd bring it up with you. And now I have."

"They own your new competition horse?"

"Horses," he corrected. "I couldn't decide on one so I'm alternating them, I offered to buy them outright, but they wanna retain ownership for breeding purposes rather than selling. There's something to be said for having a world champion depending on your stock." Sutton bumped her shoulder with his. "Or a *three*-time world champion riding their stock."

Tanna couldn't help but ask, "Do they have a competition horse in mind for me?"

"A seven-year-old mare named Madera. Natalie Finch rode her for a year, and they were close to making the CRA finals, but Natalie busted both legs in a snowmobile accident, putting them out of contention. With no rider, they decided to breed Madera, so she's been outta competition for two years."

Tanna remembered hearing about Natalie's bad luck and subsequent retirement. She'd competed against Natalie that year but she didn't have an impression of the horse she'd ridden. "Someone has been working with Madera?"

"Their trainer. Natalie Finch was a decent rider but they've never had a barrel racer of your caliber put Madera through her paces."

"Laying it on a little thick, ain't ya, bulldogger?"

"Only because it's true."

"Look. I appreciate the props, but I'm nowhere near ready to try out horses."

He leaned over the fence and spit a stream of tobacco juice. "Because you're still scared?"

Disconcerting that Sutton had said the same thing Fletch had. "I can't push the horse to perform on the level I need if I can't push myself."

"No offense, but this horse isn't *on* your level. And you gradually increased your speed over only five runs, Tanna. Five. You do five more and you'll keep getting faster. We both know it. Whatever issue you might've had with needing to build speed isn't a factor anymore."

When she didn't immediately answer, his smug smile appeared.

"Aha, you can't argue with me because you know I'm right!"

"Fine. I'll do a few more runs today and see where I end up, time-wise."

"Does that mean I can tell them you're interested? Or will you at least look at the online footage of Madera before you say no?"

"You are such a pushy bastard, Sutton Grant." She unhooked Mickey's reins and led him along the corral. "But yes. I'll consider it."

Sutton pumped his fist into the air.

"Now get back in position."

"Your wish is my command, Tex-Mex." He grinned. "And at least try to go a little faster, huh?"

Tanna flipped him off.

⚬

Fletch parked on the far side of Eli's barn. He hadn't heard from Tanna all day and he'd gotten concerned, knowing that Eli and Summer had gone to an auction in Rock Springs.

Although she assured him she had a handle on her former fears, Tanna being alone with horses scared him. The demands of his job ensured he couldn't be on the sidelines, cheering her on while she pushed her boundaries. He just hoped she wasn't holding back because he couldn't be with her every day.

So his jaw dropped at seeing Tanna racing across the dirt at what looked like normal competition speed—not the turtle pace she'd bemoaned in the last week.

So what had changed? And when had it happened?

That's when Fletch saw Sutton Grant sitting on the fence, watching Tanna's every move.

Jealousy hit him like a hoof to the gut.

So he hung back out of sight.

After the run ended, Tanna focused entirely on what Sutton told her. Then she was back at it, lining up and racing into the practice arena.

It was bittersweet, watching the woman he loved reconnect with a part of her that'd been missing. A part that defined her. A part of her Fletch had known was there, but hadn't seen in action. And it was amazing to watch her doing what she was meant to do.

After another run, Tanna loped off into the pasture, giving the horse time to graze and cool down.

He walked along the back side of the corral. Upon reaching Sutton, he draped his forearms over the fence. "Hey."

"Hey, Doc. I didn't know you were here. Pull up a section of fence."

"You plan on pushing me off for bein' a little hotheaded the last time we saw each other?"

"Nah. If bein' pissed off at me made you take action with Tanna so she can do that?" He pointed to the pasture. "Then it was worth it."

Fletch climbed up on Sutton's right side. "How's she doin' today?"

"I can't believe how well. I figured she'd ease into it. But she's been hell-bent for leather." He scratched his chin. "She's still pulling back on the second barrel, but that's understandable. And Mickey is a good horse, but he's not a great horse. He's certainly nowhere near the caliber of barrel horse Tanna is used to."

"So what changed today that sent her from zero to sixty?"

Sutton couldn't hide a smug smile.

"What did you have to do? Threaten her? Or bribe her?" he said lightly, trying to keep sharpness from his tone.

He chuckled. "I knew you weren't dumb, but your intuitive side does surprise me."

"Animals rarely verbalize anything so it's my job to be intuitive." Now that had come out sharp.

"Christ, you're touchy. Alls I'm saying is most men would look at the whole picture—Tanna getting back to barrel racing—and not break it down pixel by pixel. You knew something had to happen to encourage her to kick up the pace."

Fletch looked at Sutton. "So it was just your influence that did it?"

"You'd hate that, wouldn't you?"

"Goddamn right I would."

Sutton offered another smile. "Not blaming your jealousy on something else—yet another surprising thing about the good doc. But the truth is, I dangled an opportunity in front of her. The horse breeder I use is interested in having her try out one of their prime barrel horses."

"No shit. They told you that?"

"Of course they want her. Tanna is a proven champion. So I relayed the info to Tanna. She bitched about bein' a has-been and some other bullshit about why they couldn't possibly trust her with high-end horseflesh. But the whole time she was denying it, I saw the wheels spinning. Mostly she made the choice on her own to get back up to speed. Literally. So how long have you been here watching?"

Fletch shrugged. "Long enough."

Sutton adjusted his hat. "You pissed off that in trying to get her lined up with a new horse means she'll be leaving here?"

"Never was a question that she'd leave here. Just what kind of shape she'd be in when she did." Tanna had been more broken when she'd arrived than anyone had known—including him. As proud as he was that she'd come full circle, he couldn't stop the melancholy feeling.

"Does she know you're in love with her?"

That jarred him. "More'n likely. I haven't come out and said it, but she can't be around me and not know how I feel."

"Jesus, Fletch, why don't you tell her?"

Rather than snap off, *none of your damn business*, he said, "Because she'll run. She's never had what I'm willing to offer her."

"Which is what?"

"Everything." He hopped off the fence. "I've gotta check on a horse," he lied.

"Don't leave without letting her know you were here," Sutton warned. "This was a big day for her. She'll want to share it with you."

Fletch didn't respond. He walked to the horse barn and performed a quick check on the three horses just for the hell of it. One was a former wild mustang that Eli wanted to breed with Blue, a docile mare who became a fierce mama. That feistiness might translate into good bucking stock. He'd already suggested to Renner that investing in a few wild horses would be a good place to start. Although Renner couldn't use horses bought from BLM auctions for rodeo stock, he could start breeding them with his existing stock.

He killed thirty minutes before he returned to the corral. Tanna was outside the gate ready to start her run.

Her hair was flying as she burst onto the dirt and urged Mickey to haul ass. They cleared the first barrel, no problem. He did hold his breath as she started around the second barrel. He saw her pause for a second—and knew that second hesitation could cost her... possibly seconds. They sped toward the third barrel. Mickey turned sharply enough that Fletch feared horse and rider would hit the skids, but she retained control. She rode him hard until the end.

Sutton yelled, "Turn and burn, baby. You shaved it down to twenty-two point nine!"

She whooped and dismounted. Then set to tying Mickey to the fence post.

Fletch walked across the dirt toward her. He'd made it a little more than halfway when Tanna caught sight of him. She didn't walk, she ran. In an instant he had that squirming, beautiful, elated woman in his arms. Laughing. Squeezing him tightly. And for just a moment, all was right with his world.

"Fletch! Didja see me ride?"

"Several times. How did it feel?"

"Scary. Horrible." She smirked. "Then wonderful."

He pressed his lips to her forehead. "I'm happy for you, sugar twang."

"What're you doin' here?"

"I told Eli if I was in the neighborhood I'd check a couple of things."

"Are you done for the day?"

"Nope. I've got three more stops."

Tanna sighed. "I'm in the mood to celebrate."

"By celebrate do you mean knocking back a few drinks? Or having a quickie against the horse trailer?"

"I'm inclined to take option two. But I've gotta deal with Mickey and Sutton, so by then you'll be off to your next appointment. I'll take a rain check for the naked celebration."

Fletch cupped her ass cheeks in his hands and growled, "As long as it's tonight. Been missing you in my bed, cowgirl."

"Same." She pecked him on the mouth. "Call me when you're done. How long might that be?"

"Gotta stop at Talley's and Myerson's. Then Annabeth is bringing her horse to my clinic."

Tanna's eyes—a piercing violet today—turned laser sharp. "The cutting horse queen is havin' *another* problem?"

"Her dad is out of town. She's called me three times."

"Of course she has. She'll probably show up at the clinic in a negligee and fuck-me stilettos, wearing her tiara."

He laughed, but it died quickly when he realized she was serious. "Tanna. It's not like that."

"But it is," she insisted. "She wants you and not just as her personal horse doctor. She wants to play doctor with you. Hell, she's more determined to marry you than little Miss Ellie is."

"Bull. Annabeth is a client. That's all."

Tanna poked him in the chest. "What if I said I didn't want you to be alone with her tonight?"

"Jesus. What's gotten into you?"

"Answer the question."

"Edmunds are good paying customers. I can't afford to say no." Fletch stepped back and crossed his arms over his chest. "And it's no different from you bein' out here alone with Sutton all afternoon."

"It's very different. Sutton is trying to help me get my career back on track."

"That's the same thing I'm doin' with Annabeth. Speaking of... he told me about the folks in Colorado wanting you to try out a new horse?"

That shocked her. "Sutton's got a big mouth. I'm not sure what I'll do. I'm nowhere near competition ready." She scowled. "You're clouding the issue."

"And now I'm running behind. So how about if you make celebration plans with Sutton, and I'll just go do my job? Because most likely any plans we made would get fucked up anyway." Fletch turned and walked away.

And Tanna didn't call him back.

Chapter Thirty-two

She stewed. Cussed. Ranted. Paced. Brooded some more.

Blind and bullheaded. That's what he was.

He thought she'd rather celebrate with Sutton than him?

Bullshit. The man had nothing to be jealous of and he knew it.

How could he honestly believe that Pageant Queen Barbie didn't have her manicured hooks hovering above those amazing biceps of his, waiting for the right moment to dig her claws in?

What pissed her off the most was Fletch and Annabeth would be a perfect match. He was gorgeous. She was gorgeous. Miz Maybelle's society page would read: *Local rancher's beauty queen/professional horsewoman daughter marries local veterinarian. Beautiful, perfect babies to follow.*

But Annabeth would probably make him happy—when she wasn't running him ragged like she did with her dad. She'd pop out a couple of cute kids. They'd build a big house with a big horse barn near—or on—her family land. Everyone would tell Fletch what a lucky bastard he was for landing Annabeth as his wife.

Would Trophy Wife Barbie give Fletch everything he needed in bed?

She'd been with her fair share of demanding guys. But Fletch took it to a whole new level. Not just the rockin' sex, but his insatiable need for intimacy. If they were in the same room he had to be touching her. Even just holding hands, but more often his fingers stroked any section of her bared skin. Her arm. Her neck. The tops of her thighs if she wore a skirt. He needed a woman who was physically demonstrative in public and private. No doubt Annabeth would pull out all the stops to garner his attention and affection, but once she had that ring on her finger, would Ice Princess Barbie reappear?

Tanna placed her head in her hands. Her stomach hurt imagining that life unfold before her eyes. Fletch deserved better.

Like you? A former barrel racing champion with nothing to offer him except the type of hot sex he craves?

Isn't that what they'd both signed on for?

Yes. But things had changed.

Hadn't they?

They'd definitely made a promise to each other they would be involved only with each other for as long as Tanna was in Wyoming. Well, she was still here. And Fletch and I-Have-A-Horse-Emergency Barbie needed a reminder of that fact.

Maybe Tanna needed a reminder too, not to be cowed.

So after she returned to the Split Rock, she primped. It'd been a while since she'd bothered. But like any Texas girl worth her salt, she knew how to look good. Damn good.

Big Texas hair. Check.

Sultry makeup. Check.

Cleavage baring glittery tank top. Check.

Skintight Seven jeans. Check.

Her b.b.simon rhinestone belt. Check.

Gigantic world champion barrel racing belt buckle. Check.

Custom-made pink alligator boots with Swarovski crystals. Check.

Should she slip her favorite little gun in her boot?

Nah. That'd be over the top. Although in Texas she wouldn't have thought twice about adding it to her ensemble.

Primed, she went to get her man.

◆

The lights were on in the back of Fletch's building and the garage door was open. A brand-new Dodge diesel with a brand-new horse trailer was backed up to the door. When Tanna saw the horse's nose poking out of one of the stall windows, she gave it a little pat. "You can't be held responsible for your choice of owners, bub."

She heard Annabeth's laughter and Fletch's smooth baritone. She waited for a pause in the conversation, but none came.

What the hell did they have to talk about? Shouldn't Annabeth be trotting her horse home since he was already loaded? And wasn't it past her bedtime?

Throwing back her shoulders, Tanna called out, "Fletch, darlin', where are you?"

Silence except for the *thud thud* of her boot heels connecting with concrete.

Tanna kept her smile locked in place—it felt genuine too, when she saw shock register on Man-Stealing Barbie's face. Then she suffered through the head to toe perusal.

Yeah, look and learn, little girl, because this is how it's done.

"Now please tell me you didn't get so involved helping this girl with her horse problems that you forgot about our celebration tonight."

Annabeth's eyes narrowed at the word *girl* but she wisely kept her heavily glossed lips closed.

"I didn't forget. I was gonna call you when I finished."

Tanna placed her hand on Fletch's chest. His broad, rock-hard chest—and jealousy lit Annabeth's eyes at Tanna's casual touch. Then she ran her palm up the outside of his arm. His thickly muscled arm. Next she turned her head and looked around the empty space. "Where's the patient?"

"He's loaded up. Nothin' major that required an overnight stay."

"Thank goodness. I'm so grateful to you, Dr. Fletcher, for making time for me," Annabeth said in a breathy tone. "Percival means everything to me and I'd lose my mind if anything happened to him. Especially if it was my fault."

That comment caused a tiny blip in Tanna's radar. That'd been directed at her. So Snoopy Barbie *had* checked her out after she'd accompanied Fletch to an "emergency" visit to the Edmunds ranch on a Sunday afternoon.

"You treat that horse like gold, Annabeth."

"I do pride myself on taking good care of things that belong to me. Being neglectful usually leads to big problems." She gave Tanna a challenging stare.

Oh, honey, please. Is that the best you can do?

"I couldn't agree more. I'm sure your daddy is proud he's got such a smart teenager." She smiled and focused on Fletch—his facial expression wavered between laughter and exasperation. "Well, darlin' man of mine, as long as I'm here, I'm gonna check the Ludlows' file and track down their phone number. I do believe I left my favorite scarf there when we were preg testing ewes. I'll be waiting in your office after you lock up back here." Tanna looked Annabeth right in the eye and said, "Nice seeing you again," but she clearly meant, "I wanna see the ass-end of you now, girlie." She sauntered to the door leading to the reception area without looking back.

She thought about heading straight to Fletch's office, but it was dark enough that they wouldn't see her peeking out the small window, just to make sure Annabeth was about to skedaddle her skinny butt home.

Fletch walked Annabeth to the door. The little snot stayed close enough to him that their arms brushed. Then as she said good-bye, she threw her arms around him, smashing her body against his.

Point for Fletch that his hands remained at his sides.

Point for Tanna that she didn't storm back out there and beat the fuck out of that little shit for putting her greedy hands on Tanna's man.

She blinked. Where had that violent thought come from?

Fletch pushed the button and the door began to close.

Tanna hustled to his office. She plopped in his chair and propped her boots on his desk. Her fingers twisted the gold chain hanging from her neck as she waited.

Oh, this was gonna be some fun.

He appeared in the doorway, his hands braced on the doorframe as if deciding whether to come in. "Was that really necessary?"

"Absolutely. And given the fact she still hugged you good-bye, I could've been a lot clearer."

Fletch bestowed that slow, panty-dropping grin on her. "Even if she didn't get the message, I did. Loud and clear."

"What message would that be, Dr. Fletcher?"

"That you're all woman, a woman to be reckoned with, and you're all mine."

"Mmm. But I *am* feeling the teeniest bit hurt, sugarplum, that we had celebration plans tonight, and you were too nice a guy to tell Annabeth to get lost." Tanna cocked her head. "Was it her great conversational skills or her shameless display of perky tits that held you enthralled?"

He shrugged. "She has a nice rack. I'm a breast man, if you'll recall." His eyes locked on her fingertips brushing the top of her cleavage as she twisted the necklace. Then his gaze moved to her mouth. "But I'd be more than happy to give you a demonstration of how much I love *your* rack, if you need a refresher."

Tanna laughed. "Why don't you come over here and give me a kiss. Then you can work that talented mouth of yours down to my poor neglected rack." Fletch started toward her with that gleam in his eye. "Ah-ah. Not so fast. Take off your shirt first."

He raised an eyebrow. "Why?"

"Partially because you have a fantastic chest and I can't get enough of it. The other reason is because you smell like her perfume."

Fletch stripped the shirt off and tossed it aside.

She dropped her boots to the floor and pushed the office chair back, making room for him.

His hands gripped the chair's armrests and his liquid gaze seemed to drink in every nuance of her face. "Sweet Jesus, you're so damn hot when you're jealous." His mouth crashed down on hers, owning her with his hungry, possessive kiss.

No hands. No body parts rubbing together. Just lips and tongues and passion. Good Lord. He packed so much passion into the kiss, she felt dizzy.

He eased back, their breath still mingling, their damp lips barely apart. "I need you in my bed, sugar twang."

"We'll get there, but first things first." Tanna pushed him and his butt connected with his desk. Watching his face, she hit the hydraulic lever on the chair until she was at the perfect height.

"Woman, you've got a gleam in your eye that's making me nervous."

She scooted forward, placing her hands on his knees. Then she slid her palms up his thighs. Reaching his pelvis, she scraped her fingernails up the length of his already hard cock. "Is nervous another word for antsy?" She pulled the end of his belt through the belt loop of his jeans.

"I'm antsy if this is goin' where I think it's goin'."

Tanna tugged the belt buckle, revealing the button on his jeans. Keeping her eyes on his, she said, "Ever been sucked off in your office?"

He shook his head.

"Seriously? A hot doctor like you never had a veterinary assistant follow you in here, lock the door and get on her knees?"

"Ah. No."

"Why not?"

"I've strongly discouraged anyone from hanging out in my office."

"Good." She bent forward and mouthed his shaft through the denim, blowing hot air into the material and lightly sinking her teeth down.

He hissed.

She looked up at him across the expanse of his chest. "Drop your pants."

Fletch didn't scramble to lose his pants. He stood and very methodically eased the zipper down and loosened each side, revealing gray pinstriped boxer briefs.

"Classy."

"I thought so." He slid his hands down the flat plane of his abdomen, his fingers slipping beneath the fabric and shoving until his jeans caught the tops of his hiking boots.

"How far can you spread your legs? Or are the jeans hobbling you?"

He widened his knees.

"Perfect. I can play with your balls too."

He muttered, "Christ, you're killing me," but he leaned back and braced himself on the desk.

Tanna rolled forward. She nuzzled his sac and licked from root to tip.

Then back down. With her fingers circling the base, she pulled his cock away from his body and swallowed it in one gulp.

He groaned.

She sucked, letting his flavor fill her senses completely before releasing the hard shaft a little at a time. "I love the way you taste." She tongued the tip of his cock and reached for his heavy balls. After eliciting such sexy hot sounds from him, she switched the position of her hand and mouth. Sucking his balls into her mouth and rolling the globes over her tongue while her thumb teased the rim of his cockhead.

"Goddamn, that feels good."

As much as she liked to drag out the torture, loving the power in hearing a man beg, she was too greedy this time. As soon as she released his balls, her lips were sliding down his cock.

Another groan.

Her hands stroked the tops of his thighs as his dick shuttled in and out of her mouth. Tanna wanted to bring him off with only her mouth. No hands jacking him. Just suction, friction and wet heat.

And skill.

His legs began to bounce and she had to dig in her fingernails to stop the motion. "Sorry. It's just so fucking good."

She moaned around his shaft and his entire body shuddered from the sensation. She plunged his cock completely in past her gag reflex and released it just as quickly until the tip quivered on her lips. Tanna got lost in the rhythm, in the taste, in their mutual sounds of pleasure.

"I'm close. Jesus. How can I already be...goddamn, that tongue of yours is lethal."

She shortened the strokes, only taking half his cock in her mouth and concentrating on sucking the head. Lips, teeth, tongue worked him.

His legs started to shake, but he didn't pound his hips into her face. He made that strangled groan, his body went rigid and his head dropped back.

She sucked in time to the first couple pulses, feeling the come coating her tongue. Then she deep throated him and swallowed as he moaned and cursed and praised her in the same breath as God.

Then Fletch's hand landed on her head, patting her hair so sweetly. She dislodged his cock from her throat and suckled the tip one more time before releasing him.

Tanna tried to catch her breath and find a comfortable position because her panties were soaked.

Then she noticed the damndest thing. His dick hadn't immediately gone soft. In fact, if she hadn't felt his cock jerking on her tongue and tasted his sticky cream, she'd think he hadn't come at all.

His gentle touch on her head vanished. He twined his fingers in her hair and pulled her head back to look into his face.

"Yes, I'm still hard as a fucking brick. That's what you do to me, Tanna. You sucked me off and I came so hard I thought I'd popped something in my brain. But when I look at you, or put my hands on you, or think about getting naked with you"—his cock jumped against his belly—"I'm totally hard again." Wildness danced in his eyes.

She expected he'd release her hair but he didn't.

"I've never had sex in this office. Or any rooms in this building. As I conjured depraved places I wanted to fuck you mindless, I realized you were already in the place I wanted you the most. Handy, huh?" He grinned at her. "Now ditch all them clothes you're wearing."

As she rolled the chair back, she ditched the tank top. After toeing off her boots, she shimmied out of her jeans and traced the satin edges of her plain white bra, holding back a laugh at his greedy look. "You want this off, rack-lovin' man? You'll have to do it."

"That right?"

Her hands moved down and she traced the satin edge of her matching panties. "These too."

"You're awful bossy for the one who ain't in charge."

"Who says I'm not in charge?"

Then he plucked her out of the chair, spinning them both around and pinning her to the desk. "Bigger, badder, stronger"—he flashed his teeth— "hornier; sugar twang, I'm *always* in charge." He popped the front enclosure on her bra and stripped it away. "Take off the panties or I'll cut 'em off."

She maneuvered around until they were gone. Where they ended up, she didn't care.

"Don't. Move." He snagged a condom from his jeans. Suited up, he pressed his crotch against hers, resting his cock on her slit. Rolling his hips so the ridged edge of his cockhead rubbed on her clit. Back and forth. Spreading her wetness until they were both sticky with it.

Damn man knew how to rev her up.

Fletch studied her face. "Do you want to get off like this?"

Tanna shook her head.

"You sure?" Short jabs put constant pressure on that hot spot. His pulling and twisting fingers exacted the perfect amount of pressure on her nipples. "Once this way, and once me hammering into you as hard as you like it."

"No. I want you in me when I come."

"Does wild things to me to hear you say stuff like that."

"I can tell." Tanna arched her back and widened her thighs. "How about when I do this?"

"Oh yeah. Put your arms above you. Turn your head and moan."

Tanna followed his instructions, but added in a breathy voice, "Ooh, Dr. Fletcher, you're such an animal." She moaned softly. "Please. Do me now."

"Total fantasy moment, fucking a gorgeous woman across my desk. I'll be reliving this for years."

So would she.

But he'd stopped moving.

"We playing doctor or what?"

"Look at me."

She opened her eyes at his soft command.

Oh, hello, lust. The possessive way he looked at her sent shivers up her spine. "Fletch? What's wrong?"

"Nothin'. Everything is right for once."

Tell him you love him.

But as he plowed into her all coherent thought vanished.

Chapter Thirty-three

❧

*T*anna could say one thing about Sutton, when he made up his mind to do something, he acted on it immediately. She agreed to watch a training video online, featuring the seven-year-old blue roan mare. Intrigued, she watched another, and another, until she'd seen them all.

When Sutton asked whether she was interested in trying the horse, and she said yes, then next thing she knew, he was on the phone with the breeders, discussing possible dates.

Given Tanna's schedule, she couldn't take a few days off and drive to Colorado. So color her shocked when the owners of the Grade A Horse Farm agreed to bring Madera to her over the weekend.

And now they were almost here.

No pressure.

"Tanna. Stop pacing. You're makin' me crazy."

"Can't help it. I'm nervous."

"Don't be. Chuck and Berlin Gradsky are good people. They're just as nervous to meet you."

Probably because they're afraid to let me on their horse.

Sutton sighed. "I know exactly what you're thinking, Tanna, and that's not it. Come here." Sutton dug his thumbs into her shoulders and moved outward toward the ball of her shoulder. "Maybe this'll help."

"Oh. God. That is perfect."

"Just what I love to hear when I've got my hands on a beautiful woman," he murmured.

Warning bells went off. Sutton had been saying things like that since they'd set up this test run. Was he flirting with her?

Don't be ridiculous. Sutton knows you're with Fletch. You're just feeling neglected by the man you love.

Fletch had been scarce the last week. They'd seen each other once. They'd talked on the phone twice. She understood he was busy, but they hadn't been this hit-and-miss since they'd first started seeing each other before Fletch started his sabbatical.

A truck and trailer rig eased up the driveway.

Her heart rate increased dramatically.

"Showtime." Sutton squeezed her shoulders once before his hands fell away.

She knew the drill. Let the owners unload the horse. Let the horse run free in the corral a bit. Then introduce her.

Tanna remained in the shadows and paced. She heard the horse kick the inside of the trailer. The sound of hooves hitting metal made her jump.

Eli was on hand although Summer had made herself scarce.

Tanna wanted Fletch here so bad she dug her phone out of her pocket.

You don't need a man to be strong. You can do this.

She didn't call him.

Late afternoon heat seeped into her bones. She ducked into the barn and let the cool darkness calm her. Breathing in familiar scents. Watching dust motes dance in the shafts of sunlight like bits of fading glitter. She rested against the partition that held her tack, knowing she might not need it. Some owners preferred to use their own bits and training gear, especially in a situation like this one. She forced herself to zone out and wasn't sure how much time had passed when the barn door creaked.

An arc of sunlight cut through the shadows. "Tanna?"

"I'm here."

"Thought you might be. Gradskys are ready for you."

"Okay."

Eli's boot steps thudded across the dirt floor. "You all right?"

"I'm fine."

"You don't have to do this, you know."

"I want to. I just don't know how to tell them that even if they do lend me the horse for a trial period, I don't know how I'll pay for feed."

"We'll figure something out. I promise."

Her lips flattened. "This isn't Sutton's doing?"

"We'll talk later. They're waiting."

"What do I need to bring out?"

"Just your saddle and saddle pad."

Tanna grabbed her stuff and headed to the corral.

Chuck and Berlin Gradsky were in conversation with Sutton.

Tanna came up on the back side of the corral. She thrust out her hand. "Hi. I'm Tanna Barker."

The slender, dark-haired woman, fifty or so, smiled. "I'm Berlin Gradsky. This is my husband, Chuck."

She shook his hand. "Nice to meet you both. Thanks for driving up here and for the opportunity to try out your horse."

"We're happy to be here. We've been huge fans for years. We watched you win all three championships at the MGM Grand."

Tanna smiled. "Those were good times. Anything I oughta know about Madera before we get started?"

"She's been brushed down. Since we knew you'd ride her right away, we left on her protective boots." Berlin handed over a bridle. "We've been re-introducing competition bits, but for right now we'd prefer if you'd use this transition bit."

"No problem." Tanna fingered the smooth metal bit. Then she examined the headstall portion of the bridle, noticing it had a noseband tie-down. "She always use a noseband? Or is that new?"

"She's always used one."

"Great. I'll just go ahead and get Madera ready, if that's all right."

Berlin said, "We can't wait."

She looked at Eli and Sutton. "If one of you wants to get the gate and the other set up barrels, we'll get this under way."

Madera trotted over as soon as Tanna entered the pasture. "Such a pretty girl." The mare was a striking-looking horse—bluish-gray with a black mane and tail. Tanna looped a lead rope over her and loosely tied her to the fence where she'd draped her saddle and saddle blanket. Madera seemed smaller than Jezebel. But as Tanna double-checked Madera's legs and swept her hand across her back, she realized the mare was all muscle.

Tanna stroked her neck, talking softly to her, reassuring her, petting the area between her eyes to calm her. When Madera lowered her head, Tanna slipped the bridle on without issue, tightening the buckles and checking the bit.

So far, so good.

But as soon as Tanna put on the saddle pad, Madera balked. Backing away. Acting like she was going to kick before she did a series of little crow hops. Tanna jerked on the reins and sharply said, "Hey. Enough."

That stopped some of her antsy behavior.

Almost by rote Tanna finished saddling her. She led her half the length of the corral, stopped, backed her up and checked the cinch. Loose. No surprise that Madera had expanded her belly in anticipation of being ridden; most horses did. Tanna tightened the cinch, walked Madera forward another twenty paces and checked the cinch and the position of the saddle again. No change. They were good to go.

But when she mounted up, a shot of pain burned through her bad knee. She needed to adjust the stirrups. Tanna felt like a jack-in-the-box popping off and on the horse. Finally everything felt right.

Out in the pasture, she tested Madera's stopping power. She was happy that the mare responded to verbal commands better than the reins. Then Tanna tugged out and down on the reins and the horse turned a tight circle. She tried the opposite side. Not as tight, but decent.

As soon as she kicked her heels, Madera jumped to life.

That was a nice burst of speed.

Tanna didn't let her run far. She wanted to see how the horse would react if she let up on the reins.

Madera immediately tried to bolt.

"So, you're one of those kinds. Docile acting until the moment my guard is down. Then you pull a Pony Express imitation." She patted Madera on the neck. "I'm onto you, sister. But I'm gonna wait to pass judgment on whether that's a good or bad thing until I see what you can do." She squinted at the gate and Eli waved his arms, which meant the barrels were ready.

She kept Madera at an easy trot until twenty yards from the gate. "Show me whatcha got. Let's run." She dropped her butt into the saddle and Madera charged forward. Once they hit the timer's mark, Madera was all about speed.

Tanna directed her to the right and there wasn't a hitch in Madera's smooth movement even coming out of the pocket. Still, Tanna fought the urge to rein back on the second barrel and they cut it so tight they tipped the barrel over.

Five-second penalty.

But the race wasn't over yet. They nudged the last barrel but it only teetered. Then Madera was on the straightaway and that burst of speed Tanna had felt wasn't a fluke.

Madera hauled ass. Serious ass.

They cleared the gate too far. That's something they'd need to work on—faster stops. Many rodeos were held in confined spaces with short alleyways so the horse needed to acclimate to that possibility every time.

She kept Madera on a short rein and yelled to Sutton. "Time?"

"Twenty-five point nine. With the five-second penalty."

Which meant a base time of . . . twenty-some-odd seconds? On a first run? With a rusty rider?

Holy. Shit.

What could this horse do if she was properly trained with a rider who knew how to push her to peak performance?

She could win. And win big.

One thing Tanna hadn't forgotten about the years she'd spent with Jezebel—the feisty mare hadn't started out top-notch. It'd taken dedication on Tanna's part to get her to that level. Jezebel's owners wouldn't have had a winning horse if not for Tanna's perseverance to turn her into one. Yes, horses with high price tags almost always performed better. But a good partnership between horse and rider really made a difference.

Madera made a noise.

Tanna patted her neck. "You did good."

Confidence pushed through the fog of doubt. She shouted at Eli. "I'm runnin' them again."

Each of the next six runs fluctuated between nineteen point five and twenty-one point one.

Tanna stopped to regroup. She hung back by the gate, tempted to dismount and let Madera roll in the dirt, eat some oats, because she deserved it. But she wanted to stay on just a little longer. She was excited about this horse. Had she ever thought she'd say that again? Had she ever thought she'd supplant her fear long enough to reclaim her skill? The mechanics were coming back to her—if they'd ever really left.

She returned to the training area and stopped in front of Chuck and Berlin, who wore identical grins.

Chuck spoke first. "You made our horse look good."

"Oh, I think the reverse is true. She is a sneaky one. Not balking at the bit, which I expected with the noseband, but balking at getting saddled. She's got a wicked crow hop if you're not paying attention. Her head needs to be higher in the turn but I think trying her with a browband instead of a noseband will help." Tanna patted Madera's neck. "This girl prances like an Arabian and turns like a Quarter Horse. But that burst of speed reminds me of a Thoroughbred."

"You aren't far off. Her dam was Red Rider, a champion cutting horse. Her sire, Fool's Gold, also a Quarter Horse, but he earned his name by having that Thoroughbred streak."

"You bred her?"

"Bred, born and broke at our place. We'd intended to train her as a cutting horse. The gal can run, so on a whim we contacted a barrel horse trainer and she worked with her for a year before Natalie took her on the circuit. You have no idea what a rush it is to see you riding her," Berlin said. "It's like handing your car keys to someone and them proving that your car isn't a Ford, but a Ferrari."

Truly touched, Tanna said, "There's a compliment. Thank you."

"So are you interested in training with her?"

"Training with? Meaning putting me in charge of getting her competition ready and then handing the reins to another competitor? No."

"But you'd be willing to take her on yourself?" Berlin prompted.

"I'm willing to discuss it."

Berlin and Chuck exchanged a grin. "That's what we were hoping to hear. Tell you what. We're staying in Rawlins. We'd like to take you out for supper and we can talk about it then." Chuck looked at Eli and Sutton. "You're both invited too."

Sutton said, "Great! I'm in."

Eli smiled. "I appreciate the invite. But me'n my lady already made plans for tonight."

"If they aren't set in stone, we'd be happy to have her come along too."

"That's kind of you to offer and I'll pass it along to her. But I'll still decline. She says she's been sharing me all week and she wants a night to us." Eli smiled and clapped Sutton on the back. "So feel free to keep this one out all night."

Berlin laughed. "Deal."

"You wanna leave Madera here? Or do you have arrangements for her elsewhere?"

"If you're okay with it, we'll leave her."

"Cool. Tanna?"

"I'd be happy to take care of her."

"I'm sure you will. Shall we say Cattleman's Club at eight?"

"See you then."

She unsaddled Madera and brushed her down. Such a beautiful animal and she knew it. She tossed her mane as Tanna groomed her. Then she handed the horse off to Eli to turn her out.

"You oughta ask Fletch to come to the dinner with the Gradskys tonight," Eli said.

"I don't want to put any pressure on him. He feels guilty if he has to break plans."

"True. But I thought he'd be here today. Did he tell you he'd try and stop by for a little bit?"

"No." Tanna petted Madera's neck. "But he's busy."

"He's always busy so that's a piss-poor excuse. This was a big day for you. He shoulda been here."

She'd thought the same thing but worried she might be acting like a bitchy girlfriend if she mentioned it, so she'd kept her feelings to herself. "It would've been good to have him here. But we have our own lives. He might've had an emergency."

"You cut him entirely too much slack." Eli smiled. "I'm really proud of you, girl. You've come a long way. I know you'll credit Fletch, or Sutton, or maybe me, but at the end of the day, everything you've done—it's all you, Tanna. Don't let nothin' or no one take that away from you today."

That made her a little teary-eyed. "That means a lot. Thanks, Eli. For everything."

"You're welcome. Now git."

On impulse, she called Fletch.

He picked up on the first ring. "This is Dr. Fletcher."

"You won't believe the great day I had! Madera can run. Lord, can that mare run. I pushed her hard, pushed myself hard and it paid off. Granted, she needs some work in specific areas, but we really clicked."

He didn't say anything, which wasn't like him.

"Fletch? You still there?"

"Yeah. I'm here. Sounds like everything is working out exactly as you'd hoped."

"The horse is better than I'd hoped, to be honest. The Gradskys want me to train with her, although it's not a done deal. I've yet to nail down the particulars, but we're doin' that tonight." She took a breath before she asked if he wanted to come along.

But Fletch beat her to the punch. "So you're leaving? Just like that," he said flatly. "You get a top-notch horse and then you're gone."

"No! It's not like that." He sounded angry. Really angry.

"Bullshit, Tanna. They must've liked what they saw in you if they're willing to negotiate terms after just a couple runs. Don't tell me you won't be discussing a training schedule with them, and I'm betting that training will take place in Colorado."

"So I should what? Say no?"

"We both know you won't."

Goddamn him. Now *she* was pissed.

"Look, Tanna, I'm swamped today. I've got a long night ahead of me. Calls to make—"

"And God knows you'd never say no to that, would you?"

"What the fuck is that supposed to mean?" he snapped. "I told you when we got involved that my job—"

"Is everything to you. Yeah, I get it. I just thought maybe I'd started to mean something to you too." Dammit. Why had she said that? Now she did sound like a whiny girlfriend.

"Yeah? Well, same goes, sweetheart. *You're* the one who's packing up and leaving."

Ugly silence stretched between them.

Finally Fletch spoke. "I don't have time to do this right now."

"There's a surprise. Tell you what. I won't bother you, bein's you're so *busy*. If you want to talk? You know where to find me."

"Unless you're already in Colorado."

"Unless you pull your head out of your ass, Doc, don't bother contacting me at all," she shot back.

"Tanna—"

She hung up. And cried all the way back to the Split Rock.

How could one of the best days of her life in recent years also be one of the worst?

Chapter Thirty-four

❧

"*F*uck!" Fletch was shaking so hard he pulled to the side of the road.

He wasn't mad at her; he was mad at the situation. He'd known from the start she wouldn't stay in Wyoming and he'd assured himself he could handle it.

Yeah, you're handling it real well. Getting pissed when she just wanted to share her good news with you?

His phone rang. He half expected—no, he hoped it was Tanna calling him back to slice a layer of skin off him like he deserved.

But it wasn't her. It was the answering service. He let the call go to voice mail while he tried to calm down.

Breathe. Think. What's the next logical step?

Besides showing up at her trailer, throwing himself at her feet and confessing his love for her? Begging her to stay?

That'd be a good place to start. Problem was, it needed to be more than a fifteen-minute conversation between his emergency calls, and that was all the time he had to spare right now.

He could call her back and apologize. Tell her he knew they needed to talk. That at least wouldn't leave this void hanging between them.

Fletch reached for the phone only to have it ring. Jet Eriksen's name popped up on the screen. He let it ring again before he answered. "Hey, Jet. What's up?"

"You don't want to know. I've got a remote emergency call and I won't be done in time for our dinner tonight."

"So you're calling off the meet?" He had the hope that the dinner would be cancelled yet again and he could track down Tanna immediately after his last call.

"No. Tasha is still going. Artie will probably be missing too; his assistant said he ran into complications at his last call. I still think it'd be good for you and Tasha to talk. If either Artie or I finish early, we'll show up. Either way, I'll keep in touch."

"Good enough. Thanks for letting me know." After Fletch disconnected, he called his answering service and retrieved the message. A quick stop, the client promised. But Fletch knew if the client was calling late on a Saturday afternoon it wouldn't be routine.

He glanced at the clock and sighed. He had a lot to do in the next three hours before he met up with his potential business partner.

The only way he could get through this day would be to do the one thing he'd asked Tanna not to do to him: compartmentalize. Put the lid on his anger, shove the box to the back of his mind and do his job.

But he would deal with Tanna first thing tomorrow.

✥

Tanna didn't spend a ton of time fussing with her appearance. She showered, let her hair fall loose, slipped on a denim dress, her championship buckle and her angel wing cowgirl boots.

She'd be freaking out about the blowup with Fletch if she wasn't already obsessing over this meeting. She'd have to tell the Gradskys the truth. Telling a little white lie that everything had been fine in those months she was out of the spotlight and before moving to Wyoming was doing a disservice to all she'd learned and overcome in the past three months.

The Cattleman's Club parking lot was jammed on a Saturday night. Inside the busy restaurant, the hostess led her to a table in the back. Chuck started to get up when he saw her, but she waved him down. "Please sit. I'm happy to see Southern gentleman manners in a Northerner."

"Spoken like a true Texan."

"Guilty."

"Sutton called. Something came up and he won't be joining us."

They made polite conversation for a few minutes until the waitress delivered their drinks. Toast done, they focused on the menu in silence.

Tanna had such a bout of nerves, and was still reeling over the conversation with Fletch, that she needed something to calm her down. A shot of tequila ought to do the trick. She excused herself and cut to the bar.

As she waited for the bartender, Tanna looked around the restaurant and froze when she noticed Fletch at another table. He wore that beautiful smile and was wholly engaged with his dinner companion—a female companion.

What the fuck? What happened to his claim that he'd be out answering calls until the wee hours? Why had he lied to her? Why had he picked a goddamned fight with her and let her stew? As an excuse to have dinner with someone else? And what were the odds they'd end up in the same restaurant? Pretty good considering Rawlins had about four places to eat that didn't have a drive-through.

Her emotions teetered between fury and betrayal as she watched Fletch with the blonde, their heads bent close in serious conversation. The location of the booth, and their position in it, indicated they'd chosen it for privacy. Plus, Fletch wore the cowboy hat that kept his face in shadow—and it was highly doubtful he'd worn it because he was worried about getting interrupted for veterinary advice during his intimate dinner. When the woman grinned, and squeezed Fletch's hand, Tanna had to look away.

Skulking in the shadows made her feel ridiculous, childish and like a stalker. She oughta march up to the table and demand to know what was going on. The balls to the wall, take no shit Tanna would be dragging that woman out of the restaurant by the hair, and beating the tar out of her in the parking lot.

Yeah, that'd make a great impression on the Gradskys. Sneaking off to do a shot of tequila and then starting a hair-pulling fight in a restaurant with a woman she didn't know. As much as her heart ached and her blood boiled, she had to forget about Fletch and focus on why she was here.

Tanna left the bar without ordering the shot and returned to Chuck and Berlin. "Sorry. Saw someone I knew. Now, before you guys offer me anything, there are a few things you oughta know about me, and what's happened in my life the last two and a half years."

Chuck and Berlin listened attentively. At one point Berlin reached out and put her hand over Tanna's. By the time she finished the story, the waitress had given up on taking their order.

Silence lingered, not a particularly comfortable silence.

When Berlin said, "I'm just going to see where our waitress ran off to," and Chuck followed her, Tanna had a sinking feeling. She'd probably been too honest. Sutton should've been here to kick her under the table.

Excruciating minutes passed until Chuck and Berlin returned. A waitress appeared and Tanna rattled off food without really knowing what she'd ordered.

Berlin leaned forward. "Your honesty is appreciated. So you deserve ours also. We've had half a dozen riders on Madera in the last two months and she's never performed the way she did with you. Which is why we still think you're a perfect match and could win another national championship on our horse."

"I sense a but."

"But we're sensing some ambivalence on *your* part on whether you're still interested in competing in the sport at the level you used to."

"Maybe you're sensing my fear that I won't ever get to that level again, regardless of what horse I'm on."

"Tanna, we watched you today. Quite frankly, we don't give a shit about plying you with false flattery. We're all about the performance. And that's one thing you can do: perform. Just imagine the difference even two months of training on Madera will make." Chuck's eyes twinkled. "You might shave your time down to twelve seconds at next year's CRA."

Tanna snorted. "That'd be the day. Although, during a practice run in Galveston one year, the electronic eye timed me and Jezebel at eleven point nine eight. I assumed the machine hosed up."

They laughed.

"So, here's what we're proposing." Chuck laid it all out and Tanna was stunned by their generosity. For the first time, in a very long time, and since she'd ridden Madera, she felt like she wasn't washed-up. These people believed in her, which went a long way to her believing in herself. Sutton had been right about this too—riding a horse like Madera gave her a glimpse of the champion she used to be. The champion she could be again.

"Can you be there next week?" Berlin asked. "We'd really like to do a test run at a small rodeo in Lodestone in three weeks."

Lodestone might be a small rodeo, but it was an important one—with a big purse and lots of points to be won, since Labor Day weekend signaled the beginning of the end for cowboys and cowgirls to qualify for the world finals. The best of the best in rodeo attended Lodestone. It'd be the perfect time to start the buzz that Tanna Barker would be back in action the first of the year with a new horse.

Then her hopes sunk a little. She'd assured Harper and the Split Rock crew that she'd be around the entire summer and three weeks remained. Lainie and Celia had both stuck their necks out to secure her the job. Quitting would be a shitty way to repay them.

"Tanna?"

She looked up. "Sorry. Look. This is a lot to process. Obviously I'm very interested. But I'd like a day or two to think it over, see if I come up with any other questions or concerns."

Chuck nodded. "Fair enough."

Talk turned to mutual acquaintances, rodeo gossip and always—who was riding the top of the leader boards in rodeo events. They ended up closing the place down.

After parting ways, Tanna opted not to drive back to Muddy Gap. She scored the last room at the motel across from the bar. By some weird coincidence or fate—or maybe the universe was testing her—she ended up in the same room she'd shared with Fletch on her first night in Wyoming.

That seemed like a long time ago. She never would've guessed he was *the one.*

As she stretched out in the middle of the king bed, images from that night kept flashing through her mind. Yeah, the sex had been rockin', but there was so much more between them now. Though neither of them had bucked up and said the "L" word yet, there was love there. The type of forever love that didn't just vanish after one stupid fight.

Once they both cooled down, they could discuss where they went from here.

Because she might be leaving the Split Rock, but she wasn't leaving him.

⟶

Early Sunday morning, after it'd sunk in how much of a dick he'd been to Tanna Saturday afternoon, Fletch drove up to the Split Rock. Her truck wasn't parked in front of her trailer.

A feeling of panic set in. Had she already left? He beat on the door harder than necessary. Hearing no response, he walked in, calling out, "Tanna?"

No answer.

Her bed hadn't been slept in. Her coffeepot was unused. Her laptop sat on the coffee table. He slumped against the wall, relieved that she hadn't just snuck out in the middle of the night, without saying good-bye, which was no less than he deserved after the way he'd acted in the last week.

Fletch had made up excuses not to see her after she'd told him about the horse owners being so anxious to meet with her that they were driving to Wyoming as soon as possible. Was it a petty, assholish way to react? Yep. He'd justified his actions—if he spent time with Tanna he'd most likely come off as pissy, not supportive, and she deserved support at this crucial junction in her career. No matter how much he wanted her to succeed, he feared her doing so would mean the end of them.

Fletch didn't want them to end. Ever. He should've just told her how he felt rather than being such a chickenshit. He had lied to her; he'd never been in love before he met her. He'd never told a woman he loved her and he had no idea how to do it. Blurting it out during sex seemed... disingenuous somehow.

And not telling her that you love her was somehow... better?

At least his entire day hadn't been a wash, fraught with frustration. Last night Fletch had spent a long time talking to Tasha. She suffered burnout from running a solo practice too. She swore she'd take less money—if that were possible—if it'd give her more time with her husband and the baby she carried.

As they'd walked out of the restaurant Arnie and Jet had called, asking them to meet at the diner. They hashed out an informal agreement and the wheels were in motion to combine four practices into one. They'd agreed to share the news with their employees and meet again at the potential business site at the end of the week.

He'd been so excited about this big change in his life, he'd found himself dialing Tanna to share the good news—but had hung up when he realized it was two in the morning. Oh, and she was pissed as hell at him.

So where was she?

As he scrolled through his contact list to call her, his phone rang. Unknown number. He answered it absentmindedly, "This is Dr. Fletcher."

"Fletch? It's Bran. I'm callin' from Les's phone. Holy shit, man, I've got a big fucking problem with my cattle. Several of them have died and I don't know what the hell is goin' on. Never seen this before. Any chance you can swing by? Like immediately?"

It was the first time he'd ever heard Bran panicked. "I'm on my way."

Chapter Thirty-five

❦

*O*n the way back to the Split Rock late Sunday morning, Tanna turned on the road leading to Celia and Kyle's.

A sleepy-eyed Celia answered the door. "Tanna? Whoa. Look at you all fancied up in a dress." She smirked. "Am I witnessing the walk of shame? Or did you actually get up and go to church?"

"Neither. Long story."

"Come on in. I got nothin' but time to hear it."

The dog promptly flopped in the middle of the floor and Tanna almost tripped over him.

"Sorry. Patches always has to stay between me and the door. Some protective thing."

"How's mama today?"

"Anxious to hold the little bugger in my arms rather than inside me. This last month is gonna drag ass, I just know it." Celia pointed to the living room and sat on the couch, taking up most of the space, leaving Tanna with the corner. "I can't sit in the recliner anymore because I can't get out of it."

"You are looking...rounder. But you do have that happy glow about you, so I feel entitled to hate you a little."

"And you've got that little line between your eyebrows that tells me you're upset, or annoyed, or pissed off, or all three."

Tanna laughed. "Can't pull one over on you."

"So, what's up?"

"Short version? I've been offered a chance to get back into training and possibly competing."

"What? When did this happen? That is so great!" Celia pushed her feet against the outside of Tanna's thigh. "Now tell me the long version."

So she did.

When she finished, Celia was uncharacteristically serious. "I'm not surprised someone wants to showcase your skill on their horse, but I am thrilled for you, T."

"Thanks. I really clicked with Madera. Even quicker than I did with Jezebel. It'll sound corny, but it's like we were waiting for each other."

"Not corny at all. So, what are you gonna do?"

"I've got two options. Ask Chuck and Berlin if they'll board Madera at Eli's until I've fulfilled my commitment to the Split Rock. Which I don't see happening. Or I can ask for two days off in a row, request the third day to work at the lounge. That'd give me two full days of training plus part of another the next three weeks."

"How far is their ranch?"

"Four and a half hours. A hop, skip and a jump for an old road dog like me. And I heard from Garrett this morning. It's official he's settling in Colorado too."

"Doing what?"

"He wouldn't tell me anything except security. So it could be anything from bein' a mall cop to working in an off-the-books secret military-type company, to bein' a school crossing guard."

"That'll be good for you, having him close by again."

"We've had several long talks and some things are clearer to me, as far as what happened with my dad before and after Mom died."

"You gonna try and mend fences with him?"

"Nope. The ball is firmly in my dad's court. But I'm gonna stop blaming him for the suddenness of the decision to sell the ranch when I was the one who missed the signs."

Celia frowned. "I'm confused."

Tanna patted her friend's swollen ankle. "Forget it. I'm not confused and that's a good thing. Where's Kyle?"

"At Bran's. He had a bunch of cattle get out and they ate … well, they're not sure what they ate. But five have died, and some calves are sick and some aren't. Fletch has his hands full so Kyle went to help. I don't expect I'll see him until later tonight." Her eyes narrowed on Tanna. "Didn't Fletch tell you where he was goin'?"

"I haven't seen Fletch since Tuesday." Lest Celia got it in her head to pry, she added hastily, "But I've been at Eli's training when I haven't been working, so we're hit-and-miss." She stood. "I did have another reason for coming by. I'm taking my horse trailer. It's a mess. I've decided today is the day it gets cleaned out."

"You don't have to move it to clean it out. Do it here."

"No way. You'll volunteer to help and I'll say no, and you'll do it anyway, and your husband would get upset and have my hide." She shivered. "Kyle is one scary dude when he's upset."

"When have you seen him upset?"

"At the hospital after your little bulldoggin' mishap."

Celia grinned. "We probably wouldn't have gotten married if not for those stitches."

"Wrong." Tanna kissed her forehead. "You and Kyle were destined to be together." She placed her hand over the hard mound of Celia's belly. "I love this little bugger already, so take care of yourself and baby G, mama. I'll talk to you soon."

❧

Harper showed up at Wild West Clothiers early Monday morning.

Tanna had finished a new jewelry display. The pieces of twine draped between a small rack wrapped with raffia was supposed to look like straw … but it hadn't turned out as well as Tanna had hoped.

Harper paused in front of it. Looked it up and down and said, "Nope."

Shit.

"Grab something to drink. We need to talk." Then Harper turned over the BE BACK IN THIRTY MINUTES! sign and headed into the back room.

She and Harper had a friendly working relationship, but they weren't friends. And they'd spent very little actual time together, so this felt like she was in trouble with her boss.

Tanna snagged a bottle of water and followed her.

Harper had settled at the folding table, papers spread out in front of her. "It's come to my attention that you'll be requesting a permanent switch in the schedule. Since we don't play favorites with Tierney's sister as far as her scheduling preferences, I cannot play favorites with you. But this is a timely issue since I'll be hiring permanent staff to pick up the slack after Labor Day. I'm reducing my hours due to my increased responsibilities at home with a second child. So Harlow will be staying on at Wild West Clothiers until that is finalized and you . . . are being let go. As of today."

"What? I have three weeks left."

That's when Tanna noticed that Harper wasn't looking at her. In fact, Harper hadn't made eye contact once during this bogus firing. "This is crap. I deserve to know what's really goin' on here, *boss*."

Harper looked up, a tremulous smile on her lips. "Shoot. I suck at being the big bad boss lady and firing you for your own good like Celia and I agreed—"

"What does Celia have to do with me losing my job?"

"She came over yesterday and told me what was going on with you and why I had to let you go immediately."

That little brat.

"While I admire your intent to finish out your commitment to us, I'm afraid I can't let you do that. So I'm . . . um . . . firing you."

"Firing me," Tanna repeated. "Because I won't leave you shorthanded for the rest of the summer season?"

"That does sound ridiculous. But yes. You are being relieved of your positions at the Split Rock and Wild West Clothiers effective immediately."

What the hell? This was beyond bizarre. "But . . ."

Harper's eyes were soft, but determined. "Tanna. Are you really arguing with me? This is your golden opportunity to return to the career you love—or at least loved at one time—or figure out if you're done with it on your own terms. As good as you are at this job . . . for you it *is* just a job."

"Celia didn't badger you into this?"

Harper raised a brow. "Not hardly."

"You have staff to cover—"

"Yes, we do."

"Who else besides Harlow? Is your sister Liberty returning to Muddy Gap? Because I understand if you want to give her a job since she's a veteran injured in the line of duty."

Harper laughed. "My sister takes tomboy to the extreme. She'd be horrified if she had to actually wear something besides camouflage. Her idea of hell isn't Afghanistan. It's being forced to fix her hair, wear makeup and a dress, trying to sell clothing and accessories to women who love all that *insipid frilly girl shit*—as she calls it. I'd be too afraid to hire her because she'd pull out her sidearm and shoot customers who annoyed her."

Yikes. Liberty sounded nothing like sweet, fashionable Harper.

"Liberty will find her place after her short recovery time—it's just not here." Harper slid a manila envelope across the table. "Your last paycheck. Also letters of recommendation."

"Really?"

Harper gave Tanna a smirking smile that was so unlike her. "Really. You were a great employee and I am thankful you were able to fill in. I certainly hope you won't disappear out of our lives forever."

There was an opening. "How did things end up with the cattle yesterday?"

Sadness crossed her face. "We lost twenty cows and twelve calves. Bran is just sick about it. We would've lost twice that if not for Fletch. He was there until after midnight." Her gaze met Tanna's. "Are you and he still...?"

"I don't know."

"He's a good man, Tanna. One of the best I know. He deserves a woman who'll be there when he gets home at midnight. But he also needs to know when to say when with his job."

That shocked her.

It must've shown because Harper laughed. "Get going before I change my mind and make you tear down that hideous display."

❧

Another exhausting day and night. So exhausting that Fletch had overslept.

So when Cora called to check on him at ten a.m., he'd mumbled something about being sick and told her to direct his emergency calls to Jet Eriksen for the entire day.

Fletch hadn't been lying, exactly. He was sick. Heartsick.

He dragged himself out of bed and showered. Halfway to Muddy Gap he wondered if he should've brought her flowers or something. During the remainder of the drive he hadn't come up with any great speech to give Tanna; he just hoped she'd give him a chance *to* speak.

His stomach lurched seeing Tanna's horse trailer stretched along the back fence—especially when he saw the living quarters' door open and odds and ends littering the ground. He parked behind her, essentially blocking her in.

He was *not* letting this woman go without a fight.

Fletch marched up to the door. He didn't bother to knock; he just barged right in. "Tanna?"

She whirled around. "Fletch? What are you doin' here?"

His heart gave one last thump before it rolled over and dropped at her booted feet. This beautiful woman owned him. Heart and soul. Blood and bone.

"I came to apologize."

"Okay. But it's the middle of a workday. Are you on lunch break or something?"

"No. I called in sick."

Her mouth dropped open. "What? You never call in sick."

"I know." He erased the distance between them and cradled her face in his hands. "This couldn't wait another day. I know I should've told you sooner, but I am saying it now. Tanna. I love you." Then he kissed her.

The kiss wasn't dueling tongues and unrestrained lust, although it simmered just beneath the surface like it always did with them. But more an affirmation of how he felt.

Question was: did she feel the same?

They reluctantly broke apart. She rested the side of her face against his heart. "Apology accepted. I missed you so much. I hate fighting. Especially with someone I love."

He tipped her face up. "Can you look at me when you say that?"

"I love you."

"Aw, sugar twang, that's the best thing I've ever heard."

She smiled at him. "Felt good to finally say it. Almost as good as it felt to hear it."

Fletch kissed her again. "We need to talk."

"I know." She stepped back. "Have a seat."

He'd never fit in the bench seat with the foldout table. Damn thing had to've been made for midgets. Another bench ran along the opposite short wall. He sat and tugged her onto his lap so she faced him.

"Fletch. We're supposed to be talking."

"We are. But we're gonna stay close like this while we're talking as a reminder to each of us how right it is when we *are* close like this."

"You are such a sweet, wonderful man."

"But you're still leaving me. You're moving to Colorado."

"I don't know if it's *moving*," she said in a soothing tone. "I called the Gradskys this morning after Harper talked to me and accepted their offer. So I'm goin' there to train. We're bein' fluid with plans because with all the unknowns, things can change in a helluva hurry."

"I don't want you to go," Fletch said softly.

Tanna froze. "You don't want me to go, or you're asking me to stay?"

"Both." He sighed and shoved his hand through his hair before meeting her eyes again. "I know what this opportunity means to you. A chance to get back doin' what you love, what you're meant to do. I'd never ask you not to live your dream, Tanna."

"But?"

"But there's already a big hole in my life from you leaving and you ain't even gone yet. That's why I stayed away from you. I thought it'd be easy to get used to you bein' gone. But it wasn't. Not by a long goddamn shot."

She blinked at him, wordlessly urging him to continue.

He couldn't maintain eye contact when he confessed this next part. He stared at an ugly cow figurine, wearing a grass skirt that sat on the opposite counter. "Want to know why I didn't come to watch you Saturday?"

"Why?"

"Because I'd've been happy if you'd sucked. Christ. What kind of man does that make me?"

"An honest man." A pause. "Would you've been happy if I'd succeeded?"

"Beyond happy because I know how hard you've struggled. So see? I was screwed either way. God, Tanna, I love you and it's killing me to watch you pack up even when I won't try and stop you."

Silence.

Tanna framed his face in her hands and tipped his head back. "You love me, right?"

"I've been in love with you since the night we first met." He smiled slightly. "In fact, I believe I told you I loved you that night at the bar."

"You were joking."

"Was I? When I saw you at the branding I had the feeling we were meant to be. As we got to know each other I had this hope that you'd fall in love with me. That you'd walk away from barrel racing and we'd live happily ever after. I'd even had this secret fantasy that you came to work for me as my vet assistant. But at some point, I understood that as perfect as that scenario would be for *me*, it wouldn't be perfect for you. You'd always wonder if you'd settled for me because you couldn't have what you really wanted."

"But you never said . . . you never encouraged me to quit. Exactly the opposite in fact. You forced me to get on a horse that day."

"It's not what I wanted but it's what you *needed*. I did it knowing I was helping you get one step closer to walking away from me."

Tears pooled in Tanna's eyes.

"So in the past day and a half since our fight on the phone, I had to ask myself what you saw in me and why you'd stay with me. I work crazy hours. I've broken more plans than I've made. I've put the care of animals above most human relationships. Oh, and I'm not getting rich doin' it, so there's that extra incentive for you. When I listed all the reasons why you shouldn't be with me, heck, I didn't even wanna get with myself."

She released a sniffling laugh. "I always wanna get with you. As for what I see in you?" Her eyes softened. "Fletch. You're gentle and kind, but you're rough and raunchy too. You make me laugh, you make me think, but mostly, you make me happy. In my mind that makes you damn close to perfect." When he opened his mouth to protest, she put her fingers across his lips. "Shut up and listen to me, August Fletcher. I love you. The crazy I-wanted-to-beat-the-fuck-outta-that-blonde at the Cattleman's Club with you Saturday night kind of forever love."

He eased back to look at her. "You were there?"

"For a business meeting with Chuck and Berlin Gradsky. It was a little hard to concentrate."

"Why didn't you come over and say something? I would've loved to introduce you to Tasha since we'd spent half the night talking about you." His eyes narrowed. "Did you think something was goin' on between us?"

"I was teary-eyed and all *how could he?* At first. Then I got pissy. But then I got to thinking about my friendship with Sutton and how on the outside it might appear to be more. You believed me when I said it wasn't. I decided if I couldn't trust you, then I had no business bein' with you. And make no mistake; I want to be with you for the long haul. Even when I know that we'll be spending a lot of time apart."

"I've always avoided long-distance relationships because I knew they'd eventually end. This is different." He brushed his mouth over hers. "Because you and me? Sugar twang, we're never gonna end."

"So what do we do to make this work?"

"Whatever it takes. You'll train in Colorado. You'll either come back here when you've got a break, or I'll go there when I've got a break."

"Sounds...doable. Lonely while we're apart, but doable." Tanna poked him in the chest. "You *will* get over your issue with texting. I'll expect to get texts from you at least a couple times a day."

He kissed her nose. "Anything you want. I'll be lonely for you, cowgirl, especially these first few months when you're training hard and I'm setting up the veterinary practice with my new partners."

That got her attention. Tanna frowned at him. "What did you say?"

"Here's my good news. In the next few months I'm combining practices with three other vets. It'll reduce all our on-call hours during the week. And we'd only be on call one weekend a month, maybe two."

Her grin lit up his world. "That is so awesome for you."

"For *us*," he corrected. "I foresee road trips to Colorado in my future on the weekends I'm not working. Or I can fly to where you're competing." He grinned. "It'd be a bonus for you to have a vet to help you look after your fancy new horse, don'tcha think?"

She laughed. "Yes. But this veterinary partnership thing came about pretty suddenly."

Fletch pushed a strand of hair behind her ear. "You came into my life suddenly and changed it completely. After being with you … I saw the life I wanted. The way to get it is to make some changes and this will be a good change for me."

"For *us*," she teased. "But along those same lines, bein' here, bein' with you helped me see that I don't have to be the woman who defines herself only as a barrel racer. I can guarantee I won't be on the road any more than I have to be if I have you to come home to."

"You do." Fletch placed a kiss in front of her ear. "I love thinking about you bein' in our home and our bed."

"You're gonna make me cry."

"No time for tears, sweetheart. We have stuff to do. When are you leaving for Colorado?"

"The day after tomorrow."

He grinned. "So if we get you packed up fast, we can play hooky the rest of the day?"

"Mmm-hmm. And tomorrow I'll go on calls with you, because I know you'll have a lot of catch-up to do after playing hooky with me." Tanna draped her arms over his shoulders. "Maybe I could be a naughty vet assistant and you could come up with creative ways to punish me at the end of the day."

"I'm in." He paused a little too long and a look of concern crossed her face.

"What?"

"Before we get too far into our plans for the day, I have to ask you something really important."

Shock crossed her face. "Fletch. I don't know if I'm ready for that."

Fletch frowned. Then he realized he'd made the question sound a little ominous and he laughed. "I definitely want to marry you someday—sooner rather than later—but that wasn't what I was gonna ask you." Fletch swept her hair from his face. "I wanted to ask if we could stop by my dad's sometime today so you can meet him."

"I'd like that. A lot."

"Good. Now while we get our work done, I want you to tell me all about this horse."

Epilogue

❦

Fourteen months later...

"*Y*ou'll make sure she gets extra feed?"

"Yes, ma'am."

"And spend a long time brushing her down."

"I will."

"And check her feet after you take her across the parking lot."

"I promise."

Tanna laid her face against Madera's neck. "You did good, girl. Damn good. I wish I had a wreath of roses to drape around your neck because them Kentucky Derby winners ain't got nothin' on you."

Madera snorted.

"Tanna," Berlin hissed, "you're up next."

"Ladies and gentlemen. Please welcome your CRA World Champion, Tanna Barker!"

She straightened her hat, wiped her tears and took off across the soft dirt covering the floor of the MGM Grand Arena. Two cowboys offered her a hand and hoisted her onto the podium. The podium helpers, two young cowgirls, lifted up the saddle and the championship belt buckle. Tanna waved both her arms to the crowd, her heart beating madly.

"So, Tanna Barker, how does it feel to be CRA World Champion again?"

"Amazing. Stunning. Humbling. I'm thrilled to be here."

"It's been a rough couple years for you. Did you ever think you'd make it back? And if you did, you'd make it back on top so quickly?"

"Hell no. I mean heck no."

Laughter.

"What are the secrets to your success?"

"Support is key. Chuck and Berlin Gradsky of Grade A Horse Farms partnered me with Madera, the best little horse in the world. My sponsors rallied around me throughout the year. It's been a great year in so many ways. So I'm dedicating this win to my fiancé, Dr. August Fletcher, who believed in me and supported me on this hard-fought journey getting back to doin' what I love." She raised the belt buckle. "This win is great, but he will always be the best thing that ever happened to me because I wouldn't be here if not for him." She swallowed hard, taking a moment to get her emotions under control so she didn't break down like a blubbering fool in front of two hundred thousand people. "Lastly I need to give a shout-out to my friends in my Wyoming hometown, who are sitting in the Buckeye right now, cheering me on. Next round is on me!"

"Wyoming?" the announcer repeated. "But aren't you from Texas?"

"I'm proud to be Texas born and raised. But my heart and my soul, my life, and my home, is in Wyoming."

After she said it, Tanna realized truer words had never been spoken.

Two hours later...

"Sugar twang, what did you say you do for a living?"

She smiled coyly. "I didn't say. But a shot of Patrón would loosen my tongue a whole lot."

He flagged down the bartender.

The look on her face said *sucker.*

After knocking back the tequila, she confessed, "I don't normally share my occupation because it tends to be viewed as ... a bit dangerous. But I'll make an exception for you, chief." She slid her hands up his chest, grabbing the lapels of his suit coat. "See I'm a world champion barrel racer. A *four-time* world champion barrel racer. In fact, I just won my fourth world title tonight."

"That right? Well, congratulations are in order."

"Yes, sir." She batted her eyelashes. "I won a really big gold belt buckle. But if you wanna see it, and get a personal demonstration on how well I ride, well, ace, you're gonna have to come up to my room."

Fletch laughed. "Too many people in there right now to suit my taste. But I do have a private room reserved for later tonight if you're interested."

"I'm very interested."

"So you're just killing time in a honky-tonk ... until the right man comes along?"

"Nope. I've already bagged and tagged my Mr. Right. Just waiting for the paperwork to go through that makes it official."

He grinned at his bride to be and twisted a springy tendril of her hair around his finger. Since he'd last seen her on the winner's podium, her long locks had been swept up into an elaborate hairdo and her makeup had been redone. Tanna always looked beautiful, but tonight an extra glow of happiness and anticipation surrounded her. "You look spectacular, sweetheart. I'm the luckiest man in the world."

She curled her hand around his neck and pulled his mouth to hers for a kiss. A long kiss. In the past fourteen months they'd learned to take their intimate moments when they could. It didn't matter that they were in a rowdy bar on the Vegas strip. As far as they were concerned, they were the only ones in the universe.

Tanna broke the kiss, but she held him in place, resting her forehead to his. "Holy shit balls, Doc. Can you believe I won tonight?"

"No doubt in mind you'd win since you are the very best at what you do." He snuck in another kiss. "I'm so damn proud of you, Tanna."

"I'm proud of me too. But I couldn't have done it without you."

"Nice speech, by the way." In the last ten days, he'd nearly gone hoarse cheering her on from the stands in the arena. His hands hurt from clapping so much. And when his tough and sweet Texas cowgirl had defied the odds and scrambled onto that podium to claim her victory, he hadn't bothered to wipe away his tears.

"I meant every word I said." She fussed with his bow tie. "You look hot in this tux. But I can't wait to strip it off you later in the bridal suite."

Fletch placed his hand over hers, which rested above his heart. "So alls you gotta do is slip on your fancy wedding dress and satin shoes and you're good to meet me at the wedding chapel"—he glanced at the clock—"in forty-five minutes?" The crazy woman had set their wedding date two months ago—for 1:01 a.m., immediately after the CRA Nationals ended. She'd known all their friends and relatives would be in Vegas to support her during the final night—win or lose—so it made sense to get married here. But she'd insisted on keeping what she claimed would be the happiest day of her life—marrying him—a different day from the day she competed for the world championship.

"I'll be there, giddy as a schoolgirl, nervous as a virgin, horny as a toad." She nipped the end of his chin. "This staying in separate rooms the last few nights has sucked."

"No argument from me. So, how *did* you manage to ditch Celia, Lainie, Harlow, Summer and all the Mud Lilies? I thought they had you under lock and key in the ready room."

"I wasn't sure I could get away when I got your text. But as soon as Garnet cranked up Bobby Darin, I snuck out." She smirked. "How'd you escape from the man cave?"

"At my suggestion, Eli, Hank, Kyle, Devin, my dad and your brother decided to try their luck playing Texas hold 'em, in the guise of winning us a cash wedding gift." Fletch tipped her chin up and looked into her eyes. "I wanted us to meet alone so I could give you your wedding gift before the ceremony."

"August Fletcher. I thought we said no gifts."

"This is a gift for both of us really." He inhaled a slow breath. "Renner agreed to turn that big empty building at the Split Rock into a training arena. We'll have to lease it, but your training time will get priority. And the Gradskys have signed off on letting you work with Madera there, instead of at their Colorado facility."

Her jaw nearly hit the floor. "Are you serious?"

"Completely."

"So next season I don't have to spend half my time in Colorado?"

"Nope."

"Not that I wanna look a gift horse in the mouth—ha-ha—but . . . why?"

"Guess Renner—or more likely financial whip-cracker Tierney—would rather have some income while waiting for the commercial stock-breeding program to become viable, rather than let the building sit unused another two years. As far as the Gradskys . . . they know you take better care of their horse than you do yourself." He flashed her a grin. "Plus, you've got a top-notch vet at your beck and call, day and night, to treat their newest prize-winning horse, which also weighed heavily in our favor."

Tanna shrieked and threw her arms around him. "This is the best news ever." She kissed him. "I love you so much." More kisses. "So, so, so much."

"I love you too."

Tanna's cell phone began to vibrate on the bar. "Shoot. They noticed I was missing. I gotta go."

"You promise you're meeting me in the chapel? You won't get cold feet and run away?"

"I'm never running away again. In fact, I just may run down that aisle to reach you."

"And my arms will be wide open to catch you." He kissed her. "Always."

Before Tanna and Fletch ever met, Kyle set out to show Celia he had what it took to give her a lifetime of love. Don't miss their story in

One Night Rodeo

Available now!

$\mathcal{K}$yle raced down the hospital corridor until he spied the woman pacing across from the emergency room doors. "Tanna?"

She whirled around. "Kyle. Thanks for coming."

He loomed over her. "Thanks? That's the first thing you say to me? Jesus. I've been out of my fuckin' mind the last twenty minutes. How could you call me to get my ass to the hospital and not give me a single damn detail about what happened to her?" He had visions of her in surgery or in traction. Bloodied up and unconscious. Broken in body and spirit.

The feisty barrel racer jabbed him in the chest with her finger. "Don't you snap at me first thing, Kyle Gilchrist."

"Then start talkin'. Now."

"I told you on the phone. She fell off a horse."

Kyle frowned. "Her horse Mickey ain't even here."

"Not *her* horse. *A* horse. She landed on the steer cockeyed after she launched herself at it. I think she ended up with a hoof or a horn to her head 'cause... ah... there was some blood."

"What the hell was she doin' with a goddamn steer?"

"Bulldoggin'." Tanna's eyes darted away.

Somehow he kept a lid on his temper. "Still waiting to hear the full story."

Her defiant brown gaze met his. "You know how Celia is, Kyle. Someone tells her that she can't do something and she goes out of her way to prove them wrong."

"Who's *them*?"

"A couple of bulldoggers from Nebraska. Cocky bastards, talkin' shit to us about how easy barrel racin' is compared to bulldoggin'. The next thing I knew, Celia was ponying up a hundred bucks to prove that steer wrestling ain't that hard. Then the bulldoggers got permission from the event staff so we could have us a little race."

"You've got to be fucking kiddin' me. Celia is in the damn hospital because of some stupid bet? Why didn't you stop her?"

"Because I agreed with her and tossed in a hundred bucks of my own to teach those pompous pricks a lesson," Tanna shot back. "Celia drew the short straw to ride first."

Kyle caught a whiff of Tanna's boozy breath. "Christ. How much had you guys been drinkin'?"

"Some."

Unbelievable. "How'd you get to the hospital?"

"The bulldoggers dropped us off. Celia said she was fine and walked in on her own, so I don't think her injuries are life threatening."

"Celia would tell you that even if she had two broken arms, two busted legs, and her eyes were bleeding. Damn stubborn woman." But he hoped Tanna's assessment was right.

The emergency room doors opened and Kyle glanced up as a nurse approached Tanna. "You're with Celia Lawson?"

Kyle intercepted. "Yes. How is she?"

"She's had a chest X-ray and a CT scan. You can come back and wait with her if you'd like."

They followed the nurse to the end of a wide hallway. He stepped around the curtain.

Celia was on her back, her lower half covered with a blanket. Her slim torso appeared fragile, swimming in the floral-patterned hospital gown. Her lips were a flat line. Her eyes were shut. Kyle's gut clenched when he saw the bandage on the upper left edge of her forehead and the bruises on her cheekbone. His gaze traveled the long, thick blond braid lying beside her on the bed; the end of it brushed the middle of her thigh.

Ridiculous, probably, to watch the rise and fall of her chest to assure himself she was breathing.

On impulse, he placed a soft kiss between her eyebrows. When he lifted his head, he found himself staring into her eyes.

Those smoky gray eyes narrowed very quickly. "Kyle? What the devil are you doin' here?"

"I called him," Tanna said, scooting in to squeeze Celia's hand.

"Why?" Celia demanded.

"Because you asked for him," Tanna replied softly.

Celia's startled gaze quickly hooked Kyle's. When he smirked, she said, "Don't go getting that look or I'll wipe it right off your face."

"Sure, you will." Kyle smirked again. "Just as soon as you're not flat on your back in a hospital bed, knocked loopy."

Tanna laughed. "So how *are* you feeling, bulldoggin' queen?"

"Sore. Pissed I lost a hundred bucks."

"You don't remember they paid up?" Tanna asked. "I guess if you bleed you win by default."

Celia snorted.

"Has the doctor been in?"

"To give me stitches and to give me hell," Celia grumbled. "He poked me, muttered a lot, and then shipped me off to X-ray. I tried to tell him my ribs are just sore, not broken. Guess he didn't believe me."

"You're a few years short of a medical degree to be makin' a diagnosis," Kyle said dryly.

"This ain't my first rodeo," she retorted. "I've been hurt before."

"What ever possessed you to tangle with livestock when you'd been drinkin'?"

"It wasn't like we were shit-faced, Kyle. We each had one shot." She frowned. "No, two shots."

Tanna held up four fingers.

"Four? Really? Huh. Didn't seem like that many."

"How's your head?"

"Hard, but you knew that. The doc was worried about a concussion, so they X-rayed my melon too." Once again those icy gray eyes zipped to him. "Not a word about them finding my head empty, Gilchrist."

He'd had enough of her tough-girl attitude. "Knock it off. I get that you're scared."

"How do you know that?"

"Because, kitten, you hiss and claw when you're afraid." Kyle picked up her hand, rubbing her cold fingertips against his jaw. "So hiss and claw at me. I can take it."

"You need to shave," she snapped, jerking her hand back. "And I'm not scared. I'm annoyed."

The curtain fluttered and Devin McClain strolled in, although the country music star was barely recognizable in a ratty ball cap and sunglasses. "Hey, brat. Whatcha gone and done to yourself now?"

"Devin? How did you . . . ?" Celia blinked at him in confusion.

"Kyle called me in a complete panic. Had me thinking I'd find you on your deathbed. I wasn't sure if he wanted me here to hold your hand or his."

Kyle muttered, "Shut it, asshole."

Devin raised his eyebrow, peering over his shades at Celia. "Seems you've had a miraculous recovery."

"Why won't anyone believe that I'm fine? I just got the wind knocked out of me."

"Darlin', you were knocked out cold," Tanna drawled. She offered her hand to Devin. "Nice to finally meet you, Devin. I'm Tanna Barker. I've heard lots about you from Celia, bein's you're a family friend and a Muddy Gap homeboy."

"A true pleasure to meet you too, Tanna. Great run last night."

"Thanks." She blurted, "Omigod, I can't believe I'm standing here with Devin McClain! I'm such a huge fan. Your song 'Chains and Trains' is one of my all-time favorites."

"I never get tired of hearin' that. Thank you."

When Devin granted Tanna that million-dollar smile, Kyle could have sworn the rowdy Texas cowgirl swooned.

"So what's the diagnosis?" Devin asked Celia.

"Still waiting for the X-rays to tell us."

"Have you called her brothers?" Devin asked Kyle.

Immediately Celia grabbed a fistful of Devin's sweatshirt, grimacing as she pulled herself upright. "No. And I swear to God I will beat you bloody if you do." She leveled the same venomous look on Kyle. "That goes for you too."

"But, Celia, they need to—"

"No. Do you hear me? Janie is in the last two weeks of her pregnancy and I won't upset her or Abe for anything. And Hank and Lainie are leaving for Boulder for the consult for Brianna's eye surgery. They need to focus on her and each other, not me. Promise me you won't tell them."

Surprised by her tears, Kyle bent closer. Sweet, fierce Celia wasn't upset about being beat to shit; she was just worried about her family's reaction to it. "I won't tell them as long as you promise to call them within a day or two."

"Okay. Thank you."

He raised an eyebrow. "No arguing with me? Really? That's one for the record books."

"I don't always argue with you."

"Yes, you do."

"No, I don't."

"See? You're still doin' it."

"You started it."

"As much as I'd like to stay and hear another round of your bitchy sexual foreplay—*not*—I need to get ready to ride tonight," Tanna said.

"Now that I know you're recovered enough to bicker with Kyle," Devin said, "I'll head back to the event center for final sound check."

"Would it be too much trouble to drop me off at the arena?" Tanna asked Devin. "I'm without a vehicle."

"No problem at all."

"You're both just leaving me?"

Tanna rolled her eyes. "You keep insisting you're fine, remember? Besides, Kyle will take better care of you than I have today." She squeezed Celia's arm. "I'll see you later."

"So, brat, you still comin' to the concert tonight or what?" Devin asked.

Kyle said *no* at the same time Celia said *yes*.

"Good luck with this argument. We're outta here." Devin held the curtain for Tanna and they disappeared.

"Don't give me that look, Kyle."

Kitten, you'd blush to the tips of your toes if you'd noticed how I've been looking at you the last two years.

"What look?"

"The bossy one."

"Tough, because I have every intention of bossing you tonight."

The curtain rolled back and a young male doctor stopped at the end of the bed. "Good news. No concussion. No broken or cracked ribs. No ruptured organs. You'll be sore for a few days, and I imagine more bruises will appear. My advice is to take it easy, alternate ice and heat with the sore spots. But I'm well aware you rodeo-ers don't often follow medical advice. So the best I can do on a medical front is to prescribe painkillers."

Celia shook her head. "I hate the groggy way they make me feel."

"That's how you're supposed to feel. Like you oughta be laying down resting," Kyle pointed out.

"That's rich coming from the bull rider who's ridden with a sprained thumb, a sprained wrist, a sprained ankle, a pulled groin muscle, and a mild concussion...all in the last year. You refused pain meds and I didn't see you *resting* any of those times."

He had no response for that. Mostly he was surprised she'd taken note of his injuries.

"I'm writing you a scrip for pain meds. Up to you if you fill it," the doctor said. "The stitches need to come out in a week. Any other questions?"

"Nope."

"Good. No more mixing bulldoggin' with drinking Mad Dog whiskey, okay?"

"If you insist."

The doctor laughed. "You can get dressed. The nurse will be in with your discharge papers shortly."

Celia sat up and kicked away the blanket, dangling her legs off the bed.

Kyle's eyes drank in every inch of those ridged calf muscles covered by smooth, pale skin. His gaze traveled up slowly, stopping at the equally sexy curve of her knee.

"Stop gawking at my legs like you've never seen 'em before."

He didn't bother banking the admiration in his eyes. "Hard not to stare when you're sporting such a fine pair."

"You just noticed that?"

"No."

The air between them vibrated.

Kyle invaded her space. This close to her he felt that one-two punch of something stronger than lust. "Would it be so bad?"

"What?"

"Letting me watch over you tonight?" An internal debate warred in her eyes. Kyle braced himself for a smart-ass rebuttal.

"Watch over me like a brother would?"

"The last way I think of you, Celia Lawson, is like a sister. And you damn well know it." He pressed his lips to her forehead. "I'm glad you came to Vegas, Cele. I was afraid you wouldn't show up."

"Kyle."

"Mmm?" He placed another kiss on the edge of the bandage.

"Can we talk about this later?"

"Define *later*." The skin below the bandage needed a kiss as well.

"Right after we leave here. At my hotel. You need to skedaddle so I can get dressed."

"In a second." He smoothed flyaway strands from her face. The honeyed scent of her hair filled his lungs and he seemed to breathe easy for the first time since he'd heard she was hurt. He left one last soft smooch on her lips. It totally flustered her, which was odd, given that it wasn't the first time he'd kissed her.

"Umm ... Hand me my clothes."

He dropped the pile on the bed. "I'll be right outside."

"No peeking," she warned as he ducked out.

Kyle paced the length of the privacy curtain. On his fifth pass, he heard her gasp. Worried that she'd strained herself, he poked his head back in. "What's wrong?"

Celia clutched a wad of fabric to her chest. "It was my favorite shirt. My lucky purple shirt. Now it's covered in blood and completely ruined." A little hiccup escaped. "I can't wear this."

"Are the jeans ruined too?"

"No. Just a few splotches of blood."

"Tossing that shirt in the trash ain't no big loss in my mind. I'm thinkin' its luck ran out. Never looked that great on you anyway."

Celia lifted her head, probably to snap at him. Before she opened her mouth, Kyle gently wiped her tears. "Come on, kitten, I was kiddin'."

"Pretty stupid to be so upset over a blouse, huh?"

"Somehow I don't think it's just about the blouse. And given that you're in the hospital, you're entitled to a few tears. You don't always have to act so tough, you know." Kyle popped the buttons on his long-sleeved western shirt. "Although I wouldn't mind seein' you in just your sexy bra and them tight jeans, I don't think you wanna flash the entire ER when I bust you outta this place. Wear this." He draped his shirt over her pillow and tucked his white T-shirt into his jeans.

"Uh, thanks."

Interesting that Celia couldn't take her eyes off his chest. "My pleasure." Kyle kissed her forehead. Twice.

"What's with you kissin' me all the time now?" she asked crossly.

"I hardly think a couple of pecks could be considered me kissin' you all the time." His eyes searched hers. "But I could ramp up the kisses to spark your memory from a few weeks back, if you'd like."

"In your dreams."

Kyle chuckled. "I'll be outside if you need anything."

Former small-town girl Amery Hardwick is living her dream as a graphic designer in Denver, Colorado. She's focused on building her business, which leaves little time for dating—not that she needs a romantic entanglement to fulfill her. When her friend signs up for a self-defense class as part of her recovery after an attack, Amery joins her for support. That's where she meets *him*.

Ronin Black, owner of the dojo, is so drawn to Amery that he takes over her training—and in private, her body. A sensei master-artist in erotic bondage, Ronin pushes Amery's sexual boundaries from the start, and with each new, sensation-filled twist of his rope, Amery becomes addicted to the pleasure and to him. But as she willingly gives in to his sensual domination, Amery begins to sense a secret side to Ronin he hasn't dared to share—something that makes her question her trust in him, no matter how thrilling her obsession has become.